Kid Andrew Cody & Julie Sparrow

Two boys, the sons of the same father, yet unknown to each other, growing up in the 1930s and 40s, one on the streets of New York, the other in the heartland of the Middle West.

Kid Andrew Cody & Julie Sparrow

One rising on raw nerve and savage skill through a jungle of violence to a position of awesome eminence in Las Vegas. The other parlaying good looks, talent, luck, and sweat to become a Hollywood superstar and superstud. Both moving toward a fateful confrontation.

Kid Andrew Cody & Julie Sparrow

This is their story—their passions, their power, their many women, their driving needs, and the twin worlds they conquered and were consumed by.

Tony Curtis has written a blistering first novel!

Big Bestsellers from SIGNET

☐ **WINTER FIRE by Susannah Leigh.**
(#E8011—$2.25)

☐ **THE MESSENGER by Mona Williams.**
(#J8012—$1.95)

☐ **HOW TO SAVE YOUR OWN LIFE by Erica Jong.**
(#E7959—$2.50)

☐ **FEAR OF FLYING by Erica Jong.**
(#E7970—$2.25)

☐ **WHITEY AND MICKEY by Whitey Ford, Mickey Mantle, and Joseph Durso.** (#J7963—$1.95)

☐ **MISTRESS OF DESIRE by Rochelle Larkin.**
(#E7964—$2.25)

☐ **THE QUEEN AND THE GYPSY by Constance Heaven.** (#J7965—$1.95)

☐ **TORCH SONG by Anne Roiphe.** (#J7901—$1.95)

☐ **OPERATION URANIUM SHIP by Dennis Eisenberg, Eli Landau, and Menahem Portugali.**
(#E8001—$1.75)

☐ **NIXON VS. NIXON by Dr. David Abrahamsen.**
(#E7902—$2.25)

☐ **ISLAND OF THE WINDS by Athena Dallas-Damis.**
(#J7905—$1.95)

☐ **THE SHINING by Stephen King.**
(#E7872—$2.50)

☐ **CARRIE by Stephen King.** (#J7280—$1.95)

☐ **'SALEM'S LOT by Stephen King.**
(#E8000—$2.25)

☐ **OAKHURST by Walter Reed Johnson.**
(#J7874—$1.95)

Kid Andrew Cody
&
Julie Sparrow

A Novel by
TONY CURTIS

A SIGNET BOOK from
NEW AMERICAN LIBRARY
TIMES MIRROR

Published by
THE NEW AMERICAN LIBRARY
OF CANADA LIMITED

First Signet Printing, April, 1978

1 2 3 4 5 6 7 8 9

SIGNET TRADEMARK REG. U.S. PAT. OFF. AND FOREIGN COUNTRIES
REGISTERED TRADEMARK — MARCA REGISTRADA
HECHO EN WINNIPEG, CANADA

SIGNET, SIGNET CLASSICS, MENTOR, PLUME AND
MERIDIAN BOOKS are published in Canada by The New
American Library of Canada Limited, Scarborough, Ontario

PRINTED IN CANADA
COVER PRINTED IN U.S.A.

For Leslie

Contents

Book One

THE
SONS OF CODY

Maxwell Boyd Cody

1922

The war had ended, but the memory lingered on. La Salle Street Station in Chicago was crowded on a hot summer night in August as the Twentieth Century Limited arrived.

The crowds boarding and leaving the trains were a cross-section of everything. People stumbling over boys with their shoeshine boxes, hand flowers being sold to comers to impress the lady friend, hawkers selling their wares, an armless hero still at war, rootless, lonely selling boutonnieres for a nickel. Tears. You got coffee and doughnuts for a dime. Hey, buddy, can you spare a dime? When it's due. Remember me. Let's put the luggage on and get some mags. Okay, I need some cigs. I got to get me some rubbers. Lucky Strikes means fine tobacco. Call for Philip Morris. In the air, a fine dust of burnt coal descending on everybody and the smells of flowers, chestnuts, and sweat all intermingled with the sweet smell of the times. Watching the scene, you had a sense of what life was like in this great city.

"The Twentieth Century Limited boarding on Track 9," a voice blared out of speakers.

Maxwell Boyd Cody, twenty-five years old, felt that he had been there before, but this was his first time. Iron stairs coated in cement led to the different track stalls. Trains coming and going. He saw the Twentieth Century emblem on the back of the train and the porters in dark blue and white ready to serve him.

"Good evening, sa, your tickets, please. Thank you, sa. This way, please. Let me take your luggage, please, sa. This way, sa. Beautiful weather for our run to New York, sa; it will be flat and fine, sa. Dining car forward, sa, observation and the bar to the rear, sa. Here we is, sa, Compartment 9. The name is Simmins, sa, Alfred Benjamin, if I can be of service to you, sa, just press this buzzer."

Alfred Benjamin Simmins placed Maxwell's satchel on the madeup bed.

"Now if you'll excuse me, sa."

Maxwell gave him a buck.

"Thank you, sa."

And the black prince closed the door.

Maxwell sat in the single seat overlooking the broad train window in his single compartment. A woman in a cloche hat and short coat, followed by a harried, nervous man smoking a cigar, went by. Ashes from the man's cigar had splattered on his jacket front, unnoticed by him. If it had been Maxwell, he would have brushed it off immediately. Well, you couldn't judge by Maxwell, he was a spiff from head to foot, he was looking good as the cat's meow. New York, New York, it's a hell of a town.

"All aboard."

He heard it faintly through the glass. The conductor leisurely walked past Maxwell's window to the hatchway of the train. One foot on the step, the other on the railing, he waved with his left hand and the Twentieth Century pulled out of Chicago. From the Loop to the Big Apple in fourteen hours. The train had been rolling about ten minutes when Maxwell got up. He used the portable toilet that fell out of the shiny stainless steel bulkhead, stroked his hair, turned, and left the compartment, locking it behind him. He walked to the rear of the train, to the observation car. As he strolled from one car to another he noticed preparations for the run by the porters, conductors checking tickets, passengers coming in and out of staterooms, compartments, uppers and lowers. One guy braced up against a bulkhead wigging a flask, drinking ten-year-old, old-fashioned Southern Bourbon. What he didn't know was that it had been made at a hooker's apartment, in a bathtub, by an enterprising and devoted boyfriend, while she was in the bedroom going down on a ten-dollar trick.

The observation car was crowded. The train was out about twenty-five minutes now, and half a dozen people were pissed already from their private stash. He heard chimes ring out soft but clear. The chimes could have been some religious procession in Spain or in Italy heralding the arrival of the second Messiah. Instead he heard: "Dinner is now being served—first call for dinner." The voice had started near the front of the train calling all those who wished to dine on the Twentieth Century. He found a seat and sat in the middle of the car with his back against the bulkhead.

"Your pleasure, sir?"

"That," he said to himself, looking at the beautiful young woman sitting across from him, talking to this bum with the ashes on his jacket, hat off now, receding hair, eyes that darted from one place to another. He caught Maxwell's eye and knew immediately Maxwell was sizing up his dame. He forced the thought from his mind, but his gut knew that he knew. Maxwell looked at the porter and said, "A Coke."

"Yes, sir."

The porter left. Big Tits and Ashes were across from him having cigs, she, in ladylike fashion, lifted hers from the small ashtray in front of her, pinkie outstretched, and inhaled. Ashes just sat there as depressed as he was when he got on the train. He was going to nurse his cigar for as long as he could. Ashes had found that cigars settled him a bit, that without them the ache was just a little bit more intense, the fear of living a little more pertinent, the fear of dying a little more desperate. Ashes, or Giuseppe Prima, was a two-bit hoodlum whose days were numbered. He was thirty-two, packed a .32, had thirty-two grand on his person in hundred-dollar bills, and was scheduled to leave New York the next day on the S.S. *Atlantic* for Havana, Cuba, where he hoped he could lay low for about six months. The girl with the strange accent and voluptuous figure had started out eight days earlier from New York. She met Ashes at a party in Brooklyn. He liked her; she kinda liked his roughness and his foreignness and the fact that he came from Chicago, and went back with him. They were now on their way back to New York. He had made reservations for both of them on the boat. He didn't know it, but she did not plan to go on his idyllic cruise to the Caribbean. She could manage one more night with him, she thought, but after that, good-by, Charlie. She had had more than she could stand of this foul-smelling bore, this gross animal, this benefactor. Who's shitting who? She was doing okay. After all, it wasn't too bad. Gutless, frightened, she was going home with better than five grand folded neatly in a small purse stuck in the garter around her right thigh. Musky and safe. Five days later, when she deposited the five in the local Brooklyn bank, the teller, a guy about twenty-three, would almost come from the smell counting it.

There was a guy at the end of the car with a black suit and vest, small bow tie, white shirt, rather scruffy shoes, a bulge in his right-hand pocket, and a gray cap stuck in the left. He sat there never taking his eyes off Ashes except when Ashes looked in his direction. Then he would look away or pick up the form he had in his left hand and start reading.

The Coke arrived. Maxwell left a dollar, and took a healthy gulp, never taking his eyes off Big Tits. She was a nifty piece, he thought, I'd like to get near her. Little did he know. He had left Chicago on a hunch. He was going to try out New York for a while. He wasn't sure what he was going to do yet; he just felt free and easy. All he did was gamble a lot; he had gambled all his life from marbles to dough. He found himself drawn to the erratic and mercurial life of a gambler. He found a great beauty in it and something very romantic that suited him. A cavalier traveling from adventure to adventure. Hang the responsibilities, full speed ahead. Give vent, baby, give vent. Everything looked so rosy now, so pure, so clear for him. Sometimes the aimlessness of it all, the lack of responsibility made him nervous. He couldn't believe that he could live the way he was living without having to pay some dues for it. Oh well, here today and gone tomorrow, Maxwell.

Big Tits whispered to Ashes, got up, and sashayed down the center of the observation car. All eyes stopped. Alfred Benjamin Simmins thought he'd like to do it to her Keester. Beneath that black skin and dark brown eyes, he gave no hint of what he would like to do to anybody. They could tell 'em what bathroom he could piss in, but they couldn't tell 'em where he could stick it.

Maxwell marveled at her machinery; he looked around for any other worthy creatures. There were a few, but not his style except maybe the girl looking prim and proper, sitting down near the door leading to the observation platform at the end of the train. She was sweet and wholesome-looking, about twenty-one, he thought. He passed her face and looked out the window of the observation car, the lights of Chicago were receding, and dusk had settled into a very dark night. He finished his drink, got up, and started toward the dining car. He went two cars up, passing from the third car to the fourth, where his compartment was, and was on the outer platform of the train when he saw her standing in the half shadow, looking out of the large window. She saw him, smiled, and reached for his hand. He stepped closer to her and before he knew it they were in each other's arms, kissing full on the lips. He felt her body press hard up against him. It was an incredible experience. His erection was hard and firm and she soft and vulnerable. Her mouth disintegrated into a warm, soft, wet cavern. She moaned and reached for his penis and stroked it. It was almost more than he could bear. He was pulled off her roughly by Ashes Prima, who came out of nowhere, pulled him backward across the width of the train, and slammed him into the other windowed door.

"You gigolo, cocksucker," Ashes, red-eyed and scared, hissed, "you fucking gigolo. I'm going to teach you a lesson, you prick, you goddamn prick."

He had his piece, a .32 caliber, in his hand. He was bringing it up to shoot, when the door to the car opened and there was the kid with the racing form and the black suit, the gray cap on his head, and in his hand a .38. He rapped Ashes across the face. Ashes stumbled back and fell into Big Tits.

"You guinea cocksucker, greetings from Vito."

Blam—he fired one shot from that .38 at short range and Ashes turned to ashes. The bullet broke and shattered his chest bone, blasted his heart, and it stopped beating immediately. Without even waiting for the sound of the shot to quiet, the gunsel gestured with his .38 for Big Tits to move in the corner with Maxwell, which she did. He stepped to the platform, and with his right foot he pressed down hard on the lever that opened a metal land-

ing that swung up and out of the way to disclose three
steps leading down from the train. He swung the top section flap up against the inside wall of the train and now
the hatchway was open, leading nowhere except to gravel
and earth speeding by at sixty-eight m.p.h. in the Indiana
countryside.

The gunsel reached down, putting his hand in Ashes'
inside coat pocket, deftly avoiding any blood that was
now soaking the front of his shirt, and pulled out a fat
wallet and Ashes' .32, never taking his eyes off Maxwell
or Big Tits. Then he slipped them into his pocket,
grabbed Ashes by the belt buckle, and, lifting him as one
would lift a heavy valise, edged him to the opening. Big
Tits hung onto Maxwell. Maxwell said nothing—he just
kept his eyes on the gunsel. At the first hint that his days
were over, Maxwell would throw caution to the wind and
try and fight his way out of it, but first he had to wait
for some sign. By this time the gunsel had Ashes on the
edge of the steps and unceremoniously kicked him off the
Twentieth Century Limited. His body bounced three or
four times as it hit the gravel, ricocheted off a boulder,
and finally stopped in some low weeds, half submerged
in a puddle of water. Ashes to ashes, dust to dust; don't
ever fuck with Vito Gust.

The acrid smell of burnt powder from the bullet assailed Maxwell's nostrils, but with the door open, it was
quickly pulled out by the rushing wind that enveloped the
small compartment. The gunsel waited, checking both cars
through the windows. There was no one. He closed the
outside hatchway and, where twenty seconds earlier there
had been madness and horror, there was nothing but
peace and tranquillity. The gunsel put the .38 in his right-
hand pocket, gestured Maxwell and Big Tits to move
toward the front of the train.

"Take me where Prima was gonna sleep."

Big Tits didn't blink an eye but went straight ahead.
The next car up she turned into his compartment. It
was a double, but Ashes wasn't gonna use it.

The gunsel made Maxwell and the girl sit down in the
corner. He went through all the luggage, two pieces.
Maxwell didn't know what he was looking for; neither did
the girl. The gunsel knew the money was in the wallet,

but he wanted something else. He found it. A small black diary. It was stuck in a shoe. He put it in his pocket, checked his watch, and looked up.

"I'm going to let you live; don't try and cause me no trouble and keep you mouth shut if you know what is good for you."

With that he backed out of the compartment.

"God, I could use a drink." She sounded like a countess. She opened a small valise that lay just under the berth, pulled out a silver flask, undid it, and took a swig. She handed it to Maxwell, who did likewise. They never took their eyes off each other. She reached out for him, fondled him, and clumsily let her coat fall to the floor. She couldn't get enough of him in her mouth. He quickly tore off his jacket, reached over, and locked the bolt. They made love to each other. It was an incredible affair. Neither one would ever forget the night they spent together on the Twentieth Century Limited, leaving Ashes half buried in a puddle of water. They felt the train slow down, but what they didn't know was that it was nearing Cleveland and the train was slowing to pick up mail the Twentieth Century would hustle to New York. When it slowed, the gunsel stepped off, walked into a black two-door Ford coupe, and sped off into the night.

The two of them sat in the semidarkness of the compartment. He lit a cigarette. They both smoked quietly.

"I could use a little food," he said.

"So could I, come on," she said.

They went out of the compartment and as they hurried forward they heard the chimes.

"Last call for dinner, last call for dinner, please, last call for dinner." The porter with the chimes smiled. They had steak, french fries, a salad, apple pie, and coffee. She kept pulling on her secret flask. What had happened earlier was nothing but a fuzzy memory by now. They walked back to his single compartment.

"Get my satchel, will ya?" she said. "It's under the berth. My hat and coat are hung up on the door."

When he got back, she was in the single berth naked under the sheet. They played with each other all night long. They'd rest for a while, smoke cigs, talk, then brush their lips all over the place. At about five-thirty in the morning he went to the bathroom. He passed Alfred Ben-

9

jamin Simmins asleep in a sitting position in a corner of the car. Maxwell shaved, changed his underwear, and dressed again. He went to the observation car and sat down. It was just getting light.

"Coffee, sir?" Alfred Benjamin Simmins asked.

"No, just some orange juice, please."

"Yes, sir."

He sat there and watched the sun come up. They arrived in New York at precisely eight o'clock. As they stepped off the train, he gave Alfred Benjamin Simmins a five. He turned and looked at her. There were hollows where her eyes lived, a European shade of blue, her nose soft and small, her lips full and rich, moist from life and ruby in color. Unruly hair, brown like the darkest nut, burst from her small, delicate head. She stood five and a half feet tall, a woman in a girl, full in hips, a slender waist, small back and breasts of alabaster glory. The best of 1922 yearning for a mission, yearning to dedicate her energies. Hoping for a dream. New to a country and new to a life. America, "Take me." America, I love you. Maxwell sobbed inside.

"I don't even know your name," he said.

She reached down and picked up her satchel, took the fur-lined collar of her knee-length cloth coat and hid her throat with it. She pulled the lip of her cloche hat a little deeper over her head just above her blue eyes, looked at Maxwell, and said, "Stella," then turned and walked out of his life. Carrying their child.

Good-by, Laura Mae

Laura Mae Jones, belle of the ball. Miss Gary, Indiana. Apple of her father's eye, peach of a girl, the sweetheart of Sigma Chi. When she caressed Maxwell's cock he swooned. This beautiful belle from Bashful Bend. If she wasn't Miss America, who was? She was the daughter of a stupid and rich man. Maxwell Boyd Cody was the son of a poor and stupid man. Not stupid, maybe, in the gift of life, but stupid in its practice, with a regimented and unforgiving response to life. Letting the sun shine in only on Sundays. Their families represented another period of time. It was time for a change in the country and their parents weren't up to it. He was twenty-six and she was sixteen. Even the years between them were a tragedy as far as their families were concerned. Laurie and Max eloped. Everbody shit then. Rumor had it that Laurie was pregnant and had to marry. Rumor had it that Max had kidnapped Laurie. Waiting for her after she finished her dance class at the local high school, he threw her into the rumble seat of his Packard and drove off with her. Rumor had it that Max was queer and was marrying Laurie just to cover up this affair he was having with the high school gym teacher. She would have made a great queen. Never had a chance. She was tall, affectionate, sweet-smelling, kind, and loving.

They eloped and roamed the Mississippi River, up and down its banks. Stopping at lovely small cities and large cities that ranged the center section of the United States, coursing north to south. Max met Barney Brewster one summer's day in Wichita. A farm machine distributor and manufacturer. Brewster's Brutes. Barney wanted him as a salesman and partner for five per cent and two hundred bucks a week. Hot dog . . . let's go. So there were three flourishing years for the Cody family. A beautiful house on the slopes of Forrestown. Max bought himself a Stutz Bearcat and they made love a lot. Laurie got a short fur coat. They had fine friends. Visited New Orleans whenever they could. Bought each other gifts. Stayed at fine hotels. Went to the theater. Heard some jazz. Had king crab. Time sure goes when you're having a good time. Then one night in Memphis she got pregnant.

I Think I Heard
a Sparrow Sing

Ruth was ahead of him rushing down the street.

"Stella said it would be parked between Fifty-eighth and Fifty-ninth, close to the river as you can get. Oh, come on, hurry, Morrie, please."

Morrie loved Ruth very much. This dark, strange, wild Hungarian-Jewish girl who always felt away from home. Her family was unreliable, gay, friendly, dishonest, unruly. But these were all the qualities that made her and her family so attractive to Morrie. Her family had settled in New York just eight years earlier before World War I had begun. It was a little colder that evening than usual for the beginning of May in New York City. They went down to the East River. There was nothing parked on the street except a four-door Packard reposing between two street lights in the semidarkness of the street.

"Stella said the package would be in the back seat, come on."

They got to the car, looked in the front and the back. On the back seat was a shoe box with the top neatly placed underneath the box itself. Packed in the box was a soft blanket. You couldn't distinguish what was in the blanket or what was really in the box. They tried opening the doors but they were all locked.

"How are we supposed to get inside the car . . . ? The doors are locked," Morrie said.

"She may have hid the keys somewhere," Ruth said.

"No, she didn't. That bitch just didn't think of leaving the key."

She thought she saw the blanket in the box move just slightly . . . then her worst fears were realized.

"There's something alive in that box," she said. "Quick, we've got to open the door of this car."

There was some construction going on just below one of the lampposts. Ruth didn't hesitate at all. She picked up two bricks and started walking toward the car. Morrie, not really knowing what to do, kind of hesitantly walked beside her.

"What are you gonna do with the bricks, dear?"

She heaved one brick through the front door window and threw the other one on the ground, undid the lock on the front door, opened the back seat door, reached in, and pulled out the box. There in the box was a newborn baby. He had been born four hours earlier in a third-floor apartment on Sixty-second Street near Third Avenue. It almost killed Stella.

"That bitch, that lousy bitch. How could she do this, how could she do this?" like an animal Ruth moaned. "That bitch . . . that lousy bitch."

"Ruth, please, Ruth, Ruth. Probably couldn't tell you any more on the phone than what she did."

"She could have but if she did she knows damn well I wouldn't have been down here at this time of night and neither would you. That dirty whore."

There was an envelope with two grand in it pinned to the blanket. The child fit perfectly into the shoe box. They pulled back the blanket and looked at it under the street light. It was beautiful, composed, quiet. Eyes open looking at the both of them. They half expected the child to smile and to show some sign of recognition. It lay in the box waiting for its life to begin. As they went home on the Second Avenue elevated, Ruth decided to call the child Julius after her mother's father. Morris after her husband. Singer, which was their name. They both knew the minute they looked at Julius in the shoe box underneath that street lamp that they would never give him up. He would grow up to be their child, part of their family. However big or small they would ever become. They also knew somehow this lonely, unwanted child would remain lonely and unwanted all of his life.

"*Bulond Kurva*," Ruth muttered in Hungarian. While she was diapering Julius, Morris, simple Morrie, stood alongside looking at his beautiful woman.

"Have you noticed anything funny about the kid, Ruth?" he said.

"Like what?"

"Well, he's been with us now about fifteen hours and he hasn't cried yet."

"And God willing he may never have to."

Ruth would never have any other children except Julius. Julius, quiet Julius, they would never regret raising Julius, never regret taking that trip that May night to find him in a shoe box marked "Catlado Niro 9C Aristocrata."

Andrew

Hanging right in Wichita, Kid Andrew Cody was born. He was breast fed for six months and left it only because he was asked to. There was no comparison with the other milk. Four years later the wind seemed to take his mother away. Laurie shivered one day of the cold. It had not been any colder than the previous seasons. It seemed as if she got a bad cough, bad cold, which didn't go away for a month. Specialists came and looked at her. Said there was something in her lungs that was making her feel poorly and just rest and good sunshine would cure her. Even before they could get out of town, Laurie's health deteriorated. She took smaller and smaller breaths and just slipped away. Stopped breathing. The odds of that happening to Maxwell, the accountant, mathematician, and genius in logic, were unimaginable.

Max thought a lot had happened to him as he stood there with Kid Andrew Cody by his side, four years old, standing over the open grave of his mother. The Kid remembered little of this gay, laughing, sweet, and loving woman. A driving force had been taken from him before he had a chance to realize it. She was dead. She was gone. Max felt society was the cause of this disaster. Their life was so involved with their neighbors and their friends and their family. Everyone knowing your business and you knowing everyone else's. Once you found yourself numbered in that society and establishment, why, your number was up. You were told that certain statistics proved that you would die of this disease or that disease. He took his son. Paid all his debts. Sold the house. That money and her insurance money, and his five per cent of Brewster's Brutes, which came to eighty thousand, he put away in a safety deposit box at the Wichita Federal Bank. He bought the best Chrysler they made and hit the road with the Kid and five thousand in cash.

They moved around like gypsies. The Kid picked up whatever education he could from the people that he met and knew or would get to meet briefly. He learned to count from the cards in a deck. He picked up an understanding of math by watching twenty-one played. He learned to read from the tabloids of each city, reading the cartoons, and Max swiftly teaching him reading, writing, and arithmetic. One season on the road with his father and the Kid could read and write with the facility of someone two years older than himself. Besides just being around was enough fun. Those summer night walks. Those strange little town streets. Looking in windows. His father let him walk around until nine o'clock, then up to their room in the local hotel. They always stayed in a good hotel.

The Kid never got enough of Max. Whatever city they were in, Max insisted that the Kid go to every museum in town. If there were operas or any matinees playing, why, the Kid found himself there, listening to arias he would never hear again, listening to actors he would never see again. What kept his interest going were the people that sat around him more than what was put on stage. The people that sought out this sort of entertainment. By this time everybody was running to the movies; so was he whenever he could. But to go to the theater was really something special. Just going out was nice to the Kid.

Whenever it got really bad for the Kid, Max somehow sensed it and changed his life drastically. They'd go off the road for a while, pull into some quiet town, and Max would take the Kid and they would go fishing or they'd go hunting for rabbits or they'd camp out for two or three nights. He knew how to treat the Kid good, and when he could, he did. The time they spent together enriched both of them, and the Kid looked forward to these little jaunts that they took together while his father got the devil out of his soul, drove the monkey off his back.

Life on the Road
Can Be a Lot of Fun

1934

Maxwell Boyd Cody was his name, gambling was his game, and he'd tell anybody that would listen. All he asked you to do was bring a bunch of money to a table; he'd bring the cards. He was six foot, loose, and fancy-free. Packing the Kid with him was no indisposition. The Kid was clean and quiet and did what he was told. Besides, on nights when he wasn't shacked up somewhere with some local filly or getting his cock done to in a local whorehouse, or bullshitting with his cronies down in the lobby, or shooting pool, or playing poker, five-card stud, five-card draw, seven-card stud, lowball, jack and a dame, or out eating in some fancy restaurant, or dressed up and looking like a spiff—he was with the Kid.

They'd share a hotel room and a bath. The Kid always slept in the same bed with his father. If the Kid went to bed early, he'd try to fall asleep, lights on. He rarely could, for the pain of loneliness would reach deep inside him. He'd sit up in bed alone, eyes wide open, looking toward the ceiling and the one light that shone above his head, and shudder with a sob. He wished his father was lying in bed now with the lights out. And, just when it seemed more than he could bear, in walked his pop, looking swell and dandy, a smile on his face win or lose. Maxwell Boyd Cody was his name and gambling was his game.

The kid cleaned up his room on the fifth floor and went up to Room 907. When he walked in the game had already begun. There were six men around a table covered with green felt. A white bulb with a green shade swung just over their heads and put an unblinking harsh light on the green felt. The light was so bright that the Kid could see the individual fuzz on the felt. It was a green oasis in this sea of dark brown and black.

Harry the Ace Slaughter, black as the ace of spades, looked up from his stack of fifties, twenties, tens, and fives and saw the Kid.

"Howdy, son. How's it pullin'?"

"Okay, I guess."

"Does your father put any money in your pocket?" Ace asked, as he flipped a silver dollar to the Kid.

"Thanks, Ace."

Ace flicked a glance at Max, who was opening a new pack of Lucky Strikes. He did it like a surgeon. He flipped the end of the red cellophane strip in one circular motion and the cellophane top of the pack was gone. With delicate care the silver wrapping was stripped down the stamp that rested in the center of the pack. He lifted the silver wedge up and tore along the line at the top of the pack completely around to the other side of the stamp. One swipe across the stamp and the silver wrapper was gone and the cigarettes were exposed. He tipped the pack upside down with his right hand, tapped gently on his forefinger and out slid one newie, as he called 'em. He took it and rested the case on its edge. The matches were open, a match torn out, scraped, burning, and now lighting the cigarette for Maxwell. He inhaled, looked around at the players. How many nights had he sat like this, using all of his energies and talent and genius? All those incredible powers that rested inside this man, pissed away on a three-hundred-dollar pot.

The guys he was sitting in with tonight were no match for him. Maybe Ace. But even Ace over the long haul couldn't beat Maxwell. Max used one simple principle in playing poker: observation. He could remember every card that fell face up. He observed everything about the pack, starting with how it was shuffled. He tried to follow cards, through the shuffling, to figure out approximately where they could be resting in the deck. He'd always spot the bottom card of the deck. If a guy threw his cards over, every card seen was marked in Max's head in the order in which they rested in the pack. In that way, he could recall them instantly. He was also frugal. He'd never chase his money or anyone else's. Unless! He'd just sit and wait for the cards. Unless! He never stayed without at least a pair of tens. Unless! In five-card stud his hole card had to be ten or over for him to hang in there. Unless! If the second card dipped to an eight, he'd throw his cards and fold. Unless!

With all of this knowledge, power, and genius for the game he had one flaw. He could never judge character. He was the most gullible mother-fucker that ever lived. No one could beat him on those nights when he played his own game. But if by chance he caught the glimmer, the agony, the hate, the envy or all the other emotions people seem to respond to, why, it always intimidated Maxwell. Then, depending on how he was provoked, he would respond almost mathematically. If he felt any animosity, his game would fall apart or change. He'd stay with cards he shouldn't. Instead of dropping out, he'd call. Instead of calling, he'd raise. He felt he not only had to beat the logic of the game, but also the emotions of the game. To win a hand was to come, beat his opponent. To lose a hand was to be made a fool of by the guy that won it. When he could maintain his concentration and play his own game, he invariably won. Some nights he'd play for the exercise. Call when he shouldn't. Raise when he shouldn't and just stay in the hand when he shouldn't. He had no place to go. The Kid was sleeping. See if he could hit an inside straight. Try to fill a flush by drawing two cards. He was thirty-seven years old. Old before his time. And yet younger than the Kid. He had blue eyes. And no patience. A king without a kingdom. A man without a throne.

As the cards were shuffled and spun out to the different players from the Kid's eye level, he could barely glimpse a color or the actual card itself flying to the six men who sat around this green table. When a guy dealt, he had his own particular way of dealing. Some flicked the cards out. Others let them just float out of their hands. Others seemed to deliver each card as if it was a special delivery letter. Some flung them out with promise and some with despair. Almost breaking even was normal for most of these guys. Two hundred was a loss, no more, no less. Losing six hundred was just feeling the pain. After a thousand it was amputation without any anesthetic. If you were lucky, you made three to five hundred dollars in a poker game and played four times a week, traveling a hundred to two hundred fifty miles a day just to play five-card stud in another nameless room. If you were top notch, you could make twelve thousand dollars a week in the season. If you had a flaw, and Maxwell Boyd Cody had a flaw, you could do five, seven thousand a week, sometimes win fifteen thousand a week; other times lose your kip and have IOU's floating all over the place. Trying to catch up to them as you went through the eighteen cities that you played in. Running across the same gamblers, eating up your IOU's, and laying out a few yourself.

My Daddy

"Come here," Max said. "Let me comb your hair."

They were in New Orleans and Maxwell and the Kid were going out to a smart French restaurant for dinner. Chez Louis Ami on Bourbon Street, not far from Cat's Row. Max had bought the Kid a blue serge suit, white shirt and a blue tie, and a pair of low black shoes. The Kid had a haircut and he looked fine. Max wore a dark blue suit as well. They were identical except one was bigger than the other. There was a strong resemblance between the two. You could spot them anywhere and know they were related. Max was a fine-looking man and the Kid was going to grow up to be one as well. They slipped out of the hotel room, took the elevator from the twelfth floor, and went down to the lobby. The Kid followed Max. Max went to the desk, deposited the key, and told the clerk they were out for dinner, possibly the theater. Any messages, just put them aside. Max had his tin box with him, which he gave to the clerk to put in the safe. They walked to the door.

"Your car's ready, Mr. Cody."

"Thank you."

A Cadillac limousine pulled up with a driver. He stepped out and opened the back door and in slid the Kid and Max. The Kid loved going on the town with his father. He sure knew how to do things. The driver's name was Charlie Burrow. Max called him Charles. And Charles called him Mr. Cody.

"Chez Louis Ami, Charles."

"Yes, sir, Mr. Cody."

Off they went. That beautiful city of New Orleans. The restaurant was packed with the sporting type, the social type, and the money type. Max knew an awful lot of people.

"Hey, Max, you going to the Derby?"

"There's a big game two days from now in Chicago."

"Who wants to go up there in that lousy weather now? There's enough action down here."

They sat in a booth on the side, facing each other. A lot of people looked at both of them. Max and the Kid knew why. They were good-looking guys. The Kid and Max were pleased that they were each other's father and son. The Kid looked at Max. Max's face beamed. His blue eyes shining love down at the Kid. He reached across, took the Kid's hand, and gave it a squeeze.

"You're my boy, Kid," he said, "you're my boy."

They ordered king crab salad, baked potato, some corn on the cob, a bottle of imported water for Max and Pepsi-Cola for the Kid. A beautiful woman passed by, and Max immediately got to his feet.

"Please don't let me disturb you," she said. "Sit down, please."

"This is my boy, Andrew. This is Miss Eloise Layton, Andrew."

The Kid leaped up as his father had done.

"How do you do, ma'am?"

"He looks just like you, Max."

Max smiled and said, "I look just like him." The Kid blushed. Eloise said, "Please sit down, don't let me disturb you." They just stood there.

"How long are you going to be in town, Max?"

"Oh, a couple of days. The Kid and I are on a little holiday together. Shall we try to see each other?"

"Yes, I'm at the Brewster, 1206," she said. "Call me there." She smiled. "Good-by, Andrew, nice meeting you."

"Good-by, ma'am."

And she left. They sat down again and continued their dinner.

"To the theater, Charles."

"Yes, sir."

Got there twenty minutes before curtain. Time enough for Max to get a swig and for the Kid to read his program from top to bottom. Shakespeare, *Twelfth Night.* "If music be the food of love, play on; Give me excess of it, that, surfeiting, The appetite may sicken, and so die." An actor sat onstage in this huge chair in tights and a sword at his waist, ruffled collar and shirt, two huge dogs resting at his feet while three musicians, playing a flute, a harpsichord, and a clavichord, played this haunting Elizabethan melody. Do I stand there? I never had a brother. Sister and brother being reunited, ending up with who they wanted. Beautiful story. And the Kid loved it. After the theater, they went to Maxim's and got a plate of chocolate ice cream with syrup and some walnuts. They were at the hotel by twelve-fifteen.

"Go to sleep, Kid. I'll see you in an hour."

And there he was alone again.

In the morning Max was sitting by the window in a chair, slumped. He looked old and unhappy. He hardly noticed the Kid was there. Max was feeling bad. Alone and depressed. The Kid couldn't understand how his father could cheer up his spirits so much by just being in his presence. It made him feel good and happy. And yet, every now and then the Kid didn't feel part of his father's life even when his father was around. Sitting there now so sad and unhappy even with the Kid there, and it wasn't because his mother was dead, either. The Kid couldn't and didn't understand. Why just the presence of his father brought him joy. Wasn't there anyone that could do that for his father?

Max didn't drink much. He had stumbled on cocaine five years before in Baton Rouge. And now, he liked to snort it every now and then. No one knew about it, though. And when he ran across it, he'd pick up a little and pack it. He liked wine but that was about the size of it. He sat there by the window crushed by the weight of his own thoughts.

Cody

How am I going to find my way if I haven't any way to
go? And I'm tired of pinstriped, double-breasted suits and
two-tone shoes. And I'm a Yankee doodle dandy. I loved
her so and she's gone. She said Stella. Her nipples the color
of apricots and moonbeams. Oh, God! I came on the
sheet. Find me, please, and make a home for us. Forget
it. No one knew you stole it. Andrew, you shouldn't have
made the trip without your mother. She gagged taking me.
Stella, she said. Laura Mae, open up thy arms and let me
in. It's cold out here and I paid my dues, eh. What about
the Kid, eh? Tied to his bed with a leather belt. Come,
come, come. Long smooth licks with nary a thought. Gone
and never to fuck you again. Hair and blue eyes. Wet.
Warm. Smiling sweetly for the joy of it. I cannot go from
here to there. The ice is cold. There is no chair. Don't
let Papa see you. My sister took me when I was twelve, and
I never was the same since then. Deborah. Gone like the
dust of flowers. Also dead before her time. What about sis-
ter-fucker. Filth. Base. Animal. Come. She looked different
from then on. Smug. You warmed yourself there before
anywhere. Oh, God! I'm paying now with two pair, sevens
over. It was jerking off with yourself. Without an image.
Coming in yourself. Leave me, God, and let me be. Get
my breath. Long time no see. We met on the train, remember? I can't believe it. You haven't changed, my son.
My ass. Just because I came. It's got to have more meaning than that, don't you think? Okay. I'm wrong. I
want to be Andrew. Let him take care of me. I'm sick but
I can't. Learn to tie a Windsor. Mother, you'll never know.
Like a countess. God! I could use a drink. I should have
followed her. I'd be with her still. At the end of the platform she turned. I should have. Yeah. And if the queen had
balls she'd be the king. Take me and lay me down and
stroke my brow. Not you, son. Her! I want to be the Kid.
I never was when I was a kid. Allegheny is your uncle and
the Valley is your aunt. I should have stayed in New York.

There would have been no Andrew. Perhaps another boy. Tear it out of your throat, you scum head. Open your eyes and see your boy. He stands before you without your joy. Andrew, I'm sorry. I'm sorry.

The Kid came over and put his arm on his father's shoulder. His father took it from his shoulder and held his hand and looked up. The Kid saw the anguish in Max's eyes. He couldn't understand why. Was it his mother? Was it that poker game? What made him so sad sometimes? What broke his heart sometimes? It was only later that the Kid understood that his father wasn't finished. It was as if his father had not been given all the organs that were necessary to function as a human being in a happy state of mind. Max was always trying to find out the reason for his existence. He needed a reason. A hedonist, his father said, was only interested in the flesh, only interested in his biological needs. He wanted someone to love him when he was a kid. But no one did. His parents treated him as if he was going to come every second. Someone to chase around with a big towel to catch any of the seepage. Any daily function of his body was frowned upon by his parents. Max still couldn't imagine his father taking a shit or his mother wiping herself, not his family. If only Max could accept his joyous weaknesses which were his strengths. Chasing a pair of aces was just as profound as chasing Socrates.

My Daddy's Eyes
Are Blue

They were traveling down the river road in that big Chrysler on their way to Vicksburg. The Kid was holding Max's silk handkerchief out the window of the car as they sped along at about forty-five miles an hour, letting it stream out.

"Bring that handkerchief in, Kid," Max cautioned him.

The Kid halfheartedly nodded. Max kept his eyes on the road driving. The Kid kept the handkerchief out another five or six more seconds. It slipped from his fingers quicker than a nun's kiss. And there it was gone behind them somewhere. He quickly turned and looked at Max. Max looked over. Didn't see his handkerchief.

"Where is it? What happened?"

"It slipped out of my fingers, Dad."

Max pulled the car over, looked at the Kid hard. It frightened Andrew. He had never seen his father look at him like that.

"Always take care with other people's goods," Max said as he slid out from behind the car seat. "And always keep your own stuff together."

They walked back to about where the handkerchief had been pulled out of his hand. There it was caught in a bush. None the worse for wear. Max stretched a bit. Undid his fly, started to take a leak. The Kid did likewise. Father and son, pissing together on the banks of the Mississippi.

"Come on, Kid, we got a poker game to make," Max said. And they were off and rolling again.

Everybody chipped in and paid for the room and for whatever food, and medical supplies, hookers, bootleg whiskey, and payoffs that were necessary to keep those floating poker games going all over the Midwest.

The unending variety of ways cards fell into Max's hands never ceased to amaze and titillate him. He had never yet, in all the years he had been playing poker, ever had the same poker situation happen twice. And he had squeezed a lot of cards in his day. The whooshing of the cards had a joyous rhythm and a melody for Max. He loved the low sweet sound of chips, and coins, the cracking of paper money, and the burring of a shuffle.

"I call ya."

"Two pair aces over."

"I got a flush."

"Shit."

"Come on, whose bet?"

"How many cards you want?"

George took two and opened. He has three of a kind, Max thought, or a pair of jacks or better, and a kicker. If he has three of a kind my two pairs are beat, but if he doesn't he's bluffing, trying to improve one pair with just drawing two cards. The odds were greatly reduced in beating two pair. If he's keeping a kicker, it better be an ace, that's all. If it is any less than an ace, he's an asshole and will soon be out of the game. Or was it three of a kind?

This was closed draw poker, and there were no cards to be seen and remembered except the nine of spades, ace of hearts, and three of clubs, inadvertently knocked over. Play your own. Just play your own. Max had nines and fours and a queen. He hoped George had queens, because the one in his hand cut down the odds considerably for George to draw another. He got a jack for one discard. That helped his side. If this guy had jacks or was reaching for a jack, there was one less to be found.

George got his two cards; without looking he bet two thousand.

"Shit, man, I'm gonna take a leak."

"Call room service, get a sandwich up here."

Not a flicker on George's face.

"Nines over . . . eh . . . and he wants two . . . eh . . . shall I flush him for another five or just call? If those nines were jacks he would have raised," Max said to himself. He loved the drama of it. He started to reach. He took out ten one-thousand-dollar bills wrapped in the center with brown paper and marked in pencil "10." He took the stack and held it over the center of the table. They waited. He held it in his hands for three seconds.

"No. I'm just gonna call. I got nines over fours."

"Well, if I didn't better it, I haven't got it," George said. Turning over two kings to show openers from the three cards he had kept, searched in the two new cards he just received—nothing—turned over the kings and tossed them with the other discards.

"One down and twenty-three more hands to play."

If Maxwell Boyd Cody had known that that was all the poker hands he would ever play in his life, just twenty-three left, he would have gotten up from that game and never come back. But he didn't. Four nights later, the Kid was sobbing over his father's body, shot in the heart, and dead instantly. Max was as surprised as anyone at that table when that crazy kid from Biloxi, Mississippi, pulled out a Colt service revolver and shot him through the heart. Max had caught him cheating over a fucking pair of deuces. It was lucky for the Kid that his friend Slaughter was there.

They buried Maxwell Boyd Coty, age thirty-eight, on a hill outside Vicksburg. A pocket watch, a gold cigarette case, a tie clasp, ring, some photographs, and a birth certificate, twelve hundred thirty-two dollars and two hundred bucks from each player for the Kid. Tears. His father wouldn't be coming to his bed anymore, his sweet-smelling father. Top lip pulled tight over his upper teeth, mouth slightly opened. His father had never looked like that, as if the pain of it was just too great. Dispirited and lost, alone and afraid, the Kid had no one to turn to. Slaughter put him up with a gambling family in St. Louis. When Slaughter left, the family became disinterested in the Kid. Let him roam wild. He didn't like it. He ran away. Turned himself in, in Denver, Colorado, after hitching for three days. Shipped back to his foster parents. Then the judge and his foster parents recommended that maybe an orphanage would be the best place. The Kid felt so too. At least he could hide among the other kids and nurse his sorrow and heal his wounds. Physician, heal thyself. The Wichita Home for Boys, it was, and still is.

And never pull on an inside straight.

Book Two

LIFE
WITHOUT
FATHER

It Was Summer
and They Lived on

Sixty-seventh Street between First and Second Avenues in those days. They'd get back to their apartment around ten. Julie'd jump into the bathtub and take a cold bath. Meanwhile, Ruth would take his mattress from his bed and put it out on the fire escape. On those hot nights in New York, Julie slept out in the open. Morrie and Ruth would pull their bed over close to the window. They had an inexpensive electric fan turned on, blowing over a cake of ice that they took out of the icebox onto the fire escape. Julie'd stretch out, put his arms behind his head, and cross his legs. He didn't even need a blanket with his *gotkes* on, nothing else, and try to see things in the sky. With the sounds below and the silence above he'd finally fall asleep and wake up early to the smell of coffee coming from some unknown apartment drifting past his face. Ruth would make a bowl of coffee in his cereal dish with a lot of milk and sugar with matzohs broken in it.

Later this period of time in Julie's life didn't seem to have really existed. They were always memories to Julie. Even when they were happening they were memories. While he was experiencing them he felt as if it had happened before. Life was funny. They'd go to Central Park, the three of them, Morrie, Ruth, and Julie, in the summertime and end up near the Mall. Hot, sweltering nights in the city, some half-ass band playing something, children laughing and playing, ice cream being sold, couples on the grass dry humping each other, pretzels with salt on them, ices being sold, hot dogs and soft drinks on pushcarts. They'd sit, listen to the music, and walk around looking at other people, while other people looked at them. Then they would walk down to the zoo, keep walking until they got to Fifty-ninth Street and Fifth, turn left toward the East River, and down Fifty-ninth to First Avenue, and left to Sixty-seventh Street. Ruth and Morrie always talking, sometimes holding hands, forgetting Julie was along. Julie'd walk ahead or behind them, a cotton white shirt with buttons, short pants, thin belt with a long leftover, socks at his ankles, and low-laced scuffed-up shoes all wrapped around a skinny, dark-haired, blue-eyed kid. If they had a little dough he'd take them all to California, Morrie said. But Ruth didn't want to go. She wanted to be around her fucked-up relatives in New York. So on they stayed and waited.

In the summertime, Julie helped Morrie by delivering clothes. A funny man with a big dog who lived in a town house between Lexington and Park on Sixty-fourth Street kept sending clothes to Morrie's tailor store just so Julie would deliver them. But Julie was onto him and never let him get close. He once delivered some dresses to a woman on Sixty-seventh Street who asked if he loved Jesus instead of tipping him. He said, "Yes," so she gave him a small crucifix and a kiss on the lips. Her tongue almost choked him. He loved this encounter. She had big tits. One summer when he was very young, maybe about eight, he went to the Henry Street Settlement House summer camp, and found himself away for two weeks in the country. There were cows, and horseshit, big fields and cowshit, apple trees, and bullshit. All kinds of fruit trees and the smell of new-mown hay. That's the way it was in the country. But by that time Julie had poison ivy all over, including his genitals. He lay in the infirmary, swabbed all over with calamine lotion. It was worse than the cures of the vampires. And by the time the two weeks were up he had just barely recovered and couldn't wait to get the fuck out of there.

Julie Vanilla Malted

1935

Julie was in this trench with another kid, called Herbie. He had a carbine. Herbie had a submachine gun, four hand grenades, balloons filled with water, a canteen of flour, eight flour bombs, small brown paper bags of white flour wrapped loosely with string, and a knife. They were trying to determine where the rest of their troops were. Sal, Frank, and Angie. They knew Vito was dead because his jacket front was splattered white. This was Julie's chance. If he got this patrol through the war of mazes, he would have Seventy-fifth Street all tied up. It would be his turf. His. His. The bastard kike frrom Abilene. They were on patrol from the east end of the lot to reach the west side of it to the street and freedom and two-bits a head. Both to the north and south of them were seventeen enemies, ranging in ages from seven to fourteen. They had maneuvered their way through no man's land through trenches, in and out of foxholes, over boxes, and ash cans and corrugated metal and were about halfway through the maze. Neither one had received any fatal or crippling wounds. Julie sustained a blow, a wound of flour on his shoulder high and to the left of the chevron on his sleeve. Then above the noise of the city, and the noise in his head, he heard his mother's voice. High, clear, and sweet, calling out his name—Julie . . . Julieeee. When mother called he knew he had to go. She was reliable—not flighty—and wouldn't call his name unless she needed him for something. Without hesitating he stood up, pulled out a handkerchief so they knew exactly what his hype was and that he wasn't bullshitting anybody. Everybody froze and he nimbly walked through the maze.

"I'll be right back," he said, as he passed members of the enemy.

He dropped his carbine, the instrument of war, into a wooden crate that rested on the side of the lot, nimbly leaped over a fence, and was on his way to his mother's call. It was just before school was starting in New York City. Hot and muggy. About eleven years after he was born. Julie had been in the streets playing war in two empty lots that sat between two huge tenement houses on the East Side of Manhattan. He bounded up four flights of the tenement house where he lived with his mother and father, came up to the door of his apartment, pushed it open, and walked in.

"Hi," he said, "you want me?" There was no unhappiness in his voice as he waited to know what dear Ruth wanted of him. There was another woman in the kitchen. She looked like his mother.

"This is my sister Stella." His mother blithely turned and said, "This is your aunt, who's just come back from a trip and wants to say hello to you."

Julie smiled and said, "Hi." Stella seemed a bit undone and a bit nervous. He noticed many women reacted that way when they saw him. He was a nice-looking boy and he knew it.

"My sister is here for a few days and she wanted to say hello to you since she's never met you," Ruth said.

He thought it was odd that his mother never mentioned this sister before but that was okay too. Ruth was kind and sweet to him and anything she said was all right. So he decided to be on his best behavior. Showed Stella his room. Neat. Orderly. She seemed genuinely pleased to know him. His aunt took him out later in the afternoon to the candy store and bought him a malt, which he appreciated and liked. She was pleasant and civil with him. He was quite bored after the first five minutes. He thought there was a strong resemblance between him, this woman, and his mother. There was nothing in his face of Morrie. He was taller than both Stella and Ruth, and more refined in features.

Stella looked at him, not sure what she saw. That spiff on the train. Yes. He was an eleven-year-old boy beautiful in features, a handsome child, yet she sensed a remoteness, an awkwardness in him. His eyes were alert to everything around him, so were his ears; every sensing device he had was used. Julie at eleven and Julie at eighty would never quite be reconciled to the fact that the world was good and pleasant. To Julie there seemed to by a trap in every relationship, in every gesture, in every stance.

Stella, beautiful Stella, twenty-eight years old, as beautiful as they come and she was beautiful and she came, those orgasms placed her in this predicament. A beautiful son, yet unable to claim him because of the fire down below. Stella was intelligent enough to know her emotions and their needs. She knew after Julie was born that she could never really claim him, for her kind of life would be no place for a boy. She had the itch; she wanted to get it scratched. She wanted the most out of life and no snot-nosed kid could fit in them der plans. So this nafka from kafka would do it her way. She had the mind for it, the body for it, but she didn't really have the guts for it. She would almost move in with a guy, almost go to Florida with this one, almost go to Chicago with that one. She left the family early to go make it in the world, but she really wasn't prepared for it. She fell deeply in love every time she had an affair, whether it was Ernest Kaplan of Leahman, Kaplan, Katz & Caruthers, senior partner, married, forty-six, Central Park West penthouse, wife, four children, three boys, one girl; or big Harry Jackson, black gambler, with five apartments all over Manhattan.

There had been a lot of one-night stands for this girl, but she just wanted the experiences of living; nobody and nothing would stand in her way, least of all her blue-eyed boy. He sure was good-looking, she thought.

She felt uneasy around Julie for some reason. His gaze was unwavering and gave her no time to compose herself. She looked away, outside Rappaport's window onto the busy street to Third Avenue between Seventy-fifth and Seventy-sixth streets. She caught glimpses of herself behind the pushcarts in the crowded street, people screaming out the sale of their wares, vegetables, clothing, shoe polish, dead chickens, garters, spools of thread, five-dollar watches, ribbons, and loneliness. Julie ordered a vanilla malted. They tasted good enough, maybe

a little bit better than the chocolate malteds. What he
liked most about them vanilla jobs was the color with
the white straw, a raggard glob of white ice cream floating like some circular iceberg in a sea of white. They
sat in two metal-backed chairs in the corner of the candy
store by a makeshift table. There was another table a
few feet away that could seat four, maybe five. That was
the extent of the restaurant area of Rappaport's Candy
General Store. The rest of the room, which was twenty-
five feet long and fifteen feet wide, was crammed with
every conceivable medicine, cosmetics, rubbers, Kotex,
stamps, movie magazines, crayons, and school supplies,
but the major business of Rappaport's was candy. The
wall opposite Julie and Stella was crammed with shelves
of boxes of candy of all varieties, shapes, colors, sizes,
and tastes. Most of the candies cost you a penny. If you
bit into a right one and it was pink, you got a nickel
candy bar. Usually they were all white inside and chocolate covered outside. In all his runs into Rappaport's
Julie hit a pink only once and he'd been living in this
neighborhood for two years now.

The schools of the neighborhood were rapidly empty-
ing their young charges now, and their first stop usually
would be a candy store and Rappaport's was one of them.

Rappaport, overweight, overworked, overstimulated,
bald, apron from the waist down, gray linen jacket, the
pockets crammed with dollar bills, receipts, slips, chew-
ing gum sticks, pencils, phone numbers, a semi-hard-on
always. Incredible what candy would get him. There he
was, somewhat stooped, somewhat aged, somewhat tired,
three sons and two daughters. They were all giving him
heartburn. Fuck 'em, feed 'em fish, smile, and keep selling that candy. When he is an old man at forty-five perhaps he would retire, but now thirty-four—looking fifty-
four—he dreamed of retiring at forty-four. He set the
vanilla malted in front of Julie, the chocolate job in front
of the zaftig job that sat with Julie. Wow, was she hot!
He knew Julie's mother. This was not his mother. It
looked like the mother, maybe the sister or relative. He
would like to give that piece, a schtoop in the tochis.
Maybe if he gave them the malts for nothing she would
have to look up in surprise, and perhaps in the quick

glimpse into his eyes she would feast upon his lust, his majesty and maybe, miracle against miracle, hope against hope, he would say, "I noticed you the moment you came in—you're most attractive. Perhaps we can meet somewhere. Is there someplace that I can call you? Please, I hope you are not offended by my bold response to you, but I find you devilishly attractive. Please spare me the anguish of saying no. Just leave your number. Put it in the ashtray on the counter when you leave. *Au revoir, my dove.*" He got turned down a lot, but every now and then there was a number in that ashtray, and his cock stuck somewhere.

Each individual candy screaming to be smelled, all blended together, to give Rappaport's a distinct and curious smell. Stella's senses were so assailed and provoked by her surroundings, the smells, the people, the children, the outside pushcarts, the noise, that it was most difficult for her to concentrate on Julie, who sat before her. It took every ounce of energy to drive out all the other responses that were bombarding her to pay attention to this frail young boy who was her son, and give him even a few minutes of her undivided attention. It was tough for her. She could never concentrate on anything for long.

"Ruth says you're a good boy, Julie. Last time I saw you, Julie, you were just a tiny baby. You were cute and didn't have any hair."

Why is she being so nice to me? Julie asked himself. I hardly know her. He tipped over the straw just a shade, taking every precaution not to break it or chew the end that was in his mouth. He had had enough experience with straws to know that a chewed end is not good for sucking. She looks like my mother. Why is she so nervous about me? More nervous than the other ladies. She's sweating, too, and she smells—not a bad smell. Smells hot but it's not. At least I get a malted out of it. Rappaport's got a little too much vanilla in it this time. That shmuck is hit and miss with these fucking vanilla malteds. You'd think he'd learn by now. He must've made a lot already. She's beautiful, my tanta. She makes me feel hot. Jesus, no hard-on now—not with my aunt—and these pants, have you no shame? Her hair is wet. Holy Mary, why is she sweating so much? Must be wet in her armpits, too. And down by her bush.

He looked at her face again. Her eyes were clouded with other thoughts, other images. Occasionally she would snap out of her reverie, her fantasies, and focus in on Julie. He could see her slowly come back from where she was. She recognized him suddenly and smiled. He smiled.

"Where do you live, Aunt Stella?"

The Aunt Stella threw her.

"In Philly—you know where Philly is—about ninety miles from the city. What do you do when you have a good time, Julie? What do you like to do?"

"I like to look for shells at Orchard Beach."

"I didn't know there were any shells around like that at Orchard."

"Oh yeah, but you got to go early. You got to be there when the sun comes up. Once in a while in the summer, Mamma lets me do it. I go down with Angie, he's a friend of mine. I see him every now and then. He picks me up or I pick him up on the subway. Sometimes I leave at five in the morning. Ma is nervous, but I tell her not to be and that I'm okay. Well, maybe they're not shells —more like clamshells than sea shells—but they come from the sea; like they smell fishy. I got a collection in my room. I think I would like to go someplace where you could get a lot of shells. There must be places like that."

"Where was that?" she said.

He knew he was dealing with a ding-bat. He knew somewhere in the middle of his explanation he lost her somewhere. He saw it in the eyes. She just seemed to have left him sitting there alone, just some hulk sitting across from him with black hair, blue eyes, a face longer than it should have been, full lips, and a gentle cleft just like his mother, smelling like Friday night at Nedick's. This is getting me nowhere, he thought. Let's get the fuck out of here. He cleared his throat and she was back. It was too late to get back in the war so he decided to hitch on a trolley downtown to a five-and-ten-cent store on Fourteenth Street and steal something.

"Excuse me, Aunt Stella. It was sure nice of you to buy me this vanilla malted. Really nice meeting you. I got a ball game that I can catch and if I can get there now, I may even get to play. I don't hit too good yet, but I like to play shortstop. You don't mind if I go, do you?"

"Please, don't be silly." Stella was so relieved. "Of course, I know how a boy is when he likes to play ball." She plunged her hand into her purse and grabbed a number of bills. She crushed them into Julie's hand and said, "Please take this. Buy yourself something from your Aunt Stella."

And with that, she impulsively reached forward and grabbed him in her arms and held him tightly for a second, let her lips brush past his cheek ever so lightly. For a second there, when they were just inches apart from each other's face, both saw what it could have been, or what it might have been, and knew who they were. For a moment there, their feelings were complete. He would have stayed, but she got frightened, afraid to face her orgasms, and pulled out of the reverie of their closeness and turned and looked out of the window. Julie spun around and walked out of Rappaport's with seventeen dollars in his hand. When she turned back into the store, Julie was gone and Rappaport was standing there instead. Yes, the candy man can.

Alone Again Andrew

1937

"Cody, you've wet in your bed six nights in a row and you've only been here six days. No more water or liquid after four o'clock. Nothing."

At four-thirty, they served hot chocolate and a nice simple sweet cookie that was the only thing he had found somewhat acceptable at this new orphanage he had been sent to the week before. Dear Andrew, numbed by his despair and abandoned. Darknesses in his head that he knew nothing about or understood.

Mrs. Alma Rescall, spinster and the wardeness of this orphanage in the northern part of Nebraska, which housed two hundred boys and had facilities for fifty, tried to make it as pleasant as possible but was very stern and hard. Life was not made for play but for diligent preparation. Not so much for a life of study and living but only preparing for the great drama—death.

He tried not to piss in bed but he couldn't help it. He tried hard not to but couldn't control himself. He tried staying up, biting the inside of his mouth until it was raw and bleeding. Anything to keep him from falling asleep, but he couldn't. And when he'd wake up he knew instantly that he had wet the bed again. It shamed him. He didn't understand why he would do anything like that. When he was with his father he never did or hardly ever did. He got strong in those lonely years. Chopping wood, bringing water in, up at the crack of dawn, falling exhausted into bed by seven-thirty in the evening. He liked to go down to the orphanage's sitting room and read. There were a lot of books on the shelves, adventure stories. He read whatever he could find and lost himself in the fantasies of other people, while he was a guest of the county orphanage that fall and winter of '37.

After he had been at the orphanage for two years he had his little section of the world well organized. He chose the outdoor jobs because they seemed freer. He worked harder. But that was okay too. He had nothing but time on his hands now to work. He tried not to think of his father, but he couldn't help it. Sometimes the thought of Max would make him hold his breath. He'd shake his head as if to try to fling out this memory. Let it be nothing more than just a fantasy. Don't be gone, Father. This pain and anguish is more than I can bear. It came in waves. Sometimes during the day he didn't think of it at all. Then he'd be overcome by waves of despair for his father. It overwhelmed him sometimes. He would sit in the corner and crumble. In time the feelings got less intense as he found himself more involved in the environment around him. He was still quite alone and didn't want to share anything with anybody. A lot of the orphans came and went. There were a few that lasted five or six years, but usually these boys would find some home somewhere on a farm or a ranch or another orphanage and would leave this motel for children. If he had wanted to leave he could have, but right now it was all right for him there and he didn't mind it at all.

The hot chocolate was made with water. He ate onion and tomato sandwiches and drank whatever milk they got. The orphanage had its own farm, which produced enough dairy products to take care of a small portion of the young people at the orphanage.

The only kid he had any relationship with was Lefty Quine, a one-armed kid from the Midwest. They called him Lefty and that's all anyone knew about him. There were rumors about the arm and what had happened to it. From the right shoulder down there was no arm. The city police had found him unconscious on the road. They had rushed him to a hospital, blood transfusion, and an infection had to be stopped. He was in a state of shock. Nothing was ever seen of the arm. They searched for it in the vicinity, but nothing. He had arrived two weeks after the Kid, pale and belligerent. In three months' time, the Kid had learned the maintenance and upkeep of a tractor. He was given the privilege of choosing a team of two other boys for the gardening and harvesting and cutting of whatever was necessary on the back ten acres of the orphanage's land. He chose Lefty and Frankie Watson, the illegitimate son of a wealthy tobacco farmer outside of Versailles, Kentucky. Frankie didn't know it, would never know it. He knew absolutely nothing about a mother. He'd never had that experience. Those three kids with five arms got more work done than four kids with eight arms could.

Lefty did all the driving. If Lefty had to shift, he'd push the clutch in and with his right foot kick the gearshift into second, third, and reverse or whatever gear he needed. He sure got it smooth after a while. They were smoking corn silk. Frankie Watson reached to his hip and pulled out a pint of Kentucky Bourbon. Took a swig, handed it to the Kid. The Kid drank from it, gave it to Lefty. Lefty took a healthy slug and passed it back to Frankie again. Frankie took another hit, put the top back on, and let the bottle rest between him and the Kid on the grass.

"I'm sneakin' into town tonight to go to a movie. You wanna come?" the Kid asked.

Lefty shook his head. Frank said yes.

"Okay," the Kid said. "We'll go right after dinner. It'll cost ya two bucks, but I can arrange it."

"Does that include the movie?"

"Fuck, no. Movie's fifteen cents. Somebody'll cover for us for the bed check, and at eleven o'clock tonight when the two-day-old bread and pastry wagon arrives, we arrive too. Okay?"

"Hell, yes."

"You want anything from town, Lefty? Some cigs?"

"Nope. Just a root beer," Lefty said.

"Okay."

They sat at six for dinner. Six-twenty everybody was finished. The orphans who were on kitchen detail had eaten a half hour earlier. They were now poised and ready to clean all the dinner dishes in a snappy ten minutes. You could tell what they ate a week and a half ago by some of the stains on the plates.

At six-twenty-five the Kid and Frankie made the run. The back entrance to the home was a simple chain-link fence affair that was opened and closed by the orphanage personnel in charge of vehicles. In this case it was Tim, a forty-five-year-old idiot who would stay on there as long as they'd let him. He loved it. The food was good and people took care of you. Tim was going to make his local rounds to pick up any junk and old clothes that found their way into the boxes marked "For Orphans" placed in a number of retail stores around the city. Frankie and the Kid held on underneath the back step of the small Ford pickup until they were out of the gate, and then quietly climbed over the back railing, lay down on their sides out of the wind and out of the view of Tim, and rode peacefully into town.

They didn't wear uniforms at this orphanage because they didn't have any. What they wore were castoffs from everybody. So the two boys looked just like any two boys from the city. Likker Bill, a character around town, juiced, for a few bucks would arrange anything for kids that had some money. No one knew it, but the Kid had about fifty bucks in a hole he had put in the back of his heel. The rest of the almost two thousand dollars he had gotten when his sweet daddy got shot was kept behind the photograph of his father and his mother and him in a cheap leather frame. He was in a baby carriage, sitting with only his head and upper shoulders appearing over the edge of the carriage; his father was standing with his left thumb in his vest pocket, leaning on his right foot, his right hand holding the hand of sweet Laura, her beautiful legs ending just above the knees of some chiffon material. Three beautiful people, worth at least seventeen hundred thirty-four dollars, plus frame and picture.

The movie was *Charge of the Light Brigade,* starring Errol Flynn. What a movie! How much the Kid loved to see those people jump around up there. Sitting in his chair, he'd forget everything around him. He had no sense of his body at all, just perceiving pictures on the screen, sounds and noises. He loved them.

Did it happen? If it did, he was lucky. Seemed like a dream. Couldn't have been Frankie, because he was sitting on the other side of him. On the left side. This girl was on his right. He almost discovered her there. When they sat down she hadn't been there. He felt that if she had come in on the other end of the aisle he would have felt her coming in or at least looked up and spotted her. But he hadn't. Probably so engrossed in the film he didn't notice. The next thing he knew their legs were touching, then their hands. He reached for her and put an arm around her waist. She leaned closer into his shoulder. Slowly slid her hand across the upper part of his right thigh. Her small finger just touching the inside seam of his shorts. Less than an inch away from his cock. Oh! The joy of it! He found himself getting a hard-on. He tried hard not to, but if he was going to concentrate on the movie and enjoy that, he'd have to let it just hang out. Otherwise, forget it. He wanted his cake and he wanted to eat it, too. And he did. They groped at each other. He came in his pants. She squirmed as if she must have done something. Her face pulled back, moaning so softly. His hands inside of her blouse tripping over a nipple that was as firm as an eraser. If Frankie knew what was going on, he didn't crack. They sat there side by side for more than a minute as if they were strangers. Then she turned and looked at him. He looked at her. In the reflected light from the screen, she was certainly as beautiful as Olivia de Havilland. She leaned forward toward him and said good-by to the Kid. Then she was gone, disappearing into the black hole.

Outside the theater, he looked to see if there was any sign of her. Nothing. All gone. All shadows. He'd come in his pants, all right. But that could have been only in his head as well. But it wasn't. The pressure of her lips was still on him. He still tingled from the softness of her skin. And he still smelled her.

They rode back with six crates crammed with two-day-old bread, pastry, doughnuts, apple and cream pies. Once inside the barricade of the orphanage again, while dumb-dumb Tim pulled up and promptly dropped the ignition key and was scrambling on the floorboards to find it. The Kid and Frankie took two trays laden with pies and pastries and hurried across the dark lawn to the back of the two-story ranch house where they lived.

By four the next day, Frankie, Lefty, and the Kid and whoever they felt pity on had devoured and finished an assortment of coffee-cakes, coffee rolls. Danish pastry, doughnuts, and six pies. They were saving two apple pies for a rainy day. They were also sick.

Frankie also drank a lot of cheap Bourbon sold by a guy named Clancy Halmes, who delivered all the fresh fruit and vegetables the orphans ate. At eleven, Frankie could put away two fifths a week. He didn't last long, that Frankie. Died of consumption, he did. That's what they called it just two years later.

The last year that the Kid was there, they fitted Lefty with an artificial arm. He wasn't as conspicuous now as he used to be. There were some women whose husbands were too busy for them, so they spent all their time with charity organizations. These middle-class arbiters of good taste and culture, slumming in the orphanages and homes in their local neighborhoods. Oohing and aahing and moaning over the conditions and wellbeing of these orphans. Giving dinners for them in their local school gym. Raising twelve hundred dollars of which one hundred thirty went to the orphans. The rest was stolen, eaten by some committees, or whatever. Four of these women came to the orphanage, driven by a portly man in his fifties with a waistcoat and a watch fob, arrow collar, and a perspiring bald head. Lefty and the Kid were just leaving a building that housed the crafts room, where all the orphans made wallets for the local constabulary. It kept them busy and they were able to make six cents a wallet. As they stepped out, Lefty reached under his shirt and undid the buckle on the artificial arm that hung in a casual manner from his right side. The Kid, almost on cue, separated from him when the women being shown the facilities of this glorious orphanage came closer. They made it look like they had met by accident.

"Hey, Lefty. How are ya?"

"Fine."

The women couldn't help but see the two young boys greeting each other. Lefty kind of swung his shoulder and this useless artificial arm with the hinge at the elbow, snapped up as if it had a mind of its own, and stuck out an artificial hand whose color was a shade lighter then Lefty's own. The Kid grasped it firmly, and they stood there shaking hands and talking just for a couple of seconds. One woman found it charming and tender how these two pals met. The boys separated to leave. The Kid never let go of the artificial hand and arm. He just turned and went. It slipped out of its sleeve and just dangled there in his hand. Lefty turned and walked away. One woman screamed. Another moaned audibly. And one of the women felt some heat in her pants.

Three months later the Kid had all his gear packed. He was leaving for a farm somewhere with some foster family. He and Lefty were quite fidgety in those last few days. They both felt that maybe they'd never see each other again. Lefty Quine would leave the next morning.

"How'dja lose your arm, Lefty?"

"A boxcar refrigerator door slammed shut on it when I was trying to get off. The train was on a downgrade and for some reason the engineer slammed the brakes on this hundred-twenty-car caravan. The jolt made me hold on tighter with my right hand. If'n I'da let go, I'd have two good mitts now."

But he didn't. And this huge three-hundred-pound door with its edge as sharp as a dull knife came slamming down at twenty miles an hour.

"I didn't even know what happened. I found myself lying alongside the track. The train waiting for the light or whatever it was that made it stop so fast to change. I still didn't even know it. I kinda thought it but I didn't believe it. I walked about a mile. I couldn't delay it anymore. The pain, and I guess the loss of blood. And I didn't remember anythin'. Once in a while, I found myself crawling with my one arm. Then I was in the hospital. The guy that opened the boxcar the next day musta shit when he saw that arm holdin' on for dear life . . . only there was no life on the end of it."

Gone but not forgotten. Raise your right hand and repeat after me.

Julie

Thirteen, and Never Been Kissed

Dear Parents, Relatives, friends and Rabbi Suhmulovitz:
On this day of June the 3rd, I leave my youth behind me and step into the world of men, prepared to bring honor and respect to my heritage. As a son and a Jew, the greatest aspiration I can strive for is to bring pride and admiration to my Judaic heritage and at the same time, give my mother and father the greatest joy a son can give and that is love and faith in my years ahead as a man and a Jew. I thank my mother and father for their patience and concern in my years of growing up. I tell them to always know I shall never disappoint them during my years as a man and a Jew, but will only bring them the best their son can give them, with the help of God, trust, honor, and respect for our laws and traditions. In closing, I look at my youth that has passed before me even before I knew it was gone. I glimpse the future's unmade memories with anticipation and not without some fears, but know I pass from boy to man with my heart, and head held high, with compassion and dedication. I do not say good-by to my youth but ask it to join me in my quest for my manhood. AMEN.

Julie's Bar Mitzvah was beautiful. He really was doing it to please Morrie and Ruth, who seemed to look forward to the day that their only son was going to have his Bar Mitzvah, but he liked it himself, too. He read from the

Torah and said the prayers beautifully. Made a speech in which he accepted the responsibility of being a man. He praised his mother and father and hoped that they would always be proud of him not only as a son but as a Jew as well. Morrie's brother gave him a watch. Ruth's cousin Ilona gave him a fountain pen. Morrie made him a blue serge suit. Ruth gave him some white shirts, a blue tie, and a red tie, and a number of relatives gave him some sweaters and some money in little envelopes, thirteen bucks. He gave the money to Morrie. Morrie at first wouldn't take it and then finally he did. He didn't have much money in those days and every little bit helped. Julie and Morrie didn't begrudge each other anything.

Morrie invited some musicians to play at the house that evening after the Bar Mitzvah. By ten o'clock all the relatives and guests had left the party. Morrie had paid the musicians to play until midnight, and they were going to play until midnight. Julie had the radio on real soft listening to *The Shadow*. Ruth was cleaning up the dishes in the kitchen. Julie was looking over the gifts that he had received. Morrie made those three musicians, two violinists and a cymbalist, play till midnight. He sat in a soft upholstered chair in the corner of the room while the three musicians played in front of him. His dark brown hair combed flat and back, a trim tapered mustache nesting under a large nose, and two brown eyes, a single-breasted suit with spats, and brown shoes with taps, brown shirt, tie, and tiepin, a ring on his finger, a glass of wine in his hand. A bold feudal lord just finishing off his evening thoughts.

* * *

The kid's name was Webber. He was bigger than Julie, and he hated Julie. He'd bump Julie while they were lined up outside P.S. 82, with the morning traffic screaming up First Avenue, hoping to knock that kike cocksucker under a beer truck. "We got enough sheenies now as it is." Once Webber did succeed in bruising Julie up his left side, knocking him against some old wagon that was rustling by the street at that time, rapped him up against an old lamppost that he was frantically holding onto after his crash with Webber. He knew then that his life wouldn't be safe or tolerable with this prick Webber around. He had to do something. He didn't know what. Figure out some way to equalize Webber, something to give him back the peace and quiet that he wanted. At the snappy age of fourteen, that fucking Webber was a Nazi, a pure all-American Nazi German. Webber dogged him in his classes . . . Hey, Jew kike. Hey, asshole Hebe. Jew boy, Jew boy. Hitler will get you if you don't watch out. Christ killer. Come here, kikie. Sheenie fuck. Fag Jew. Cocksucker. While Webber tormented him, Julie knew that it wasn't natural. He knew something must be boiling inside of Webber like an open sore to make him strike out like that at another kid. It was more than just a fever. It was a madness inside Webber. You could look into those red beady eyes and you could see that he meant business. There was an earnestness about him.

Sometimes when Webber wasn't looking, Julie'd catch a quick look at him. The way he stood there, kind of at ease with himself, attractive in his own way, his attention directed elsewhere, at something going on in front of the class, a smile on his face, he looked nice. It was hard for Julie to believe that this was his tormentor. This quiet, calm-looking boy that sat across the room from him, this dark angel. Julie knew that he couldn't take too much more of it though. He had to decide quickly. Otherwise he'd have no life at this school. He'd become the butt of every bully in the school, and everybody was a bully. He would eventually be sought out by the other two thousand-odd fucking nuts. Who knows what his life would be then? It was fucking miserable now. So Julius Morris Singer, aristocrat without portfolio, decided he must act. He didn't know what to do exactly, but he knew something had to be done. He was afraid of the idea, but it had to be done. The next time Webber picked on him, he'd try to get even.

Julie decided the best place would be in the assembly hall, during general assembly in the morning. What better place for all the kids in the school to see the shit that this crazy Hebe kid had been taking from Webber and to give it back to Webber in front of everybody. Let everybody see what Webber could create. So he decided it would be done. He'd have to maneuver himself close enough to Webber so that Webber would be obliged to taunt him, knowing full well that this Jew-kike coward wouldn't dare start anything in general assembly. Wouldn't he? Oh, yeah. Well, that's the last time Webber would ever try that bullshit. That Nazi Heinie Wienerschnitzel.

Friday morning at nine-twelve Webber found himself with a man standing in front of him. At the slightest provocation, Julie spun around and grabbed Webber around the neck like a vise with his left arm and wouldn't let go. With his right arm and hand, he started beating Webber furiously on the head. He stuck his fingers in Webber's eyes, nose, ears. Julie's legs were planted firmly on the ground. Webber tried everything in his power to stop Julie. Webber grabbed him and hit him up against some chairs. He banged him off the wall. They rolled between the seats in the long central aisle that lead down to the stage in the assembly hall. Julie never stopped smashing, screaming, punching, biting, doing everything in his power to put an end to Webber. It took four students and a teacher to finally pull them apart. Webber hysterical, his face white and bloodied, his hair matted, was completely undone. For Julie, it was exhilarating, something he had never experienced before. To be able to express yourself in a way like that, to know what you're doing, to plan something like this and let it erupt like that and have it come off as successfully as Julie felt that it had was something beyond his wishes.

Perhaps he should have never pushed himself to that extreme. Perhaps he should have found another way to help himself through that awful situation. Perhaps if it had been done in any other way it wouldn't have had the dire effects it had on Julie for the rest of his life. For Julie had the Power. He knew it and he could feel it. He sensed it with the people around him. People that up to now didn't even know he existed all of a sudden looked at him with an immediacy, with an intent. He was someone among them screaming to be heard, asking to be looked at, wanting their attention, striving, seeking it. It must have had a profound effect on everybody in that room that morning. Julie never forgot it and Webber never forgot it.

The boundary of German town in Manhattan was from about Seventy-ninth Street and First Avenue going up

Manhattan to about Ninetieth Street. The main artery of German town at that time was First Avenue. All the German shops emptied into it. And during the late thirties until the start of the war, this became a rabid German Nazi neighborhood. Very nationalistic German Americans, really. They had parades up and down First Avenue with young people and old people of German extraction wearing swastikas on their arms, goose-stepping up and down First Avenue with the American flag and the German flag and the Nazi flag alongside of them. All Jews or anyone who looked Semitic were fair game in and around this neighborhood. These Aryans who beat up on anyone who dared to come into their private preserves. It was during this period of time that Angie and Julie tried to venture as close as possible to the neighborhood. In their eyes, they could not imagine how people could be so overtly violent and angry, as if Webber had multiplied, like rabbits, into thousands and thousands of people, and there in that area of First Avenue centering around Eighty-third, Eighty-fourth, and Eighty-fifth streets were one hundred thousand Webbers. All looking to beat any kike that happened to be in the neighborhood.

Julie would take Angie with him. Angie was an Italian Catholic and really had no animosity toward the Germans. But once when Angie was walking down the street, two blond-haired kids who turned out to be Germans attacked him and kicked the shit out of him. Punched him in the mouth, really rapped him up bad. Stole whatever he had on him and called him dirty kike and Jew and Hebe and killer of their God and said he should be dead. Then after they had beaten him and torn his clothes, they chased him down the street. You see, anyone that looked like Angie or looked a little like Julie was fair game.

Angie and Julie started to accumulate milk bottles and condoms. From the river to the hospitals to the hallways, there were enough rubbers lying around to recap the recaps. They found condoms floating in the East River, in hallways, in the movies, and Angie swore he found one in church. They broke into a drugstore once and stole all the rubbers the druggist had. They began depositing their ammunition in this tenement house on First Avenue and Eighty-fourth Street. Usually they would be in the neighborhood carrying newspapers or their shoeshine boxes, always looking like enterprising young men trying to make a few cents for themselves. And whenever they had the opportunity, they'd sneak up onto the roof of this particular building and behind some of the chimneys that protruded along the edges of the brownstones and tenement houses. Julie and Angie would pee and pour whatever excrement they could find in any of the neighborhoods into the milk bottles. They built themselves a supply of fifteen bottles and ten rubbers and surgical gloves filled with the same concoction.

On the day when the German Bund had their annual parade, and were Heil Hitlering it down First Avenue, the two boys went up to the top of the roof and hurled these missiles of love down upon the populace below. Before they had even hit the ground the two boys were gone. Down the back stairs of this huge building. Through an alley. Across to the next building's side, down some fire escapes. Ending up on Eighty-third Street and Second Avenue. As soon as the shit hit the band and the Germans realized what had happened, their little storm troopers started to fan out to find the perpetrators of this foul and horrible deed. Our boys by that time were on Second Avenue. Good ole Second Avenue. Going up to the El. Under the turnstiles, and into the first train that was going downtown. Getting out of that fucking neighborhood as quickly as they could.

Julie

Rabbi Suhmulovitz
Calling

He swore he would get through the day if it killed him.
Every year up to now as far back as he could remember
he never made it. Oh, he'd get to hold it longer through
the day, but always somewhere before sunset he'd break
down for either water, some watermelon, or a cookie, or
a glass of milk, an apple, or a torpedo sandwich with a
Pepsi. He could never make the fast of Yom Kippur.
This year he would. He promised himself. He planned it
carefully. He ate as big a dinner as you could possibly eat
the night before. As a matter of fact, the two days before he had gorged himself eating all kinds of junk foods
in and around the city just to build up a tolerance so that he
wouldn't have to eat on Yom Kippur. About six-thirty
the dusk before, he ate an enormous meal that his mother
automatically prepared. By nine that night he was starving.

Morrie was an orthodox Jew. Julie sat beside him, now
that Julie was over thirteen. He had bought two seats in
the shul downstairs for him and Julie and one seat upstairs
for Ruth. Julie never told Ruth and Morrie on those Yom
Kippur days that he had broken the fast early in the day.
Today he was sure he would get through it. But he was
starving. His mouth was dry, his breath was short, and his
stomach growled and yearned for something. Anything. He
put on his sweater, pants, and sneakers and climbed out
onto the fire escape and ran up to the roof. He heard the
cooing pigeons that a lot of the families in the neighborhood kept on roofs. He looked down into the wells of the
apartment buildings and saw the different apartments, some

55

lit, some not, some with shades down, some with shades up. Families eating, reading, getting ready for bed, brushing their teeth, and some young girl without her blouse on, washing herself before going to sleep. He went for a walk. By eleven o'clock he was home and had fallen asleep thinking of food.

The next morning was incredible. He was foaming at the mouth. Orthodox Jews do not brush their teeth or mouths in the morning on the day of Atonement. For days, sometimes months, he wouldn't brush his teeth, now all of a sudden he wanted to brush 'em. No, he mustn't. He must make it today. He must make it today. He said his morning prayers with Morris, and then the day started in the synagogue. The wailing, the mumbling of prayers. Standing, then sitting, then pounding their chests, then rocking back and forth mumbling those old words from another time, another place, bringing the memory of the past to the present. Time passes, passing the pain from one generation to another, from one runner to another. The women segregated, sitting upstairs with shawls or hats or sheitels on. All the boys and men down below, boys over thirteen, and boys under thirteen, and men with their talises and yarmulkas, boys with just their yarmulkas.

Julie could read a little because he had been sent to Cheder by Morrie when he was ten, three years before his Bar Mitzvah. Morrie was called up to read from the Torah. Julie joined the singing and wailing at times. Making sounds while his mind searched for shells. Milling in and out, going outside for a minute to take a breath of air or to relieve himself. Some men did nothing. Twenty-four hours they fasted, abstaining from the ordinary functions of life to prove that they had control over their bodies, their souls, and their intellects. That they controlled them and not the other way around. At least that's what Julie thought. Being a Jew was different at least. He figured that any group of people that could cause that much furor and hate and be so few in number must have something. He liked it, that's all. He was lucky he hadn't been born in Germany, and didn't know it. He tried to distract himself by counting how many people were in the synagogue, downstairs and upstairs. Morrie every now and then would look at Julie's prayer book, point his finger to a place on the page. Julie would start there, glancing over at Morrie's book every now and then to make sure he turned the page at about the right time as well. Morrie knew when Julie was B.S.ing; a gentle nudge was his cue and punishment. Morrie would allow him to leave his seat and he'd go into the anteroom of the synagogue, walk down to either the gymnasium or the small auditorium where all the boys and girls congregated. They'd size each other up. Make dates for late in the week. Maybe for the movies. Crushes. Love affairs. Hate. All the elements exchanged by young people, waiting to be able to go home and get a square meal.

Sunset would be at about six-thirty. As soon as the last prayer was sung, they would blow the shofar, and that would be the end of it. They'd close their prayer books and file out exchanging greetings in their way out to the street. Some would have dinner together. Some would not. They'd all go home and share with their families. Food made no difference anymore. He didn't think he'd make the day. He'd be the first person to faint in the synagogue. Flat out. Women would laugh, men would giggle. They'd drag him out by his feet into the gutter. Well, it wasn't gonna happen to him. He did everything in his power to keep himself calm and quiet through this ordeal of no food and no drink. He heard the sound of the shofar. He was bursting with joy and with hunger. He ran down to the bathroom . . . rinsed his mouth out with water from the tap. It refreshed him somewhat, certainly enough until he and Morrie got home. Ruth had left a bit earlier, had dinner all prepared for Morrie's cousin and his wife. Ruth's younger sister Irene came with her boyfriend. Ruth was an impatient cook but her meals always turned out wonderful, a little too much chicken fat maybe, otherwise not bad. These early meals of tutucapustah, bubledesh, cholent, palachintah, cherry soda. Foods that he thrived and grew on.

After dinner out on the streets. Still warm enough. Still early enough. Fuck around for an hour and a half or so playing johnny on the pony, war, kick the can, or kick your ass. Who could ask for anything more? Ringaleavio. Kokoko. Ringaleavio. Kokoko. Ringaleavio. Kokoko. Three times. Stick ball. Punch ball. Tag . . .

* * *

One day Julie and Angie snuck into the Gaiety Burlesque House on Forty-second Street between Broadway and Eighth. They got caught right away before they saw any naked girls. The comic was on doing some kind of a Floogle Street shtik or something. At the end, Angie and Julie were grabbed by this guy.

"Come on you hard-ons," he said, "get your asses outta here. You can't see these cooses yet. Beat it. Beat it. Beat it." He escorted them to the stage door, opened it, and said, "Now go."

No one under seventeen was allowed in. They were going to see naked girls if it killed them, so they went to Jersey, where they weren't too choosy how old you were. Just bring money. They were playing Tchaikovsky's First Piano Concerto, which starts out like that popular song "Tonight We Love." With this music out came a young girl who obviously hadn't had too much experience as a stripper. Her movements were not awkward but they were just a bit wooden. Both Angie and Julie couldn't take their eyes off her breasts, which were very white. One could see the slight shadows of a few veins that ran from the shoulder part of her breasts down to the nipples. Angie and Julie had never seen anything so clean in their lives. So polite, so beckoning, full and ready for life. The boys were quite used to women by then. They were asked on a lot of occasions to escort hookers to certain hotels and apartment buildings and wait for them. They had a lot of opportunity to learn all about ladies and their needs and their own as well. But somehow this alabaster creature with glorious breasts won them over.

Angie, crazy Angie, he fixed it up so that both he and Julie could go to this whorehouse. They were then maybe fourteen and a half. This friend of Angie's had arranged it, said it was going to cost ten bucks apiece. That was a lot of money in them days, but that was because they were young, being ripped off by the old again. They got in the house and sat down. Three girls were sitting in an anteroom. All three were quite young, fresh-looking, and wonderfully built. Any way they had been built would have been exciting to Angie and Julie. It didn't make any difference. To help make their choice easier, one of the girls voluntarily turned around and walked out of the room.

Both guys sighed with relief because they didn't wanna have to break anybody's heart or hurt anyone's feelings.

"They gotta be kiddin'," one girl said.

Angie had a hard-on by this time. With his hands in his pants pockets he leaned forward.

"I ain't kiddin', lady."

"Come with me for a minute," Angie said to Julie. "Excuse us, girls, we'll be right back."

The next thing Julie knew they were marching into a men's room that was on the same floor.

"Whatta ya doin', Angie?" he asked.

"Come on, we're gonna jerk off first and then we're gonna go hit 'em. At ten bucks a throw, kid, we gotta be careful. All she gotta do is look at me and I'll come."

And they thought of alabaster.

Later they jumped on the back of a trolley that was going back uptown, back to their neighborhood. They both held onto the back of the trolley. Their jackets zipped up right to their necks. Their stocking caps pulled over their ears. A cold and blustery night in New York City. They were just about four feet away from each other. Traffic noises and the wind were too loud for them to have any kind of conversation. At one point the trolley stopped at a stop light. For one miraculous second all the sounds seemed to quiet down to nothing and what was a screaming wild and violent place all of a sudden sounded peaceful and quiet.

"That was nice, Julie," Angie said, "that was real nice."

Andrew

1938

"I saw my sister's tits once when she came home from college. I'd never seen anybody's tits except maybe in these pictures I got."

"How come I never see your mother, Slim?"

"She's away in a hospital for the mentally deranged."

"Sorry."

"That's okay. I don't miss her. After my legs went bad she did too. Where did you come from?"

"My father got shot in Vicksburg."

"Shot. How?"

"With a gun."

"Somebody shot your father?"

"Yep."

"Was you there?"

"Nope. I just saw him after. Dead."

"Wow. Was he a policeman or a soldier?"

"Nope. He was a gambler, a gambling man."

"Why would somebody wanna kill him?"

"He caught somebody cheatin'."

"How'dja find the Stewarts? Are they related to ya?"

"Nope. A friend of me and my father's named Slaughter sent me to a family he knew. They didn't want me. I didn't like them so I ran away a lot. They sent me to an orphanage and I stayed there until I came to live with the Stewarts."

"Let's build a raft and go somewhere. I heard about somebody that built a raft and went down the Mississippi. Some kids."

"You probably mean Tom Sawyer and Huckleberry Finn."

"That's it! Where'dja hear about him?"

"This Slaughter told me about these guys that went down the Mississippi River. Just kids. Built a raft."

"That's a story?"

"No, that's in a book. I read it. Called *Huckleberry Finn, Tom Sawyer*. Written by Mark Twain. His name was Samuel Clemens and he used that as a pseudonym."

"A what?"

"That's a phony name."

"Oh."

"That's a name that ya made up, like a nickname."

"Oh."

"I got a nickname."

"Yeah."

"Everybody calls me the Kid."

"That's a funny name for a kid."

"Shhittt."

"You know what a whorehouse is?"

"Yeah."

"They got one outta town. A couple of guys work for my dad go down there on weekends. My father goes every now and then. Wish I could go. But I don't wanna yet till my legs get stronger. I don't wanna have anybody lift me on and off."

"Who done them pictures?"

"I did."

"Ooh, you draw beautiful."

"I use pastels and crayons."

"I got me an oil set ordered from a big art house outta Chicago. It's got all the colors of the rainbow and you can make any color that you want."

"I can do that now with my pastels. Gimme a color."

"Blue."

"What color blue?"

"Well, Slim, just gimme blue."

"No, no. You gotta give me some color of blue. Like dark blue or sea blue or true blue."

"Ha."

"Okay, what color blue?"

"Sad blue."

Slim mixed some blue and white until the blue was pale.

"Yep, that's pretty sad-lookin'. What time of the day do you like the best?" the Kid said.

"The night," Slim said without waiting. "You?"

"I like the day."

"We should be one person—you like the day, I like the night."

"I miss my father at night and you miss your father during the day."

"My dad and I don't spend much time together during the day. Once in a while he takes me to town, but I don't feel he likes people to see me."

"He's probably busy."

"Bullshit, Andy, he ain't that busy."

"I hear them whores let you put your cock in their mouths."

"Why do they do that?"

"Some of the guys seem to like it."

"Jeezuzz!"

"I hear tell that some of the guys, once in a while if you get 'em drunk enough, will bend down and kiss a woman's . . . you know."

"You mean her . . . ?"

"Right."

"Jeezuzz!"

"Uch . . . I'd hate to be a woman."

"Me too . . . even with two legs that worked."

Slim hobbled over to his bureau, which rested against one wall of his bedroom. His window overlooked the wheat fields of Kansas. He opened the top drawer and under some skivvies and underpants was a brown envelope. He handed it to the Kid.

"Look at these."

There were twelve black-and-white pictures of a naked girl in provocative poses or what she thought were provocative poses. She was lying on a couch with a cake on a tray beside her. The twelve poses were different shots of her eating the cake. Slabs of it in her hand. Licking some from the cake itself. A long sliver of the spongecake just touching her parting lips. Sometimes her bottom facing the viewer, sometimes her breasts. Legs pulled up. Arms pulled up. The Kid couldn't keep his hard-on off.

"I'll be back."

And Slim hobbled out of his room and down the hallway. You could hear his braces clomping as he went farther away. The sound of his movement finally stopped. The Kid had his cock out in Slim's bathroom and a towel wrapped around it. The twelve photographs neatly placed on top of the basin and there the Kid traveled to Babylon.

*   *   *

"Give me a hand, will ya, Kid?" Nelson Hargrove said. "Right, Slim."

They were sitting alongside the river, just outside of town. The boys lived just two miles from each other. The Kid would take Slim down to the river and they'd swim. Only in the water were they equal, because Slim was crippled by polio. His legs were as thin as his wrists all the way from the hipbone down to his toes. He wore steel braces with leather cushions around the bendable joints, knees, and ankles. While Slim undid the heavy leather around his waist, the Kid undid the straps around his ankles and his knees. The Kid dove into the river, spun around, extended his arm, and gently eased Slim into the water.

Now at last Slim and the Kid were equal. Swimming in the water, they looked identical. About the same size, the same height. They looked a lot alike, like brothers. Each boy saw in the other what might have been or what could have been. Each saw the pleasure and the pain of it. The Kid tried as hard as he could to project himself so that he could be looking through the eyes of Slim, to see him swimming there. But he could only think himself so far; after that he just gave up.

Slim's family was wealthy, owned four thousand acres of land, raised cattle and grain. The Kid lived with a foster family named Stewart. The Stewarts were proud of their foster son and he thrived both physically and intellectually with these extremely intelligent people. He was always being asked how he felt, what he thought of things, what he felt the purpose of existence was, if any. Was it a mistake? Was it divined? Was he an accident? Or, was he the King, the God of gods? The Kid was slow in school and didn't pick up on subjects quickly. He was a half year behind in his educational development. Slim was a whiz. He used to help the Kid whenever he could.

They did something else that made them almost equals. Bareback riding. There were two mares that Slim's father,

Gregory, kept tied up close to the ranch house. He'd pick Slim up under the armpits and gently ease him onto the back of the horse. The Kid would pull himself up on his horse and they'd start off together, wearing just denims and no shirt. They'd usually ride the range down to the county line. The Kid slid off Chexter to undo the gate so they could cross the road that the county had assessed for a local throughway. Parked about twenty yards from the gate was an old Packard pulling a small one-door camper. Some old guy, or at least he looked old to the boys, was fixing a flat tire. The Packard, held up by an old jack that seemed ready to buckle at any time, tilted about twenty degrees. The old man cursed as he tried to undo the bolts that kept this old wooden-spoked wheel tied to his old and exhausted car.

"Goddamnit . . . shit . . . I just can't get that bolt clear."

The Kid rode up.

"Can I help?"

"No, you couldn't help me. A scrawny kid like you. I can't get this bolt off. There! Shit, man, I did it."

He pulled the wheel off the axle and started to replace it with the tire that he carried as a spare.

"How far is Grand Falls from here?"

"Oh, about four miles down the road," the Kid said. "You'll see it. It'll be off to your left in a small clearing."

"Well, that's where I'm going tonight. I'm gonna spend the night. Do a little helpin' and a little prayin'. You boys live around here?"

"Yes, sir, we do."

"Well, I figger it would be good if you showed up tonight and bring your parents. I'm the Reverend Sinclair, the Reverend Jeremiah Arlington Sinclair, the preacher extraordinaire. I can heal what aches ya and soothe ya soul."

Before he finished this little speech, the door of the camper opened and out stepped a barefooted girl of about seventeen.

"Come along, Elvira. I got it all fixed. This here's my disciple and one of the sisters of the Lord."

Elvira slid in opposite the Reverend Jeremiah, but not before the boys caught a good long look at her snatch, which she accommodatingly let them see. Poor Slim, that's

64

about as close as he had gotten to a girl all summer and what had he got to see but her magic mound?

Down the road the Packard went. Well, the boys were gonna see this religious ceremony tonight and, who knows, they could even be touched by God and do a little touching themselves. The Kid ate at Slim's house that night and at seven-thirty sharp they were at City Hall Auditorium ready to meet Jesus. Almost everybody in town was there. Families brought their young children along for an inspirational and divine experience. Mayor James Jamison, also the butcher, made a short speech extolling the small community and the presence of God among them all. There was still a depression all over the country. But it was not felt as profoundly here in the small communities of the West and Midwest. There was always enough to eat, always enough clothes to wear. And these people couldn't understand why all those big city folk couldn't make ends meet. That's because all them big cities had foreigners in them and aliens and undesirables who were trying to usurp and take over the American way of life. Reverend Sinclair was introduced by the Mayor; neither Slim nor the Kid recognized him at first. That scrubby, grunting man that they saw changing a wheel on his car was now standing tall, white hair flowing, face shaven, white clerical collar, black suit, black shoes. He looked beautiful. The Kid now had some idea why that good-looking girl hung around this very powerful, energetic man. There was an organ onstage on the right and the girl was now sitting demurely in front of it, dressed in white. The dress falling just to her knees as she sat, high-necked, her hair pulled back, socks that came just above the ankles, and a pair of low-heeled white shoes with a strap across the arch where it buttoned.

The preacher put out his arms.

"My friends, let us pray."

On cue the girl began to play "Nearer My God to Thee."

"Oh, Lord, sanctify us, care for us, as we care for Thee. We look to You for guidance and help. We look to You for peace and understanding. Accept the blackness of our souls, the sins of our parents, the hate of our minds and help us find salvation in Your Presence. Give us the peace we wish. Give us the strength we need. Give us the love we crave, dear Jesus. Cure our ills and we shall cure each other."

Slim's father, Gregory, was sitting next to the boys, his gray eyes shut, knowing God had punished him for copulating with that transient farm girl on that hot summer night five years ago. The next day Slim had a fever. A week later he was paralyzed from the waist down. So the dear Lord did stretch his long finger down and punish those who broke the laws of God. If he could only tell Slim how sorry he was. If he could only purge himself of these terrible aches and pains he suffered.

After his opening sermon and half a dozen songs, a plate was passed around and everyone reached into their kep and came up with whatever money they had to give. It wasn't too bad, about eighteen bucks. Finally the moment of truth came for a lot of people who suspected this would happen. The healing. Mrs. Coalsman's insistent and permanent headaches were cured by the outstretched big hand of the Preacher. He laid it on her forehead with fingers extending into the hairline.

"Dear Lord, pass the pain from this body. Pass the ills from this head. Dear God, purify this creature."

She couldn't feel the headache because of the pressure that the preacher held her head in. The pain was unendurable. Suddenly it was gone. She felt nothing. A little giddy perhaps, but there seemed to be no pain in her head. She was so relieved he had let her go; anything was better than the pressure of his hand. There were a few ahs.

One of the ranch hands on the Jamison spread had an elbow that had become infected when a spur was accidentally driven into the joint. It was swollen, red, turning a light color of blue. The Preacher looked at it, realized what it needed was to have the remnants of the spur removed. The center of the wound was now marble-shaped and looked as if it was ready to burst. The Preacher knew that a good doctor would have cured that a long time ago. The doctor in this small community was either incompetent or dead. The Preacher wasn't about to ask. He took his left hand and put it in the same position on the rancher's head as he had done with the woman before him. And he put enough pressure on the man's head for him not to feel anything except the big hairy hand of the Preacher, laying down heavy on his head. He had two towels folded on the small podium for just these kinds of occasions. The man's elbow was held up high for all to see this ugly infestation. He took one of the towels and put it over the elbow and he squeezed with his left hand. The rancher felt nothing but those five fingers of God, driving themselves into his skull. The Preacher simply popped that wound as one would pop a cherry or a grape, the contents flowing into the towel that was covering it. The discharge that had been building up in the elbow for the last two weeks exploded from it and the ranch hand felt immediate relief. The Preacher felt a shudder go through his body. He held the elbow. Pulled away the towel, almost afraid to look at what was in it himself, and held the ranch hand's arm up in the air, rapidly bending the elbow up and down five or six times.

All one could see was a light red mark where just a few seconds ago was a purple-red infection. Cleaned by the finger of God.

"Does anyone else need the healings of the Lord?" he asked.

Before he even knew it himself, Slim was being prodded down the center aisle by his father, Gregory.

"Go on Son, do as your daddy tells ya. Do as your daddy tells ya."

Slim was embarrassed but didn't dare disobey his father. With his two crutches he started hobbling down the aisle to where the Preacher stood on the low stage. Every eye in the auditorium was on Slim. He felt it and hated it. He hobbled down, moving one arm and then the other, leaning forward on his crutches. He stopped in front of the Preacher, who now stood about eight feet above his head on the platform. The Preacher hopped down from the stage in front of Slim. Everyone was tense. Slim had beads of sweat dripping down his forehead, as did the Preacher. The girl stopped playing the organ and turned and looked in Slim's direction. He saw her piercing blue eyes and almost fainted from desire of her. And yet he stood in front of this madman who put his hands on Slim's head.

"God, listen to me," the Preacher said. "Hear me, God. Cure this sinner."

Slim's father could feel the pain of the remark strike inside his gut. The Preacher had both hands on Slim now. Both hands resting on his forehead.

"Now, God . . . now."

On each word, Slim could feel the pressure of this man's hands, trying to drive him into the ground. He held on tight to his crutches.

"Throw away one crutch," the Preacher said.

Slim took one crutch and dropped it to the ground. The Preacher took both hands off Slim's head now like a magician just disclosing the rabbit in the hat. He stepped back about three feet. There wasn't a sound in the auditorium. All eyes were on Slim and the Preacher. He backed away another foot.

"Now, boy, throw away the other crutch."

Slim let it drop and stood there on his braced legs. Slim's father was crying.

"God, dear God," the Preacher said, "hear this boy's plea. Let him walk."

The Preacher looked at Slim, looked at him with those dark black eyes of his.

"Walk to me, boy, walk."

Slim stood there, took a step forward, and fell right on his ass. The rubber end of the crutch was near his outstretched right hand. He pulled it toward him, grabbed it with both hands as one would grasp a baseball bat, swung the fucking thing, and knocked the Preacher flat on his ass, knocking out two teeth in the process. There was screaming. Two women fainted. Gregory rushed down and picked up his son, with tears streaming down his face. Slim crying. People hysterical. That girl sitting on stage looking cool-eyed over all the activities below. Gregory carried his boy out the door. The Kid hung back. The place was in a shambles. Seats turned over. People running out. The Preacher just slowly coming to his senses. He reached up. Took the other towel down from the podium. Used it to wipe the blood pulsing from his mouth. The Kid went down the aisle to the right and in the pandemonium leaped onto the stage and went up to the girl.

"Come on with me."

She didn't wait, blink an eye, or take a second thought. She followed him down the back stairs out through the back door of the auditorium.

"I got twelve dollars here," he said. "Been saving it now for the last year. I was gonna get me a horse. But I'm gonna give it to you if you'll . . ."

She looked at him coolly and calmly.

"If I'll what?"

"If you'll make love to me and my friend."

She caressed him and kissed him and made love to him down by the banks of the river he and Slim swam in. They rode bareback. Slim was home by now, brought home in the buckboard by the head ranch hand. The Kid had the girl up the stairs and in Slim's bedroom before Gregory, who was still in town talking with the Sheriff, trying to decide what they were going to do with the Preacher, got back to the ranch. Slim moaned with the ecstasy of this incredible experience that he now had in the middle of Kansas on a hot summer night. Legs out of braces. He cried for the beauty of it. She stroked his hair, calmed him down, and was out of his room ten minutes later, sitting behind the Kid as they half trotted back to town.

By the time the Preacher had had his mouth treated and got his gear into his car and camper, Elvira was back and hardly missed by the white-haired, silver-tongued devil. They were bundled into their car and on the road by eleven-fifteen that night with a stern warning from the Sheriff never to come back again. The Kid stood on the sidewalk as the Preacher drove past. One street light shining harshly picked out the face of Elvira as she went by. Her eyes were looking at the Kid, his at hers. They smiled and she threw him a kiss. That twelve dollars safely stuck away with another sixty-three dollars in a small chamois sack that rested warmly in her pubic hairs unbeknownst to anybody. Perhaps with the exception of God.

Julie

Why Do They Always Have to Be Jewish?

Angie looked Jewish; Julie didn't. Angie's nose was long with big nostrils and so was his face. His eyes weren't as big as they should have been for the size of his face. So they always gave him a look of distrust, which was the last thing that Angie was. His hair was black and straight and so was the color of his eyes. A thin neck, big Adam's apple. Shoulders and arms a little narrower than they should have been for his height, which was the same as Julie's. He looked frail, but he was the toughest motherfucker on the block. Tenacious. One of the great miracles of life for Angie happened when he discovered he could jerk off. To be able to amuse himself like that was better than any free ticket to any movie in town. And Angie loved the movies. Angie's haircuts were always bad, either too high above the ear or uneven in the back. Clothes meant nothing to him. He just liked his mother's food and jerking off, and Julie. Not necessarily in that order.

When Angie smiled the world smiled with him. You had to be dead not to be infected by it. He lit up anyplace he was in with that glorious smile of his. His eyes disappeared completely when he smiled or laughed. Whenever Angie and Julie found themselves hysterical over something, Julie would have to lead him around until he stopped laughing because he'd invariably run into the fucking wall or knock over a vase or fall into somebody. What Julie liked about Angie was how spontaneous he was about everything. He and Julie would always embrace and clasp each other's back. Angie was very

70

physical, always digging his fingers in your ribs, pinching your cheek, grabbing you around the shoulders. Or, if you were a girl, caressing any part he could get ahold of. He had no shame for there was nothing to be ashamed of. Once he and Julie were at some girl's sixteenth birthday party in the Bronx. Angie took out his cock and stuck it in the cake. Someone told the father of the girl but by the time he got into the living room where the cake was, Angie and Julie were gone.

A mystery to Julie was how families come up with different people. Oh sure, Angie and Joey looked somewhat alike. Joey was four years older than his brother. And one could tell a Vittucci when they saw one, but there the similarity ended. When Joey smiled you got garlic, when Angie did you got love. Once in the late summer when they were about nine Angie and Julie went to a movie called *Showboat* in which this guy and this girl cut their wrists and passed blood between them. When the picture was over, they went to Julie's house. Ruth was out. Morrie was downtown working.

"Let's become blood brothers, okay?" Julie said.

"Okay . . . how're we gonna do this?"

"I'll show ya, Angie. There's a box of matches on the stove, get 'em."

Julie went to Morrie's sewing machine and got one of the finer sewing needles.

"Light a match, hold it over the point of this needle. That way ya kill all the germs."

"Right."

"Look how black the needle's got. It's gotta get red hot, though."

"Shit, it's burning my fingers."

"All right, that's enough."

"What do ya do about the black?"

"Ya wipe it off with a towel. Get the one by the sink. There, that should do it."

"Now, what?"

"Stick it in ya finger and make it bleed. Then I stick it in my finger and make mine bleed and we put the fingers together and we hold it like that so our blood passes into each other."

"You're outta ya fuckin' mind, Julie. You ain't sticking that thing in my finger. Stick it in yours first."

"All right, I'll do it to mine first."

"What are ya shakin' your hand like that for?"

"That'll bring the blood out more."

"You got enough blood comin' from that finger already. You think you know whatcha doin', Julie?"

"I know. I know. Gimme your finger quick."

"Oh, shit, I don't like this."

"Gimme your finger."

"Here. Here, ow!"

"Now shake ya arm."

"That's a lot of blood from a little stick like that."

"All right, gimme ya finger and let's put 'em together."

With that Julie and Angie became blood brothers. And Morrie and Ruth took the boys to see *Charge of the Light Brigade,* starring Errol Flynn and Olivia de Havilland, that night at Loew's Seventy-second Street in loge seats.

* * *

They saw a lot of each other for the next four years, then Julie moved away with his family to the Bronx. First they moved to the west side of Manhattan, then the east side of Manhattan. Then they moved to upper Manhattan around Eighty-fifth Street, which was the German section of town. Then they moved to midtown Manhattan, in the basement of the Arlington Hotel, where Morrie had the dry-cleaning and tailoring concession for the building. During that period of his life, Julie lived among pipes and boilers, electrical and plumbing equipment in this huge complex of apartments. That building, the basement area, gave him a beautiful place to hide and play.

He would often pick up Angie at the subway. They would walk the nine blocks to the hotel and then Angie would spend the night with Julie. After his parents had gone to bed, both of them would sneak up into the floors. Looking through the transoms, they saw it all, all the distasteful and wondrous and ordinary functions of living.

From the time Julie was eight until he was fifteen, they moved all over that big fucking city. Wherever Mor-

rie found himself a job, his small family moved with
him, and there they lived while he eked out a living and
tried to put away some money for himself and his family.
It was in his early teens, right after his Bar Mitzvah, that
Julie and Angie started to hit the streets on their own.
During the next years both Angie and Julie started to
make inroads into the nefarious world of guns and gunsels. The people they met were interesting, unique, and
certainly the most dishonest that ever lived. They ripped
off anybody and everybody. They found themselves pimp-
ing. They found themselves running money for the books
in town. They found themselves stealing. They found
themselves at large and for sale to any gang in town
that wanted to hire two young men who were innocent-
looking, quiet, and seemingly calm enough to take care of
any kind of job.

Angie had a younger cousin who used to deliver papers
in another neighborhood. He was always getting hustled
and run around. Every now and then someone would
rob him. Some man tried to fuck him in his ass once
in the back stair well of a building. He was lured into
avarice. Another kid delivering clothes was murdered by
some madman in the entry hall of the house. His family
didn't get an "I'm sorry" from the store owner after the
death of that child. Kids and young people were always
being ripped off by adults in the late twenties and early
thirties. It was prevalent because of the Depression. They
got it from everybody. Shine someone's shoes? If the guy
wanted to give him the money, he would; if he didn't,
"Beat it, you little fuckin' kid." Kick the kid and scream
he ruined his pants or something. A child had no recourse,
no protection. Nothing. The most persecuted human on
earth was the child.

Angie and Julie saw a need for help for the local kids
in the neighborhood, and they organized all the little kids
around the block. Julie and Angie would walk in and
would go to it. There was one kid who worked for a
butcher in another neighborhood, just on the outskirts
of theirs. The butcher's name was Otto. He was a German prick, into the Nazi thing at that time. Just before
the war, you could feel a part of Hitler's madness affect-
ing the German population of Manhattan. This Otto had
been treating this poor little boy terribly. One week he

wouldn't pay him his salary. Another week he would give him his pay in scraps. He was doing this to a young child. The boy had no recourse. At the end of the day he'd come home depressed, and through the grapevine, as kids tell each other, Angie and Julie heard of it.

"That's the store," the boy said. And the next morning bright and early at nine o'clock when the butcher opened the shop—the boy didn't work there until after school—there were our boys, Julie and Angie.

"Good morning, sir. May we speak to Otto, please? Mr. Otto . . ."

"*Ja*," he said, "what is it?"

He was cutting some meat, impatient, both Angie and Julie could see what kind he was.

"Well, sir," Julie, "we've come to speak to you about Ralph, the boy that works for you in the afternoon, about the lousy treatment you've been giving Ralph. We'd like you to give us the money that you owe him at this point. Er, it's ten days' back salary, which comes to six bucks and thirty-seven cents. We want it now and we'll be on our way."

Nazi Otto couldn't wait to heap his foul ugly words at the young boys. What did they mean? Who did they think they were? These cowards who loved money before God and family. Some Jew kikes, to come walking into his establishment and making those kinds of demands.

Julie smiled and Angie smiled and didn't show any signs of being ruffled by this man's ugly abuse. Julie calmly and quietly went and picked up one of the butcher cleavers lying almost carelessly on the wooden block. The butcher got a shade nervous but he shit when the next thing happened. Angie picked up a big heavy thigh bone from a bone box and started swinging it around the place like a bat. Bam. Through the beautiful plate glass window in the front of the shop saying, "Otto's German Butcher Shop" with gold raised block letters. That went first. Then the scale went. Then the glass on the meat cases started to go. Then all the hooks on the wall lost all their meat to the floor. If it didn't look like a butcher shop before, it looked like a butcher shop now.

By this time Otto was stunned and cowering under Julie's innocent look and raised meat chopper in the corner.

"Stay, Mr. Otto, stay," Julie said.

And Mr. Otto stayed. For the *pièce de résistance*, Angie went over and picked up about ten pounds of the finest steaks you could see, wrapped them, and hoisted them on his shoulders.

"Sir, we're leaving. This," pointing to what they had done, "is what you owe Ralph. Heil Hitler."

And with that the boys marched out and started to beat ass down First Avenue as fast as they could go. Otto never called the cops. Never said nothin'. And he never fucked with the little kid again.

Julie and Angie didn't make too much money in the protection racket. They really didn't care. Joey organized them and started getting fees from kids who wanted revenge. It was the joy of power for them to get young people like themselves a little straightened out in this adult ripoff fucking world that they found themselves in and they knew that their protection lay in themselves and not in some hokey organizations.

It was during one of these incidents of child protection that Julie got hit in the ear with a baseball bat, making him stone deaf in his left ear. It kept him from going into the service. By then, they had advanced from kids to clubs, to stores, to cars, anything that needed protection. They built up their little P.R. to about seventeen thousand bucks. Not bad for three kids in New York City at that time.

* * *

It was spring and he was almost fifteen. Some kid grabbed him.

"That's the fucking kid. I'm telling ya, that's him."

There were two other kids. One of them was pimpled, mean, and ugly. The other had a glove, a first baseman's glove, on one hand and a baseball bat in the other. Julie saw an outline of a ball in the pocket of the Ug.

"Are you sure?"

"You're fuckin' A, I'm sure. I'd never forget this prick."

His hand was twisted around Julie's coat jacket and part of his shirt collar, pinching part of the skin of his back as well. Julie could feel how hard he was holding. Julie tried to pull away but this kid flung him up against the building. He bounced off and got up on his feet, school notebooks still in his hand, a brown belt tightly wrapped around the books.

"Didn't you beat up his brother?" the Ug said.

Julie didn't like the look of it. He should never have come back to the neighborhood so quickly. Days before he had come upon this older kid stomping this little kid lying between his legs between the gutter and the sidewalk. The kid on the ground was Irving the Scholar, one of his neighbors. Irving lived two houses away from Julie. A shy and gentle boy whose father was a bookkeeper for a firm uptown and whose sister was fucking half the track team at Seward Park High School. Julie had never seen the guy standing over him before. Julie didn't wait. He leaped and grabbed his collar and pulled him off the younger boy. He half dragged him to his feet. As he did, he snapped him in the stomach with a right, then he brought a short uppercut squarely across the face of this surprised kid. Flattened him with it.

The kid lay there stunned, then looked up and said, "Why, you kike son of a bitch." The kid started to get up. He was bigger than Julie by two inches, not much heavier. He started up off the ground. Julie kicked him squarely across the head with his right sneaker, then kicked him again. This time the kid got smart. He rolled and presented his backside to Julie, not his head. When he started to straighten up, Julie hit him with a left into his kidneys, which buckled this kid right up against the iron railing fence surrounding this tenement house. He turned around and faced Julie and Julie brought a right cross across his face. Julie just couldn't control himself. Should he give his opponent a second to collect himself? Should he observe any of the supposed rules? Those Marcus and Goldberger Rules. Julie, once he was threatened or something he cared for was threatened, didn't know anything except survival. Anything else was unimportant. He tackled each second at a time. Spontaneity of the situation told him what to do rather than a well-thought-out strategy. It had only helped him, never hurt him.

Julie backed up as his adversary kicked out with his

foot moving backward so that the kick wasn't as damaging as it would have been to his groin if he had stood still. The guy took off. Julie waited a second or two for the pain to subside enough so that he could run and he took off after the kid. Running just enough to keep him close, to keep the kid within striking distance. About four blocks away, Julie felt fit enough. And five blocks full out, Julie cornered him in the middle of a street.

The guy grabbed for Julie's neck and they wrestled to the ground. It was then that Julie looked up and saw two kids running up the street as hard as they could from the other corner. He knew now that he was in enemy territory and decided he had better get out of there fast. But not before he gave this kid one more good swift kick right in the ribs. He burned. Taunted these fellas enough so that they thought that they could catch him and then he took off, flat out. The grocers, butchers, and dry-goods merchant men along the street could not remember seeing a kid streak down the street faster. Faster than they had ever seen any human travel, streaking between pushcarts and trolley cars and cars and people and bikes and every sort of vehicle, every sort of human, every sort of animal rushing down a street in New York City then.

And here he was, shmuck face, back again, somehow getting lost up in the neighborhood after school was over, kind of roaming around forgetting where he was. Or did he? Did he deliberately come back again? Not even knowing it himself? Always in a strange way pushing himself to that ultimate challenge?

He threw his schoolbooks into Ug's face as hard as he could, which made Ug even uglier. The kid that had been yelling at him, this other guy's brother, was completely surprised by that action. Julie had time enough to hit him right in the mouth above the upper lip and right across part of the nose. But before Julie could stoop down, pick up the books, and start to run, this guy with the baseball bat swung it. It rapped Julie right behind the left ear as he started taking off down the street. The momentum of the hit kept him going for the first five or six seconds when he didn't know where the fuck he was. The blow created a white light inside of him. He didn't see, he didn't hear, he didn't know, he was just a light. When he got his consciousness back, all he could feel was his body and himself hurtling down the street. Sidestepping a car. Missing a pushcart. Changing direction. Cutting across the middle of the street, between speeding cars and jumping on the back of a trolley. The trolley started to slow and he could see his pursuers getting a little closer than he would like. Julie dropped off the trolley and stopped, facing them with clenched fists. They stopped, and Julie knew he had them. He sprinted off fast. It took these guys a few seconds to build up steam and speed. By that time Julie was long gone. He played cat and mouse with those guys. The three guys thinking they had him. Julie ran with blood streaming down his shirt and short jacket. He was crying, pissed off and angry. Caught in that lousy neighborhood!

He stopped off at the Jones Memorial Settlement House, used the boys' room, washed off the back of his neck, where he had a big welt and an open cut. That's where the blood had been coming from. It had dried by now but it throbbed terribly. He took off his shirt and jacket, washed them in the sink water, trying to get as much of the blood out of it as possible. Rinsed them out. Took toilet paper, wet it with cold water, and slapped it on the back of his head. Left the settlement house and started home.

At the back yard of his house, he went up the fire escape to his floor and into his room. He used the shirt and jacket to get some of the blood out of his hair so it wouldn't look too matted where the cut was, changed shirt and jacket, and left his books. Down the fire escape again. Up to the front of the house, through the door.

"Hey, Ma, I'm home."

"Where's your books?" she said.

"I didn't take 'em," he lied. He giggled inside. He thought, Shit, man, that was fast. Whew.

"Milk?"

"Yeah, man, that'd be wonderful."

"Are you all right, Julie?"

"Oh, I'm great, Ma, great."

"You know, Julie, I've the feeling that you don't always tell me everything."

78

"I tell you everything, Ma, everything that you should know."

"What do you mean that I should know? Shouldn't I know everything?"

"No, Ma, you shouldn't know everything, and neither should I."

"Come here," she said.

He got up and walked to her. She put her arms around him. He put his arms around her. He loved her so much. As she loved him.

Ruth sensed that Julie was very intelligent, and later when he dropped out of school completely, she was always tempted to cheppeh him about it. But she thought better of it and realized what must be must be. And if Julie had no more interest in schooling, well, her or Morrie's insistence certainly wouldn't stimulate it. Their faces were just four inches apart. Julie liked to look at Ruth. Her dark eyes were always laughing. Made no difference how tough it was for them. And in the late twenties and early thirties, it was tough. Ruth always gave them a nice life, him and Morrie. Their home was always clean, and although the food wasn't too plentiful at times, it was always wholesome. Once Julie had a bad cold with a very high fever. Ruth came in with a bottle of witch hazel and rubbed him down from head to toe, singing to him in a low, deep voice, some old Hungarian melody. Once he had eaten some junk food in the city and when he got home that night he was ill. He leaped out of bed and ran to the toilet, just making it to the bowl before he threw up. Ruth was there beside him, holding his forehead with her left hand, her right hand gently caressing his right shoulder. He felt as if he was going to turn inside out. Ruth never gagged and never turned away in disgust. She just held his head and soothed him, until the spasms were gone, wiped his mouth, took a face-cloth and wiped his face with cold water, and led him back to his bed.

When he saw that first pubic hair growing, Ruth was the first to see it and know about it, then Morrie. She could curse with the best of them, always in Hungarian. Yet, she always treated Julie as if he were the pretender to the Austro-Hungarian throne.

Looking at her now, Julie saw that her black hair was

quite curly. Whenever they went out, she would always pull it back, tying it behind her ears with a ribbon, twisting the rest of it, which must have been a foot and a half long, into a bun that sat neatly on the back of her head like some coiled black snake. Her eyebrows were thick and unplucked. Her lashes fighting each other to escape from their lids. Her eyes were wide and doe-like; those eyes that made her look very vulnerable. Between them rested an aquiline nose, thin, with a slight rise in the center. Nostrils small and delicate. She always looked as if she had lipstick on; her lips were dark, moist, and succulent. Morrie must have a good time with that mouth. A slight cleft sat in the middle of a beautifully shaped jaw that rose to two small pierced ears. She had just enough neck to turn her head, no more. There was a trace of a mustache on her upper lip. Later with a little money and a razor that would disappear. She was olive-tanned, dark and sultry.

He once saw her nude, inadvertently. Ruth was short, full-breasted, and full-hipped, and full of life. As a child in Hungary, she had been abused by a father who really didn't care much about her or her sisters. This abuse showed itself mostly when Ruth was around men. She was argumentative, impatient, and rude most of the time, except with men who were over five feet five inches tall. Her father was that height and she never was comfortable in the company of short men. Right from the beginning she knew Julie would be tall and with those blue eyes she was content to have him as her son. Julie could make her laugh so easily. When he called her baby she blushed. She liked being around Julie. Julie had a strange effect on Ruth. She always felt like a little girl when she was around him. It was almost as if he was the father and she was the daughter. She never told Julie that until near the end. And she always smelled good. She was clean. Julie liked that.

Looking at Julie, Ruth thought he looked a bit pale, but as a kid he was always pale, which made the contrast of his blue eyes even more dramatic and mysterious. She could never really get used to Julie's looks. They tickled her. When he was around, she constantly had her eyes on him. It was tough being an aunt and a mother. Her mother's name was Bertha and Bertha ran her four daughters and one son like some Hungarian goulash, hot and full of spice. Bertha was taller than all the children and at least six inches taller than her husband, Alex, a pompous, embittered Austrian-Hungarian Jew. Five feet five and big-boned. A farmer by birth, a loafer by design. He felt all his children owed him a living because he had begat them. It had dire effects on all the Klein family. He could be petty, pensive, and a prick. When he finally died, everybody drew a big sigh of relief. The one thing he gave that family that they needed was a tenaciousness about life. None of them ever really gave up a situation, regardless of how difficult some experiences were. None of the Klein children ever hid from life, except Stella. Stella was more vulnerable than the rest because she was the youngest and had the best figure even at an early age, and this disconcerted her because she had difficulty handling the passions of men. Passion always overwhelmed her, and this quality stayed with her all her life. Of all the Kleins, Ruth was the most compassionate. No wonder Morrie and Julie loved her so.

Julie

So You Think
You're a Sparrow?

Julie was sweet sixteen. The Vittucci family and the Singer family were giving Julie a sixteenth birthday party that night. It was June 3, 1940. Hot and muggier than usual. Angie was shacked up somewhere and Julie wouldn't see him until the party. He left the apartment that he shared with Ruth and Morrie at nine-thirty that morning. They were living on Sixty-fourth Street off Lexington Avenue then. Julie had his own room; Ruth and Morrie had theirs. There was a sitting-dining room with a radio and books—big and little books, papers, magazines, comic books—a violin, and a big chest with glass covering the top half in which all the dishes that they owned were stored. A sewing machine stood by the window where Morrie would do any family or home work, a small rack with two or three clothing items hung there waiting for Morrie's skilled hand, a couple of couches, two easy chairs, a kitchen with an icebox, a good stove, big white sink, linoleum on the floor, and a kitchen table with four chairs around it. An entry hall led to the front door with a little eye peeper and a chain lock.

The incredible thing for Julie in this apartment was that they had two toilets. He finally had his own toilet. That toilet meant an awful lot to Julie. Today he had on gray slacks and a white shirt with a gray pullover. The points of his white shirt hung out over the gray pullover he wore. He was skinny in those days, very skinny. He stood five ten when he was sixteen. A lot of black hair over these piercing blue eyes, long scrawny neck, and his nails were clipped good and short. He had about a hundred twenty bucks on him in a paper clip. He was going to travel in high society today, and he looked forward to it. Dressed like this and with a little money in his pocket there wasn't anyplace that was not allowed him. Who the fuck would know he was a Jew? He'd go to a baseball game or a museum or an art show or family party or a friend's party, or even a movie. He would more or less aimlessly travel through the city. He'd pick a neighborhood he'd like to try and that's where he'd end up.

Carnegie Hall. He had passed it many times, but today he was going to pay it a little closer attention. By eleven o'clock he was at Carnegie Hall. He went in and sat down. There was a rehearsal going on. Fifty girls singing. Some chorus. Some girls were arriving, some were leaving. He listened for a bit then got up to leave. As he walked up the aisle, he heard a girl's voice.

"Oh, sparrow."

He stopped and turned to see where the voice came from. There seated in one of the seats was a blond girl whose hair was the color of wheat. They locked eyes, hers green, and looked at each other for just a beat.

"What made you think I was calling you?" she said.

He blushed.

"I dunno . . . I just thought . . . maybe you meant me."

He walked closer and sat down in the aisle seat. There was an empty seat between them.

"Do you sing with these girls?"

"No, I go to Hunter College. I just wanted to take the day off today, I guess."

They both listened to a very beautiful piece of music being sung by this chorus of girls. He sensed her sitting there. She wore a pleated skirt to about her knees, a beige sweater to her neck, around her neck a gold chain with a small cross at the end of it, and simple dark brown shoes with a low heel. Looking at her, you could feel summer coming on and you knew too when summer was over she would be a woman. She looked at him again.

"So you think you're a sparrow."

"No, I don't think I'm a sparrow, and I don't think I've ever seen one, either."

"It's a small gray bird. Very independent. Always moving. Not too intelligent and always getting caught by cats."

"Mr. or Mrs?" he said.

She didn't crack.

"Let's go somewhere else," she said.

They got up and walked out of Carnegie Hall. He finally took her hand three blocks past Carnegie Hall, much to the relief of both of them, and off they went.

"Let's go to the Museum of Modern Art; it's beautiful."

Before he could answer, the sparrow and Pamela, that was her name, were on their way. It was quiet and solemn as they walked around. He kept looking at her tits. She kept looking at his eyes. He couldn't understand why everybody took this art shit so seriously. They were nice pictures and certainly interesting objects and sculptures but everything was so fucking solemn, so mystical. They walked and looked, holding hands. Their palms becoming moist and warm. She stopped suddenly.

"Oh, I know something to see. Come on."

She took him. They seemed to meander in a maze of pictures and walls until they suddenly came into a little room. On the wall of this room, going from one section of the wall to the other, was this huge painting. Green. White. Blue. Little touches of yellow. When he got his eyes adjusted, he could see that it looked like flowers, flowers floating in the water.

"Monet painted that," she said. "It's called *Water Lilies*."

The hugeness of it cast a spell over him. Pamela could sense his reaction and was pleased by it. She took his arm and squeezed it.

"Oh, Sparrow, I was sure you'd like it. I'm going to Europe next month. I'm going to the South of France with my parents. Maybe to Rome for a week. On the way back we're going to stop in Switzerland and then finally to London. We have some friends in London. I may even spend a year there, going to school. I don't know. Have you ever traveled, Sparrow?"

"No, I went to the country once. Peekskill. At a camp."

"I've been to California and Hawaii. Oh, Sparrow," she said.

They were seated on this stone bench facing the *Water*

Lilies. She turned and brushed his cheek with her mouth. He turned and kissed her ever so lightly. He could have swooned for the joy of it. He loved and was moved. He loved her so. They went to a restaurant and had some omelets. After lunch he took her in a taxi to Broadway, and they went to see a movie, *Gunga Din,* with Cary Grant, Douglas Fairbanks, Jr., and Victor McLaglen. They necked and held hands or anything else she'd let Julie hold and vice versa.

They were in the streets walking, quickly. They were on Fifty-ninth Street. Across the street from Columbus Circle. It was about three o'clock.

"Nobody's home," she said.

They were in her room in this huge apartment building. He didn't know how many rooms were in the apartment, he never saw them. They'd come through a hallway in the back and directly into her bedroom. They were in each other's arms and into each other almost before the door finished closing.

They were walking in the streets again.

"I'm to meet my sister at Carnegie Hall at five," she said.

They walked to Carnegie Hall. A few minutes after five, Pamela's sister Pauline, who was maybe twelve, walked up and said, "Hi."

"This is the Sparrow," Pamela said. She turned and looked in Julie's eyes and said, "Good-by, Sparrow." And this tawny creature turned, walked out of his life, never to be seen again.

He never told anybody; he never told Angie. But from that day on, he called himself the Sparrow.

*   *   *

He finished work one morning at around two. He and Angie had gone upstate to pick up a rig of French wines that had been delivered through Canada. Through Feinstein, a liquor dealer and distributor in New York, Julie found out about this rig. Feinstein promised him fifty per cent of its value if they could deliver. Feinstein said it would be worth around forty thousand bucks. Not bad for about eleven hours' work. Angie broke his fist on that gig, and part of his wrist. The driver of the rig had

called him a stupid guinea cocksucker. Angie looked at
Julie and that was his mistake. While he looked away,
the driver rolled up his window. Angie really didn't even
look; he just doubled his fist and threw it right into the
glass. It didn't shatter the glass but it really fucked up
his fist. He was hopping mad, threatened to kill that son
of a bitch. Julie pushed him away and calmed him down.
The guy in the rig got out, really white now, frightened
by the ugly look in Angie's face. When the guy was gone,
Julie chided Angie.

"Now what the fuck are we gonna do? You busted
your arm throwing it at that asshole for no fuckin' reason, Angie."

"I can drive, Julie," Angie said. "Don't you worry
about it. I'll either drive the rig or the car."

"Fuck you," he said. "You're drivin' the car. I'll drive
the rig."

"No, Julie. I can manage the rig."

"You can't manage no rig, Angie. Now get in the fuckin' car. Don't give me any more bullshit. Now git in
there."

Angie looked at Julie and saw that Julie was really
pissed off, he didn't want to antagonize him.

"Okay," he said, "okay, Julie. Anything you say, pal."

"Can you drive that car?"

"Sure I can drive the car. I only hurt my mitt."

That crazy fucking Angie drove all the way down to
Manhattan with that broken hand, followed by Julie in
a rig he had never driven before. Julie took off two lampposts, wiped out one car's fender, and miraculously was
not stopped by anyone. But that was a long rig and Julie
just didn't know where the ass end of it was half the
time he made a turn. By some miracle, though, they got
to the warehouse on Sixty-first Street and First Avenue.
Julie got out of the rig, sweating and exhausted. He
turned the contents of the truck over to Pasquale, who
handled all of Joey's contraband in and around town,
told him to tabulate it and wait for Julie to call him.

"Right, Julie. I'll take care of it," Pasquale said.

He walked out to the car and said to Angie, "Slide
over."

"Look, you wanna ride to your place?" Angie said. "I'll

take you there, but I'm drivin'. Climb in on the other side."

Julie was too tired to argue. He climbed into the car and they drove to Julie's apartment. Angie said he was going back to Brooklyn. He knew a doctor who would fix up his mitt and he'd call him tomorrow sometime.

"Good night," Julie said. "Watch yourself, you crazy guinea."

"You too, you fuckin' kike."

As Angie pulled away, and as Julie started walking into his apartment building, they both smiled to themselves. They sure liked each other. When Julie opened the door of his apartment, he knew somebody was inside. He sensed the vibrations were not hostile, so he proceeded to act as if he didn't know anyone was in the apartment. Went straight to his kitchen. Put on the light. The light shone out into the bigger room. Julie went to the sink and poured himself some water, quickly glancing into the room he had just come from that was now partly lit by the light from the kitchen. He saw something in the reflection of the mirror that sat across the room and reflected a corner of the room that Julie couldn't see from his position. He was sure it was a girl. On the kitchen wall was the light switch for the sitting room. He switched on the light. He didn't pull his gun. He was prepared to. And there stood Maria Teresa Vittucci, sister of Angelo, sister of Joseph Nineteen years old and never been touched, frail and voluptuous. Frightened of life by her religion, ready for any experience by her inclination.

Julie, cool and detached like a surgeon, deflowered Maria Teresa that night. Deflowered her good. Her pimples disappeared. And a need to confess every twenty-two minutes also went. They never mentioned Angie or whether Julie should mention it or not. Julie never presumed to tell Maria Teresa anything. She had black hair and black eyes, white skin, hair under her armpits, a musky and intoxicating smell, but she was nuts. Mashuga.

The third time she arrived at Julie's apartment, she was teaching him and showing him some experiences that he had never even imagined existed. Oh, tongue, where is thy string? And just as suddenly, Maria Teresa disappeared. He didn't see her again for months.

He was out at the house with Angie one day. Maria Teresa came in and took off her coat, went over and kissed her brother Angie, and kissed Julie on the cheek.

"Hiya, boys, want something to eat?"

They followed her into the kitchen. She made them each a sandwich and a glass of red wine. She had started school. She was really going to try to make it at college. Maria Teresa met a postgraduate student who was teaching at City College. Philip was thirty-two and full of the stuff about art and artifacts and archaeology and digs and government grants and Ford Foundations and trips to Mexico and Egypt and Sinai and Sicily and Italy.

Two years later in the tomb of some ancient Pharaoh that was being excavated by the Ford Foundation, Maria Theresa and Philip were humping on a makeshift bed inside this cool and calming tomb. She thought of Julie then. Julie could never figure out Maria Teresa. Just as well. They could never have made it together.

Julie

1942

The war was still raging and Julie was nineteen years old and a good-looking son of a bitch. Ruth and Morrie lived in the same apartment they had all lived in for five years, and Julie had just rented and furnished a new apartment on Seventy-fifth Street, just off Lexington Avenue. It was away from everyone and he thought that possibly here was an opportunity to create a life of his own. Maybe meet a nice girl somewhere and have a place to take her. Wherever he lived, though, there was really no peace or quiet. He was always on call twenty-four hours. He and Angie had worked out a system, a code, simple enough but it worked for both of them. If their phone rang twice and stopped, they were to call Angie's home. The Vittucci family was living in Brooklyn now. Angie's sister Maria would pick up the phone because it was in her room, and Maria would give either Julie or Angie a message from each other. Neither one trusted anybody in the world that they functioned in, except each other.

It gave Angie and Julie a lot of power to know that they could rely on each other that way. They could make pickups. Tail each other. Back up each other. They were like two gunfighters in the Old West, standing back to back, confronting the posse.

What Julie was doing more than anything else was driving around in a Cadillac hardtop, checking five points in the city each day. He would check the illegal offtrack betting rooms. Their books combined had a total cash receipt of over two and a half million dollars. And no taxes. This money was constantly moving to cover all bets that came into the local syndicate. Julie, for patrolling it and seeing to it that no outside prick or outside organization stole any money or tried to bust in and hurt any of the runners, trackers, bookers, and bettors, got ten per cent of the action. If someone got hustled or rustled or buffaloed by anybody that was connected with this booking syndicate, Julie would trace down the guy or the woman, find out who was harassing them, and usually, if this person ever came back, that was the end of that mother-fucker.

For this Julie had a couple of guys traveling with him. One was a Polak called Stanislow, or Boom Boom Palchik, as he was affectionately called by his friends, and a guy named Dizzy Kleiner, who was the first cousin of Irving the Scholar, a kid that Julie knew when he was a kid. Both Kleiner and Palchik were mean but considerate. If they were going to bust up somebody who wore glasses, they'd take his glasses off. They never punched where you could see it. Always in the kidneys or a good shot in the gut. If someone needed a bit more persuasion, a right knee in the groin seemed to show them the light. If that still didn't work, a pair of brass knuckles seemed to be an excellent convincer, particularly if you were zapped in the shoulder blade. After that, it was out of Palchik's and Kleiner's hands. If anybody was not intimidated by these two bulls, why, Julie would contact one of Joey's associates and somebody from New Jersey would be brought in for either compound fractures or fractured skulls. In some instances they broke necks.

It was harsh and unrelenting for seven days a week. Once in a while the action in Julie's life would taper off, and he would have a few hours to call his own. Besides keeping his booking syndicate in good order without making it look like a police or strong arm organization, he ran protection for fifty beautiful creatures. Count them. Fifty beautiful creatures, who through fucking and sucking were able to send brothers through college, mothers to cooking schools, put fathers in hardware stores, boyfriends through engineering schools, and keep baby sisters in candy and dolls. These delectable ding-bats got between twenty and fifty bucks a trick. Half of which went to the madam, Olga, and a half of that to Julie. A dora could make a thousand smackers safe and sound every week, with all the customers she wanted. And no taxes. If any of the recipients of the goodness of these creatures would have asked where the money was coming from, why, each girl was a model and had photographs to prove it. The recipients each month waited anxiously for all the magazines to come. Bought them all to see if they could find their loved one somewhere in the pages of these books, but no such luck.

These nymphs came from Cleveland, Ohio; Walla Walla, Washington; St. Louis, Missouri; Denver, Colorado; and twenty-five other cities that were in the Midwest and South. No one manhandled any of these girls. Joey had another crew that took care of these creatures. The best guards were Italian boys. Somehow their very Catholic upbringing, the respect they had for mothers and sisters and women in their family, and also because they were afraid they'd catch a dose, they laid off all the girls that worked there and did whatever servicing was necessary. But they kept their flies shut.

The girls were spaced all over mid-Manhattan. Julie kept trying to get all the girls to move closer and closer together. If he had his way, they'd all occupy the first five floors of Rockefeller Center in immaculate and clean little bedrooms with as nice a toilet as you could get. Julie checked every lovely lass himself. His lieutenants would always be in touch with the madam, who saw to it that seven to ten of these girls were always around, clean and accommodating.

If they had any problems, they always went to Olga. Sweet Olga. She ran it all. She not only took it in the ass, but probably gave the best advice to these girls that anyone could give. Julie relied on Olga to let him know that everything was in shape with all the girls. Any rumble that occurred would always end up on Olga's phone and a minute later into Julie's ear, and maybe five minutes later there would be the three Italian cardinals, always alert, always gentlemanly and well mannered. By the time Sunday morning came around, Olga had fifteen hundred dollars, tax free, put away in an envelope that she kept for herself. That fifteen hundred plus the four years of fifteen hundreds each week were put away in a safety deposit box. Olga had no expenses.

Julie had to be available for Joey's beck and call and that was quite a beck and quite a call. And it could happen anytime day or night; Julie would find himself talking with Joey on the phone.

"Some guy just calls me and tells me he's got a truck full of new radios, Philcos, just across the George Washington Bridge. Fifteen hundred sets that are scheduled to end up in Cincinnati somewhere. We can rustle 'em but we gotta act fast, Julie. I think ten thousand buys the whole rig. But I figger if you get out there, Julie, we could pick it up for five. At five, it's a bargain. Take Vito with ya; he's not doin' nothin'. Angie's havin' dinner with my mother tonight. Go make the deal."

"Okay, Joey, I will."

Ten minutes later, a black four-door Ford sedan, late model 1942, would pull up at Julie's place. There was a slight tap on the horn, and Julie was on his way. They got those sets for five grand, but a little persuasion was necessary. The guy that was selling was ripping off both sides. He was ripping off Julie and Joey because the sets were hot and couldn't be moved for a good six months. By then the sets would be dated and lose their value unless they moved them out of the state right away. This guy had hijacked the rig and contents with nothing more complicated than a duplicate key in the ignition and away he went. The kid who drove Julie out to the load climbed aboard the rig and pulled out following Vito and Julie across the bridge to a warehouse in Brooklyn.

By twelve that night Julie was free and would be dropped off wherever he wanted to be. He went by Olga's. He didn't have to be in love to come.

Julie

Not So Standard Oil

Radkovitch was the biggest bootlegger this side of Canarsie, short and tough. On the Jersey side of the bay, two 50,000-ton tankers were tied alongside each other at Piers 11 and 12. Very rare and valuable unrefined oil was inside them to be used by the Atomic Energy Commission for research and experimental purposes. The head of the Atomic Energy Commission had called President Truman to ask if they could divert some crude oil for their program. It was agreed upon. The two tankers were sitting on the west side of New York City waiting for assignment to Los Alamos. Radkovitch found out about it and in passing mentioned it to Julie. Hoping against hope that maybe Julie, this clever Jew kid that he had become friendly with, who he knew he could trust with any moving job, to move anything anywhere, Julie could do it. Julie was the man. Lucky for Los Alamos, there was more oil where that came from.

Julie told Angie he would need sixteen men and three four-door sedans for two hours' work. The men were to be told absolutely nothing but that their presence would be needed. There would be no trouble, no hassles, no shit. They would be told what to do and they would do it with no questions asked. For this he was willing to pay one hundred dollars an hour. Through Radkovitch's brother-in-law, Meyer, Julie hired two river pilots of the New York City Harbor Patrol. He met the two pilots with Angie at Lefkowitz & Laibowitz, the Jewish delicatessen in the West Bronx on the Grand Concourse. He offered them twenty thousand dollars apiece for thirty-six hours' work. They were both to do what he asked with no questions asked. The captains of both oil tankers were Greek. Through Angie's cousin Mario, who was going to City College, Julie got hold of two Greek-speaking exchange students who were staying in America during the war years. The parents of these young Greeks were very wealthy and wanted their children out of harm's way during the war that was raging in Europe and in the Mediterranean. Partly for the adventure and partly for the excitement, they decided to help Julie in his plan. He told Angie to pack his .38. This and Julie's would be the only pieces they would need on this caper. Everybody else would be unarmed.

By the time the cars got organized on the east side of Manhattan, it was eight o'clock that evening, and there were now four cars. Three cars carried the sixteen assorted gunsels and a car packing Angie with his cousin Vito, the Greek interpreters, and Radkovitch, who just had to go out and see how Julie was gonna do it. Joey was along as well.

Away on the eastern shore of the Bronx, just beyond the Bronx Beach, there were a dozen abandoned piers that had been used during the great immigration surge to America. These were now used mainly by business concerns to store some of their freighters before the ships were loaded again and sent off. They all set off. Staggering their departure by fifteen minutes. At nine-thirty, the first car arrived at Pier 11 and, almost as if it had been planned by Albert Einstein, the moon set as each car arrived exactly on time. By a quarter to eleven, everything Julie had planned was ready and the caper began. Everybody was told to get out of the cars. When Julie waved, and only when Julie waved, the men were to come up the gangplank, single file. When he waved again they were to leave, get back in the cars, and wait for orders.

Julie, Joey, one of the interpreters, and Angie came up the gangplank. Spoke to the Greek officer of the deck, who asked to see some official authority papers and Julie then asked to see the Captain immediately. They were ushered into the Captain's quarters and the Captain came in a few minutes later. Jacket off, tie undone, and with what looked like a Greek newspaper in his hand. Sitting in the Captain's quarters by the porthole on the port side was his desk and sitting on the desk was the ship's clock, a beautiful 1890 chronometer that had been built in England. Without hesitation, Julie pulled his .38 from his waist, adjusted a silencer to it, pointed it toward the Captain, pointed past him at the chronometer and blew the clock to smithereens. He then asked the shaken Captain to sit in a chair, explained to him that in half an hour they were to depart from the pier. The ship was now being hijacked. They invited the Captain to the bridge. They went onto the bridge. Julie waved and the sixteen men started coming up the gangplank led by the pilot. The pilot proceeded up to the bridge, where he was introduced to the Captain and then they went into the Captain's room, where they rejoined the interpreter and Angie. The Greek Captain gave orders to all crew members on board the ship. They were to set sail in a half hour. Start engines. Prepare to depart. Julie went out on the deck again and waved. The sixteen men marched down the gangplank, climbed back into the cars, and waited.

Julie left Angie with the Captain and told Angie he would be back. Didn't tell anybody anything else. He got into the lead car and the four cars again pulled around, out through the gate that they had come in five hundred feet to the next entrance, flashed some papers to the port guard there, and drove in front of the other tanker that sat directly astern of the first. With precisely the same movements, same directions, Julie went on board to the Captain's quarters, blew this Captain's chronometer to smithereens as well, and told him through the interpreter that they would be leaving in a half hour. The Captain came out on the deck; Julie signaled for the men to come on board. Did everything he had done just twelve minutes earlier. He left Joey on board this tanker. He himself left, down the gangplank, into the lead car and back to Pier 11.

At Pier 11 he told Vito to meet them on the east shore of the Bronx piers in exactly thirty-four hours. Three of the four cars then departed. Julie went back on board the first tanker and saw that they were practically ready to set sail. The Captain, of course, not knowing that the men that had come on board had since left. Bow and stern lines were thrown off and the ship slowly started to drift into the mainstream of the bay of New York City. As the ship pulled away, the car with Radkovitch drove back to Pier 12. Radkovitch went on board and saw that tanker number two was ready to set sail. Radkovitch's arrival was Joey's signal to tell the Captain to drop bow and stern lines and the second tanker slowly started to drift into the mainstream and the current of the river itself. Both pilots were to keep each other in sight, one directly behind the other. In the next phase of the operation, all Greek personnel on the two tankers were forced to stay below decks. Not to poke their heads above deck at all at any time. For the next thirty hours the tankers sailed out of New York Bay, past the Statue of Liberty, and made a huge circle. Then headed back up in through the bay this time on the other side of Staten Island and up the Hudson; they now went up the East River, underneath the Brooklyn Bridge, past Welfare Island, up to the bridge that separated Manhattan from the Bronx. The bridge obligingly opened and both tankers very delicately passed through the open bridgeway and into the small inlet that led to the eastern shore and the remote Bronx piers.

Six thirty-five, just as dusk began to fall on the city, both ships were tied alongside each other to the piers. Vito and four men left from last night's caper helped tie them securely to the piers. Ten minutes later, four cars arrived with four drivers hired through the local teamsters' union office. The cars were large and roomy big four-door sedans, not particularly opulent but clean and well running. The crews of both ships were told to pack their gear and disembark, which they did. They piled into the cars. The captains, who happened to be twin brothers, found themselves in one car by themselves with some fine whiskey, two identical chronometers, and a beautiful luncheon arrangement for them. The windows, which had been painted dark, were rolled up and this caravan of Greeks left the piers in the Bronx not knowing where they were.

The drivers' instructions were to drive them to Norfolk,

Virginia, where they were allowed to take an hour's stretch at the local teamsters' union office. They could then relieve themselves, then back into the cars, back to Manhattan, delivered promptly to the Greek Embassy from the most baffling and bizarre trip they had ever taken. They had no idea where they'd gone at sea, where they had tied up. They did not know that they were at Norfolk, Virginia, at one point. The only thing they knew was that they were now at the Greek Embassy in New York City.

Radkovitch loved the sea voyage. Actually, it was wonderful for all of them. Those few hours by themselves in the gently turbulent sea gave them all a chance to reflect on how they thought their lives, their families, and their friends were doing. It was a nice change in their very hectic and provoking lives. After this Radkovitch said that Julie could do no wrong. There was nothing that Julie couldn't do, and nothing that wouldn't be his if he just wanted it. Radkovitch had a big mouth and he found himself embedded up to his ankles in cement. Twenty-five feet below the pier in Staten Island with a look of amazement on his face. If Radkovitch had only kept his big fucking mouth shut. It was Joey who did Radkovitch in without telling Angie or Julie. Radkovitch, at one of his Rumanian dinners, had blurted out this incredible experience of stealing so many tons of crude oil.

Julie and Joey didn't like each other now but Julie was smart enough to see the expediency of what Joey had done although he couldn't have done it or wouldn't have done it to Radkovitch. Joey had done it without even batting an eye. Julie sold the United States Government back its oil for seventy-five dollars a barrel. It was worth forty-five dollars on the black market if you could get it. An official from the government was blindfolded and brought to the two tankers. He examined the quality of the oil, reported back to his superiors, and two two-suiter suitcases full of one-hundred-dollar stacks were delivered to Julie in the back seat of the sedan used at the beginning of the caper. Once the money had been counted and they determined that the serial numbers were not in sequence, the government agent was then driven back to the two tankers. His blindfold was taken from him and he was left to his own devices. Julie's split was seventy per cent. The rest went to Angie and Joey and a sum to Radkovitch's Rumanian Independent Lodge. Posthumously.

Julie

Leaving Time

Julie stepped out of his car and a big arm grabbed him around the neck, in the garage underneath the building where he lived. How could he be so careless? His arm shot up to this burly arm that had his neck exactly in the crux of it, applying pressure ever so slightly, and if Julie's hands were not dug in there, pulling that arm a bit from his neck, why, he would have fainted away. He faked it and relaxed.

Julie's groan disconcerted the guy. Julie knew he must be big by the size of the arm around his neck. He felt it give, relax as if not knowing what to do, this nameless arm. Then Julie took one hand off the arm, reached down and had his .38 out before the guy behind him had a chance to squeeze up on Julie's neck. Julie twisted his head. Then the arm took control again. As the arm started to squeeze, this time in earnest, Julie pumped this shadowy figure with two slugs from his .38. For a second or so Julie thought he had missed because that arm didn't relax at all. It just crumbled with him onto the ground. Julie found himself still held by this nameless arm. It was a struggle to get his head out of that position.

Twenty seconds had elapsed from the time he was grabbed to the time he finally escaped from the arm. The shots reverberated and were still ringing in his ear inside the basement. Julie, out of breath, panting a bit, listened. Julie didn't hesitate. He took the wallet from the arm man. Then he took the keys from his car and opened the trunk. There was a large plastic bag which kept the trunk of his car clean. He lifted the guy from under the armpits and dragged him to the car. He lifted him up and folded him into the trunk of his car. Julie drove a big Chrysler in those days. He jumped into the car, started the ignition, backed out and onto the street. It was late and nobody was around. Julie drove up to Fifth Avenue and Central Park, pulled over on the right-hand side of the street.

Julie checked himself to be sure that there was nothing on his person that could in any way tie him to this dead gunsel. Then Julie drove down Fifth Avenue for two blocks, then turned east on the first block he could and sped down to the river as quickly as he could go without attracting too much attention. Julie wasn't sure whether the guy was carrying a piece or not. In the haste and rush of it all, he didn't get a chance to take a good look. He got down to the river, pulled up, left the motor running, opened the trunk, and reached in and pulled this gunsel out of the car. Julie sat him down on a bench overlooking the river, turned, and looked around. It was a quiet neighborhood, but Julie could not be sure that the flatfoots would not be pulling down that street and now was no time to meet anybody.

Julie picked up the gunsel, and threw him over the railing. He heard the splash as the body hit the East River, turned, and ran for his car. He got in and started to travel calmly up to his apartment.

He pulled into the garage for the second time and stepped out of the car wearier than he had been a half hour ago. He checked his trunk to see if there was any blood. There was none. Seemed clean. But tomorrow he'd have the car completely cleaned out. Walked up to his apartment, picked up a metal box in which he kept all of the valuable papers that he had and some money. Walked out of the apartment. Down to his car. Pulled out and went to Ruth's and Morrie's. He figured Joey was trying to tell him something. He could have taken on Joey, but that would mean taking on Angie, and he could never do that. So Julie, that night, decided to deal himself out. Later at Ruth's, he went through the wallet of the dead man. The name was Aldo Pepino. He knew then it wasn't the B'nai B'rith that was after him.

So Joey had made his move.

Joey and Julie never liked each other. Maybe it was because they were both very much alike—vain and uncomfortable in the presence of equals. Julie never trusted Joey. They felt secure with each other only because they had one strong tie that kept them together—Angie. They both loved Angie. There was something in the look in Angie's open face, the trust, the kindness one could see, the shyness. There were times when he would blush, and this impressed Joey, and certainly impressed Julie.

Angie was a rare breed, a rare breed indeed.

The next day, Julie went back to his apartment to pack. As he stuffed his things into two suitcases, five guys came into the room. Julie had them covered with his .38. He leveled the gun at Angie's stomach, looked in his eyes, and said, "Sit down, Angie."

Angie and Julie. They loved each other. It was difficult for them to express it but they did. They admired each other. They liked each other's style. Each one sensed in the other something unique. There was an ungrudging admiration that made it easy for them to like each other. They didn't feel as if they were being outdone by each other. Maybe with some other people they would, not with each other. Angie and Julie were quite content to be friends and pals.

"Angie, I can't cover you with a piece."

Julie handed Angie the .38. Angie took it, put it on the table.

"Julie, there can't be two bosses," Angie said. "Either you stay or Joey. Joey wants to buy you out. He's willing to pay you top dollar for every one of your holdings, Julie. Julie, take the money and run. You're twenty-eight years old. You could pull out with a million. You could go anywhere, do anything. You could be anybody. You wanna be on the hustle, go to Vegas. Beautiful spot for a guy like you. Be a big gambling spot one day. You watch. Go, Julie, don't fuck around here. You're not gonna pick up anything around here except a dose. You gotta go."

Poor Angie, caught between these two powerful boys. Julie could sense Angie's discomfort and realized he could never cause him any pain. Julie smiled, looked at Angie, and stretched out his hand.

"Let me think about it. Give me a little time to get myself together."

Angie was relieved. Julie was wary. Julie never really kept a close tab on the kind of money he had accumulated with Joey and Angie. So he shook hands and said, "Just a little time, pal." He had no idea what to expect.

The next afternoon, Angie came by with a valise.

"Joey wanted me to give you this."

Julie opened it and there was $1,250,000 in cash. Julie was a millionaire and he didn't even know it.

If it hadn't been for Angie, Julie would have been wiped out long ago. Julie would take his share and move to Vegas. December 18, 1951, found Julie on the Super Chief, traveling west to Las Vegas. A bag full of money and a bag full of clothes. On his hip, a new .38. Before he left, he bought Ruth and Morrie a beautiful home in New Jersey on the Palisades overlooking the river, a house they would live in for the rest of Ruth's life. Joey wanted him out. He had gotten out. And he was going West.

Ruth and Morrie saw him off at the train along with Angie. When he got on the train that night in New York City, he was sure that his life in the city was finished. Everything he wanted out of that area he had taken with him and now, still a young man, he took off without once looking back. Angie and he embraced. Looked at each other. Smiled. And then split. Good-by, New York. Good-by. Give my regards to Broadway. They would never see each other again. Angie was shot and killed in a Brooklyn basement eleven days later because of Joey's carelessness. Angie never knew what hit him. The slug tore a hole as big as a fist through the back of his head, and that was the end of Angie. Joey knew all the time there would be trouble. He should never have sent Angie. He was always careless. And it cost him his brother's life. Angie, sweet Angie . . . in the prime of his life, in control of his power, down the river of no return. You never know anyone by words, you only know 'em by being with 'em. You only recall. Never relive. When Angie died, Julie forgot the past. It was only with Angie's death that Julie changed; they had shared a lot together. Angie was someone Julie chose to love and be with. With Angie, Julie always felt complete. He was now alone again. Julie tried to figure out what he was doing when Angie died. As close as he could figure, he was sleeping. What he didn't know was that Angie was smiling at him in a dream when the bullet hit. Julie never remembered it. And another kid bit the dust.

He had a compartment on the Super Chief from New York to Las Vegas. Also on board was Samuel Solomon, head of Pacific Pictures. Traveling with Mr. Solomon was a very beautiful young woman named Sally Tarlow, Mr. Solomon's male private secretary, and a screen director and writer named Ference Nagy. They used their trip to California to develop and prepare a future motion picture to be made for Mr. Solomon's company. Sally, eighteen years old, out of Pennsylvania, looking for some kind of success, anything, met Solomon at a party. Solomon, besides fucking her, was going to launch her on a film career. She definitely had something, this girl. Vivacious, stimulating, interesting, a good head, great body.

By the time the Super Chief hit the plains of Kansas City, Julie was fucking Sally in the upper berth that belonged to the director-writer. And don't think that Solomon didn't know all about it. He could determine character immediately. He saw the kind of power and drive that Julie had and was pleased to be able to meet him at the beginning of his career. When Julie got off in Vegas, he had Sally's number and also Solomon's number in Los Angeles, which were the same. He told them that he would be pretty busy in Vegas until he got his business set up, but the first time he was in town, why, he would call them. And if by chance they had any occasion to come to Vegas, to call him. Right. Right!

Book Three

KID
ANDREW CODY

Andrew

1943

Baltazar Sloane, his friends called him Bart. He'd been in the Marines now two eight-year hitches. He was in the first assault on Guadalcanal and had been injured badly by shrapnel. He was sent to Hawaii to recuperate and finally to Camp Pendleton as a drill instructor. He had a wife and four kids and he lived in National City, just outside of San Diego. On his days off, which he spent with his family, you wouldn't think he was a World War II hero in the United States Marines, decorated with a Purple Heart, Presidential citation, the meanest mother-fucking drill instructor on the base. He played bridge with his wife and neighbors, liked to do crossword and jigsaw puzzles, helped his two sons make model airplanes and liked to barbecue. He was jovial, kind, and considerate to everyone he ran across, until he put that fucking hat of his—that cavalry felt hat—on his head. He was thirty-two years old and hard as nails. There were fifteen hundred recruits at the Marine Base in San Diego that spring of 1943 and Kid Andrew Cody was one of them. He and twenty other kids drew Drill Instructor Sloane as their tormentor and patron saint for the next eight weeks. Of these fifteen hundred men Kid Cody ranked in the top five in general demeanor and in the top three going through the obstacle course, which was a grueling test for anybody and took six minutes, full out, to complete.

The first time Kid Cody did it, it took him five minutes and thirty-five seconds and he eventually shaved that down to just under five minutes, which was the unofficial record at the base at that time. There was nothing he didn't do without a great deal of energy. This made no impression on Sergeant Sloane. He just goaded Kid Cody a little harder than the rest. But it didn't phase the Kid. He was used to these kinds of responses from people. He just kept himself together and didn't allow anyone to phase or undo him. About three weeks into his boot training, having dinner at the mess hall, some kid named Alfred, sitting about five seats from Kid Cody, went apeshit. Get off, he screamed, get off me. He started pulling at his blouse as if some animal was crawling inside of him. Everybody sitting around him froze and hoped Alfred would calm down finally. But he didn't. He got louder and went more berserk. He finally picked up a knife from the table and started slashing out at anyone near him. Everybody tumbled away from the table and started to run. Finally, Drill Instructor Sloane and the Kid pinned him down to the ground. Alfred wouldn't be held down, kept struggling. Drill Inspector Sloane yelled, Cody, gimme a hand with this asshole! Cody screamed, Yes, sir! He got hold of Alfred's feet and promptly got kicked in the balls for his efforts. He held on for dear life. Eventually Alfred would calm down. He did. His energy spent, his chest heaving, gasping for air. They picked him up and hustled him out. Took him across the parade grounds to the infirmary, which had been alerted. Two orderlies grabbed Alfred. A nurse came running in and gave him a shot. When Cody left, Alfred was sitting in a chair, kind of glassy-eyed and docile. They walked out and went back to the mess hall. Sloane walked ahead of him with his cavalry felt hat still in place on his head, hat pushed forward, chin out, chest out. The Kid pulled his shoulders back, lifted up his chin, fell in step behind his drill instructor. That was the first time he felt like a Marine, marching behind this hard-nosed son of a bitch. There was nothing he couldn't do. The Kid loved those eight weeks. Testing himself and the times.

Once when he snuck out of boot camp he met a girl at a USO dance held in downtown San Diego on Friday night. Her name was Mary Lee Anderson. She was beautiful. She wore a satin dress that clung to her. Long legs, beautiful body. After the dance he took her home. They necked on the couch. Rubbed hard up against each other until he came in his pants. He had no way of getting to the base, so she drove him back. It was now morning. He had until six. She gave him her telephone number and the Kid told her that he probably could get out next Saturday night and Sunday. She said, If you do, call me. Maybe we'll do something. He said, Okay, good-by, Mary Lee. She said, Good-by, Andrew. She drove off, leaving him standing there at the entrance to the base. It was quiet with an occasional car driving in, a couple of sailors checked in; three Marines, pissed, staggered up to the gate, flashed their I.D.s, then entered this huge training camp. He made it to his quarters. He got undressed, took a shower, took his dirty skivvies, went into the bathroom, and washed them out in the sink, squeezed the water out of them, and hung them to dry on the line outside his barrack. And then it was bright and early, and he was getting his head blown off by Drill Instructor Sloane, screaming what an asshole he was, didn't know his left foot from his right, and if he was looking for trouble he was going to get it from him. He called Mary Lee that night, and she said she'd pick him up at six o'clock Saturday night near the base. Bring a bathing suit. She came driving up in this Packard convertible. The fastest kid on the base. She didn't tell him then but they took off straight for Ensenada, which was about a two-hour drive into Mexico.

They arrived at nine-thirty and checked into a motel that had bungalows right on the sea. They went to a restaurant that served clams, lobsters, and fish caught off the coast of Mexico. They went dancing in this nightclub not far from where they were staying. She rubbed up against him, driving him crazy. He could tell she liked him and so he tried to control himself, at least until later. They were dancing close. She said, Oh, Andrew, it's so beautiful to be here with you. He was almost speechless with someone like Mary Lee. Someone as outgoing and giving as she was. He was sure there was some catch to it, that she would probably have some ax to grind, some reason to take him. He was a nice-looking guy but he didn't figure he had much to offer anybody, least of all a woman or a girl. But he was content to bask in her warmth, in her generosity. She whispered to the clerk at the motel when they got back. Ten minutes later, in their bungalow with the glass doors open and a sea breeze cruising the room, there was a knock. He got up, went to the door, and there was the clerk with a package. He gave it to Mary Lee. It was a lid of marijuana. She had some paper in her purse, glued two sheets together, and made about the best-looking joint you've ever seen. The Kid had heard about locoweed but he'd never tried it. Well, he did that night. One thing for sure, that weekend, he didn't come in his pants. They spent the next day, Sunday, walking miles and miles up and down the beach hunting for shells. It was so beautiful and so detached from what his life really was, with this sweet girl standing alongside of him, sharing it with him.

Then there he was, Monday morning, lined up ready to go on a ten mile hike, at a trot. Adjusting his gear, sorry he hadn't gone to the toilet, and realizing that it was going to be a tough day, a tough, fucking day indeed. The day and a half he spent with that beautiful girl was now nothing but a memory. They had made plans to talk later in the week as soon as he had a chance to call her. Boot camp was finished and he was shipping out. He had orders to go to Mare Island, near San Francisco. He knew he was going to be shipped to the Pacific somewhere. He didn't know where but he knew he was leaving. Monday morning, at nine o'clock, he had graduated from the Marine boot camp at San Diego. He had orders to report to the Marine Adjutant's Office at Mare Island at 0800 on Wednesday morning. The Kid and Mary Lee spent the last day they had together on the beach at the Coronado Hotel just outside of San Diego. At five that afternoon he was to meet three other Marines, one of whom owned a car. The four of them would split expenses and drive up to San Francisco. It would take them all night. Mary Lee and the Kid hurried into each other's arms and bodies at another motel. Memories of love in rented beds. She drove him to where he was to meet his buddies. The last he saw of her, she was driving down the highway, going south, tears in her eyes, top down, hair streaming back. This beautiful girl from National City. Gone out of his life forever. He reported to Mare Island at exactly eight o'clock Wednesday morning and four days later he found himself on a troop transport on his way to Honolulu.

Andrew

1945

Your lep. Your lep. One, two, three, four. Your lep. Your lep. One, two, three, four. Your lep. Hup. Hup. Hup, sang out the Sergeant as they paraded before Admiral Nimitz in Pearl Harbor. The Admiral had arrived earlier that day from Midway and was now reviewing the Marine Base in Pearl Harbor. There on the drill field fifteen battalions marched by in close order. Kid Cody up front carrying the emblem of the Corps. It was beautiful. These boys so eager to please their father, who stood benevolently by on a platform. This almost old man looking at these almost young men marching before him, ready to die for the good old U.S.A. Your lep. Your lep. Your lep, right, lep. Your lep. Your lep. Your lep, right, lep, he sang out in a clear, resonant voice. Five different voices counting cadence at five different places on the field, all reverberating back to each man who seemed to be marching to echoes on this hot, harsh day in early 1945. There were nothing but ripoff joints in Honolulu then. These young recruits came in and out of that town like a good laxative. He got a few days at Waikiki. Got to the island of Maui on a tour given by the USO located at Waikiki. Three hundred sailors, Marines, and some Army. As soon as they hit Maui, these three hundred men had only one thought in their minds, one burning desire, one aim; to get laid.

They were shown sections of the island where some natural geysers erupted, and the huge pineapple fields that ranged all over these islands, making the one or two families that owned them richer than the city of Los Angeles. Artifacts of the old times on the island, canoes, huts, beautiful places to swim, a luau for everybody, some ice cold beer. Still, all these kids would have given it all up for just one piece of ass to be raffled off to one lucky son of a bitch.

He ended up on the *Saratoga*, an aircraft carrier. As a private first class, he found himself standing guard duty primarily on board this aircraft carrier. At sea, four hours on and four hours off. Tied up somewhere, four on and eight off. He kept his gear clean and neat. Worked out every day in a section of the carrier rigged for a gym. Found himself stationed topside on the bridge as admiral's aide and runner. He carried a .45 as a sidearm. He was a fine marksman. But he could no more kill anybody with one of those bullets than he could crap in his pants. He hoped he would never have to do either one. He bunked with thirty-five other men in the third quarter of the upper starboard side of the *Saratoga*, at water level. He could have rigged a hammock and slept in it but he chose the bunk instead. Although they were stacked on top of each other, four high, he still found the bottom bunk the quietest and the most private.

They were somewhere in the Pacific and he'd just come off his four. It was midnight. He decided against getting something to eat. Went down to his bunk and changed. Took a towel and wrapped it around his waist, and put on some wooden sandals that were almost regulation gear because of the crabs and other animals that floated around the ship. It was quiet that morning. He saw few, very few personnel up or around, an occasional sailor sitting in the coffee room, a couple of guys bullshitting in a corner somewhere. But down around where he was now there were very few men up or on duty. On the way down he saw the Navy Chief Gunner's Mate. They nodded. Stepping into the shower, he heard something hitting the metal bulkhead. Thought he barely saw a shadow. The shower was cold and brisk. He dried himself. Heard a rustling sound in the other compartment. Brushed his teeth, shaved, dried his hair. The first book he could remember really enjoying was the book he was reading now, *Anthony Adverse*. He thought he'd put in an hour with the book and then try to get some sleep. As he stepped through the compartment hatch he sensed somebody was standing by the side, but before he could even turn, one arm had grabbed him around the neck, another one around his waist, and pulled his buttocks up against strong hard muscles and somebody with a hard-on obviously trying to drive it between his cheeks.

It so stunned the Kid that for a second or two he didn't resist. He just hung there, in mid-air, as if in limbo, as if carried off out of the ship and projected into another world where the only senses that were responding were the senses down below him where he felt only flesh against flesh. The Kid was strong but until that night he never knew how strong. He seemed to vibrate, vibrate so hard and shake so hard that this figure behind him started to lose the strength it had and he could feel it weakening. When he knew that whatever was on top of him in the back was off balance enough, he planted his bare feet firmly on the ground, leaned forward, and lifted the body clear off the deck. The Kid then turned to his left, pivoted on his feet about forty degrees, and literally threw himself and whatever was hanging on his back into the metal bulkhead that stood three feet away. He heard a groan and a whooshing sound. The Kid swung around quickly when the arms relaxed after the smash into the bulkhead, and there was the Chief Gunner's Mate with a navy-blue robe on with nothing on underneath. The robe itself opened and the Chief's genital area was exposed. The Chief was about forty or so—just a shadow of gray in a closely cropped head of hair—kind of a soft gut and big flabby arms. He was three inches taller than the Kid, who was then about five ten and a half and weighed about a hundred forty pounds. This guy was a hundred ninety. The Kid threw three punches in less than two seconds. He drove his right into the stomach and had it away before this man could crumble. He then threw his left in an arc upward and before the Chief even felt the pain of that punch, the Kid brought his right straight out and across the Chief's jaw and bottom lip. He caught the Chief standing and defenseless with that last right cross. Before the Chief hit the deck, the Kid had the towel wrapped around his waist again, and his small ditty bag with his toilet articles in his left hand again. He looked around the small chamber. There was no one there and no sound in the semidarkness of this passageway leading from one chamber to another.

In the Chief's sandals were stenciled his name, Brenner

T, and the insignia of his rank, Chief Gunner's Mate. The Kid walked back to his bunk and got dressed. He checked with one of the sailors on duty who he knew.

"Hey, Ralph."

"Yeah, Kid."

"Find out where the Chief Gunner's Mate by the name of Brenner T billets out, will ya?"

"Sure, Kid."

He stood in this room that was lit only by a red light which prepared a man to go on duty. If you went from light to dark, as many of these men did when going on duty, it took your eyes a minute to adjust to the darkness. A minute could mean the sinking of a ship. This red room prepared your eyes so that the transition took but ten seconds. It was quiet and the Kid was sorry he wasn't going on duty now and he was sorry that this had happened to him. Or had it? Was it just a memory or a dream or something he wished would happen to him? He couldn't be sure.

"He's in Compartment 33, port side, amidships."

He dressed, checked out his sidearm, the .45, and started topside to go on duty. He had fifteen minutes before he had to report for duty. He went to the Chief's compartment. Took him a few minutes to find it. He finally did. He saw down this corridor five individual staterooms, each one housing a chief. There was a small name plate and there was Brenner's name. The Kid didn't hesitate. He turned the handle of the door and it opened. He stepped easily inside and shut it behind him. There sitting at the desk with a number of papers, bed undone, clothes folded over the bunk, sat the Chief still in his navy-blue robe. He had on a pair of glasses which he immediately took off to see who was in the room. The Kid, with holster open, took out the .45, pulled back on the chamber mechanism. He released it and placed a .45 millimeter shell into the chamber. He released. It slammed back. He raised his arm, held it straight out and stiff. The .45 was six inches from the Chief's temple, aimed right between his eyes. Oh, God . . . no, he uttered. The Kid just looked at him, blue-eyed and steely, not quivering, not wavering, just standing erect and stiff as this chief's cock was a little while back. He held that position about ten seconds. Ten seconds of agony for the Chief, and then just as quickly pulled back the .45 and put on the safety, put it back in its holster, turned, and started out the door.

"We gotta stop seeing each other, Chief. People are starting to talk."

Andrew

1945

The personnel officer on board the *Saratoga* thought it wise to transfer Kid Andrew Cody, Private First Class, from the *Saratoga* to a land-based Marine battalion. Fourteen days later, the *Saratoga* was docked at the Navy Marine Base on the island of Guam. The Kid spent two days at Camp Ealey, a rest camp for submarine sailors returning from patrols. He was reassigned to his original battalion, which was doing patrol duties on the island of Saipan. The next morning at nine-twenty, he was at the air base and flying out on a B-26, as gunnery replacement. There was always a regiment of Marines who were doing overlapping jobs needed by the Navy and by the Naval Air Force. Saipan wasn't much different from Guam, much more primitive at this point in the war. The Marines patrolled the foothills of the island to try to keep marauding Japanese patrols from stealing supplies and killing whatever men were around. This existence was altogether different from the dry and clean, almost antiseptic way of life aboard the *Saratoga*. Although this portion of the island was secure and the base itself was well guarded, everybody walked around half expecting to get their asses blown off. He was billeted in a quonset hut with sixteen other Marines. And before he knew it, he was on patrol.

He was flat on his belly in the middle of a jungle somewhere blowing holes through leaves and shrubbery with an M-1 carbine. The enemy was nothing more than sounds, movements of bushes, and occasional smells. They were on patrol going up a small ridge, spaced about twenty feet apart. On the left and right of them were low bushes and rocks, heavy foliage, thick and dark, even under the bright sun which burned down on top of them.

The Kid looked to his left and there he was, looking at him. He was the same age and passionate. A bit more ragged-looking than the Kid, but mean. He was Japanese and almost as tall as the Kid. As the Kid fired his carbine, he dove for cover, as did the Japanese soldier. The two shots made the men in front of and behind the Kid dive for cover. The Kid heard some rustlings from the direction in which he had shot at the Japanese soldier. He pumped four or five more rounds as quickly as he could into the area and waited. He was astounded at how hard his heart was pounding in his chest. He heard somebody yell.

"What are we gonna do?"

"Stay covered," another voice said.

The troop commander, Marine Lieutenant David Simon Ward II, decided not to try to get to the top of the ridge. He came down the trail, half crouching, passing each man, followed by his scout. He'd gone down about seventy yards and had corralled all his men, all sixteen of the patrol, and instead of heading straight down now, he started west in the same direction that the Kid had seen the Japanese soldier. Traveling in this direction, they came to a low mound. As they came to the top of it, they saw a dirt road ranging down from the top of the hill. They held up on the east side of the road. Lieutenant Ward checked all his men. They seemed alert and ready for action, and he decided to wait there to see if there was a movement of any kind across the road or down in the little gully. They all heard it at the same time; a strange, staccato-like, harsh sound erupted in the air. It was a voice and obviously Japanese.

There, two hundred feet up the road, coming around the bend, was this Japanese officer with a samurai sword resting on one shoulder. The Lieutenant raised his hand to all the men to hold their fire. The Japanese officer dressed in puttees, leather boots, short khaki jacket, army belt around the waist, packing the equivalent of an American .45, left hand swinging and empty, right hand holding the handle of this samurai blade that rested unsheathed on its flat side on his shoulder. He was a young man, wearing a small visored cap. He was stepping quite smartly down the center of the dirt road. When the Japanese officer was about a hundred feet away from him, Lieutenant Ward stepped out into the middle of the dirt road facing his Japanese counterpart. Lieutenant Ward drew his .45, cocked it, held it out, bent his elbow up to waist length and in a very relaxed manner menaced the Japanese officer. The Japanese stopped ten feet from the American. The Japanese officer lifted the samurai sword from his shoulder, held it upright, at the same time, clasping the handle with his left hand as well. Before you could draw a breath, he brought the blade flying past the Lieutenant's lower chest and abdomen. He sidestepped and started walking again down the road. Marine Lieutenant David Simon Ward II, crumpled to his knees, not even recalling what had happened to him. Three seconds later, his heart fluttered, spasmed violently twice, and stopped beating. He had died under the hot sun, in the middle of a dirt road, without even knowing it.

Sergeant Salvador Fachetti, Chicago born and raised, stepped up on the ridge of the road. The Sergeant was holding up the rear of this small troop and was twenty feet away facing the Japanese officer when Lieutenant Ward crumpled. Salvador Fachetti was the best pitcher Chicago University ever had. His pitches were accurate and fast and if the war didn't last too long, why, he could possibly play in the National or American League one day as the star pitcher for the Chicago Cubs.

Sal was standing fifteen feet from the Japanese officer as the officer continued past Salvador down the road, acting as if he didn't even see him. His samurai sword once again resting on his shoulder, clean and sparkling, reflecting the rays of the sun as if it had never passed through the entrails and guts of a man just fifteen seconds before. Salvador dropped his carbine by the strap onto the ground, reached to his right hip where a small canvas bag hung housing six hand grenades. He took one out, pulled the pin, held it in such a way that the small metal safety bar could be released by just lifting his fingers. He knew these grenades were timed for seven seconds and were pretty accurate up to six, rarely went at five. He timed it for six and a half. He released the safety bar and took a breath. He checked the pitching mound. One second. Checked where the Japanese officer would be when he threw. Never taking his eyes off the officer, he drew up his right hand with the grenade and cupped it with his left hand as well. Two seconds. He let his right hand swing with the grenade in a short arc, brought the grenade up to his chest. Shifted the weight to his right leg and leaned slightly in that direction, just lifting the tip of his left foot off the ground. Three seconds. Leaned back on his right foot and cocked his right hand and arm that held the grenade. Four seconds. Then he threw with all his might in the direction of the Japanese officer. Five seconds.

The trajectory, speed, weight, wind conditions, the Japanese officer's head, all joined into this mathematical miracle equation and at six seconds point two, it just touched the back of the Japanese officer's head when it exploded. The head disappeared almost immediately. The body stood poised there for a second with the samurai sword resting on its headless shoulder, took one step, and pitched forward and fell. His red blood staining the road in front of the body. The American officer was bleeding now and dead. Both men were dead. The whole experience had taken forty seconds. That was the first and the last time the Kid would see anybody die during World War II.

Andrew

1948

Kid Cody came out that summer. There was a lot of haze that year in the Los Angeles Basin. The valley of the tears. It was only at the end of fall that the weather in the basin turned hot, clear, and dry. The blue-eyed devil was twenty-four years old, lean and tough. He had behind him three years in the Marines, ten years in two orphanages and three foster homes, six years drifting around with his father, and five years living with a mother and father who had no knowledge of life at all. None of the practicalities of it.

On the island of Guam, just eighteen months earlier, he had met a guy by the name of Spencer, who came from Los Angeles. Spencer told him, when the war was over, if he was ever in California, to look him up. It was an Oldfield number—Oldfield 6-3849. He had been discharged from Camp Pendleton, the Marine Base in California, because it was in San Diego that he had enlisted. He had said good-by to Ollie just a few hours earlier before he started to hitchhike up to L.A. Ollie Kahn, out of New Orleans. All but three of his teeth had been pulled out while he was in the service, and he had been given dentures. He was twenty-seven years old, rushing back to New Orleans to pick up the pieces. Three years was a long time in the life of a gambler. Even so, he was getting back to his home town with eighty-five thousand bucks. Eighty-five thousand bucks that he had picked up gambling all across the South Pacific, sending money orders home to his bank in New Orleans. Ollie was an orphan. Here's my number, Kid. You can always get me there in New Orleans. If you're ever around there, and get homesick for them good old days on Guam and Saipan, call me. I ought to be pretty well set up in a couple of years. See ya. With that, Ollie turned and walked out. And so did the Kid. One going east. The other going north.

He called the Oldfield number and asked for Spencer. There was no Spencer there. They didn't know anyone by that name. The Kid stepped out of that phone booth with about two hundred twenty dollars to his name, a pair of socks, a pair of shorts, one T-shirt, comb, toothbrush, a tube of Colgate toothpaste, and a double-edged razor all nicely housed in a small brown leather bag that he carried under his arm. He had a pair of Levis on and a brand new pair of short cowboy boots that he bought in a Western store in San Diego, a short denim jacket, a light blue cotton shirt, and the best-looking white Stetson you could buy for thirty-five bucks. The piece of paper that Spencer's name and telephone number were written on fluttered out of the Kid's hand. He watched it waft its way onto the street. As a car passed over it, the gust of wind that was generated blew the paper in the air where it caught another gust of wind and then another and just floated away into nowhere. The Kid watched it for a few minutes. Saw it disappear. Then he turned and started walking.

He was left off at Pico and Western by a Bible salesman driving a prewar Plymouth, who kept swigging on a pint of cheap Bourbon as he extolled the virtues of God to Kid Cody. The Kid listened with interest as the Bible salesman kept pumping out the gospels of God. Did you know, son, the Book of Revelation reveals the past, the present, and the future? If you want to know what your destiny is, just read it in the Book of Revelation. The good Jesus was no priest, no prophet, no wise man who walked this earth. Sweet Jesus was the Son of God. He gave us our divinity. His teachings govern us. For without these teachings, what are we, son? Before the Kid could answer, he said, Whiskey-guzzling bums. That's what. In my case, it's Bourbon. Sex-craved men, who crave after succulent, beautiful, gentle young creatures. He took another gulp. Shit, kid, I'd sure like to get laid. The Kid looked straight ahead and said, Well, don't look at me. The Bible salesman grunted. He let him off at the corner, wished him good luck in this sin-ridden city, and took off in his Plymouth, looking first for a place where he could get laid; second, a place where he could stay for a few days and sell his Bibles.

It was ten-fifteen on a Wednesday morning. The Kid walked north until he got to Sunset, then he turned west and started toward the sea. With a couple of rides and by walking, he was down at the Santa Monica pier by a little after twelve. He felt hungry for the first time that day. Sat down in a diner he found along the sea, not far from the pier. He ordered eggs, up and down, two orders of crisp bacon, toast and butter, a glass of fresh orange juice, and java with a lot of cream and sugar. All for eighty cents, including tip. He wanted to bed down somewhere. At least have a place to put his few belongings. He didn't want to walk around looking like a greenhorn. In those days, there were a lot of small, wood-framed houses all along the sea going into Venice. Every now and then you'd see a "For Rent, One Room, Furnished" sign. The Kid found what he thought looked like a nice house, clean and well cared for. Walked up the four wooden steps. Rang the bell. She was forty and her name was Alice. She had a daughter Maria who was twenty. And Maria couldn't call Alice Mother or Mommy or Noo-noo. She had to call her Alice. The house belonged to Alice's mother, Irene, who was fifty-eight. And if you didn't call Alice Mamma, you certainly didn't call Irene Grandmother. You called her Irene. The Kid took off his Stetson and said, I'm looking for a room to rent. Alice thought he looked clean enough.

"You just get out of the service?"

"Yes, ma'am."

"What were you in?"

"In the Marines, ma'am."

"Where you from?"

"Somewhere in Kansas, ma'am. Wichita, Kansas, ma'am. That's where I was born."

"How long you planning to stay?"

"Well, I don't really know, ma'am. Thought I'd just stay around for a little bit. Maybe get connected here or head back to Wichita."

"Twenty dollars a week and I'll give you breakfast. Two weeks in advance."

"Right, ma'am."

"Don't call me ma'am."

"Okay," he said. He reached into his pocket and peeled out forty bucks from his small bundle, handed the money to Alice.

"Don't you want to see the room first?" she said.

"I guess it's going to be okay."

"You guess, huh, kid?" She smiled. "Well, don't guess about anything."

He walked into a clean and tidy foyer with a staircase leading to the upper floors, of which there were two more. To the right of the stairs was an archway beyond which there was a room. It looked like a sitting-living room. On the left was another doorway, leading to what looked like part of a dining room. And at the far end of that he could see the kitchen water basin through an open door. She started up the stairs in front of him, the Kid obediently following. Her behind was jiggling just a foot and a half away from his face. She sure was good-looking, the Kid thought. He had better wait though until he was sure this was the place to stay before he made any move, if any. He had good luck. The room he got overlooked the sea through two big windows and there was a small terrace as well. There was a single bed. The room was about ten feet wide and twelve or fourteen feet long. She said, My name is Alice Rodriguez. She turned and left. The bathroom, which was down a short hall, had a bathtub, a shower fixture, a john, a small basin, and a window that looked into a house alongside. He went to the bathroom, took his clothes off, and took a warm shower. He put on his clean underwear, washed out a pair of shorts he had with him in the basin, and looked up into the mirror. He had an oval face, light brown hair, blue eyes, and a cleft chin. His mouth was somewhat irregular but full. He weighed a hundred forty-five pounds.

*　　*　　*

It was after breakfast. He stepped out into the haze of Los Angeles. Thursday morning. He turned north and started up toward Pacific Palisades, walking, trying to catch a lift if he could. If not, he was content to walk up along the ocean. Pacific Ocean Park sat out on a pier about a half mile long. With the war over, he could already see the hustle and bustle to put it back into shape for the postwar years. During the war, a small detachment of sailors was lucky enough to be based at the edge of the pier where they kept a lookout for that lone submarine with a suicide crew of Japanese that would come and blow up the Los Angeles Basin. That was the rumor. These sailors would bring whatever girls they could corral from around the basin and down at Santa Monica out to the pier, and everybody would fuck their heads off. They called the pier "the snatchiary." The pier sat about a twelve-minute walk from where he lived. He stepped onto the pier and loved it immediately. There were all kinds of rides and shops ranging the whole length of the pier, which was facing due west. It was a carnival in the best sense. Half the rides were open. There were families down here already, trying to distract themselves and their children by giving them the pleasures of the rides during midweek, instead of just weekends. There were a lot of people still out of work.

The Kid ambled down the pier until he got about halfway down, saw what looked like an office, walked in, and asked the girl behind the desk if there was any work around. She gave him a quick look, told him to keep walking down to the end of the pier, there was a construction firm and maybe he could find something there. Thank you, ma'am. He walked out, turned west, and walked another two hundred yards to the end of the pier. There was a small construction hut on the corner. A guy named Malone was running the outfit. He was the head contractor, head carpenter, and head mother-fucker. Whatever you got paid, you gave him five per cent of your action. It was him that got you the job, no one else but him. Malone had the Kid sized up before the Kid even got to his desk.

"The job'll get you seven dollars a day, two of which is dues. So you clear five. I made a deal with the hash joint on the edge of the pier about a hundred yards up the right—Marie's. She'll give ya three square meals for a buck and a half a day. A lot of joints around the neighborhood you can flop down, if you want. General construction work. I need a kid that's strong and stupid. Are you strong and stupid, kid? And don't talk much, and keep your eyes on the job that you're assigned to and nothin' else? If you're that kind of a kid, say so."

"I reckon no one gets to talk much around here."

"Tex, you're hired. You look strong and stupid and sound stupid."

"My name's Cody, Kid Andrew Cody. Where do I sign up?"

Malone smiled. Great, he thought. He liked this kid already.

"Can you swim?"

"Yep."

"Okay. Come on. Charlie, I'm goin' down below. Hold the fort."

"Right."

Charlie was busy in the corner. The Kid noticed him now. He was short, bald, and fifty, skinny, mean, lived in the valley, married to a pretty good-looking woman who at that very moment was going down on some motorcycle cop she met four days earlier when he didn't give her a ticket. He and Malone ran this company. He was the paymaster and general deal maker.

Come on, Kid, Malone said. They walked up the pier going east another twenty-five or thirty feet. There was a railing that overlooked the ocean with a staircase leading down. The door was locked. Malone took out a key, opened the lock. The two men passed through. He relocked the gate, and down they went underneath the huge pier. Just a second before there was gaiety and laughter and children and grownups. Old men fishing off the pier. Guys vending hot dogs and peanuts and Cracker Jacks. Mothers looking after their children. Kids looking at themselves in the fucked-up mirrors. Sea gulls shitting on some of the people. Kids with bathing suits on and sand stuck everywhere, buying soft drinks and popcorn. There were a lot of tits around. In California, girls wore their brassieres just a shade looser and their sweaters and blouses were opened and tighter. The smell of food. The smell of virgins. And, the cool breeze coming out of the west. He heard calliope music, the rattle of a roller coaster scaring the shit out of the twelve people sitting in it. One guy in the roller coaster loved it. He was sitting with a girl he had just picked up and as the roller coaster hit the steep dive doing a snappy sixty miles an hour, she grabbed his cock. Now as they reached twenty feet below the pier, the world above stopped. It was as if he had been swallowed into another world, into the pier's mouth, swallowed into its guts. And, there, below him as far as the eye could see, were pier posts embedded into the water which in turn allowed these posts encased in cement to rest a good twenty-five feet below the sand. It was colder down here and he heard the sea beating up against the huge stakes which held this pier at this point in the ocean. He could see how truly fragile the whole rig looked. There were some catwalks where one could manage to go from section to section, but primarily the only way you could get to the pier posts in the center was by a little rowboat kept another twenty feet below them tied to a smaller pier. He could see about ten or fifteen guys ranged all around the different poles, scraping away at barnacles.

"Hey, Skip, how's it goin'?"

"Okay. We still got another thirty-five or forty yet. We'll get 'em."

"This is the Kid. He's workin' for us and he can swim."

"Okay."

Malone turned to the Kid and said, "I'll pay ya every Thursday." And left.

"Didja ever wear a frog suit?"

"Yep."

"Were you in the service?"

"Right."

"Marines?"

"Yeah, right."

"Well, you oughtta know a little about diving."

"I reckon I do."

"Okay. We got some Navy surplus underwater equipment. Go get yourself fitted out with a wet suit, some fins, a mask. I'll try you around the surface today and if it looks like you can handle yourself, I'll give ya a tank tomorrow."

"Thanks."

"You're welcome." Skip, broken-nosed, potbellied, and forty-five, looked at the Kid and grunted. "Huh . . . look in that shed. You'll find everything you need."

The Kid turned around and walked to a small shed that stood on the side of a platform that rested between four of the huge poles. The area was about a twenty foot square. He found a top and rubber pants that fit pretty good. The flippers he found were a little big but he stuck a hole through the back portion of the fin, got some shoelace, passed it through, and tied that around his ankles. That way the flipper couldn't fall off. Not bad, he thought. Found a rubber cap that only exposed his face from his forehead to just about his chin. It fit him okay. He found a swim mask that was adjustable and he flopped out to Skip. Skip told the Kid that he wanted him to work on one pole about a fifteen-foot swim from where he stood. He gave the Kid a scraper, told him to dive below the surface of the water to see how thick the barnacles, and whatever other things there, were and the general condition of the pole. The Kid dove in. He was surprised at how menacing and angry the water under the pole looked, as if it yearned to get out and bask in the sun instead of being stuck under this pier day after day. It was angry, much stronger than where the pier was not. He dove under with the mask on and didn't see a fucking thing. He came up. Spit in the mask, cleaned it off. He knew it was going to be tough, but he didn't realize it was going to be this tough. He had no way of anchoring himself to get a good grasp on the pole and start hacking. The surf kept slapping him against the pole or holding him there, making it impossible for him to cut away at the barnacles. The smell was tough too. It smelled like rotten eggs and rubber. He slashed away as best he could. Would surface every fifteen or twenty seconds for another breath of air and down he'd go. Took him a couple of hours to get that one pole clean, a foot below the surface. The Kid figured at that rate it was going to take him the rest of his life to get all of those poles cleaned.

It was lunch. He was called over on the side by Skip. Got out of the water, still warm underneath the rubber suit, but his feet and hands were wrinkled and blue. Skip said, You got a half hour. The Kid went over to the shed, took off the rubber suit and all his equipment. Dried himself with a dirty towel that hung on a peg. Dried his hair. Got dressed. Walked out. Skip said, You made a big mistake, Kid, you gotta be back here in fifteen minutes now. Kid turned and looked at Skip and said, I don't gotta be back nowhere. Turned again and walked up the steep wooden stairs to the top level, where once more he heard the joyous sounds of the living around him. He vaulted over the gate with the lock and saw Malone standing, talking to one of the workmen. Malone looked surprised, walked over, and before he could say anything, the Kid said, Them two hours down there was on me. He turned, walked down the pier, passed Marie's. It was crowded but he found a place at the counter, sat down, some girl came over, short brown hair, blue eyes, tough nose, tough mouth, a nice heavy figure.

"What'll ya have?"

"Just a hamburger, please, and a Pepsi."

"Okay."

It cost him twenty-three cents. He left thirty cents, got out on the pier, turned east, and walked to the end of it. An hour and twenty minutes later, to be precise, Kid Cody was fucking a beautiful redhead at a beach house in Malibu.

Julie

He used to like the fights in New York. He went to one of the local gyms in Las Vegas. Saw a kid with the Star of David on his trunks working out. Went up to him and said, What's a nice Jewish boy like you doing in a place like this? The kid said, Well, gotta make a living. Julie looked at him. He was about six feet tall, very strongly built, intelligent blue eyes, and a flat, broken nose, a perfect middleweight. I'll show you how to make a living without having to get your nose busted anymore. Put on your coat and come with me. The kid didn't even bat an eye, went over and put a coat over his trunks and taped hands, left everything else behind him, and followed Julie right out into the main street of Vegas.

"What's your name?"

"Rosie. What's yours?"

"Julie."

They shook hands. From then on, they were friends and associates. Rosie was the strong arm of the 711 Casino. The No. Two Schtarker, as he liked to call himself. He looked over everybody, saw everything; no one could come into their place without having first to check through Rosie. This old ranch-type casino was about four miles out of town. Julie opened as quickly as he could, spruced up the place. He had a big neon sign outside the club with two dice totaling the number seven rolling from one side of the sign to the other, changing from seven to eleven. In the early fifties, there was a lot of action to try to buy him out because everyone could see that he was developing a very good clientele and a very good business. In a very firm but gentlemanly manner, he resisted all offers of partnerships, semipartnerships, limited partnerships, up-your-ass partnerships. He ran his business tight and close to his chest. No one else was going to be part of it.

Once, when the club was pretty busy with about thirty people who had come up from Los Angeles for a long weekend, three guys with handkerchiefs pulled across their noses, one carrying an Army .45, the other two carrying .38 callibers, walked into the casino and quietly and calmly announced that it was a holdup.

"Nobody move and everybody lie down on their stomachs."

Julie, who was in his office at the time, knew immediately that something was wrong. He quickly looked through the peephole and saw that Rosie had a .45 aimed at his temple. So he knew that Rosie for the moment was incapacitated. He quickly ran down the back steps, through the kitchen area, past the place where all the garbage and trash were burned, ran across a couple of places where some ash cans stood, picked up an old baseball bat, old but still in good condition, taped in white adhesive from the edge of the bat to about nine inches up. He grabbed it without breaking stride and kept running until he came to the entrance to the club, where there was a small mailbox-grocery area where things to be delivered were brought. He arrived exactly ten seconds before the Chevy four-door sedan came driving up with a driver and the three men with handkerchiefs which were now pulled down around their necks. Between them was a large bag with money, watches, wallets, whatever they had taken from the customers and from the management of the 711 Casino. As the car drew adjacent to this post office-grocery, Julie swung the baseball bat so that it came square across the front windshield of the car as it came by at a snappy thirty miles an hour, getting ready to go on the open highway where it could hit the road to dreamland. The force of the bat shattered the windshield and killed the driver. The car veered to the right, smashing into the wall, much to the shock and horror of the three occupants of the car. The fella sitting alongside the driver started out of the car with his hand on his piece. As he did, Julie nailed him right between the eyes and he crumbled immediately to the ground. Simultaneously, the back doors of the sedan opened and out tumbled the two other gunsels, one rolling on the ground, the other running in the opposite direction. They thought they would draw Julie's fire from them. They were fucking with Julie and Julie was mad. As the first gunsel rolled out of the car and hit the ground, Julie pegged him right through the top of the head. As the fella rolling in the opposite direction drew up and fired at Julie, Julie just barely ducked and pumped two bullets into the man's twisted body as he was running. Bim. Bam. It was over.

Rosie came running over. Julie said, Get rid of these stiffs and the car. Clear all this shit out of here so that nothin's happened. Got it? Get all the money back where it was. Tell all the clientele how sorry we are for the inconvenience and that their gambling debts were on the house this evening. If any of the local constabulary gentlemen arrive, tell the customers to just say that nothing transpired. The management would deeply appreciate it.

"You mean to tell me that there was absolutely no disturbance here tonight?"

The local Sheriff had arrived and had already been halfway through the casino. They were now down in the kitchen area.

"Nothing, Sheriff," Julie said. "I don't know what would make you think there was."

"Well, I had a report that you were held up by four guys, that they were driving in a Chevy four-door sedan. You don't know that car?"

"No, I don't know what you're talking about."

"Well, that's the damnedest thing. I got a report that absolutely stated the fact that this is what happened on your premises tonight."

"Well," Julie said, "you've been through the casino. You saw nothing like that happened, haven't you?"

"It's the damnedest thing, the damnedest thing."

"Sheriff, who was it that gave you that information about tonight?"

The Sheriff took a second, looked at Julie.

"Oh, some concerned citizen who wishes to remain anonymous."

"Wait a minute, Max, give the Sheriff here some nice steaks for his family, will ya? It's the holiday time and I want to thank you for your help. Whenever I needed you for any kind of altercation, you've always showed up, so I really appreciate it. And on your way out, if you'd like to pick up a bottle of booze, please do. And I'll see that a case of some fine whiskey is at your home now for the coming year and a present for your deputies."

"Well, that's mighty nice of you and I sure appreciate it, Julie."

"That's okay, Sheriff. My pleasure."

Max went into the deep freeze to wrap up four steaks for the Sheriff. As you looked beyond Max, you saw four other pieces of meat hanging from hooks in pinstripe suits, hats on. Outside, the Sheriff told his deputy that for a kike that Julie was a tough son of a bitch.

Andrew

1948

In the morning on the beach in Trancas at nine-fifteen, September 3, 1948, Kid Andrew Cody got into the movies. He was wearing old frayed denims and that's all. What skin you saw was brown from Southern California sunshine. His hair was streaked lightly by the sun and the sea. He had his knees drawn up and his arms around them watching an honest-to-God movie being made. They were lying in each other's arms as the ocean surf beat upon the shore. The wave half dragged them into the sea. Only their passions kept them afloat, as they hugged, kissed, held onto each other. Before he could engulf her completely, she pushed herself away from him, held him at arm's length for just a beat, pulled back, stepped up, and ran toward the water, tearing off her flimsy top as she went. As the crack of her ass reached the level of the water, she let the flimsy covering go and dove into the sea with nothing on. He rose, seemed ready to run, he heard somebody yell, Okay, that's a print. Cut it. Cut the camera. A young man raced and leaped into the water and started swimming toward the girl. The girl meanwhile had turned around and started back. They passed each other. He swam as fast as he could to retrieve the flimsy covering. That was the only one they had.

That cheap fucking wardrobe department wouldn't buy two, the assistant said, and they couldn't because they turned it down in the production meeting. She stepped shamelessly from the sea, glistening and beautiful. The wardrobe woman's arms outstretched with a warm white terry-cloth robe extended to her. She slipped it on effortlessly, wrapped it around her waist, and came walking up the beach.

Her agent-manager, Barry Stone, was sitting in a collapsible chair. She came walking up in the robe, her head and face still wet. He got up.

"I knew you could suck, but where'd you learn to swim like that?"

She smiled looking at him; how crude, she thought.

"Don't be cute," she said.

The Kid saw the guy that looked like he was in charge of everything gesture to the girl to come closer down to the water. They started getting a tripod set up right at the edge of the water and proceeded to aim the camera at the fellow that was standing looking out to sea. Before the take, he reached down and wet his head and shoulders and stood there looking wistfully as this creature dove into the water. The Kid edged a bit closer. No one seemed to stop him, and he was quietly watching the work anyway. He heard a commotion. Voices a little louder than they should have been. And the guy that looked like he was in charge of everything seemed quite exasperated. He came walking up in the direction of the Kid. The Kid sat still and tried to remain as inconspicuous as possible. They were about fifteen feet from him now.

"Well, didn't anybody check with his agent when you hired this asshole? I told you I needed somebody who could swim. Dive out after the girl. I mean, you read it in the script. It's explained there quite explicitly, isn't it?"

"Yes, sir," the assistant director mumbled.

"Then who the fuck is responsible for this? We schlep all the way out here and now I can't get the key shot of the day—the two of them swimming off into the sunset. This is fuckin' impossible. Forget it. I'm . . ."

"Please," the assistant said, "maybe we can work this out. Wait. Just give me a minute."

"Well, get somebody to double him, then."

"There's nobody here that can double him. Nobody looks like him enough."

"Why didn't they put this on the call sheet?"

"Well, they all knew about it in the production department."

The production chief took it upon himself not to have to hire an extra person, a double. They knew the actor couldn't do this particular stunt. Wasn't particularly dangerous. But they wanted someone that looked good diving into the water and swimming swiftly. This actor just couldn't have done it. It would have cost maybe a hundred bucks more, but they wanted to save the hundred. And this director was obstreperous enough not to take no for an answer. They knew it and they had to come up with somebody pretty quick to double the actor or they would just have to sit around and wait until they got one. Because that's the next thing the director proposed.

"You call Central Casting. Tell 'em I want a guy down here, six feet tall, sun-streaked hair. Well, just give them a description of the actor because I'm not turning film until you get somebody to double him. He isn't gonna do it."

He produced a cigarette and someone produced a light. The assistant glanced in the direction of the Kid. He started toward him. The Kid wasn't quite sure what was up. He got up as the assistant director, about thirty years old, receding hair, thin, nervous, and always a little nauseous, came toward him.

"You know how to swim?"

"Yep."

"If I get you this job, you wanna make fifty?"

"What do I have to kiss?"

"Never mind that bullshit. You want fifty bucks? I see you been watching. All I want you to do is put on this guy's trunks and when this guy tells you to go, just dive into the water and swim out to where the girl is and just keep swimming alongside of her. Fifty bucks. Whatta ya say? Come on."

"Okay. You got it."

"Come on with me."

The director was as surprised as everybody else when the assistant director, Art, came walking up with the Kid.

"What took you so long?" he said. "Shit, man, it's a miracle. Where'd ya find the kid?"

"He's been watching us all morning."

"Can we take a waiver here? Are we gonna get in trouble with the union?"

135

"No, we won't. We'll just tell 'em it was an emergency, and we hadda do the best we could and . . ."

"Oh, shit," said the production manager. "We give 'em enough work. They'll give us a little grace."

"Okay, tell him to change trunks with the actor."

The Kid walked down to one of the portable campers that was sitting on the beach. As he walked over, the actor seemed a bit perturbed. But not so much that it created any ugly vibrations. The Kid didn't mind any of it, except getting into this guy's trunks. He didn't know how clean or dirty this was but . . . The blue swimming trunks were wet from the water and in a second he would be diving into the water so whatever crabs were around would either die from the cold or drown, whatever. He took off his denims and the jockey shorts he had on underneath and slipped on the blue trunks, stepped out of the camper, and walked to the spot that they showed him right on the edge of the water. He noticed that the camera was behind him and to the right. The girl was about twenty feet from him at the edge of the water, standing in a robe. The assistant director nodded. The girl took off the robe, again bare-assed, gently walked to the water, dove in, swam out. When she had swum out ten yards, the director hollered, Action.

Just before he heard Action, the Kid was told not to turn around and just to listen to the voice of the director and do everything he told him. The Kid stood there and waited.

"All right, kid, just stand there looking. Just keep looking. I want her out about eight, ten more feet. Get ready, kid, now just keep looking out there. That's it. Move your right shoulder back a little bit. That's enough. Okay. Now take one step forward, now another. Take a deep breath. Let it out slowly now. Now start moving into the water. Okay, now, faster and faster. There you go now. Dive in, and swim out to her. Go ahead."

He swam strong and swift and was beside the girl in a few seconds. They swam together, matching stroke for stroke. Both were excellent swimmers. From the time he was a kid, he loved the water and while in the South Pacific he swam every chance he got. You could lose yourself in swimming. He felt the brisk sea sting his body. He was relatively calm. He'd exhale in the water.

Pull his cheek over and inhale as his lips reached the surface, then back down into the sea again. Every three and a half strokes. He never looked up, just kept swimming and thought of nothing. Swim into the sunset. For fifty bucks, what a score for nothing. He peeked over his shoulder and saw that he'd lost the girl a long time ago and must have been three hundred feet from shore. He turned, some hands were waving at him. He turned around and swam back strong. The company, by that time, had started to put away all its equipment, folding up all the collapsible chairs, apple boxes, tripods, battery boxes, wardrobe woman's bag, make-up bags. Everything was slowly being lifted and marched up the beach to the road and into the trucks that waited to take the equipment to a new location.

Most of them were still on the beach as the Kid finally touched bottom. He started to walk toward the assistant director.

"I thought I'd come out and say good-by."

Art laughed.

"Okay, okay," he said. "Here's your fifty. Thanks."

There were two twenties and a ten. The Kid looked up at Art and said, "Thanks."

"What's ya name?"

"Kid Cody. Yours?"

"Art Taylor. Ever work in pictures before?"

"No. This is the first time, Art."

"Better get up to the trailer and put on your denims. Come on back when you finish."

He was out of his trunks and into his denims and alongside Art three, four minutes later.

"Where ya livin'?"

"I've got a room down by the sea, near the pier."

"Here, I'll give you my number. Hollywood 3-0974. And my answering service, Hollywood 7-9144. We're going to be hustling on this picture for another week or so. There's a call later in the week. We're gonna try to pick up some of the locals just outside of Santa Barbara in a big cove. Call me Wednesday night. If we're still on schedule, we'll be driving by here Thursday morning at six. Sunset and the Coast Highway. You get a ride up there and back for free and maybe pick up a hundred. I got an easy stunt, but I don't wanna pack any more people than I have to. If you do good up there, Kid, then maybe I can get you a card."

The Kid said, "Thanks," and Art was on his way.

The Kid wasn't sure what a card was and what all that movie talk was, but he liked the swiftness of it and the way that Art had arranged it all. And on top of that he had fifty bucks. That was the biggest score he had made yet in one day.

He stayed a week with the company up on the Monterey Peninsula, not only doubling the actor or the actress but the propman and the second assistant director. He was a general runner. He made himself useful to any of the different crafts that needed him. Art got to like him a lot and he started to like Art. All they did was put each other on. He liked the idea of conning Art or fooling him about something. Art was not the kind of guy you could fool easily. In his job he knew how to do everything; he knew every guise and trick anybody tried to pull on him, except the Kid's. His were a little more ingenious. He had gotten his screen actor's guild card by then and knew a little bit about all the different professions that made up a movie. He paid attention to what the production department was trying to do as well as what the director was trying to do. He got a pretty good part in a Western being made out at Republic, playing the boyfriend of the sheriff's daughter. When the sheriff is shot to death in a gunfight in town, the boyfriend sees the sheriff killed and now he must tell his girlfriend that her father is dead. When he said, Your pa's dead, the girl screamed and started to cry and he started to laugh. It just tickled him, this playacting. The more passionate it got, the funnier it got. The director did it in two shots with the script girl reading the girl's part. Now that he had calmed down a bit, the Kid was able to read his lines without much trouble. But he looked good, with his Stetson in his hand, looking down at the daughter of the sheriff as he arrived in town. As he walked up to her, his first line in the piece was, You must be the new schoolmarm.

He was sent to acting school immediately.

They called it sense memory. He had to recall the feeling of a box or object of some kind. To try to recall the exact response you received when you held a glass ball in your hand or felt the fabric of your tie. It was valid enough for you if you were a young actor because it gave you something to do. Acting was the only profession you thought about a lot but did very little about.

There were six people in that class besides the teacher: Tack Armstrong, the all-American boy; Leslie Trent, cool and classic; Paula Pembrook, funny and gay; Lucille Ryder, long and luscious; Vinnie De Carlo, singer and poet; and Barnabus Berger, the teacher artistic, vain, waiting for his big break, a way of acting named after him called the Berger Approach. But, to that chosen few, it was called Berger's Bullshit. He assigned these young people scenes to do from one-act plays, two-act plays, three-act plays, from the newspaper, from anything. He didn't give a shit, he didn't have to do it. He'd just come in the next day and hem and haw, smile benevolently or look solemnly, and then give you a critique. How he reacted the next day depended on whether he was able to screw that starlet the night before. And these poor kids were subjected to his whims and fancies.

Kid Cody had been given a seven-year contract four days earlier, fifty bucks a week. The studio thought it wiser to pay him weekly than fifty bucks every day he did a stunt. The Kid was co-operative and gentle with everyone he met. In those days they had a lot of people under contract because they made a lot of pictures each year. Lester Pearlstein was the most important producer at the studio. Mr. Pearlstein liked him ever since he saw him do that stunt out at the Tanner Ranch. They had him dressed as the leading lady with a fur coat to the knees, black stockings, high heels, a cloche hat pulled tightly around his head. The girl had to fall backward out of a second-story window and land in a fireman's net being held by six odd hands that they could find around the neighborhood. He came out backward out of the window as requested, but the assholes with the net were just a shade late running up with the net. He hit one guy, the rim and part of the webbing of the net, ricocheted from there against the wall of the set, then bounced off that and landed on the flower vendor's wagon into four clay pots of artificial flowers. When the dust finally settled, he just lay there, didn't move at all. The director and the assistant directors came rushing over as did the nurse and Mr. Pearlstein. A couple of other stunt men working that day came rushing over as well. The Kid just lay there looking up with the blond wig askew, hat held on for dear life, coat ripped in two, the dress he was wearing up around his waist, his hairy legs hiding in these black silk stockings, one shoe heel broken, the other still intact. Someone asked him if he was all right. As the Kid got up on this one shoe and brushed himself, he said, It would have killed an ordinary girl.

Pearlstein thought that was funny, and when his name was brought before him as a possible choice to be under contract to his company, he chose the Kid.

Julie

Julie liked Los Angeles. In the early fifties Julie came down to L.A. with regularity. The 711 Casino was operating smoothly by now. Julie could trust Rosie while he was gone, and Rosie had a couple of guys working with him that he trusted. The head bookkeeper in accounting at the 711 Casino was Pat Mahoney. Julie knew Pat Mahoney from their school days in New York. Pat had also known Angie. Now that his club was running, Julie liked to get out of Vegas every now and then. He liked his life in Vegas. This club that he was fashioning out in the desert meant a great deal to him. It was something he had put together on his own. But before Julie bought the one hundred acres running alongside his place, he wanted a general understanding of the offer he had to make in order to buy it. He decided to go to Los Angeles on a beautiful March day to look up Samuel Solomon and ask him if he thought it was a good deal or not.

Julie took the first flight out of Vegas for Los Angeles and as soon as he arrived he went to a phone and called Solomon's office at Pacific Pictures. He spoke with him immediately. Solomon said, Get your ass down here. Julie jumped into a cab and went to the studio. He loved the place. He passed a cemetery with oil wells pumping around the perimeter of it, hot dog and hamburger stands galore, six gasoline stations all of different companies on four corners, a lot of people on motorcycles. From the air, Los Angeles looked like a flat plateau in between some hills. On the ground he found it a lot hillier and rollier than it looked from the air. All the houses ranging up the many streets they passed through were white and private. Each had a small green lawn, a place to drive a car, a garage in the back; the lawns and back yards were bursting with flowers of the season. He found himself on Wilshire Boulevard, a wide and sedate street which ran practically the entire length of Los Angeles. He passed through Beverly Hills, banks, department stores, equipment stores, banks, hotels, shoe stores, Cadillac dealerships, banks. There were a lot of banks. They went up Doheny north to the hills, cut right on Sunset Boulevard, then down through the strip, a lot of bars and restaurants, and all those nightclubs: Club Gala, Mocambo, Crescendo, Ciro's. The people on the streets all looked prosperous and healthy. The young people looked very handsome. They passed Schwab's, which was the unofficial western boundary before you started into Hollywood. You could hide in Los Angeles. If you thought you could hide in cities like New York or Chicago, you could really disappear into the hills of Hollywood and L.A. By the time he reached Pacific Pictures, which was right in the heart of Hollywood, he was crazy nuts about this big sprawling city, and he made it a point to get down here as much as he could. From the airport to the studio took almost an hour. They were expecting him when he walked into the building. The cop sitting behind the desk seemed to recognize him.

"Mr. Sparrow," he said. "Here, sir, let me hold your bag down here. Mr. Solomon is expecting you."

Julie said thanks but took the bag. Julie went through a glass door, walked to an elevator, went up to the second floor, turned right then left, and there at the end of the hall were Mr. Solomon's offices, a two-door affair. Solomon's secretary's name was Agnes Morrow, haughty and cool. A man and woman were sitting in the office anteroom. Julie was immediately ushered into Solomon's office. Mr. Banks, head of the story department, and an agent called Waxie Shapiro, five foot two and eyes of blue, the toughest mother-fucker this side of the Pecos, were sitting with Solomon. Waxie knew where everything in Hollywood was buried, and who was buried into whom. The story editor, Alistair Banks, was cordial and fifty. He left almost immediately.

"Waxie, this is Julie Sparrow," Solomon said, "a Jew boy from New York. Owns his own joint in Vegas. Julie, this is Waxie Shapiro, agent. If you want to know anything about this town or anyone in it, call Waxie. Between you two guys, I ought a have all the land west of the Mississippi locked up."

Waxie never cracked. Extended his small, well-manicured hand to Julie. Waxie was dressed immaculately as he always was and always would be. They liked each other instantly because they knew they would never have to rely on each other.

"How long are you here for, Julie?" Samuel said.

"Oh, just a couple of days, Sam. Haven't had a chance to come down into town yet. Thought I'd kind of case it out."

"Sally's on location in Honolulu, and if you need to know anything, call Waxie. Waxie, give him your number."

"Sure, Sam."

Waxie produced his billfold and handed Julie his card.

"I had a nice ride from the airport. I love this town already."

"You're staying at the Beverly Hills Hotel," Sam continued. "A car'll pick you up tonight at eight, bring you by the house. I'm having some drinks and we'll see about dinner later. Maybe we'll eat at the house. No, no, Julie I'm taking you to Perino's tonight. It's a fancy guinea restaurant on Wilshire Boulevard. If you want, you can go to the hotel now and fuck around the pool. I got a better idea. Why don't you hang around the studio all day today. Didja ever go to the movies when you were a kid?"

"I didn't have the time. Besides, I don't like movies."

Waxie loved him already, and Sam loved him even more after that. Julie roamed around that whole studio that late morning and early afternoon, walked on the stages, was shown the back lot, saw in that seven or eight hours all the elements that make a movie. He saw a film being shot in the middle of its production schedule, one film just starting, another one three quarters finished. And finally one that was finishing. Each film he saw shooting was a different kind. One was an adventure film from what he could gather. A lot of men dressed in funny clothes, milling around wearing bloomers and swords, talking, gesturing. One guy looking very much like another guy. They could have been twins, except that if you took a closer look you would notice that one of the twins was a little more wrinkled maybe, a little tougher. He couldn't figure out who was the stunt man and who was the actor. They were working out some piece of business, some action that they were going to do. These twelve guys were going to come flying into this room, all with their scimitars in their hands. He saw some guy halfheartedly kissing some girl on another stage he stopped at. He guessed they really didn't care about each other, which probably was the problem. He saw some very beautiful girls dressed in some kind of abbreviated costumes, like in a nightclub, hurrying past onto a set, a couple were giggling, one was flirting. A couple were walking by themselves listening to no voices but the ones inside their own heads. He felt that they were all comparatively happy, working in a production company. No, you knew right away that with all the bullshit that was thrown around in the business, all the awards they gave each other, all the eight balls they gave each other, all the digs and all the hate that they heaped on one another, all the jealousy and envy they exerted on each other, very few friends were made. You ended up with a lot of observers who were afraid to commit themselves.

To Samuel Solomon, it was a business. The business of making movies and that's what he was doing, making movies. Thirty-five pictures a year. You were always sure that at the end of a year out of the top five or ten Samuel Solomon's pictures would be up in there, maybe three or four. That's the kind of a business Samuel Solomon ran and he was making himself a lot of money. Waxie, through Samuel, was able to put away two hundred thousand dollars a year, clear, with a lot of deductible items. Shapiro was single and lusted after big wenches. With the power he had, he would get the biggest. They were all dedicated to him, all ready to die for him, loving him, just so long as they ended up in the fucking movie.

By five o'clock that afternoon, Julie was at the Beverly Hills Hotel, checked in, halfway through his bath, reading the Los Angeles *Times*, in a small bungalow which rested on the eastern corner of the hotel. It had a sitting room, small kitchenette, and a bedroom, and what Julie really liked the best was the toilets in these fancy places that he now traveled to. That always impressed Julie more than anything else. The toilets in a house, or the toilets in a store, or the toilets in a restaurant. He could judge the kind of a place he was in by the toilets and how they were kept. That gave him more insight into a place than anything else. At exactly seven forty-five the phone rang. The desk wished to notify Mr. Sparrow that his car and driver were waiting for him. Julie was dressed and ready to go. Julie always dressed beautifully. Always had good tailors making him really fine-looking numbers. Morrie always looked after his clothes when he was a kid, and Julie was always accustomed to a good piece of cloth rustling between his legs. The unit he had on tonight was a black suit, a white on white shirt, a medium-sized black tie with a large Windsor knot, the tie front just below the belt buckle. Julie never wore jewelry. Just a pocket watch. He carried nothing more than a driver's license and a hundred in twenties. He opened the small black bag that he had been traveling with and took out a pocket .32 caliber, snub-nosed handgun. He slipped it in a pocket inside the waistband which fit comfortably over his right ball and cock. You couldn't see it. He dressed to the left.

Julie was skinny and with this pistol where it was, no one could ever tell he was carrying a piece, in frisking him you had to really be a pro to shake out that .32 caliber. Julie walked out of that hotel with a soft black felt fedora and a black, double-breasted military topcoat cut at knee length. He knew the impression he made as he walked through the lobby of that hotel. It gave him a fire inside him, a fire which he always loved. They were off in this black Cadillac limousine, climbing gracefully up into the hills of Bel Air. A big iron gate, green bushes and trees, shrubbery of all colors just bursting there, even in the dark. Two minutes, time it, two minutes' drive from that gate up to the front door of Samuel Solomon, Esquire. When Julie hit the door, Samuel was there. Sam must have been forty years older than Julie then. Sam was no kid. Julie was just thirty then. Sam was pretty close to seventy. You'd never know it. His energy just dominated everyone but not Julie. Nor did Julie's energy overpower Sam. If anything they complemented each other. If one super-Jew could do 'em in, can you imagine what two could do? The party was going strong and there were a lot of people there. Sam took Julie by the arm and introduced him to everybody and everybody stopped when he walked over with Julie. After cocktails, Sam took a chosen eight to dinner at Perino's. Julie was one of them and so was Waxie. And five of the greatest looking bimbos you'd ever wanna see.

Waxie immediately staked out this gorgeous redhead and would not be deterred. Like the little suckerfish that follows sharks around. Waxie loved that redheaded dame and she was his tonight. He hung on every word she said, every little whim, any nuance, anything and everything was hers. He had a half-dozen fur coats hanging in his apartment which he'd lend to whatever girl he was going with. While she was going with him, she was wrapped in his furs. When she finally decided she'd like to roost it up with someone else, that was okay by Waxie, just as long as she brought back the coat. They drank Dom Perignon champagne and had the best dinner that you could have anywhere in town. After dinner they were back at Sam's house, and Brandy, that's what she called herself, left with Julie for the hotel. The car parked on the east side of the hotel and Brandy and Julie were able to walk directly to the bungalow, which had a fire going and was warm and friendly right in the middle of the wilds of Beverly Hills.

He spoke to Sam the next morning about ten. Sam had been in the studio since six in the morning, rousting out all the guys that worked in their offices in New York, where it was nine in the morning. Told Julie he wouldn't be able to see him because he was busy getting ready to preview a film that afternoon to run that evening.

"Use the car," Sam said. "Go anywhere you want. Stay as long as you like. I'll probably see ya in Vegas next week."

"Oh, Sam, I can buy one hundred acres alongside my club for $5,000 an acre. I'm offering seven per cent prepaid interest for five years which is $175,000 grand, which is ninety per cent deductible on my taxes for this year. Which means only $17,500 cash from me. In five years, I pay the principal."

Sam said buy it.

"Thanks, Sam. Take care of yourself. Give Waxie my best when you see him or talk with him."

"Right."

"So long."

"By."

They stopped off at Brandy's apartment in the hills of Hollywood. She ran and changed her clothes, picked up a towel and a bathing suit, got back in the car. They drove back to the Beverly Hills Hotel. When they got there, he said to Brandy, Get out. She got out of the car with him. Julie walked to the driver's side of the limousine and said, Get out, will ya? The driver said, Yes, sir. The driver climbed out of the car. Julie slid into his seat, beckoned for Brandy to get into the other door of the front seat of the limousine.

"What's ya name?" he said to the driver.

"Willard, sir."

"Willard, I'm taking Brandy to the beach and we'll be gone most of the day. I'll be back here around five. See ya then."

With that Julie and Brandy took off in this Cadillac limousine with dark-tinted windows. They changed in the back seat, fucked in the back seat, had a little lunch in the back seat. They were back at the hotel at five o'clock. They brought the luggage down to the limousine. Willard was there and the three of them pulled out of the Beverly Hills Hotel. Julie all checked out and ready to go back to Vegas. Brandy came along with Julie to the airport. He said good-by to her.

"Brandy, when you're in Las Vegas, you know where I'm at."

"When you're in Los Angeles, you know where I'm at," she said. "Please, Julie, call."

She gave him her number. He thanked Willard and turned toward the plane. He never saw Brandy again.

Andrew

1948

Art gave him some tickets to see Eugene Ormandy at the Hollywood Bowl playing theme songs from two dozen films. He asked Maria to go with him. Irene slept on the third floor of the house in a little turret room. Irene's bed sat in the middle of the room, facing the sea. On the walls were photographs of muscle men in different provocative poses. Flexing muscles. Bulging out chests. Show you the pectories originalis, the gluteus maximus, the maximus gluteus. Hard muscle was what Irene liked. A beige circular rug rested underneath the bed. There was a bureau and a make-up table. A door led to a closet where Irene had an overabundance of pedal pushers, blouses, and wedgies. She had a couple of dresses but hardly ever wore them. There was never really an occasion. Her bathroom had a bathtub, a basin, a toilet, and a hair dryer. On her make-up table were three wigs, all sitting at attention ready to be worn. Her own hair was lifeless and sparse, but with those wigs on, she looked softer and more vulnerable. Without them she looked like Confucius or what you thought Confucius would have looked like.

Alice's room was just below her mother's, overlooking the sea as well. Her room was sparser and more practical. It was square. Wood painted white. Alice slept in a single bed in a corner. On her wall were prints and reproductions of famous paintings. Once she saw this series of eight pictures being sold at a market in Venice, California. There was Van Gogh's *Chair*, Gauguin's *Tahitian Woman*, Pissarro's *Village on the Seine*, Manet's *The Picnic*, Cézanne's painting of Aix en Provence, a Braque still life, and Matisse's *Turkish Woman*. Alice liked black stockings and black shoes. Wore dresses just below her knee, nylon panties, a soft bra on her medium-sized breasts. She liked poetry, particularly the *Rubáiyát* of Omar Khayyám, poems by Edna St. Vincent Millay, and the stories and poems of Edgar Allan Poe. She liked wine and liked to get high and take baths.

Maria's room was on the first floor and had a private entrance so she could come and go as she pleased. Her room was small and untidy. Maria didn't know yet who she was. Her environment wasn't as important as what she did in it. A couple of pictures of a sailor and a Marine that she was corresponding with sat on her dresser. Maria went to business school, learning shorthand, typing, drafting of letters, and an occasional kiss on the lips from a business ad teacher, Mr. Kimble. Archie Kimble knew figures better than anybody and was a devil with the ladies at that school. One of the reasons he took the job was the fucking privileges he derived. A certain grade made it possible for these girls to audition for the better jobs around town. Ones in Beverly Hills and Los Angeles for attorneys and business offices. A certain grade made you eligible. Anything from a thirty-six bust up would automatically find herself somewhere in Beverly Hills or West L.A., but only after Archie, in his simple but well-appointed apartment in Santa Monica, saw this would-be secretary doing things to Archie and Archie doing things to her that you only saw in stag movies. That Archie was quite a man. Maria never fooled around with him because she didn't have to. Her grades were excellent and she was waiting to pick her own spot. Not that Archie wouldn't have liked to because Maria was a fine-looking girl. Maria Rodriguez had made love six times to one man. He was thirty-two and sold her her stenography books at the stationery shop where he worked in Westwood. Smooth-tongued, smooth-haired, he took her to Lake Arrowhead one Saturday morning, hoping to spend the weekend. They made love to each other six times over that weekend and she never saw him again after that. It was exciting making love and it seemed to ease some of the tension. But six times in two days was a little too much, she thought. It freed her somewhat and she didn't look upon sex as some ugly, frightening experience. But she was going to pick and choose a little more carefully from now on. Her hair was black and she had it cut short

to her shoulders. Brown eyes, straight nose, and a full
mouth. They called Maria's father Chico. He'd come out of
nowhere once in a while. Didn't speak to Alice at all.
Nodded to Irene. He drove a truck and looked mean.

They listened to Eugene Ormandy that night under
the stars. They held hands. He put his arm around her, and
his right hand felt the beginning of the softness of her
breast. It was warm and beautiful. Alice had loaned him
her Packard and with that car the Kid had some wheels
in L.A. They stopped at the pier when they got back from
the concert. They walked to a seafood counter down at
the end of the pier. Had some fried shrimp. Maria ordered
wine. He ordered a Pepsi. She said, Park the car a block
away from the house. He did. They walked to the street
that the house was on, looked at the ocean, turned west,
and walked down to the beach. Climbed over a railing
and found themselves in the warm sand. They could see
Irene's and Alice's lights were on. The rest of the
house was dark. She said, I'll be right back. And before
the Kid could stop her, dear Maria was up and running. He
sat there looking out to sea, the warm sea air wafting
over him. About fifty yards away he saw a small fire on
the beach. Some guy was walking along the beach down
by the water's edge. He noticed some bonfires to the right
of him as well. He thought it a bit unusual for so many
people to be up and around at that time of night. The
beach way on the left and to the right seemed crowded
with people almost waiting for something, although the
spot that they were in was sheltered, much quieter.

When Maria returned she had a bucket and a blanket.
He didn't say anything. He helped spread the blanket out
on the beach. She climbed on it. Sat down and looked out
to sea, holding the upper portion of her body up by her
left hand, resting on the blanket. The Kid sat down cross-
legged, took off his shoes. Just sat there in a kind of half-
assed yoga position, contemplating her navel. He was
shaking with joy and anticipation. As soon as Maria felt his
hands, she knew. They just blended into each other's
arms. Her dress was up. She had no pants on. And before
you could sing the first verse of Mareseatoats and Doeseat-
oats and Little Lambs Eat Ivy, the Kid's pants were down.
They held each other tightly and as he heard the screams,
the grunion are coming, the grunion are coming, he came

as well. Maria leaped up and said, Come on. The kid had his pants on following Maria down the beach to a small cluster of people up ahead with flashlights. People started to chant, The grunion are running, the grunion are running, in a witchcraft whisper. And like some miracle, the waves rushed in and delivered hundreds of the most beautiful white, silvery fish he had ever seen in his life. Just glistening under the moonlight and the flashlights. Being picked up by bare hands and put into the buckets that people had with them. Maria and the Kid started scooping up the grunion. Another wave, another group of grunion leaped onto the shores, flapping, flipping around. By the fourth wave, Maria and the Kid had their bucket full. They gathered up the blanket, and slowly walked back to her house. He told her he'd get the car and pull it into the garage, which he did. By that time, Maria had the light on in the kitchen and there were the grunion. Alice and Irene had come down. Broke out a bottle of red. They made delectable eating, lightly fried in vegetable oil. You couldn't ask for anything better. Alice told him that the grunion ran once a year, and you could time it like clockwork. The fish and game department gave the hours the grunion would run. Only at night. It was based on the tide and the mating habits of these small silvery fish. Fascinating. We saw a movie tonight, Alice said, thinking to herself he's nice and he's clean and he's well mannered, and Maria knows how to take care of herself. Good night, Maria. Good night, Alice. And good night, Irene.

Although these three women loved each other and were related, they had no idea of each other's needs. Irene was uneducated and uninformed, not interested in anything except her own physical needs. After that, she would just vamp until ready. Alice's needs were a bit deeper and more demanding. Her curiosity was always being provoked. She was always being stimulated by some new wrinkle of life. Always surprised that things could be new even at forty. Maria was the most secretive of the three. Her name frightened her, Maria Rodriguez. Sounded like some Spanish princess. She had no ethnic response at all. Half the time when they called her name at school, she expected someone else to get up. Her father was Mexican. Her mother was Irish, and her grandmother had been born in Norfolk, Virginia, of Swedish parents. The

Kid had never lived with women the way he was living with women now. He felt he had to tread easily. He didn't really feel completely comfortable in this environment. He liked it, but it made him a little nervous, as if he was afraid he would do something wrong. It was nice living with women. The house was kept clean and warm. Women, it seemed to him, had a knowledge of living lives much more than men did. They were more practical, as demanding but less intrusive into your life.

He heard Alice sobbing one night. He got up. The house was quiet. He walked to her door and listened. She was moaning, crying. He just barely whispered, Alice. The sobbing stopped immediately. He heard a slight rustling sound and her door opened and she stood in front of him, one-eyed. The light from the entry hall ricocheting off the ceiling down to her tear-stained face. He didn't know what came over him, he just stepped into the room. Maria was the motivating factor of their love-making. She executed things. She initiated them and the Kid just followed suit, letting Maria explore on her own so that she wouldn't be frightened away in their exploring of each other. He instinctively knew that with Alice it was going to be another relationship. He closed the door behind him. He was as hard as he could remember he'd ever been in his life. In the semidarkness Alice looked young and vulnerable. The Kid led her to the single bed in the corner. The shades were drawn up and the moonlight reflecting off the water gave her room a soft gray look. She moaned, low, soft murmurs. Suddenly she held her breath and then let the air leave her slowly. Her legs were spread, one leg hanging over the edge of the bed and the Kid eased into her. His arm outstretched, balancing himself on his fingertips. Resting on the bed itself. Balanced like some huge tripod. Praying mantis about to lose his head. He rolled her over, moved her. She just lay there and submitted to the Kid. Arched and strong, he looked up once. Saw the blackness of the sky and the stars shining through it. He heard the sound of the surf and the stillness around him. He found himself suspended in space. Time had come to a stop. He got off for a while and looked around him. He saw the Kid and Alice copulating. He went out the window and looked in. He saw the Kid and Alice from the water's edge, two tiny figures, two specks. A small vibration sitting by the sea. He tried to go higher, to see the shoreline, the tops of the houses that surrounded the neighborhood. But couldn't. He never could get out of himself as far as he would like to. He wasn't sure he wanted to or not. Perhaps one day he'd do it and never be able to return. But these were no thoughts for fucking. Back to the job at hand. Into the breach. His arms relaxed and he fell upon her. He was awakened by Alice, gently with a kiss. He got up. Kissed the inside of her palm and left. He found himself in his bedroom half asleep. He wasn't sure whether or not he had dreamed what had happened.

"Is it difficult for you to think that I've made love to the same man as you, Mother?" Maria said at ten-twenty one evening at the house.

"It's not that, Maria."

"Well, then what is it, Mother? Is that so terrible, do you think?"

"No, it's not terrible, but . . ."

"But, what, Mom? Can't I come like you?"

"Please, Maria, you don't have to be so explicit."

"But why, Ma? Is there something unique about when you come and I don't? Do you think there's such a big difference between that and being hungry for a hamburger, or listening to a concert or reading a book? It's all part of living, Mother. I don't deny you, so don't deny me."

"I don't. I haven't."

"Yes, you have. Just by your behavior, your attitude toward me. You've always treated me less than what I am. Maybe it's because you think I'm a half-breed."

"Oh, Maria, please."

"Mom, I've got as much of a thirst for living as you do and I won't let anything stand in my way. If you want me to move, say so. But you're not going to frown or disapprove of anything I do. Just as I don't disapprove of or frown about anything you do."

"Maria, we shouldn't talk to each other in this way."

"But, Mother, if we don't, we'll never talk to each other again. Let's become friends, you and I. Let's share these secrets with each other. I haven't anyone else to share them with. Why drive me into the streets—drive me away from you? I don't want to call you Alice. I want to call you Mom, Mom. I don't think less of you or more of you because we made love to the same boy. Our relationship is much deeper than that. And I won't let you cheapen it, Mother, by being jealous."

Alice looked at Maria. Tears welled in Alice's eyes. She reached out and hugged Maria very close to her.

"I love you, Maria. Let's begrudge each other nothing."

Maria pulled back, tears in her eyes as well.

"Oh, Mom, it's so nice to call you Mom."

Meanwhile the Kid was up in Irene's room. Doing the Hootchy-Coo.

Andrew

1949

They were on location in Kanab, Utah, and Chuck Derringer challenged him to a duel. Chuck was the star, and when he wanted to play, everybody played. No one could outdraw Chuck, but everybody tried. It never interested the Kid and he never found it necessary to try to outdraw Chuck. The Kid was challenged. The draw consisted of the opponents holding a bandanna or handkerchief between them, the tips of the handkerchief or bandanna being held by their teeth. Whoever dropped the handkerchief first was allowed to draw. By the time you let go of the handkerchief and started to draw your pistol, Chuck's six-shooter would be out and resting nicely in your belly button. With the Kid, he added another wrinkle. As he put the six-shooter into his navel, he had one six-shooter loaded with blanks behind his back, and as that gun nestled up and touched the Kid's stomach, he fired the one behind his back. All the Kid heard was the explosion, smelled the acrid smell of burned gunpowder, thought of Max, and waited to see him. He fainted instead. Everybody had a big fuckin' laugh and thought it was the funniest thing that ever happened. When the Kid pulled himself together Chuck came over and apologized. The Kid told him to stay away from him. He didn't want any part of him. It was only just before Chuck died in a plane crash that the Kid spoke with him again, and that was by chance.

August of '49 on location in New Galieses, New Mexico, a hundred degrees in the shade. Big Boy Johnson, senior stunt man, head wrangler, head everything, had not been able to defecate for three days. The combination of food and booze and whatever else made him a walking ad for constipation. Finally, one of the wranglers gave him a laxative that they gave the horses as well, and one morning at ten-fifteen, in the hot, broiling sun, sitting in the middle of nowhere, eight guys on horseback, the camera three hundred yards away, they had to go galloping across the camera over a crest of hills. The only ones on that ridge, waiting for the charge and the action and the fear, were the eight men on horseback, which included the Kid and two other actors. All the rest were stunt men. They were all making about the same money. There was Waco Jones with a long-handled shovel, ready to catch whatever horseshit fell to keep this particular area in which they were to ride as clean and virginal-looking as possible. His instructions from his brother, Gype Jones, the production manager who knew where every penny went and really ran the whole picture outfit, were: Keep the fuckin' place clean. Before the shot he was to duck behind a bush. There was some hitch down at the camera and the assistant screamed up that there'd be a five-minute wait.

"Goddamn, they're workin'," Big Boy said to no one in particular. "I'm gonna take a couple of minutes."

He leaped off his horse and ran to a small clump of bushes resting about ten yards from where they were waiting. Some of the guys got off their horses. Some wondered what the night would hold, if there would be any local girls or if there were going to be fights with the locals about them Hollywood fags that were in town making a movie. As Big Boy hustled over to this bush, Waco, with the long-handled shovel, scurried around behind him without Big Boy knowing it. Big Boy dropped his pants and squatted. Waco slid this long-handled shovel quietly under Big Boy. Big Boy sighed with relief. His evacuation was immense and took a while. When he had finished, Waco Jones carefully pulled that long-handled shovel, loaded, out from under Big Boy. He quickly disappeared behind some other bushes and hid the evidence in a hole that he had prepared, covered it over, and there, this valley had not been fouled by anyone, and Gype Jones, his ass-chewing brother getting back at him after all those years, could go and fuck himself. Big Boy used some leaves from the same bush and as he pulled up his pants and looked down, there was nothing. He was shocked. No shit! His first thought was that he had done it in his pants. But there was no evidence of that. He kept looking back to the area that he had been in. Everybody said their Hail Marys. The director screamed. Action. The assistant waved the red handkerchief. Off they went, screaming past the camera on these half-crazed horses, these frightened young actors, two drunken old pros, and two young stunt men trying to make their mark and one stunt man-wrangler-cowboy whose only thought at that moment while galloping at twenty-five miles an hour was what happened to that shit. The horses pulled up, they fell off, and this stunt man wheeled around on his worthy charger and galloped back to where that bush was. He must have looked for fifteen minutes before everyone started to feel sorry for him. People were screaming and laughing hysterically. The question was, who was going to tell him? Waco wasn't. When Big Boy was finally told by Art Taylor, he chased Waco around for half a day and finally cornered him by the lunch wagon and stuck his head in two barrels of ice cream that was to be shared by the whole company. That got everybody right where they lived. But it all ended up good-naturedly, everybody loving everybody else by the end of the day, and that night in this little camp in the tent that served as the mess hall, the Kid saw maybe forty grown men drunker than any equal amount of Bowery bums. He then knew that those men were as scared as the kids.

In his early days in Hollywood, the Kid found out that having an orgasm was an exhausting experience, not from the actual orgasm, but from the experiences leading to one. Jerking off, masturbating, wanking yourself, was not for him. The Kid liked skin, a lot of it, and soft. There was no theory to his selection. If there were a machine that could play back the orgasms he had had, the Kid would have to think hard about getting involved again. These unchosen, voluptuary virgins looking for success in films or in my lady's chamber. Example, he had delectable Delilah almost bedded one night after hours of pursuing. The minute she walked on the set one morning for an interview for a part in *The Mighty Mormon* (he was playing the son of the Mormon), he knew she had a knockout figure, and with the figure, there was a madness in her eye that captivated Kid Andrew. One of her brown eyes was just a bit off center, giving her the look of someone that was stoned all the time. She was about eighteen, he thought, and she must have landed in the city maybe a week ago at the latest. He smiled and so did she.

"Art, did you ever see that filly before?"

Art looked over where the Kid was gesturing. He didn't need to gesture. He spotted her right away.

"A good-looking baby."

Her back was as good-looking as her front. She was luscious and she was fresh. By the Kid's reckoning, five foot eight, bam! Art, a little more experienced, rated her bim. Art knew right away he didn't have a chance. To bed that beauty was gonna take a lot more than just screaming, Quiet on the set. This is a take. Quiet back there. Ready? All right, roll it. Art and the Kid were getting to be good chums now; they had made a dozen films together, directly or indirectly. Art either up in the office or working on the floor, trying his hand at everything, absorbing everything the second he saw it, assaying immediately what values there were for him, pro or con. It took Art less than half an eyelash to come to that conclusion. Arthur Gayle Taylor, Art never took no for an answer. Tenacious, wily, and a pushover for a sad story. He had more money hanging around town in the pockets of extras, bit players, stunt men, assistant directors, propmen than any other man in town. No wonder a lot of people loved him. He was supporting half of them. Give me five, he said to the Kid.

When the Kid stepped out of the action at the Oakwood Cafe, he was surprised and delighted to hear her name was Delilah Jones. She came from Alabama and was staying at the Hollywood Club for Girls, a safe place to stay in the City of Sin while aspiring to be the greatest tochis taker in town. She was standing beside a gobo being used to shade a corner of the set. Behind it blazed an arc, harsh and hot, about ninety degrees where the light was concentrated.

"Hello, Delilah," the Kid said as he stepped alongside her.

"Hi."

Her voice was light and airy. She looked even taller

standing alongside of him. She turned and looked into his eyes, or he thought she'd looked into his eyes. It wasn't going to be easy to hold her interest. He could feel that she was very friendly and that stimulated the Kid. The Kid waited while they adjusted some of the lights, the sound boom's shadow was in the shot, and it had to be taken out.

"Looks hot in there."

"Yes, is this your first time on the set?"

"Yes, it looks like nice work."

"Nice work if you can get it, and you can get it if you try."

She smiled.

"Is it hard to memorize the lines?" she asked.

"Not if you tie it in with a piece of action you're doing."

"What do you mean, action?"

"Oh, some kind of business, some movement, some reason to cross the room, maybe make yourself a drink at the bar, tie your shoelace, anything like that. It's tough to memorize it sitting in a room."

"I'd like to try it."

"You'll do okay. You're smart and you've got the body for it."

He figured he was half right. She looked at him, or he thought she looked at him.

"The better proportioned you are, the easier it is to do your job."

"Mother knows someone here in Los Angeles, and she gave me the address and number of an agent named Louis Murray Limited. Well, I called Mr. Limited only to find out his name was Murray, and Limited was the name of a company. I went to see him and he gave me the names of five casting directors at five different studios. He said he'd call them and all I had to do was call in a day or so and go see them all. If anyone wants to hire me for films, Lou said, I should call him Mr. Murray, but he insists I call him Lou, he'd handle everything for me and charge me ten per cent. He said that was standard. I signed a Screen Actors Guild contract authorizing him to be my agent."

"Did you join the Guild yet?"

"Well, I tried, but they told me at the Guild that I

can't become a member of the Screen Actors Guild until I get a job, and Art told me before that I'm not going to get a job until I become a member of the Screen Actors Guild. I just don't see how it's possible to get into pictures."

"Well, theoretically that's true, but if it looks as though you are going to get a job, why, it's quite easy to join."

"Thank you," she said.

"You're welcome, and what are you doing for dinner?" he said.

"Nothing, but I have a very busy day tomorrow. I have two other directors to see and my schedule for the week is quite full. I'll be getting up very early in the morning, so I can't stay out late at all, straight and true."

"It's five-twenty now." He couldn't believe it yet. "Why don't you wait, if you don't mind, sit around and get to know what it's like on the set? You got a good chance to be in the business, so have a look around. I'll finish here about a little after six. There's a place I go to for dinner called Domino's, a small joint, great food, and you're out early."

"Okay."

He swung around and was ready and back at the Oakwood Cafe before they called him.

The next thing he knew he was looking in the face of some big ugly man whose breath was stale from food and liquor and cigar smoke and who was spewing obscenities into his face, having collared him by his throat, his huge right fist doubled up like a ham ready to knock him into oblivion. He gurgled something like, Wait a minute. The huge hand around his throat relaxed and set him gently on the floor. As he touched the ground, Stacy's right fist and arm were on the way, doubled up hard as nails, bam into the midsection of this giant. It didn't stop him, but it slowed him down. Stacy Armstrong had his vicious left ready and cut hard across this giant's head, arcing it three inches above his own head. It connected hard and solid. Slammer Cartwheel looked more surprised than hurt as he felt his chin move over three inches from under his face, and before he got over the surprise, a right cross came flying, sending his chin back in the direction it had come. Slammer flew over a teakettle into a table of frightened prospectors and gamblers and barmaids. Two guys who had been standing alongside the Slammer were now in a very agitated state. They both knew that Stacy Armstrong, the doctor's son, could not handle himself. Jake, the thinner of the two men, stepped back and at the same time drew his Colt .45. Before Jake had that gun clear of the holster, Stacy had drawn, fired, and as Jake's gun came up into a shooting position, Kid Stacy had holstered his gun and now stood empty-handed in front of Jake, who didn't have much time to think about anything. He clutched his chest with his left hand, slowly lowered his right, dropping the Colt, and crumbled to the floor. Kid Stacy now turned his attention directly to the remaining bandido, Alvarez Gonzales. He stammered something in Spanish and tried to put a smile on his face, made a rather exaggerated gesture of his hands away from his guns, and slowly backed away. At twenty feet, Kid Stacy said, Drop them. Alvarez gingerly reached in both holsters at the same time and with his thumb and first finger gingerly let the pistolas drop to the floor, relieved finally of those awful things. He turned around and walked to his freedom.

"Cut," the director said. "That's a print, and I want to do it again."

A couple of groans, one grunt, and then they started to reconstruct the set to look as if it were brand new.

"You've done great. You're famous, people know your name, and you can get a nice seat in a restaurant. A lot of people envy you. Do you love it?"

"I love it," he said. "I love it."

"That's what I'd like to have," she said, "without having to give up too much."

With the salad and grilled chicken, she smelled heavenly. He couldn't take his eyes off her. Her shoulders, the beautiful form of her breasts, her very thin arms dissecting that chicken as elegantly and as perfectly as a surgeon. Her manners were beautiful, she laughed a lot, he was almost embarrassed because he had that throbbing hard-on in his pants. He just couldn't help it. He was as horny as Kansas in August. When he finally got her to his apartment after dinner, he was a nervous wreck, but he knew he mustn't rush her, for she had a few things to attend to this week and had no time or inclination for anything but success. Lay back and read, he thought. Don't be greedy.

The next time they saw each other, they kissed a little in the car, but that didn't help his condition at all, and that orgasm ended in his pants. The third time he saw her, it was at Barney's place for drinks, dinner, and dancing; then after that to Andrew's place, which was on top of the hill.

"Oh, no you don't, Andrew. Not in this house, not here on this couch, on your bed, or anywhere around here."

"What?"

"I don't want to be just one of many. And I don't mind that even, but it's got to be someplace that you don't know and I don't know."

"But Delilah, we're here already."

"No, Andrew, please."

She got up and walked to the door.

"Please take me home."

He drove her down to Hollywood and drove back to his house in the hills. Stymied. He finally had her on a blanket down at the beach, and at the height of his joy she shoved him away and screamed, Don't come, don't come. Her sudden convulsion unhoused him and he found himself buried in the sand. Please, please, she said, be careful. He said, I'm careful. I'm careful. A ship was pulling away from the dock and he was on it.

He ran across her again at a cocktail party. After that she wasn't around for about a year and that was the end of that. She had disappeared. No one knew what ever happened to her, whether she married, didn't marry. They knew she worked in four movies, but that was all. There was never any hint of scandal or drama about her, just a nice girl who never learned how to take it.

Then there were Sandra and her husband. She kept insisting that she was divorced, and this guy kept arguing with him that she wasn't. Telling him that she was his wife and she was a good girl and not to hurt her. Hurt her? While she was using Kid Andrew as a decoy, Sandra the shimmer was stripping for three producers and a director in town and neither one of them knew that they were being had by Sandra at the same time.

It took the Kid three dates to find out that Stephanie

Lattimer, would-be starlet, Palm Springs habitué, Las Vegas regular, two films to her credit, *Modern Screen* introducing her as the girl most likely to, was a guy. No one ever really scored with her in the usual way, but she sure showed all the guys she went out with a good time. No one ever really took her out more than once or twice, it seemed, and that didn't make too much difference anyway. There were so many guys and gals around that you hardly remembered them from one day to the next. She may be sexy but she's naughty, were the catch phrases they used in the ads for her last picture, *The Ravaged*. She played a schoolteacher gone wrong, or right, as the case may be. Well, Stephanie Lattimer was a guy. She had all the machinery necessary to be a guy, maybe not the biggest, but that's the way it goes. Salvador's body just didn't have the muscular delineations usually found in a boy's figure, or if he did, it lay beneath a series of fat layers. When encased in women's apparel, he could be the sexiest looking wahoo in the neighborhood. Exquisite fine features. Charlie Chaplin wasn't as funny as he was. Salvador Rocco Gang Bang. Salvador was rough and ready and so was the Kid. When Salvador was Salvador, he sounded the same as Stephanie, except with Stephanie the ends of the sentences were light and airy. Each word ended up in the air, melodious and pleasant to be around. Salvador's oldest sister, Margo, had been around about ten years earlier. Everybody had had her one way or another somehow, all the bucks in the neighborhood, that is, and some of the doves as well. Her Catholic background and upbringing didn't seem to deter her at the beginning, but as she got deeper into that society, she started to lose control of herself. She'd suddenly raise her voice and start screaming. She wanted to try everything and became aggressive about it. She tried to tear the steering wheel out of a guy's hands one night. Jumped in a pool at a party, just wouldn't come out of the water, lying face down. Somebody finally hauled her out. When she finally came to, she looked up at the guy who'd saved her and said, Now why did you do that? She's away somewhere now, poor chick.

Salvador's plan was that Stephanie was going to ball it with all the guys and girls around for about ten years, then write a book, mention everybody's names, have recordings, some still photographs, documented, authenticated, computerized, finalized, certified. Saga of the sex life of all animals. He would dedicate it to his sister, and when he had published and sold movie rights to Monogram, he was going to buy a yacht and sail under the Golden Gate Bridge and watch all those producers, writers, actors, actresses, business managers, agents, doctors, singers, dancers, and secretaries come leaping off the bridge. He had cared a great deal for his sister. She was the only one who had really been kind to him as a child. He swore revenge, but Salvador, or Stephanie Lattimer, would never get the chance.

Stephanie begged no the first night out with the Kid, but relieved him anyway with stroking. On the third night, just as he was ready to come:

"Kid, I've got a surprise for you, and I'm doing this only because I like you. This is gonna hurt me more than it does you. Look, you haven't lost a girlfriend, but gained a boyfriend. Don't take it so personally. What I'm saying is, I'm a man. You might not want to trust me from now on, but please, Andy, I'm on a mission and cannot be deterred, so keep your fuckin' mouth shut and keep out of my way, or I'll get you good."

The Kid was introduced to hookers for the first time when he went on tour with his movies. He'd visit a lot of cities exploiting the films with radio interviews, newspaper interviews, meeting the press in most cities, who by and large were hostile. Ben Saphire, the press agent who toured with the Kid, cleared all the interviews, arranged all lunches, dinners, and appearances, and introduced him to that all-American dream, the Hooker. What was natural, an impulse and a need, was now big business. There were a lot of them in his tour years. The flesh and faces, smells and sounds had by now blended into a montage of memories; he was never able to put them back in their original form anymore. There was no real reason why he enjoyed the company of hookers. It was just easier for him to communicate with a female for those drives that were constantly tantalizing him. If they were as full as that, he gave in to them gladly in the most economical way that he knew, paying for it moment by moment,

He wasn't sure when it started to happen. All he knew was that he started to like it. Maybe liking it wasn't the right definition, more fascinated and awed by its magic. There were so many elements to remember and then to forget them as you did it. There wasn't anything particularly complicated about doing it, either. It was a matter of forgetting your own existence and allowing the situation, the physical locations, the strangers who were supposed to be lovers or enemies, friends or strangers, to become part of your whole existence. To be suspended, so to speak, in another world from a few seconds' duration to sometimes five or six minutes. After doing it for ten years acting took more stamina than anything else, the Kid thought. Strong legs, learn your lines, and not let anyone or anything interfere with the moment at hand, for there he would be surrounded by seventy people from all the departments of the studio. Propmen, directors, a producer, an occasional writer, script girl, art director, set director, messenger girls, special effects, clapper boys, assistant directors, extras, other actors, actresses, production managers, their assistants, all of their collective energies and concentrations poured into one small set in the corner of a sound stage surrounded by fifteen to twenty other sound stages on this huge studio complex. Main offices out near the front gate, commissaries, dressing rooms, offices, newsstands, gym, secretary pools, garages, parking lots, huge prop department, set department, horses, a Western street, a wrangler in charge of the horses, a lake, and a small run of a river. Portions of planes, cars, boats, wagons, cannons, Arabian streets, Paris streets, tenement streets, London streets, mythical streets, Midwestern streets, all ending by a waterfront overlooking a lake. Half of a steamship, the fronts of buildings held up by crutches of Dali, furniture, glassware, linenware. If they didn't have it, they would rent it, and when you came on the set that morning to shoot the scene in your lady's boudoir, man, you were in a lady's chamber with hot and cold running water. It wasn't that these artifacts were unreal, it was just that they started nowhere and ended nowhere, of nowhere.

"Don't get so close to her, Kid, or you'll cover the eye light set to clear up some shadows around the young lady's eyes," a cameraman said.

The director said, Closer, Kid, closer. Closer, Kid! He got closer because the director was King Shit and what he said goes. Sometimes there was a director who was weak and gutless, postured a lot, sounded like a director: Quiet, for Christ's sake, how am I going to get this work done if all you are chattering like chickens? Screw you, Mr. R., Andrew thought. Another basket case sent in to direct a movie. No talent, just a bad memory. His title, Mr. R., was a nickname for Mr. John Ratch, who had memorized every phrase in the book connected with pictures. He knew all the lenses, how the camera worked. That was about the size of it. He knew nothing about continuity, following a story from beginning to end without getting lost in the details.

The Kid found himself making entrances through doors, windows, cellars, rivers, roofs, chimneys. One day he would be in bed with a dark-haired girl, riding a horse with a blonde, having champagne with a redhead, taking a brunette home to Mother. He got to observe other actors and actresses in their profession: some came to work stiff with fear, or stiff with booze; some prepared and knew every word; some didn't know their names. Big-titted, small-titted, big ass, small ass, men, women, children, dogs, cats, pigs, chickens, snakes, cows. These were his companions in these countless scenes that had been played and filmed.

Photographs upon photographs were taken. Photographers from all over the world descended. Andy didn't know it, but he had become an international star. They treated him like shit in good ole Hollywood, where the race was so intense there was no time to take a breather, but constantly to fight the forces of envy, avarice, and hate. Everyone was branded a fag as soon as they arrived, anything to demean and cheapen so that the other person could have a little better shot at it. It was all the precious things in the world rolled into one, and was being sought after by thirty thousand people; men, women, children, dogs and even a pig, all looking for that sweet smell of success. Agents, lawyers, press agents, columnists, sooth-sayers, producers' wives, plus secretaries and all the other related crafts of the picture business were mixed together in some minestrone soup that was always bubbling, always ready to erupt. Vying for roles, consulting the stars, doctors, agents, and the itch in their pants, and what was the next step toward their success? Do you sleep in the nude? Yes, I think the expression is "raw." Dinner parties, here, there, and everywhere, this executive's house, that studio's première dinner, dance after the screening, but only for the chosen few la-de-fucking-da. Come on down to the Springs and spend the weekend with us, said Ruthy, the producer's wife, ah ha ha. Why don't we fly to Vegas Friday when we've finished work? We'll take that Sunday afternoon plane; just tell the old lady you're out scouting locations. I'll cover you. Sit-down dinner parties given on the lawns of these houses covered over with a cellophane contraceptive to keep out the cold or keep in the hot, with burning gas heaters smelling of kerosene mixed with beef Stroganoff, Chanel No. 5, and menopause no. 3. Hey, Charlie, hey, Billie, hey, Mary, hey, Jane; hi, Tommy, hey, baby, what's happening? Cain! Cain, I got to go. What? It's six already, baby. I got to be in the studio in an hour. I got to go home and change my clothes, feed the dog, shave. Can't you stay just another ten or fifteen minutes? I can't, baby. You know how mad your husband gets when I'm not on time.

"What do you think it is, Doc?"

"Well, it looks like a sty, but I think it's a cyst."

"My eye's swollen pretty bad and I'm supposed to work this morning."

"Well, let 'em just photograph you from the right side."

"Don't you want to go to Santa Anita on Saturday and give out the eighth race cup?"

"The silver screen award for the most promising new-comer, the winner is Andrew Cody."

KID ANDREW CODY

Each day went thataway. Muse and fuse. It was extraordinary, the Kid thought. The next thing he'd remember he'd be doing something. Being made nervous by this unreasonable actor standing in front of him. Looking for some psychological edge so as to be able to dominate the scene, and not just the one in front of the camera or just the one made expressly for films. Him, meanwhile, playing tense, being rough and arrogant, sharp and witty, like the elder statesman watching the neophytes go through their stuff.

"Kid, don't shuffle so much if you don't mind. You see, then my eyes are always wavering."

Him didn't want the Kid to move around at all, because the Kid was cute and knew what he was doing. Maybe fleshing it out a little bit more than it should have been. Him was no help anyway. Him who knew better was afraid to tangle with the Kid. Knew Him would be eaten up. So Him came on with all the old numbers that have been used ever since that movie camera began. An inch over your line. The heat of the light leaves his right eye. The Kid looks. That inch that Him is over the line forces the Kid a little to his left. It pulls the camera around ever so slightly and the Kid around ever so slightly. The two moves compounding each other puts the key now four inches away from where it should be. Instead of an overshoulder two shot, Him's now in a quarter-profile position. The cameraman digs but refuses to speak to Him, because the last time he gave Him advice, Him chewed him out in front of the crew. The Kid moved four inches to his right by shifting his weight to his right foot. Him now was covering the Kid.

"If you don't stand still, Kid," Him said, "they can't light ya."

"Archie's lit me," the Kid said, "but you're standing in it."

Don't mistake it. It was the battle of the wits as well as the brawn.

Every time he won an award, or was singled out for one reason or another, or was announced for another film in the trade papers, he could feel the tension in the commissary. So he didn't go anymore. Two-week tours of one-nighters to exploit his last picture, *Farmer's Daughter's Revenge*. I'm at the Roundhouse Hotel, 907, come on by after for a drink. A local secretary, beautiful. She got to 907, two drinks later she was pissed off for coming 'cause you're an actor, think you're cute, huh? Well, I'll tell you something, I'm no pushover. All this was going on while she was taking off her clothes. She started down on him and halfway through a lick, stopped, looked up at the Kid, and said, Wow, if my mother could only see me now. A gala première for the *Pirate's Treasure* and the theater was decorated like the interior of a galley, up and down all the aisles ranged burly men with huge arms and a whip snapping, and treating all the audience in their seats as the crews for these galleys. Avast ye, mates. Quiet, or the Captain will have your head. Row, you varmints, row. A tempo and a beat-beat on a tom-tom came on you slowly, amid the sound of wind and rain. The theater darkens and you could feel yourself almost at a sea. And there on the screen, lo and behold, were Captain Cruck and his pirate crew on the deck of their galleon, as they sailed the seven seas in search of bounty and boobies.

When the film was over, which was not fast enough for ninety-five per cent of the audience, they adjourned to a plastic balloon bubble with rubber grass on the parking lot of the theater, with those oil heaters again, while David Gamble served them his famous chili con carne with broads and beer, cheap and effective for that crowd. Beautiful young girls dressed up as pirates, their skirts split all the way up to their bloomers, blouses opened up down to their navels, short swords tied to their waists and a patch on one eye. Of the twenty girls who served as hostesses, eighteen gave their telephone numbers to assorted directors, producers, exhibitors, producers' wives, and actors.

It'll be glorious, Andy, do come. I've got a bongo player, some grass, we'll pop a few uppers, some wet towels. Giggles. A midnight swim, all nude. Another giggle. And at dawn, breakfast and watch the sun rise over Pacific Palisades. Who's going to be there? Just you and me. Against this skimpy tapestry, he had to whisper to the girl, I love you, my darling. She smelled awful. He always made a point of cleaning himself very carefully before he went to work each day. He watched his diet as much as he could, so that he wouldn't be belching, farting, or generally passing any kind of odors that were unnecessary. He found them occupational hazards. This girl smelled bad and sour. Don't hold me too close, please. It's against my religion. I shouldn't be doing this without my dueña here. I'll go to the drugstore and get you one. Jesus, he thought, hold her too close. I don't even want to drink her water. But at ten grand a week, beggars can't be choosers.

It was in situations like these that he began to appreciate the art of acting, or the artlessness of acting. To him it was like being there but not being there. If he believed it, then they believed it. If he had doubts about himself or the people he was working with, it was impossible to hide, and it always permeated the scene. Sometimes the director wasn't smart enough to realize where it came from. He just knew something was wrong. The Kid knew, Andrew knew, Kid Andrew Cody knew. Was there anything more to it than just memorizing lines, listening carefully, and looking soulfully to this profession of his? What did he like about it so much? Sure, there was the money, the fame, fortune, the dames, the yachts, the plots, the games, the gems. In the early days, he was only concerned that his hair looked okay, was his suit cut all right, would they finally give him an eye light and wipe out the circles of the night before from around his navy-blue eyes?

In an early picture, he needed a pocket handkerchief and the wardrobe man stuck a Kleenex folded casually and elegantly in his pocket. It was tough for him in that scene, walking around like a wealthy dandy, barking orders on the phone, making passes at the secretaries, acting tough with his fellow competitors, with a fucking Kleenex in his pocket as a handkerchief. If the lapels on his suit were too big, it distracted him; if the shoulder pads were too much, that distracted him. He just couldn't find himself comfortable and at ease, words seemed clumsy pouring out of his mouth. He was easily distracted by noises coming from around the camera and from behind it. He was being bombarded then by outside influences, the fringe benefits of his profession were nickel and diming him to death. But he was afraid to use his power, or perhaps didn't know how to. If he couldn't hold on, drive all that bullshit out of his mind and concentrate on the moment, he would end up washing cars on Sunset, serving hamburgers on the Hollywood Strip. On the one hand, the producer wanted his best; and on the other, he had hoped the actor would have the worst. They were usually jealous and envious of the actors. They made the most money, got the best-looking girls or the guys, as the case may be, weekends in Palm Springs or

Las Vegas or fly to Acapulco, or nip in to London for a gala or even New York for a telethon, or fly to St. Thomas, on a yacht in Sardinia, or collecting shells in Jamaica, snorkling in Hawaii. He could sense their envy and avarice. A lot of guys and girls he knew buckled under the intense pressure. They started popping pills: pills to sleep, pills for energy, to be able to run through the day, nervous, irritable, angry cats, finally coming late for work. Stuck in the traffic, believing all the bullshit that they wrote in the papers. Being intimidated by lady columnists, those dried-up harbingers of old herrings, printing ugly and unhappy things about people, not able to understand and accept that intelligentsia anonymous making a hundred and a quarter a week or a day, it made no difference. It was enough to make some of those newspapermen and women take another belt before Christmas.

When a scene went well, it was worth the price of admission for the Kid, all the lights around him were forgotten, cameramen, the prop department, the script girl, all of them faded into nothing. If he got laid that night or not, it didn't make any difference. Whether he sat next to the hostess or the host at the next dinner party didn't make any difference. There he was, like surfing, like skiing, like swimming, able to drive all of those pretty, ugly, unhappy, and also pleasant and wonderful memories out of his psyche, out of his head, out of his mind, out of his soul. He just found himself attacking the problem at hand, and when he finally said I love you, he believed it. That sour, garlic-smelling object in front of him believed it; the director believed it; he was free. He had so much time in which to accomplish the task of the scene. He had to walk across the room while he explained the reason he felt that his automobile was a better design than his competitor's. He had to stop at the bar, get the champagne bottle from the fridge, get two glasses, open the bottle, all the while explaining the difference between his fuel injection eight cylinder carbureted V-8 as opposed to his competitor's, always sensing the girl's affection and warmth for him. He was torn by his need. She was warm and desirable, she wanted him, he wanted her, but he had work down at the garage, the car had to be ready. True, all of it had been done, but he somehow felt uneasy, and wanted to check it out carefully. She asked him to stay a bit longer, he would, but only for a little while. Still uneasy, not knowing why. Meanwhile, back at the garage, his competitor, that prick, was neatly eliminating one of the integral parts of his carbureted V-8, and this warm, desirable, beautiful creature, in her cozy apartment in a penthouse down in Malibu overlooking the Pacific Ocean, was trying to keep him distracted for another hour or so.

They toasted to his luck with the champagne, he had opened the bottle on an exact cue. She said, Stay, stay, Steve, stay for another few moments. Karpathy, the director, said, A moment, there should be a beat, then I want that bottle opened, pour yourself a glass, pour Rebecca a glass, forget the car, let yourself go completely. You walk toward her. Rebecca reached up, put her arms around his neck, he sank smoothly to one knee which he placed on the couch, the other remained on the floor, and they kissed with both his arms outstretched, holding the champagne glasses. He waited a moment, would he or wouldn't he? He leaned forward and dexterously put the two glasses of champagne, still in the kiss, delicately on the table behind the couch, never looking, and swooped down on her into the soft creases and cushions that they were lying on. The camera waited a moment, and slowly rose above them to settle on the window, and for the first time you saw the stars, the thin line of the horizon over the ocean. A bit later the horizon started to light up and the sun came up.

There were a lot of acting schools around, all looking to pick up a little money by teaching you something that everyone did naturally. There were fancy schools and dinky schools. They were all the same, trying to make a score out of something that came simply and in some cases effortlessly from the person himself. You needed confidence, calmness, intelligence, and an uncluttered mind to record all the instant pieces of information that you had to store away. Pick up the glass, stay out of the girl's light, don't knock over the chair when you come in the window, jump in the car, and go away immediately. Don't sit there fucking with the ignition because you can't start the car. Make sure you have half-rubber heels on your shoes so you don't slip jumping from the window to the top of the van. Learn your lines, and when you think you've learned them, learn them again. Don't let anyone trap you or fool you. Always be early, never late, for a cue. Be ahead of everybody. Sense everybody's needs and wants and desires, and try to orchestrate it all together so that when you read the line, when you look, when you respond, it was just as if it was happening at that second, spontaneous and real, responding to the moment now, the action, and not to some direction coming from another person's mind. It was cruel work. He saw young people and old people and animals crumble under the pressure, not able to remember from one line to the next, apologizing, using blackboards to read lines, sweating, throwing up, asking for five minutes, not able to take all of those instructions, and make it pour out easily.

At the beginning, the Kid felt if you had to be angry in a scene, you really had to get angry, but how exhausting that was, how sad. He realized then that to become really proficient at his profession, he had to be able to have all these emotions, traits, thoughts, images, at his fingertips. I want you to be a little angry here, but not enough to kill the joy of love in case we need it later, got it? Just walk in and say hello. Got it? Now in this scene, I want your emotions to be turned inside out. I want you angry, mean, but still moved, knowing full well that Harry will be back later in the evening. Miriam won't know how to respond to Nancy, and Phil and Charlie aren't back from the yacht in time for Sally's birthday party for Edna and Phil. I'd like you to be a bit contrite, but yet on top of yourself, not allowing anyone to disturb this perfect balance of equilibrium of souls and spirit and mind. Got it? You want me to come and smile, right? Right.

This method actor asked the director of the film what was his motivation. The director replied, Asshole, you don't do it like I tell you to do it, I'll get another asshole. The method actor looked at him with half-closed eyes and mumbled, That's my motivation.

The only thing good about acting schools was that they made it possible for actors to hang around with each other. A lot of information passed between them in schools and an occasional professional job was found. In one of his earlier film experiences and experiments, he was asked to deliver a telegram with the line: "It looks like it's followed you halfway across the country, ma'am." He tried variations emphasizing each word separately. It looks like it's followed you halfway across the country, ma'am, and on and on until the director saw him pacing up and down. Karpathy walked up to him and quietly said, All you want is a tip. Bim, bam, thank you, man. It started to make some sense to the Kid. All you wanted was a tip, hot damn. It was the best advice he ever got. A stunt man, Dave Sharpe, gave him another piece of information that he needed. All he had to do was to practice it. Once when they had to arrange a bit of action to go before a scene, David said, Don't walk if you can run. Don't run if you can fly. Be early rather than late. Settle only rarely to make a point. Never stand still, always move a little. After all, you're in a moving picture.

He loved those early days, waiting for the light, waiting to reload, waiting for the leading lady, waiting for a prop, waiting for the actor to learn his lines, waiting for the director to make up his mind, waiting for the director who was waiting for himself. They were on location in Brazil. He got $2,000 a month expenses besides his salary. It cost him $15,000 to rent a beautiful villa five miles from the location work. They were there for ten weeks. Just before they left the location to go back to the States, the third assistant, a Turkish chap named Adil, told him that the guy that owned the villa had rented it to the production manager of the company for $350 a week. Somebody had moved better than ten and a half thousand out of his pocket on that location. When he got back to New York, he told the head of the studio to give back the money or he wouldn't go back to work. They did, and then promptly bum-rapped him around town for holding them up for money before they started to shoot again in Hollywood. Blackmail, they call it. He called it chickenshit. Once they hired a fleet of cars from a local private limousine company, a smoothie, who of the ten cars they hired used three for the company, and the other seven to pick up tourists from the airport and take them to the hotel and show them around the beautiful city of Roma. When his partner turned him in to the company, the producers fired the limousine company immediately, but had to pay him off for ten more weeks. They had a contract.

The partner, now a big man with the production department, was given the contract. He was hired at the same price and also for another ten-week contract in which he gave them back the same cars. They just fired his partner. Meanwhile the partner went to Hollywood for a holiday. And they call actors shmucks.

Or how about the time when they had fifteen thousand men on horseback, dressed, ready for war? On Action, they would come across a huge crest, down into a valley where mines would be detonated, and men and horses would go flying. From one side of the chasm rode blond Hardy Anderson, the all-American boy, sidestepping bombs and shells and falling horses and soldiers and swords, cannon, and bayonet, and shrapnel, and sabers to fight his way to the top of the other ridge, where one of eight cameras was situated. Ready when you are, Mr. De Mille. The girl, Ginny something, girlfriend of the producer, sitting on horseback, waiting for her lover. When he finally arrived at her side, they were to turn around, turn to the camera, and ride off together. When he arrived at the top of the crest she threw up. It was either morning sickness or the El Rancho Vega dinner she had last night with her producer boyfriend, either one, that shot was going to go down the toilet. And with all the blanks that didn't go off and the make-up that smeared, marks that were overshot, and the camera running out of film, and the wind blowing her hairpiece, and the champagne bottle not popping, the doorknob coming off in your hand. And in your great love scene kissing Madam, she quietly slipped some of her doublemint-flavored gum into your mouth. That ought to teach you a lesson, my cocky lad.

But it was all worth it. He knew of no place where he could enjoy himself as much, feel as full and alive, as in these fantasy worlds. To be many places, many things, many people, on the back lot in the San Fernando Valley. He was doctors, lawyers, Indians, women, children, animals; he was strong men, deaf men, blind men, brave men, cowards, thieves, murderers, and was paid for it. To find yourself in the middle of a scene, to find yourself confronted by a beautiful woman, angered by a violent man, made brave by your action, was something joyous, for those few minutes a day, to forget your very reality, even though you enjoyed being who you were. To be someone else, someplace else.

> Don't be glad
> Don't be blue
> How do you know
> You're even you?

Lila London

At a very early age Lillian Lansky decided that life was filthy and disorderly. Lilly tried to bring some organization into her life. In a brownstone flat outside of Philadelphia, in a busy and very enterprising family, Lillian, now known to the world and showbiz as Lila London, columnist and newsmonger, grew up.

She was graceless, clumping around on feet a little too big for her. She had aversions to a great many things: heights, depths, highs, lows, sour cream, bananas, frilly underwear. She didn't like brassieres but it didn't make any difference, she didn't have anything to fill them with. She had a keen mind, remembered everything. She was a solipsist and didn't even know it. Her favorite subject was history. Where she got some of her historical facts no one knew, but she would regale her girlfriends or some acquaintances at school or at home with her information. Cleopatra was a nymphomaniac; Madame Pompadour was a Lesbian; Marie Antoinette, while taking care of the King, was also seeing after a few guards; Catherine the Great's great love affair with a pony named Alexi; and Mahatma Gandhi had a beautiful wife and children and a home in Beverly Hills which he visited when everyone thought he was going off meditating. These tidbits about the great were what fascinated Lillian Lansky and set the pattern for her future life.

She studied journalism and deluded herself into thinking that she could write about styles or review books and movies. She was ugly. Sloping forehead, sallow skin, small eyes accentuated and slightly bulged, a short stubby neck over something with two arms and legs, and dark hair with shots of gray. If she couldn't act in them she would write about them and particularly about the beautiful people that surrounded her. She couldn't bear their success. She either loathed them or hated them. There was no in-between. She was either at their throats or their heels.

Picture people were a perfect choice for her venom

and fantasies. Anyone she came across in the picture business was fair game. She was a virgin until she was fourteen, when she blackmailed the butcher boy into fucking her. He was overcharging her family.

She started working in pictures doing anything she could. She finally got a quarter-page column in the trade paper and then her power began to increase. One guy out of Cincinnati, fucking her at her beach house, put a pillowcase over her head when he came. That was the last time they ever heard of him in the Hollywood Hills, and in Cinn-ci-fuckin-ati. She would wear two pairs of pantyhose. She liked it tight down there, and it fattened her calves.

When she first started writing her junk, she was about thirty-five pounds heavier than she was now. She'd had her hair streaked, cut in the most fashionable way, wore clothes that she thought fit her figure. To be kind, her figure was an extra closet with some clothes on it. Still, there was a vibration which came from her that fascinated some people. She was tenacious and believed in herself. She had as much right as anyone to be alive. What size Tampax Sally Tarlow used or what went on in Vinnie De Carlo's penthouse suite at the Sands Hotel in Las Vegas, or who was the latest enamorato of Fiona Phillips, the new protégée and singing star of Arnold Class Productions. Mr. Class being politically inclined, hoping one day to use his producer's mantle as a steppingstone to the governorship of California. All these personal variations and problems, needs, wants, and hangups that each individual had the privilege to enjoy were fair game for Lillian Lansky. To this bitch, if it happened in the movies, it was fair game.

Hooker (she added a new wrinkle, she paid), extra, bit player, starlet, Lila London, now columnist getting even with everybody who didn't believe in her or did numbers on her. Out of nowhere going nowhere. If someone snubbed her at a party, well, shit, there would be an item in her column the next day, testifying that if he wasn't married he would be soon and if he was, he wouldn't be soon, their marriage was breaking up or it wasn't. She was pregnant or she wasn't. He was on dope or he was fucking some drum majorette. Rumors and innuendoes. Lila London grew from all that, the way a horsefly grows from horseshit. She had everybody petrified. She thought.

The studios paid court to her; producers, directors, writers, actors, law firms, agents, top studio executives, their wives, girlfriends, and secretaries. Press agents creamed and reamed her, cushioned her with daily calls about her health, her well-being, her bed-wetting, her rash.

"Oh, by the way, did you hear that Sally was taking it up the ass from Fred while Miriam was doing it to Sylvia, and Charlie had his tongue in Bobby's ear, while Peter was doing it to Paul and Mary?"

A couple of people were smart enough to realize that it was all just so much bullshit. The thing to do was to get the name of the picture printed right and when it was going to be released, who the actors were and to spell their names right. If the major studios in the forties and fifties had to pay for all the publicity that was spewing out of the film capital, it would have cost each studio fifty million dollars apiece. As it was, they just paid a fraction of that and there were eight major film companies then. Their paid advertisements, which meant ads in the newspapers, trailers in the theaters, ads in magazines and all publishing forms, commercial time on radio, and the huge ads on billboards and in front of theaters, were the only legitimate paid advertising that they were prepared to do. Each studio had an additional fund for trying to interest the wire services in stories emanating from Hollywood and the film industry. It made better sense for the studios to try to get connected with a newspaperman or woman by sweetening their individual kitties with gifts of liquor, trips, and paid-for holidays. It sure was tough to turn them down then. And so the film industry, by having a few columnists in their pockets, had privy to newspaper columns and radio air time without having to pay the exorbitant rates that they were charged for ads.

The executives, quietly holed up in Palm Springs, let whoever was writing the column call the actors or anyone they wished any names they liked, just as long as they spelled the movie's and the producer's and the distributing company's names correctly. For any news was good news. Press agents were handling the stars. The same stars were under contract to studios that were paying their press department to publicize them well. The studios needed a lot of writers to write copy about pictures. The polls they had, the awards they gave, the ads they took were the only way to get your name in print and let people know what you were selling.

These newspapermen and women who worked exclusively off the film industry came from colleges of fine reputations, fine newspapers; first-rate journalists who were now shills for the motion picture business and getting paid good for it. Whether they liked your picture or didn't like your picture, who gave a shit, just so long as they printed it? A couple of these movie-newspaper-television critics, assholes, really diddled themselves into thinking that they were doing the picture business a favor. Bullshit! They were nothing but hacks. The ones that realized this were easy to get along with, pleasant, and accepted their fate. No wonder so many of them drank. They couldn't face it. Now, Lila London was a little bit of everything. She had a little poison from them all. She knew it better than anyone. What she was doing was just so much bullshit. That probably made her even meaner. She used the printed word to throw people into spasms, depressions, elations, agony, ecstasy.

Twenty people were only indirectly related to what came out of the news mills of Hollywood. These twenty people were the most important actors and actresses, four directors, two producers, and one writer in the profession. People went to see films because of them. They were hated, and envied, and adored by the actors, by the writers, the directors, the producers, the producers' wives, the production managers, the cops at the gate, the executives of all the distributing companies. What started out as the simple exercise of capturing life, movement, and sound became a big biz, a miracle. Brought alive by the performers that imitated life. People may have written them and directed them and cut them and put them together, but still the experience was captured by the actor's physical expression. Good or bad, he experienced it. He knew it. Time was the great gift. To take the time to re-create life as spontaneously as possible before the camera was a true gift and not the preparation that went before it or behind it. Two things were primary: a means to record and something to record.

These chosen few in films were pampered and petted and pawed and ravaged and raped, if any of them allowed it. To come from nowhere with nothing, no credentials of any kind, and to have a chance to get lucky in the good old summertime, to make it. A way of life of ease and comfort. Money, fame, respect, admiration, love were all part of that gamble.

Andrew

1950

They gave him the lead in *The Preacher's Son*. A twelve-day wonder to be shot by one of Pearlstein's reliable picture makers, director-producer Zoltan Worth. All shot in Lone Pine on location. Bim-Bam Thank You Ma'am. He was thrilled. He thought it was going to be a great Western, and on top of that, he would get to do all them wonderful stunts which he loved to do. He was as good as anyone around in the business. Maybe he lacked the experience that some of the stunt men had, but he had imagination and was intelligent, which added to his craft enormously. The stunt men he got to know were fine men and boys, and he always liked to be in their company. Some were ornery, some were mean, some were just swell folks. He got along with everybody, though. No one could pick a fight with him. Who'd want to? You couldn't stay mad at the Kid for very long. He learned a lot from Rube, Dave, Paul, Bob and Gary. Into the first day's shooting up at Lone Pine, he found he had to go with one unit of the company to do all the dialogue sequences sitting on top of a horse. At the same time, the second unit was shooting the action of that sequence in another valley just five miles away, using a double for the Kid, and paying him fifty dollars a day.

The Kid started the movie. By the end of twelve days' shooting, he had earned one hundred dollars while his double earned five hundred and twenty plus a couple of fifteen-dollar adjustments. The head of casting, Robert Barclay, tried to convince the Kid that he benefited from being under contract to Mr. Pearlstein's company. The fringe benefits were many. Free publicity, a half-dozen dinner parties around town, Mr. Pearlstein's Palm Springs house could be used for two weekends during the season. Always a new cutie put under contract. Mr. Barclay would put him down now for a weekend he wanted. He wouldn't even have to wait the customary six months. And, the Kid had a father to call whenever he would need one. God forbid he should ever, but if he ever did, he could call Mr. Pearlstein. The thought of a father melted the Kid. He thanked him for the few fringe benefits he was offered. And for the final *pièce de résistance*, Mr. Barclay told the Kid that a couple times a month he could sit down and have lunch with Mr. Pearlstein at the emerald table in the Rainbow Room, where, with his back to the wall, Pearlstein looked into the Sunshine Suite commissary of Studio Block One. Tough to turn it down. Especially when it was free twice a month. Delicious chicken soup with matzoh balls, boiled chicken, and onion-flavored matzohs sitting in a neat stack in the middle of the small table resembling old parchments of law. Eat all you want. Nobody to stop you.

He met Perry Rose, the press agent, that fall in the commissary. He was seeing this starlet named Linda Long. She was some distributor's girlfriend who was getting a six-month contract with an option for another six. The distributor arrived in Hollywood three or four times a year. And, during that time, if the young actress was diligent in her drama lessons and her dancing lessons and when the distributor was in town, her sucking lessons, why, she could last a little longer than the six months. She was living with Pearlstein and his wife, who were looking after this beautiful creature for their distributor friend from out of town. She'd sneak off and meet the Kid under the pretext of acting, singing, painting, music classes. Everybody was going to classes in those days, improving themselves. She and the Kid would drive down to the beach. They'd eat at Bill's, a seafood restaurant. Finish eating and out in the sand by seven, seven-thirty. Perry Rose had access to a beach house in Malibu. And it was there that Linda and the Kid would spend a few nights a week. The press agent said he'd look out for the Kid and plant whatever items he thought would be necessary. And the Kid wasn't obligated.

He hardly got a chance to see Pearlstein's house in Palm Springs because in the next few years he found himself going from one picture to another. He made sixteen films. Time sure goes when you're having a good time. He was laid, relaid, double-laid. Whatever he was after he got. In that three years it was all telescoped. After the twelfth week under contract and two and a half pictures made, he was raised from fifty a week to two hundred fifty a week, which calmed him down a bit, and he insisted on doing some stunts, which they gave in to reluctantly. Not because he didn't do them well. He did them damn well, better than anyone else could do them at that time, but they took time away from the shooting of the dramatic portions of the film. So the Kid tried to get those stories with less dramatic impact and more falling off your horse on your ass. His name had been mentioned a number of times in the columns now, taking Lois Lamour to dinner at Perino's, or June Madison to Chasen's, or Wendy Baxter to Billy Gray's Band Box. Lila London saw his photograph on the cover of a movie magazine. She liked the looks of him immediately. She checked around town and found that Linda Long's press agent, Perry Rose, looked after him. She called him and said, I want that boy. I'm ready to do a Sunday piece on that boy. Bring him by. She made a date for later in the week, she was busy digging up dirt about some actor who was living in the Valley with his agent, and it didn't look kosher to her. Vile, ugly fag trying to rob this town of its beautiful men. One day she thought she'd do an exposé about the ugly things that went on in this town. Meanwhile she never stopped stroking Erica's bush and finally went down on Erica and lost herself in the warmness of the place and forgot about the mundane problems of her profession.

Erica sat there taking notes while the Kid spoke with Lila London. Hollywood columnist extraordinaire. He kind of stumbled through all of this, all the questions that were asked. His answers rambled. He gave a little of his background, his likes and dislikes. Shit, he couldn't tell her. Never get in the paper. So he liked to walk on the beach, liked to read a lot, went sailing once in a while when he wasn't working, chopped down trees like a lumberjack. Glory Glory Hallelujah bullshit. He was just interested in getting fucked in those days, nothing else. It'll be a week from next Sunday, she said. They'll take some pictures of you tomorrow so I can run it with the story. As Perry Rose and the Kid were leaving, Perry said, Lila, we just got a beautiful shipment of kosher hot dogs out of Chicago. You know those real beauties. They were sent by special plane. I thought I'd send over a dozen or so, if you'd like them. I would adore them . . . adore them, she said. She should, she ate enough of them. She was cheap. She'd save on anything. Just send it over, dear, send it over. She was thirty-two and talking like some *grande dame*. Oh, by the way, she said, come down to the beach house on the weekend and have a swim if you like. I'm outside of the colony up in Trancas. The colony's too boring. Too many rumors flying around there. Nice to get away with oneself, isn't it? Yep, it sure is, he thought, and said, Yep.

He had bought a secondhand Buick Roadmaster with Dynaflow drive. Four hauler, convertible. He had to keep the top down all the time because it flapped in the wind and kept tearing. It ran okay and life was carefree. The house was a California beach house, lots of wood and rustic. The terrace overlooking the sea. Steps going down to the beach. Two bedrooms, bath, kitchen, living room, sitting room, dining room overlooking the terrace, which overlooked the ocean. Practically all the furnishings in the house were gifts; couches, beds, sheets. Gordon Gross, another press agent, had a brother who was in the home-furnishing business, and he could get it for you wholesale. Lila was penurious. She spent money only when it was absolutely necessary and then she'd try to bill it to someone else. She once went to Palm Springs to cover a golf tournament of the stars and stole all the towels, soap, sanitary napkins, and anything else she could find in this luxurious suite at the hotel in the desert. The studio had to replace it, of course. But what was a handful of towels in comparison to the headlines that studio got that following Monday morning? "Star Tournament-Star Studded." "Stars," by Lila London, was her column heading, it was her trademark. "The Annual Stars Tennis and Golf Tournament in Palm Springs was a star-studded sensation. Tommy Benson was funny as usual and outdid himself Mcing the night of the banquet. Benson and his bottle of Jack Daniels became old friends before he went on and his Bourbon husky voice was a treat to our ears." And on she'd ramble taking swipes at anybody she wanted to and praising only the uglies. She was the queen of the uglies and anybody that was good-looking was fair game for this bitch.

The Kid hadn't been around too much, but even if he had, he would have been completely unprepared for this weekend. By ten-fifteen Sunday morning, he was in his open chariot. He found himself speeding back over the Malibu Canyon Road on that quiet haze-covered Sunday morning. After last night, he didn't want to be alone. He started to drive to Leslie's house. Leslie Trent had a house this side of Mulholland Drive, high in the hills overlooking the Valley and parts of Beverly Hills as well. It was a beautiful spot. Yesterday afternoon had started out pleasantly enough. There was Erica, London's German secretary. And David Kliner, executive producer for Dream Productions, a half-assed pornographic film company that made only tit and sand movies, a lot of tits and very little sand and a lot of Vaseline, without any of the majors knowing it. He was making more money than any three of the majors combined. David constantly eyed every girl he saw, looking for the perfect breasts. And if he ever ran across a pair, he pursued them until he had conquered them. Perry Rose showed up a half hour after the Kid arrived with Rebecca Ryan and Liza DeLongpre. Both under contract to Dream Productions. Ten minutes later, Betty Beaumont arrived, first assistant and head executive secretary to Steven Shechter, production executive at Rialto Studios. She was thirty-six and had an itch all the time. She didn't care what or who or where, just so long as that itch could be tickled and calmed. It was a fire she couldn't quench. She kept waiting for the miracle that would stop this itch from driving her into the streets, into the bizarre and strange experiences that she was living.

At eleven-thirty, after some whiskey and downers and one furtive joint of marijuana were passed around to all the guests, out stepped Lila London from her bedroom, looking like Rudolph Valentino. Black boots to the knees, white flowing pants, white satin shirt opened on her no-tit chest, her head in some white turban, and a piece of costume jewelry that had been used in a film called *Ali Baba's Revenge*, and worn by Maria Maiven, the sultry queen of the Ali Baba films. Somewhere Perry Rose got her that jewel, which was worth twelve dollars and eighty-seven cents. Out she stepped with a short curled whip. Everybody took it quite calmly, didn't pay too much attention to it with the exception of the Kid. The head secretary settled into a soft, comfortable lounge chair overlooking the water. She spread her legs and moaned, being done to by Roberta, the actress that came in with Liza. David Kliner of Dream Productions kind of moseyed his way over to the delectable corner and disappeared into a mound of flesh. Andrew found himself in a maze of pubic hairs being done to and doing it at the same time.

By two-thirty there were bodies all over the place, half naked, some out, some not, some hot, some not. Every hole he found he put it to. That Erica, she was something else. She seemed to want to please everybody that day, that night, and she just about did. By five-fifteen everybody was out for lunch except Lila London and that whip. He had taken a moment's pause over the buttocks of Liza and was dozing when that whip bit into his shoulder. When it bit into his ass, he leaped off and spun around and there she was. Rudolph Valentino the Second. She drew back the whip to hit him again. He punched her in the mouth, which is the last thing in the world you do to a Hollywood columnist. She went ass backward over the couch and landed in the middle of the living-room floor. The Kid figured now, was the time to split. He went to the bathroom to clean up. First, he searched for whatever clothes he could find that belonged to him. Got them together and made his way to the bathroom in one of the bedrooms. There he was confronted by Perry Rose, who begged the Kid to please let him go down on him. The Kid in a very gentlemanly fashion thanked him, but said, No thanks. He felt he'd have to go now. Perry could see the resoluteness in that Kid's eye and had witnessed that punch so he was in no position to pursue it. The Kid backed out of the bathroom figuring it was the only way to make it safely out of the place. He went out through the terrace doors and down to the water. Walked about a mile down the beach, took off all his clothes, and dove in. It was bracing, clean, and cold. He swam a hundred yards straight out into the surf, turned, and looked at the California shoreline. There it was all before him, sunrise just turning deep orange. Another day in Southern California. How quiet everything looked. No cars, no sounds. He squinted while he floated in the water, looked at the shore, and tried to imagine what that shoreline looked like before man had ever gotten this far. Now his surroundings were so permanent, he thought. This sea, how many millions of years had it helped float someone that swam in it. How friendly it could be. How destructive as well. He just hung in the water with his face above and tried to drink in the energies of his planet. He felt at one with it and it with him. Both an extension of each other. He was the best of the breed but he didn't know it then. What meaning did life hold? What was he destined to do? Dear Max, where are you now? In that great poker game in the sky, playing with Capone and four or five other studs he never saw or knew. Max would have loved it out here with him in California, dreaming. He thought of his mother. He had an image of some woman with long brown hair wafting over his entire body and face. She smelled so much like a woman. Floating in the water he recalled his mother when he was two or three years old. He closed his eyes and felt her lips brush across his cheeks. He tried to project himself back to that time so that when he once again opened his eyes there would be his mother and all this would have been some fantasy or just a memory of things passed. Gradually he felt his face warm up as if the breast of this all-woman, this mother-woman, had opened herself and was going to take him and caress him and hold him. He got stiff again at the thought of her. He let his eyes open slowly and there was the sun over the Malibu hills, warming him. He started swimming ashore now as fast as he could. When he got to the sand, his heart was pounding in his chest, and he felt giddy. He lay down on the beach and let the sun dry him. He dressed, walked up to the road, and started walking north to where he had parked his car. The seat was wet from the night's dew. Everything comes in California. He smiled. He drove to Paradise Cove, dipped down to the water again. There was a small diner. He had an eight-ounce glass of fresh orange juice with pits. Jumped back into his car and started to drive back to town.

When the word got around about what the Kid had done, he was finally the biggest celebrity in town. They started to talk about him. It made him hotter than ever. To knock a cunt like that on her ass was no minor achievement. Lester Pearlstein decided to put a bankroll on Kid Cody. He had a script on his desk called *Hanging*. The story was about a twenty-year-old kid accused of murder outside of Vicksburg, Mississippi, in the late 1800s. It told of his trip from where he was apprehended to where the hanging was going to take place, and in flashbacks in between that story were scenes of him before the murder. When they got to the ending, Pearlstein shot it both ways; with the Kid getting hung, and with the Kid escaping and galloping off into the sunset. Perhaps to return as *Son of Hanging*.

They hired a Hungarian director named Martin Klinger, learned, cultured, elegant. He brought a picture along as if he were teaching a cooking school, one ingredient at a time. His pictures always appeared a bit detached. Not connected really to anything solid. Even when the stories were very tough and uncompromising he felt that pictures should be shot quickly, not to think too much about them. He was only prepared to give so much time to the project. After that, fuck it, feed it fish. Klinger was spontaneous and used the environment around him like a good conductor. Nothing missed his active attention from eight until seven-thirty right after rushes. After that he was not available to anyone until next morning. Everything that came into a frame of his film had a reason, a purpose. The cameras found themselves always in the best position to be in when a piece of action was going to be done or someone was going to speak. His films had style, there was no question about it.

Pearlstein wanted a little of that big-time action. The *Hanging* was going to separate him from the boys. Wait until those fucking Frenchmen see this. If we win Cannes Film Festival with this, I'm gonna tell 'em to shove it up their asses. Feels right, it looks right, thought Pearlstein. He'd make something now that would make him feel good. Pearlstein had been in films fifteen years. Coming out of Chicago, a distributor's son, trying to make it on his own. Worked in accounting. Had extensive knowledge of bookkeeping. Was up to date on all the tax laws.

Assistant director, assistant cutter, assistant story editor, assistant to the associate producer, assistant to the producer, and finally, the producer. He was given the money to make some movies. He owned fifty per cent of them, and he knew how to make them so every penny counted. And he had a story sense, an idea of the kind of movies he would like to make; the two things combined gave him a big edge. Married to Adele. Father of Robin and Sherrie. Art Taylor would marry Sherrie and wouldn't be an assistant director for very long.

The schedule was three weeks outside of Vicksburg, where Max was buried, near Broken Jaw Canyon; two weeks back in Los Angeles, one week at the Tanner Ranch, one week interiors. Twenty-five days. Bim-Bam Thank You Ma'am. In Technicolor, mit sound. Scored. Dubbed. And a final print previewed and ready for release that summer. The Kid and Klinger liked each other and the picture blossomed because of it. The Kid for the first time had a glimmer of what acting in movies was like. When he knew what he was doing and believed in it he could do a scene over a hundred times if they asked him and get it right each time. He learned to concentrate, shut everything else out of his mind. It was just like all the other pictures he had made, except the dialogue didn't sound funny coming out of him. He believed what he was saying. The next thing he knew, it was finished, scored, dubbed, lip synced, first print, first cut, previewed, now color blended. This is a major studio preview, it said on the screen before the picture started. He sneaked into the back of the theater in the Valley and this major studio preview audience felt a little bit better that night. Felt as if their lives weren't wasted. That they weren't just a mass of nothing. Always getting the leftovers. Treating the audience as if they were some kind of joke. Making movies for all reasons except maybe for the audience. Here tonight, God bless 'em, they weren't being ripped off. They were being asked. In a nine-hundred-seat movie house, the audience was going to make the producers shit just a little bit that night. If it was excellent, it was just all right. If it was just all right, it was bad. They didn't like the people, they didn't like the clothes, they didn't like the story, they didn't like the prose. The picture finished, the executives would hover underneath the marquee outside of the theater in front of the four black limousines pulled up alongside of the street. Don't think for a minute those executives didn't love this kind of an evening. Pulling up in a black car, jumping out, sitting in, looking wise and noble and profound. The arbiters of American taste and mores and culture. Hey, Eddie, look at the tits on that kid. Go on, Fred, ask her. Maybe she wants to be in pictures. You don't know. Go on, do like I tell ya. There these men would stand solemn-faced, talking among themselves while some fifteen-year-old kid with pimples, ready to burst, comes out and with his greasy hands writes on your questionnaire, It was a lousy, fucking movie. That hurt. Pimples folded it neatly and handed it politely to the son of a producer. The men took their coveted droppings, shoveled themselves into the cars, and split. Somehow the Kid survived all of that. The Kid found himself as hot as they get in the movie business. He bought a Yamaha 350; pulling up those canyon roads at forty and fifty was no mean trick. He rented a small house in the Beverly Hills area, high, over-looking the basin. He bought the biggest Chrysler they made and drove it every now and then. He had a maid twice a week. Then Perry Rose called him.

Aces Again

1953

"Dear Kid. I saw you in this here movie the other day in Kansas City, Missouri. You sure growed up to be a fine looking boy. The minute you came on and asked that girl if she was the new school marm, I knew it was you. You sure was a sight for sore eyes. I always liked you, Kid, and I'm glad you're doin' good. I think back on them days with your Pa and you, runnin' up and down the river. They're over now. I've been sick. I'm in a hospital outside of Wichita, about thirty-five miles south in Pottsville. If this letter gets to you, here's my telephone number. I wish you would call me. I got something for you. Your friend from the good old days, Harry Ace Slaughter."

It was written in simple hand. In his excitement, Ace forgot to write the telephone number down. But the letter was sent with the address of the home on the envelope. He called information and had the number ten minutes later.

Tell Ace Slaughter it's long distance from Hollywood for him, he heard the voice on the other end of the phone say. Harry Slaughter. Ace. Friend of my youth, a voice from another world.

"Ya sound good, Kid, how ya been?"

"Oh, swell, Ace. Been working here in California. Got out of the Marines. Been hanging around here ever since. Got to work in a couple of pictures."

"Man, it sure was nice to see ya in that picture. You've growed so tall. Look just like your father. The minute you stepped on the screen. I knew it was you. There he was, Maxwell Cody. Wow. Kid, I'm glad for ya. Ya happy?"

"Things are just fine, Harry, just fine. I got a lead in a

picture called *The Preacher's Son*. That picture ain't out yet and I'm gonna be in Vicksburg in about a week to do a picture called *Hanging*."

"Sure would like to see ya, Kid. I got somethin' for ya. It's a miracle that I run across ya now 'cause I didn't know what to do. I guess I would have found you eventually. I didn't know whether you went into the service or not, but I was gonna check the different services and see if they had anyone listed by the name of Andrew Cody. You gonna be down here, you say, in about a week?"

"That's right, Harry."

"Well, it'll wait till then. You know I'm not too far from where Vicksburg is, you know."

"I know, Harry. I remember Mississippi real good. I'm gonna be able to get me a couple of days off on the location. Suppose I try to get up to the neck of the woods where you are. If I don't, maybe you can join me down on the location."

"That's where Max is buried, you know, outside of Vicksburg. Broken Jaw. Do you remember?"

"I remember."

"Sure miss that crazy son of a gun. I've missed him a lot these years."

"What's ailing ya, Harry?"

"Just getting old, and nobody to care about. That's about the size of it. Soon as you get to Vicksburg, you call me, hear?"

"The minute I get in. I look forward to seein' ya."

"I gotta go now. I talked a good-looking nurse here into giving me an enema."

"See ya, Harry."

"So long, Kid."

"Mr. Pearlstein, I'd like to get to Vicksburg about four days before the company arrives. I got a few family chores I'd like to do."

"You got folks down around there?"

"I did, and I got a friend I wanna see."

"Well, go ahead, Kid. Miss Ornstein will give you your plane ticket in advance. Art is going as associate producer this time."

"Great," said the Kid.

"He'll tell you where to meet the company. Just be sure

you're there by Sunday. We start shooting on Monday."
"Right, Mr. Pearlstein, thanks."

It was a Monday. He had to close up his house and put
his bike and car away. He called Linda and said he
would see her when he got back. Still had that Stetson,
new denim suit, nice pair of shiny brown boots, and a
new zippered bag that he had bought to carry a few of his
holdings. He got down to the airport. Got in the belly of
big iron bird and found himself flying to Chicago. He got
to Chicago at two-thirty in the afternoon. He was heading for Vicksburg but just on a hunch decided he would
go to Wichita. Went to a newsreel theater near the airport. Then found himself in a DC-3 arriving in Wichita at
six fifty-five. The plane circled Wichita. As it did, its
flight plan brought it over part of Slim's ranch. The Kid
looked down and smiled. Wow, is Slim gonna be surprised. If he could find him. The DC-3 touched down,
came to a stop, and the Kid was out with his luggage
and a rental Ford in twenty-five minutes. He drove out of
Wichita. Nothing had changed in this cattle city. It was
as if he hadn't been gone at all. He wondered if the
Stewarts were still around. Well, he'd know soon enough.
He couldn't tell much at night, driving out to the Hargrove
spread. Fences looked up to date. The first sign of any
change occurred when he drove up to the big wooden
gate that said, Hargrove Ranch. Written across the mailbox
in neat print was N. Hargrove. The last time he'd been
there it was G. Hargrove. It looked as if Gregory Hargrove
was in that big corral in the sky. He could see the house
from the road. Some lights were on. He opened the gate.
Drove in. Stopped. Closed the gate behind him and drove
up to the front of the house. As his car came driving
up, the occupants had no idea who he was and so they
moseyed out onto the porch. No one expected anybody
that time of the night anymore. He pulled up. One was a
ranch hand named Harvey Gallagher. He had a two-year-
old boy's hand in one hand and a loaded shotgun in the
other. The boy had dark hair and even in that semidarkness the Kid could see a strong resemblance between
him and his friend Slim. He felt a certain tension begin
to leave him as he knew that maybe Slim was okay. He
got out of the car and walked up to the porch. Two dogs

came sniffing and barking up at him. Gallagher shushed them.

"Kin I help ya?"

"I'm lookin' for Slim Hargrove."

No one called Mr. Hargrove Slim anymore except if you had known him when he was a kid. Gallagher looked closer.

"Are you that orphan kid Mr. Hargrove used to hang with back years ago?"

"Right. I'm Kid Cody."

"Hell, yeah. I remember. And I seen ya in a picture, too. Well, come on in. Mr. Hargrove'll be sure glad to see ya."

Screen door opened and the wood door opened in. The Kid walked in and there at the other end of the long hallway in the dimly lit corridor sitting in a chrome wheelchair was Nelson "Slim" Hargrove.

"Hey, Slim."

"Kid . . . It's the Kid. Sure good to see ya. Come on in."

Slim had married a poor local girl named Allison Smith, well-educated, well-mannered woman. She was about twenty-five. Slim hadn't changed at all except the upper portion of his body was just stockier and stronger, and in comparison his legs looked even thinner than he had remembered them.

"You see my boy outside? That was Daniel. Hey, Mike, where are you?" Slim yelled.

He heard a child's footsteps come hustling down the stairs and there was Michael, two years older than his brother. Both dark-haired, both looking like Slim. A big smile on his face. He embraced Mike.

"This is your daddy's friend. They call him the Kid. He's a cowboy and works in the movies."

"You seen any of my pictures yet?" he asked Slim.

"Hell, yes. Saw you in that Western with that girl where you said . . ." He and the Kid read the line together . . . "You must be the new schoolmarm."

"You're okay, Cody, okay. Have ya eaten?"

"Not yet."

"Well, come on."

Slim wheeled his chair around and effortlessly rolled it into the dining room. The family had finished eating but almost by magic there was a setting at the table, and before you knew it the Kid was eating prime rib, mashed potatoes, some beer, a salad, a beautiful sponge-cake, and some milk.

Allison was a very beautiful woman, solemn and very respectful of Slim and his household. Slim was quite content now with his two boys growing up and maybe hoping to have two or three more. Maybe that would help him forget that he was a cripple. Maybe through his children he could see himself travel all over this world and do all the things he had dreamed of all these years. They talked of days gone by and days to come. And the Kid fell asleep at eleven-thirty that night in the room where he used to sit around with Slim. The very room where Slim gave him them dirty pictures. In the morning just before dawn he heard the wheelchair coming down the hallway, stop at his room, and heard somebody rap gently. The Kid said, Come in, Slim. Slim opened the door and rolled in. He was in pajamas and rolled right up to the bed. The faintest hint that the day was coming could be seen in the hills. The Kid didn't put on his bed lamp and these two men, one lying, one sitting, one crippled, and one not, sat waiting for the dawn to come up.

"How goes it?"

"Okay."

"Slim, I still miss my pa. Wherever I go, I half expect to see him coming around the corner. I think of him a lot and he gives me a lot of courage. California is nice. Beautiful girls. Climate sure nice. One of these days you and Allison gotta come and visit me out there. Lots of roads. Lots of cars. Lots of space. I was in the Marines. I don't know, there were a lot of times when I wanted to write ya, Slim. But I just didn't. Please forgive me."

"I wish you would have, Kid. It would've meant a lot to me. Knowing where you was and what you were doin'. I was stuck here. Couldn't pull out. I thought you was my friend."

In the darkness, the Kid started to cry. How thoughtless he had been, how selfish, how only interested in his own self. Never thinking of anyone but himself. Or if he did, never doing anything about it. Slim knew how the Kid felt. He reached out, touched the Kid's arm, and said:

"That's okay, Kid. We're still pals. We'll always be, you and I. You got me laid and that's more than a lot of people in this world have ever done for me. With the exception, maybe, of Allison."

They both laughed.

"My pa died soon after you left. He was acting funny in those days. He never drank and he never smoked, you know. But there was somethin' eatin' his guts. He'd run off and show up a few days later. We'd never know where he went. Made everybody nervous. He died in an automobile crash. They said he had been drinkin'. But I knew my daddy. He didn't drink. Anguish drove him into that bridge. Nothin' else, just anguish. I think he blamed himself for me being a cripple. I sold a thousand acres just a year and a half ago. Made me over two hundred thousand dollars in that sale. You see, Kid, I'm doin' pretty good."

It was getting lighter.

"Funny, the first time Allison ever saw me was the time that preacher tried to make me walk. We got to know each other the next year and everybody, including me, felt she only went with me because she was sorry for me. Or, maybe needed the money. I don't know. How could I know? I was just a kid then. I really treated her like dirt. A lot of studs around town were looking to knock her off, but she hung in there with me. Married six years ago. She's a fine woman and I love her. And I'm lucky. And I'm feelin' good. And you wanna know what makes me feel better than anything?"

"What's that?"

"I can get a hard-on. That's a lot more than a lot of guys around here can do."

The sun was creeping over them low hills now.

"What was the Marines like?"

"Okay. Saw a lot and did a lot. Ended up in the South Pacific. Got out in San Diego. Just hung around Los Angeles last four, five years. I'm on my way to Vicksburg. I'm doing a picture there next Monday."

"Well, shit, man, you can hang in here for a while."

"I don't think so, Slim. I got a couple of errands I gotta do. A friend of my pa's is in a hospital in Pottsville and I wanna find out where my ma is buried. My pa's in Vicksburg. I'm gonna go see Harry Slaughter. He used to gamble with my dad. Maybe this morning. Thought I'd leave my gear here and just drive down. I wanna ask him about my pa."

"When you fixin' to go?"

"Well, as soon as the sun gets a bit higher, thought I'd have somethin' to eat and just kind of slide down and see the Ace."

He was shaved, dressed, and having breakfast with the family, with Michael and Daniel ranging all over his frame, riding his shoulder, smiling and giggling around him. He was in his car and on his way to Pottsville at quarter to eight. He drove west into Wichita, took State Highway 307, heading south. Sixty-three miles later he was pulling into the outskirts of Pottsville. He asked a gasoline station attendant where the Pottsville Home for the Aged was. Traveled a mile south, then due east, turned, and went south. He stopped at a drugstore and bought a box of cigars and three or four girlie magazines that the store vendor was trying to hide behind the *Cosmopolitan* magazine rack for fear some of his customers would think he was a dirty old man. There was Harry sitting on a bus bench outside the main grounds of the hospital. Just waiting for the Kid. He knew he would be coming around one of these mornings. After breakfast he had dressed and decided to wait out there. Two strong crease lines came down from under his eyes to the jawline. His skin was dried out and made him look a lot older than he was. He still had a good head of hair but it was all white now. And his body was frailer than the Kid remembered it. But he'd never forget them hands. Those strong, powerful poker-dealing hands that could palm a deck if he wanted them to. He pulled up across the street. Got out and walked up the street toward Harry. Harry kind of turned around and looked and here come that good-lookin' dude in a denim suit, brown boots, and a white Stetson hat, open white shirt, smilin'.

"Shit, Kid," he said, "you're lookin' good."

They never went into the hospital. He sat on that bench for an hour with Harry.

"Your pa could be mean. I saw him slap a girl once 'cause she took twenty dollars instead of ten that he said she could have. And he could be generous. He once got his shoes shined by this little black kid and he gave him five dollars. And I said, 'What are you givin' that nigger five dollars for?' and he said, 'He could use it more than I could.' Strange fella, your dad. I sure liked him. Had a lot of style, he did. Knew a lot, too. The thing I liked most about your dad was the way he looked at me. His eyes smiling. I used to tell him, you gotta take me more serious, Max. But he didn't. After your ma died, I don't think he took anything serious."

"Whatcha doin' here, Harry?"

"Oh, I got a bum ticker. I had a seizure just about five weeks ago. I don't play much anymore. I got a little kip somewhere. Not much, but enough. Come on, let's get outta here. Take me for a ride, Kid, will ya?"

"Sure."

"Before you do, I wanna get something from my room first. I'll meet ya out here. Thanks for these," he said, and left with the cigars and magazines.

Harry kind of shuffled up the steps leading to this private hospital. The Kid watched him go. He looked the same except he'd shrunk all over. He was just a little smaller but still a fine-looking man. The Kid went and got his car and drove it in front of the hospital so Harry wouldn't have to walk too far. When Harry came out of the hospital, he smiled, appreciating that little gesture of friendship. He opened the door and climbed in.

"Come on, Kid. I know a nice place."

They drove about a mile to a lake. Both men got out and walked to a park bench with chairs that was used by the chess players in the neighborhood or by families out on a picnic. Harry pulled an envelope out of his pocket and handed it to the Kid. There was a letter and a key. The letter was addressed to the Kid. His hand started to sweat. He could feel his tongue at the base of his mouth get dry. He swallowed to give himself a little more moisture. It was from his father.

"Dear Andrew. I wanted you to have this after you had grown up. Life's uncertain and improbable. I know no way of organizing it. You're a fine boy and I love you. Perhaps when you read this letter, we'll be sitting somewhere together, smiling and joking with each other. Perhaps I'll be dead or perhaps you will. If we're both gone, there'll be nothing left but this letter. Here's a key to a safety deposit box and all the papers necessary for you to get in. It's at the Wichita Federal Bank. Go pick it up, Kid. I hope you're a man when you read this. As I'm writing this, you're sleeping in the bed twelve feet from me. You look nice. I love you, Andrew, and I wish I could give you more. But I have nothing more to give you than just my presence. I thought you'd like to know that you had apple pie and vanilla ice cream tonight for dessert. You always loved that dessert. And I made love to a beautiful woman. Your mother is buried in Cole's Hill on the west side of Wichita. Grave registration number 0976. We're leaving at six in the morning for Vicksburg, you and me. After that, you and me are going to go down to New Orleans and do some fishing and swimming. My son in the future, that's what my son and I in the past will do this coming week. Dear Andrew, never pull on an inside straight. Ha, ha. Your father. Maxwell Boyd Cody."

The Kid got up from the table, walked to the lake's edge, and cried. He drove Harry back to the hospital. Took him in. Met the nurse that gave enemas. She was good-looking. Seemed ready to give the Kid an enema. She was a good-looking piece and she was going up to Wichita that afternoon and he'd drive her up. He gave her Slim's telephone number to call him when she finished in town. He embraced Ace, Ace hugged Enema, said good-by, and told him he'd be in touch. He was up in Wichita by eleven-fifteen, left Enema off, and went to the bank. They checked the papers he had with him. All seemed in order. He had his Marine discharge papers with him, his driver's license, and whatever else was necessary for them to give him the safety deposit box that his father had kept for him. He found eighty-seven thousand dollars in cash in that box, a dozen or so photographs of his mother, his father, and himself, in some unnamed forests by some unnamed bridges, in some unnamed houses. The money was in a envelope and attached to it with a paper clip was a small memo page and on it, Don't spend it all in one place. Your dad. He took the money out. Went back to Slim's. Got a call from Agnes, the enema queen, at five. Picked her up in town at the bus stop at five-fifteen.

Had her fed, washed, and bedded by ten-fifteen in the Wichita Hotel.

She was big and wholesome, that enema queen, and they did it to each other all night long. At seven-thirty the next morning, he was in his car, stopped off at Slim's, told him he was going to visit his ma's grave and would be back later. At ten-twenty, he was sitting alongside of her. She, six feet below him. The short red flowers that were growing on her grave looked like her and almost felt like her. He sat there an hour, recollecting nothing, just letting the vibrations of his mother try to reach him, but nothing did. He vaguely remembered this sweet woman and vaguely cried for her. He got up, looked at the hills surrounding the place, turned his back, and walked down the slope. He wouldn't be coming to these parts again. Allison thought that maybe the Kid ought to move his father and bury him next to his mother. But the Kid didn't like that idea. They were separated by maybe seven hundred miles, but that was okay. He wouldn't want to disturb them. He bid farewell to Slim, Allison, the two boys, and Gallagher on Thursday morning. He was in Vicksburg Thursday night. Friday morning found him standing looking at his father's grave. It hadn't been kept as well as he would have liked. He went into the director of the cemetery's office and asked why his father's grave was weeded over. The man was very apologetic and said he would see to it from now on that the grave was kept good and clean. The Kid said he hoped so. He gave him a check for twenty-five bucks and his address in California. The Kid was all cried out. He looked at his father's burial spot with a detached and remote sense. Enough with the dead, he thought. On with the living.

Lynn

Lynn had always been a beautiful child. The recollections she had had, as a child, hardly had made any impression upon her. She always lived for the present. She forgot names quickly and old friends as well. She was like a yacht sailing up a calm and quiet river, smooth and flat, reaching into infinity in front of her and, behind, turbulence and commotion, leaving countless never-ending waves as she proceeded through life. Her schooling was choppy and short and not very profound while she was growing up in Gary, Indiana. The daughter of a man who drank a lot, and couldn't have cared less about anything, and certainly not his daughter. Her mother, on the other hand, sought solace in the Book of the Lord. Went to revival meetings, Billy Graham meetings, Reverend Shmearcase meetings. Always searching for the good Lord's little gifts that he laid upon people as he went along, curing illness, pain, and anguish. Her mother's name was Shirley and that's about all she could remember about where her mother came from and what kind of an early life she had had.

Lynn moved from Gary to Chicago, one cold winter's night. She arrived on a Greyhound bus, and had the name of a friend who had gone to Chicago two years earlier to try to make a life for herself. She called her. Came by. Stayed with her for a few days until she got a job working as a ticket seller in a movie house. Sitting in that glass booth out in the middle of an empty street on those cold and wintry nights in Chicago. Irving Burkett saw her there for the first time. He thought it was fate. She thought it was cold. He had been walking by with Paul Allistair-Carter, his new administrative aide in the film distributing company that Irving, or Mr. Burkett, was the head of and son of the founder. He owned the theater where this beautiful creature from Gary, Indiana, sat in that glass box. As soon as he got to his office he called and found out what her name was, social security number, and just about everything else he could about her. He came down to the theater now more than he used to.

"Oh. Good afternoon, Mr. Burkett. Surprised to see you here."

"Why's that, Jimmie?"

Jimmie was the local manager. Jimmie Ellis, young man from around Chicago, dissatisfied and horny. Didn't make enough money and didn't get enough fucking. It didn't take Jimmie long to realize that Burkett had hot nuts for the girl in that glass box. Lynn saw an opportunity. This Burkett chap was gentle and kind enough. And Jimmie ended up as Paul Allistair-Carter's assistant with a fifty-buck raise.

"I was wondering, Lynn, perhaps you would join me for dinner tomorrow night."

"That would be nice."

"Please call me Irving."

"Please call me Lynn."

And they did.

"I love it. The apartment's beautiful. Look at the view. Irving, please! Wow—all of Lake Michigan."

Irving came over and put his arm around her waist and both of them looked out the window of this apartment in this building along the lake, fourteen stories up, unfurnished. It was beautiful. This was his first affair, so please be kind.

Burkett flew to the coast a few times and took Lynn with him. She liked it and he liked her a lot then. He spoke to Pearlstein and then the next thing you know, Lynn-you-know-who had a seven-year you-know-what with six six-month options starting at a hundred bucks a week plus the six she got from Burkett to maintain a nice *pied-à-terre* somewhere in the hills of Hollywood. Well, there she was in Hollywood outfitted and ready to go. Classes here, classes there, evening classes everywhere. She was beautiful, Lynn was. Her shoulders down, her neck long. She was perfection. Stately and tall. She was soft yet firm. Her skin was fair with hardly a blemish anywhere. Andrew had just broken for lunch and was trying to beat all the sets down to the commissary, when he came upon this beauty called Lynn. She had just fin-

ished one of her classes with Berger. Andrew by that
time had graduated from that kind of nonsense. He eyed
her fast, checked her up and down, and saw that she was,
in fact, new to the studio. If he didn't move quickly every
stud on the lot would be staking a claim.

"I'm not really in the mail room. It looks like I work
here but I don't. You see, I'm really the son of the son of
the president. The producer gets all the information
that he needs from me."

"Actually I work in the production department but you
see, I, uh, am in charge of the production. Right. What
are you doin' for dinner tonight?"

"Oh yeah, really, I've directed a lot of films, really.
Uh-huh. Yes, well, I'm on the set really most of the time
as an observer. You see they use my abilities. Every now
and then the director will check with me. You'll notice
now and then he looks at me. Yeah, right. Well, technical-
ly what they call me is the associate producer to the associate."

"I don't know who's handling ya. But whoever's doing
it is doing a lousy job. Here you are and no one's ever
heard of ya."

That, coupled with Berger's bullshit, kept Lynn busy as
ever trying to figure out who was saying what to who
about where. Andrew moved true and fast, right to the
heart, no nonsense. That comes from experience and an
almost constant erection.

"Excuse me, my name's Andrew Cody. Yours?"

"Oh, wow. I'm Lynn."

They both smiled. She blushed. He moved a shade closer. This time he took off his Stetson.

"You looked lost and alone and I thought I'd help you
out."

"Thanks. You're the first movie actor, star, I guess."

"Oh well, I guess I am a star but not really big yet but
I'm moving toward that way."

"Oh, you are, Mr. Cody."

"Please, call me Andrew. You can call me Andy, if you
like. Even call me the Kid if you want. Call me anything
but please, just call me."

She laughed.

"Where you going?"

"Well, I had some time off before my dancing class and

I thought I'd maybe go to the commissary and have some tea, or—"

"Come on, kid, I'm takin' ya for some apple pie and milk. Or anythin' else you're hankerin' for."

With that he took her right elbow and started walking toward the commissary, nestled between two huge cypress trees down a small path, past the newsstand and the barbershop, in through a little lobby with the cash booth where you paid your Rainbow Room bill. Beyond it were tables and chairs of the unreserved section of the room and there in the middle was a high bar where you could have breakfast and lunch and read the trades and quiver and quake. Everybody was vying for a little action in those days. Any commotion was a good commotion. You don't locomote, you don't note.

"Come on," he said, "we'll sit in the corner in the Rainbow Room."

There was a table for two that sat in the far corner of this large room. It got its light from a large, circular window that had potted plants arranged very nicely around it outside the building. When you looked out you didn't see the studio lot or any of its artifacts, only above it and the blue sky. Around noon in the summertime when there was no haze or any kind of clouds, fog, or anything else, the sun's rays would bounce off some of the slanted roofs and windows and reflect into the room, broken up enough to make rainbows. One never knew in what part of the room they would hit, but if they hit you, it was better than the lead in Louella Parsons' column. She didn't tell Andy about Burkett in the beginning.

"I've got to go tonight, Andy."

"Why? You're always duckin' off lately at these odd times."

"Now, don't be unfair. We've been seeing an awful lot of each other. But tonight I've got to go someplace."

"Come on, baby. I had us clocked out for tonight for a screening at Freddie's and then on to the Crackerjack."

"Andrew, I can't."

This was something he couldn't understand. He was getting angry. He had been angry before and hurt before and left alone before. But I don't want to be lonely tonight. He took it the best he could. He acquiesced, of course, and left her up at the house. At some point he wanted to follow her but, shit, that would only tear his insides out even more. So, let it be, boy, let it be. He wouldn't call her for a day or two and then by accident they'd run across each other on the lot.

"Hi. Did ya get the part?"

"No, I didn't. They wanted someone taller."

"Who told you that?"

"The casting director."

"I know this guy, Kevin, I could ask him. After all he's the producer of the picture."

"Please, Andy, don't. I don't want it that way."

"Okay. What are ya doin' tonight?"

"What would you like to do, Andrew?"

He sighed. A knot released in his stomach. He smiled at two wranglers who were walking by on their way to the commissary. He put his arm around her and looked into those sweet blue eyes of hers.

"Nothin', baby, nothin'. I just wanna be with you."

It looked like he was sleeping, but he wasn't. He was watching her. She was taking a shower in an open stall, in a room that was conceived for a shower, with basins on the side. The door was far enough away so that no water ever splashed outside of the bathroom into the bedroom. It was all marble and it was hers. She knew he was awake. They both played the game. Both played the images of their minds, the desires of their fantasies, the slivers of someone else observing without really being there. She was pure and clean, he thought. Andrew got used to it but never over it. His heart would pound. He'd get a lump in his throat. He'd break out in a sweat. A nude woman melted him. Especially if they didn't know he was looking. He didn't like the daylight or too much light in seeing a woman. He liked looking at them in soft, diffused light. He liked chiffon, soft, caressing chiffon. He peeked at Lynn again in her bathroom. She killed him dead with her beauty, her womanly beauty. He wanted to be her then, caressing herself, anointing herself. He would have loved to be her then, to feel herself, to look at herself. She was lucky to be her, he thought. Shheeet, man—Slim, Max, anybody. If you could see what I see now. Andrew felt his eyes could come from the ecstasy of her being. Blind, he would have sensed her beauty. What Andrew didn't know then was that her youth was half the battle won. That during those early years at the bursting of the bud even ugliness was beautiful. So long ago, fleeting and gone in an instant. She had a joy then, naïve and vulnerable. Her hair auburn and unruly, nestling her head as if it were a crown, strands of it bursting in all directions. Smacks of it curling down and up and around. Her eyebrows arched like a lopsided bow, the same color as the hair on her head but not so intense. Taut, ivory-toned skin outlined her beautiful blue eyes that were clustered by her long and curly and thick lashes that always needed shaping. Her nose sat exactly where it should, complementing her eyes by being straight and gentle. Her lips were another story, sensuous and bawdy, full and tender to the touch. Her chin ended her face gracefully with a hint of a cleft. A long neck molded to her exquisite shoulders. Her breasts rose high and mighty with nipples the color of the palest rose. Beneath those glories rested a flat but shapely abdomen nestled between her welcoming hips. Her mound protruding a shade in front of her, auburn in color as well. Her bottom tight and curved like a cello's curve. The legs below were as well proportioned as could be. Her feet, perhaps a bit small for her height. She stood five feet seven and a half inches and she could cook like Mama Verde on Saturday night. The only flaw she had, if you want to call it a flaw, was that she was a pushover.

Why not? He'd have somebody to come back to every night, take on locations, go to parties and premières with. There must be a lot you're missing by being by yourself.

He's cute. I could go for him but I won't. He's going to be nothing but grief. But he sure is cute.

"Oh, Lynn, dear."

She had turned off the water by now and was drying herself. Blinds were pulled back and their view through the window was through a canyon, a remote and empty canyon, with beautiful shrubbery, green, moist, and lush, growing between them and infinity. She brought a warm, wet towel in and bathed him. They kissed. She brought a bowl of guavas from the table that rested near the bed, put it between them on the bed, and sat cross-legged and gave herself and the Kid a guava apiece.

"Andrew, I'm going to tell you something. Mr. Burkett, who is a distributor out of Chicago, and a very good friend of Mr. Pearlstein, is my—my patron."

The Kid was halfway through the guava when "patron" hit him. He tried to cool it and not look too surprised. Swallowed that chunk of guava. As delicious as it was it slid down heavy.

"What do you mean by patron?"

"Well, it's because I know him that I got to be under contract to the studio from back East. And you see when he comes to town I somehow feel I'm more or less obligated to—er."

"You mean to see him."

"Well, yes, yes. Certainly to see him, yes."

"And what—what do you mean?"

"Well, er—"

"Are you tellin' me that you're nothing but a whore?" Lynn flashed on him, hard and true.

"And you, kind sir, how does your whoredom manifest itself?"

"I'm sorry, Lynn, I didn't—"

"Forget it."

They sat silently for a long time. He touched her leg. She didn't move or respond. He moved the fruit away and tried to kiss her. She just sat there looking out the long window to nowhere.

"I'm sorry, my love, I'll take whatever I can of you. Let me be with you when you want me to be with you. I won't ask any more questions and I won't call you any more names."

She looked at him, her eyes full of tears.

"Promise?"

"I'm sorry, Lynn. I'm as lonely as you are."

He took her in his arms and they made love among the guavas.

Andrew

1956

"I wouldn't wanna break your pretty face, you cock-sucker."

The pain was sharp and clear. A searing surge through his guts, reaching as high as his heart. His arms held back by some karate expert. He was being slashed by this blond, pink-faced kid, maybe the same age as the Kid. The next thing he knew, he was face down in Coldwater Canyon with his head, left shoulder, arm, and leg in the gutter. The rest of him overlapped on the sidewalk. By the time the Kid stumbled onto his feet, twelve cars had passed by. And now that the people in the cars realized that he wasn't a stiff, they were more inclined to stop.

"You all right?"

"I'm okay . . . yeah fine . . . thanks."

The Kid tried to hide himself so he wouldn't be recognized. If he had been recognized, it would have been all over town in the morning. The Kid would give them the stories they wanted to hear but there was a portion of his life that he kept to himself, that no one shared. No one. The less press the better. He felt all right, he thought. Except how the fuck did he get here? He had no idea what time it was, he didn't carry a timepiece, and for a few minutes there he didn't know where he came from. Those minutes in limbo were unique. Foot-loose and fancy-free, I love to wander. I got the gypsy in my soul. Ace. That was the first sound or image he thought of that brought him any peace. Why am I all of a sudden worried about Ace, or where I came from, or who I was? What difference does it make? He was cooling it now. Out of sight, out of mind. High again, looking at himself from high. I mean what more did you want out of life than to be able to cool it every now and then?

He straightened up and started to hitch down Coldwater Canyon. A young couple, a boy and a girl, picked him up with no questions asked and dropped him off at the corner where the Beverly Hills Hotel stood. There was no answer at his house and the service told him there were no calls. He told the service that if the Ace called him, he was on his way up to the ranch house.

The Kid took a cab and had the cab park a half block from his house. He walked up cautiously to where his house sat. He could see a car parked about a hundred feet away. The lights were out and everything seemed normal, but the Kid knew somebody was around. There were always a lot of bird and animal sounds around his pad. He had about three and a half acres behind his house that ranged down to a slope. He had it full of fruit trees, and all the animals in the neighborhood would congregate there for breakfast, lunch, and dinner, night and day. Birds, rabbits, muskrats, rats, and crickets. If you could quiet all that wildlife noise around you, then you had some bad vibrations because they would sense someone that they didn't know. He knew somebody was holed up in his ranch house waiting for him, just hoping he'd come walking through the front door, and that's just what the Kid did. He walked right up to the front door, put his key in the lock, and opened it wide. He pressed a button that turned on bright lights outside and bright lights inside. Suddenly you were at an indoor tennis match, hot and sweaty. It certainly surprised the two occupants of the room. They were standing about twelve feet apart. One six feet from the Kid, the other nine. The dark one needed a shave and had nicotine stains on his thumb and two fingers. The blond one needed a bath and a mouthwash. His breath was a mixture of Bourbon and burned onions. As the light went on, the Kid was fast, and while they took time to be surprised, he planned his strategy. As the look changed on the face of the first man, the Kid had him with a left and a right cross, folding him like some ox being slaughtered. The blond looked as if he was starting to reach for something but he didn't get far. The Kid spun and was at his throat. They both fell to the floor and before this blond guy could recover the Kid hit him with a right while he was still flat on his back. The Kid got up, went to the closet, and got a lasso. He threw it around the blond's head and pulled it tight around his neck.

"Keep it tight or I kick your balls off," the Kid said. He could feel the tension leave the room. He didn't seem as hard pressed as he did before. Even Blondie relaxed.

He held the end of the lasso. But what the fuck happened last night, or earlier, or whenever it was? Harry Ace Slaughter popped into his head.

"We got no beef with you," the blond one said. "Come on, man, untie me and let me be free."

The Kid walked up to the dark-haired man, looked down at him, reached in his coat, and came up with a .38. He was maybe thirty-five, lean, and mean, a coward. He stirred and opened his eyes.

"You know Harry Ace Slaughter?"

"No."

"He's six foot and gray-haired and wrinkle-faced and black."

"No, I don't."

"Comes out of Kansas."

"Don't know him."

"Wherever I was last night, he was with me. Then I'm dumped on Coldwater and you're here waiting. I reckon you're trying to tell me something. Well, I'm listening."

He walked to the bar and splashed water in his face.

"I'll tell you what. I'm gonna give you a much better chance than you gave me."

He aimed the .38 and said, Dump your wallets slow. They did and he picked them up. Blondie was packing a .38. He opened the .38 and took out the shells. Put them in an ashtray on the counter of the bar. He put the open gun on top of the bar as well. He snapped the lasso and it flipped off Blondie's head. The dark one dove at him. The Kid hit the darker-haired fellow hard enough to send him through the fucking window, which lucky for him was open. He hit the concrete resoundingly and that was that. The Kid turned his attention to number two. Blondie was using the rope as a whip. The blond belted him across the right cheek, putting him down. Followed by a vicious kick aimed straight for the Kid's teeth. The Kid turned his head just enough so that the shoe passed his cheek, but before that foot reached its full arc, the Kid was on his feet. He threw a left hook into Blondie's kidneys and Blondie went flying into the fireplace, grabbed a poker, and got to his feet. The Kid walked to the bar, took the .38 Colt, and put one shell into the chamber. He spun it, then aimed it at the blond one.

"Now, Blondie, talk."

Before the blond one could talk, the Kid pulled the trigger. Click.

"Oh, shit," the Kid said.

And the blond one did.

"My name is Terry Farraday. I live at 1832 Formosa Drive."

The phone rang. The Kid picked it up.

"It's Perry."

"Hey, how are ya?"

"Okay."

"What's going on?"

"Did you read the nominations?"

"Yeah, I saw 'em yesterday."

"Whatta ya think?"

"Bullshit," the Kid said. "They're just payoffs."

"I think I can get ya on as one of the presenters."

"Hold on, my other phone's ringing."

He put Perry on hold.

"Yup."

"You okay?"

"Yup. Where you at?"

"Randy's," said Ace.

"I'll see ya."

He pushed in on Perry.

"One of the presenters?"

"Not me, Perry."

"Never mind, Kid. I think somebody's got a contract out on you."

The Kid laughed. That Perry had a way of dramatizing everything.

"Perry, I gotta go now."

"Lila ain't gonna take what you done to her lying down."

"She'll take anything that's done to her lying down."

"You know what I mean."

"Yeah, I know what you mean."

"She told me that she was gonna ruin you in this town."

"I got a feeling that yenta's gotta be fixed again. Did you know, she's got a license that says Ms. Lila. It should read 'Ms. Take'!"

"Jesus, Kid, don't do anything you're gonna be sorry about."

"I won't."

"And Kid . . ."

"Yeah, Perry . . ."

"You got enough bimbos around town, don't fool with any jailbait."

"Now he tells me."

"I got a feeling that's the way they're gonna try to get to ya."

"Thanks, Perry."

"It's okay, Kid. I spoke to Lynn."

"Yeah . . ."

"She's bustin' up with Burkett."

The Kid was partly responsible. The Kid and Lynn were having dinner at Chasen's when in came Irving Burkett and his wife, Pearlstein and his. Pearlstein couldn't avoid seeing Lynn and the Kid. All six people in this classic Greek drama behaved admirably, except the Kid, who found himself giggling, like he did when he was doing that scene with that girl in his first picture. Irving Burkett loved Lynn. He never knew anybody that gave of herself so freely to him as she did. He knew he was paying for her career, but she knew it, too, and was appreciative. Always treated him like a gentleman. Never embarrassed him. And when they were alone together, she acquiesced to all his wishes and demands, which were very few. He seemed to need more affection than lovemaking. He saw life afresh and anew through her eyes, like windows to the future for him. She knew the latest songs, the latest records, the latest in-people, the latest out-people, the latest styles. And Irving Burkett liked that. He started out in Milwaukee, Wisconsin, and now Chicago. And who knows tomorrow? He didn't think there was any tomorrow for him. He was on his way to the grave. He could see it already. Children's weddings and brises. Brother's children's Bar Mitzvahs and marriages. Two weeks a year in the Bahamas. One week a year in

Miami. Four weeks a year, maybe more next year, for his Hollywood conferences and meetings, bim-bam, thank you, ma'am. Five social events of the year, black tie, twelve other affairs, dark suit, a dozen or so, casual attire, soirees, doing buffets to the boffos, to sneak previews, to some screenings. There was always a good funeral around somewhere. Now with Lynn leaving, he'd act a little heartbroken to his friend, Pearlstein, but don't let Bertha know. Anyway, he had his eye on another nofka he met while he was picking up a little bauble at Tiffany's for Lynn. She was a beauty, this Tiffany, and what was even better, she was his size. He was five six, balding, and forty-seven. Everything in his affairs were taken care of. If he went down the Coronary Corral the next day, everybody would be well taken care of. So fuck 'em, thought Irving Burkett.

Irving Burkett was willing to forget lovely Lynn, and hold no grudge against either Lynn or the Kid, but his wife had other plans. Later that night, unknown to their husbands, Miriam Burkett and Adele Pearlstein discussed Lynn and the Kid.

"Miriam, I've never heard you talk this way or cry like this. My dear, calm yourself, tell me what's happened."

"Oh, Adele, Irving's nofka, you know the one I liked so much? The girl out here in California, that girl we met last night at dinner, with that cowboy, what was his name, Tex?"

"No," she said, "Kid."

"Yes, Kid. Kid Cody. Well, I'm telling you something. He ain't kosher."

For a moment Adele said nothing.

"Well, don't you wanna know?"

"I'm waiting, Miriam. I'm waiting."

"Well, she was out in the open with that boy last night. When no one knew her, it was only a rumor. Now there is this girl out with this Texan, this cowboy, this Kid Kosher. Getting pictures taken yet. You told me a long time ago that it was good to be permissive. Give Irving a little more room, you said. I have and already he's trying to move out of it."

"Calmness, Miriam. What else do you have?"

"What else? Isn't that enough? Sandra has met this wonderful boy out here. The boy is smart, good-looking, rich, and they'll have a beautiful life together. The boy's family are bolabusses. Tough momzers who want none of this intrigue or scandal or innuendo. And if there was just a hint of something not kosher in a nonkosher house, they would have no part of it. Lila London already had a blind item in her column about some distributor out from Chi, Ciceroing it with La Lynn of California. And dear Lynn shouldn't be seen out in public with an ill-mannered cowboy with a lace bed in Hollywood."

This she didn't like. Adele Pearlstein didn't. What little she saw of the Kid, he was no putz. He was smart and tough and she knew he'd fight back, if he felt it was worth fighting for. She really had no way to determine that yet because she didn't know him that well. But she was sure of one thing, he wasn't about to give up his way of living one iota. She decided to go for the win, for the checkmate. She figured she had enough pieces. The Kid would be gotten out of the way and beat and maybe beat badly, and so would the girl. She could arrange it through different people who worked at the studio. People she had cultivated personally with loans and with help in all kinds of areas: tracing some family member in Europe, sending some money to a relative behind the Iron Curtain, paying for a forest of trees in Israel. She was responsible for a lot of people's well-being and she felt like Madame God. She got everything done, effortlessly and calmly. First she decided she would talk to him. She met him the next day at the Pearlstein house in Malibu.

"Please, Kid, leave this Lynn be. There's a lot of girls at the studio. Her patron, Mr. Burkett, is embarrassed. People are already implying that he was having an affair with her. You and I both know that's not true. The best thing for Lynn would be to be quiet now. You're a popular fellow. People like to see you, they like to take pictures of you. You're in the movie magazines all the time. You're doing wonderfully well. You were practically an orphan. Raised in foster homes and orphanages. You've worked hard to get where you are today. Why bother with Lynn? If no one hears about her now it'll be nice and quiet. Lila London won't say anything in the papers and rumors won't have it all around town. Burkett's daughter is going with a very fine young man and anything implicating her father could possibly hurt this union. Please, Andrew, I hope you don't mind my calling you by your, if you'll excuse the expression, Christian name."

"No, not at all, ma'am. Go right ahead."

"Thank you. And besides, excuse me, you shouldn't call yourself Kid Cody. Your name should be Andrew Cody. Kid is too goyish, and I mean it in the best possible way."

"Thank you, ma'am."

"Certainly, if you must take Lynn somewhere, take her where no one can see you. What I'm saying is, just give us a little hand now and who knows, in the future there may be an opportunity for me to do you some kind of a service. I could be a good friend, Andrew."

"Yes, Mrs. Pearlstein, I can see."

"And a terrible enemy. So, if you will excuse me, I'm off to a luncheon."

He was shown to the door by a Chinese houseman. There were some extraordinary Chinese pieces, authentic with restoration hardly necessary; huge vases and many other striking artifacts of China rested in this house. The house was air-conditioned and dehumidified. It was a perfect combination of living style and the sea.

When he got out, he climbed on his bike. Damn, that Mrs. Pearlstein sure knows how to live, he thought. What the hell. Of course I can help Mrs. Pearlstein. I'll just stay out of the big spots in town until this thing blows over.

He was all prepared to do that until a night later Lynn got the shit kicked out of her. Somebody busted her up. Not badly, but bad enough to cause some pain and give her second thoughts about everything. And the Kid wouldn't have found out about it had he not driven up to her house and tried to get into her apartment. He just had a hunch. He couldn't get her on the phone, so he decided to track her down. He knocked on the door, but there was no answer. He kept knocking and buzzing. He went down the stairs of the duplex around to the back. The bottom half of the building had been scooped out for automobiles and on the next floor were Lynn's three windows; the kitchen, sitting room, and bedroom. They were locked from the inside and closed by a ratchet that you spun and then latched. Her car was there so he figured she had to be home. He drove his convertible, which had been completely restored and looked beautiful, underneath the garage. He climbed onto the front window rim of the car, still a few inches short of where one half of the kitchen window was open, but enough room to get both his hands on the lip of the window ledge. One hand caught the window ledge as he leaped up, and just as well, too. His legs were splayed out and had he missed he'd have come down on that windshield between cock and balls first and that wouldn't have done him any good at all. He got both hands on the window ledge now, extended his left arm even deeper into the room. Found it just barely allowed his shoulder in and, holding the outside window ledge with his right hand, he forced his left shoulder against the half frame of the window. He could feel it give, but it was going to take a lot more doing than he had expected. It gave a little, he inched in a little. He kept doing it that way until he was able to force his whole body through. He was afraid that any loud racket such as snapping the hinge off would have caused more noise than he would have wished.

He came upon her immediately, half moaning, her face white. He lifted her up. He was relieved, she was bruised but okay. It had happened maybe just ten, twelve, fifteen minutes ago. She remembered someone whispering, Cunt . . . now cool it. Then an erection between her ass. That's about all she could remember. The pain in her jaw wasn't as bad as the fact that someone had such easy access to her and that she had fallen into the trap and allowed this to happen. How foolish. The Kid lifted her and carried her to her bedroom. Now, Mrs. Adele Pearlstein, you got two pawns. Lynn didn't hurt enough not to make love. So she and the Kid did. Two hours later she left for Vinnie's place. The Kid told her to be careful, stay off the phone.

The Kid couldn't figure it. When he left Malibu there was a kindly look on the face of Mrs. Pearlstein. Was this her way of putting a period at the end of all things in the past? Was it necessary to beat up this girl? They sure didn't think much of people if they thought they could be shoved around by a little beating and for no apparent reason.

What the Kid did not know was that Lila London was behind the beating, and not Adele Pearlstein. Lila thought she would do Mrs. Pearlstein a little extra favor and teach Lynn a lesson. Lila London seemed to think she had an open license to hurt anybody she felt needed to be hurt. And she had people who could get the job done.

One was a weight lifter and the other knew karate. Maybe Mrs. Pearlstein thought that roughing Lynn up was enough, but for Lila London it wasn't. She was going to get even. No tinhorn, asshole, out of the Midwest, with a Stetson and with the butch name, Kid Andrew Cody, was going to shove her around and certainly not after that humiliating experience at her beach place. She could never live down getting turned down and punched by some cowboy. God! She called B. Shrike Martin, formerly out of nowhere, whom she met at the Artists' and Models' Ball the year before, where he promised her undying devotion and service. His hard-on was at her disposal, and if she weren't available, please direct him in the direction of anyone she thought worthy. He would do anything and had, and would, and did.

His first test came when Lila London was banned from Empire Studios. It wasn't the press department's fault; the head of the studio, Mr. Henry Younger, ordered it. Then Mr. Younger's second son, Charles, got roughed up by a hooker and two ruffians. But the boy said these fellows were pulling their punches and he was hurt a lot less by what he felt were really tough guys. Four days later, Lila London walked back on the set of Errol Jones's latest picture and demanded to know why he had moved out of the house he shared with his wife, and had banned her from the set. She now had the okay of Mr. Younger himself to visit anytime she wished. And what else could Younger do? Errol Jones showed up at his studio a couple of times a year for a couple of pictures. That was maybe eleven weeks' work. What did he do the other forty-one weeks of the year? His studio was open fifty-two weeks. So fuck Errol. If he doesn't want her on the set, let him kick her off personally, which Errol did. His stud horse, Ranger, was standing under him when he first saw Lila London come on the set. He got off in cavalry fashion and told her if she wasn't off the set in a minute, they would turn that mare in heat loose on his stud horse, Ranger. And when Ranger had the biggest hard-on she ever saw, they'd fit her on it. As much as she'd like it, she felt she had to go anyway, and she turned around and walked off. She didn't want to take on Errol, and certainly not his horse, so she forgot the whole matter. But she felt she was now strong enough to take on the Kid. The only one the Kid really liked besides himself, Lila London knew, was that ugly old nigger the Kid made his houseguest. She spied them once as they were down at the health goods store buying supplies one day. She ducked down next to this press agent that was driving her around as she passed them. Black and white, like they were married. First this old drunk, then the Kid.

Meanwhile, back at the ranch the gutless partner was just regaining consciousness when the Kid gestured him over closer to the blond. He kind of half dragged himself back into the room and sat down in a chair. The blond one was sitting yoga style in the middle of the room, having by now found his true self.

"We don't know anything. We were called by B. Shrike Martin to do you up. We're gettin' five hundred apiece. I swear to ya if I figured it was gonna be as heavy duty as this, I'd never done it. I'm not prepared to hurt anybody bad. Neither is my partner. We're just lookin' to make a little money."

The Kid had gone through both their wallets, and both were well documented. The Kid threw them back their money, but kept all their cards.

"If anything ever happens to me, all these papers go to the police with a note from me. Get up."

The two men got up. He gestured them toward the front door and the Kid walked them out of his house. He could see that a car was still there. He figured it was their car. As they stepped off his front step, he punched the blond one right across the mouth and sent him sprawling.

"Now don't you two cocksuckers ever come near me again, 'cause if I see you anywhere even by accident, I'll embarrass ya. So flee."

He waited in the shadow of his door, with Blondie's pistol in his hand, with the street light glancing in under the portico and lighting the lower portion of the Kid's body and his hand holding the gun. As the two men drew alongside the house on their way down the hill in their car, the Kid raised the gun and pulled the trigger. Click. The guy driving almost fainted and off they went into the night, never to be seen in that neck of the woods again.

Kid Cody

1958

The Kid drove onto the lot at 7:45 in his Buick to start his new picture, *Crimson*. He was ready to work at 9 A.M. Sally Tarlow showed up to work at 11 A.M., ready to shoot at 2:25. It was the first day of shooting. At 5:30 the same day, Pearlstein decided to give Solomon's star back to Solomon. Solomon's company was to receive twenty-five per cent of distributor's fees, thirty-five per cent of the receipts of the film *Crimson*, and $500,000 of which Sally Tarlow, under contract, would receive $22,500 and a sore ass. Obviously, if Solomon couldn't keep his star in line, then how could he expect Pearlstein to do it? But he brought to the pot Kid Andrew Cody and maybe if the Kid was turned loose on Sally, maybe he could calm her down. Sally was mean and bitchy and unhappy and looking for a fight. She thought she'd found her match in the Kid.

"Would someone ask the cowboy to get on his mark so that they can light me properly for this fucking shot?" delicate Sally from Tumbledown Valley bellowed on that morning of the first day of shooting.

Chuck Watkins could feel his ass tighten up. There was absolutely nothing he could do with her. He tried on two attempts to see her before the picture started. As the director he wanted to at least introduce himself. Next thing he knew it was Monday morning, he had never met her, and there he was at nine o'clock waiting for Madame to arrive, taut, tight, and nauseous. By the time they got their one and only shot for the day, it was 5:10. They had three and a half pages to shoot and somehow they ended up with only one big blazing closeup of Sally Tarlow looking into the Kid's eyes. To heighten the effect, they had the Kid standing on four-inch risers, the camera precariously balanced over his right shoulder shooting almost directly to the ground with Sally's face pulled tight from looking up. Beautiful. All of those imagined ugly lines that she thought were bursting from her face revealing to the world her depravity. She couldn't take this getting old, she couldn't take it at all, and she was going to get even with somebody.

"Cut, that's a print. It's a wrap," the assistant said unceremoniously around the camera.

Kid was in Pearlstein's office twenty minutes later.

"Mr. Pearlstein, we ain't going to get this picture made. Not the picture you want to get made. It's going to murder everybody. I recommend, sir, you dump her and get someone else, or dump me."

"Give it another day," Pearlstein said.

"Time is not going to solve this problem, Mr. Pearlstein."

"Kid, please, if we can make this picture, let's make it. So if she's a pain in the ass, big deal. You don't have to live with her unless you want to. I could arrange it if you like, a few days perhaps down at the beach, a nice girl like her, good-looking, but maybe you shouldn't get involved, just show up each day. If anybody is going to break under the pressure, it's going to be her and that Solomon. So come on, Kid, let's not buckle under that bullshit; as they say in television, hang in there."

The game started at ten after nine Saturday night.

Solomon, Vinnie De Carlo, Kid Cody, Pearlstein, Julie Sparrow, and the Ace sat down to play. King Solomon decided the picture they were running in his projection room was shit, so to help the night move along a little bit easier he thought a poker game would do it. Vinnie De Carlo was going to play. He didn't like movies anyway. He'd just come off the road playing one-night stands all over the country. His nerves were raw and his pockets were loaded. Kid Cody was having an affair with Adele's sister's youngest daughter. Her name was Cherie. She was big mouthed, big assed, big titted. What he liked about her was when she finally quieted down after a couple of joints, she'd cuddle and want to be held and to hold. They were making love three or four times a day. The Kid's kip was improving all the time. He was picking up real estate holdings all around California, and a couple of quality stocks with over a hundred thousand dollars' interest in each one. He had bought interests in an exploratory oil company using his tax dollars. He was building himself a portfolio, maybe a quarter of a million dollars' worth of oil interests. Life was sweet and sure. Pearlstein was Pearlstein, happy to be around. They didn't like the movie, they wanted to play poker. Okay, so I'll play poker. Call it, I'll do it, if you treat me like a gentleman and don't pick on me, or call me names. That attitude and about eight million dollars was not bad. Solomon had asked Julie to come to L.A. for the weekend. Things were quiet at the club in Vegas, so Julie flew in on Friday. Quiet and calm and always looking for trouble. For a man who didn't give a shit about anything or anybody, he was being bothered by some uneasiness in his gut. It made him pace, nervous as a cat, but he controlled it. Pearlstein decided to stay and watch the movie, Sally Tarlow softly snored in the corner while her rival in the movie, Sandy Loveacres, was there on the screen doing her number, being sexy and funny. There were four producers, two actresses, and one actor, three agents, and an assorted group of friends and foes from the different studios where everyone worked.

As the six of them sat around the table, they decided what they would play: five-card, seven-card stud, nothing wild, lowball, highball, or the highest and lowest hands, five-card draw, jacks or better to open. Each man had a check on an open account to cover whatever he would lose that night, each player writing on a piece of paper the stake he was prepared to gamble. Each man exposing it into the center of the table like the falling spokes of a wheel. A hundred thousand grand apiece, leave whenever you want, a royal flush beats four aces, right? Right.

The chips were a different shade of blue, four distinct shades, from dark blue to sky blue. The dark blue were a thousand, the next shade five hundred, the next shade one hundred, and the sky blues were the twenties. Angus Hobbs, the English butler, had already arranged all the necessary drinks and liqueurs for the game and had supplied a small table alongside Mr. Solomon. On this table he kept his chips, a pad and pencil, a place for a drink, and a dozen brand new packs of playing cards. Six were blue packs, six were red packs. Solomon chose a red pack, took a small penknife, slit open the pack, took out the cards. He took the jokers, threw them aside with the two other blank cards that come in the pack, and began to shuffle the cards with his manicured fingers.

"Pearly, a script came across my desk today. I don't know how good it is. I like the guy who's making it. Story's a little rough for me, about a dying priest, but maybe you'd like it. I told him to have a copy on your desk tomorrow."

Pearlstein nodded. He didn't like to be called Pearly, but what could he do, with the King there? He called you what he liked. The Kid was dressed like Pierre Cardin wishes he could dress, and drove the girls wild. He was pinstriped all over. Pearlstein was shades of gray. Everything that Solomon wore was silk, silk mohair suit, silk tie, silk shirt, silk underwear, silk stockings. Vinnie in jeans and denim, long hair and losing it, a pair of worn Tom Mix boots, a white cotton shirt. Julie's name should have been Autumn, because that's the way he looked. And the Ace like a preacher come to town, all in black except for the white shirt and no Bible. Every hand opened with twenty and with jacks to bet, you kept feeding the pot until you could. It was five-card draw and Pearlstein and Slaughter both waited until the third card fell before they picked up the first two. Then when all the cards had fallen, they neatly stacked them and picked them up and squeezed them. Six different sets of five cards out of a possible fifty-two cards. Each man had his own ideas of what he thought the laws of playing poker were. Solomon could follow cards excellently, remember which cards were turned up, track them from the ones that were not turned up, matched against his five cards, it gave him a pretty good idea of what kind of chances he had of improving his hand. Each played an occasional hunch. None would pursue a hand unless he really knew or thought he had a damn good chance of nailing it.

It was five-card stud now and, when the third card fell, Ace, Julie, and Pearlstein were rubbed out. Solomon called De Carlo's raise of three hundred dollars. The Kid had made the original bet and also called De Carlo's raise. The next card fell and the Kid dropped. Solomon bet his pair of kings, five hundred dollars. Called by De Carlo. Solomon on his next card didn't improve his pair, and Solomon didn't need to show his third king. Fitting, Solomon thought, King wins on king.

The movie was long since over. Sally Tarlow had been scooped up by the houseman, dumped gently in the back seat of a limousine, and driven to her condominium penthouse apartment on Wilshire. Adele Pearlstein came into the game, smiled at the men playing, and sat next to her husband. Most of the guests had left right after the film. A half-dozen stayed on to watch the poker game. A girl named Mara was sitting at the bar on a high cane-backed chair. Pearly felt lucky, the Ace opened, Solomon stayed for the draw. There was eight thousand dollars in the pot by the time Ace and Pearly were the only ones left. Pearly had drawn for an inside straight and low and behold, he had picked it beautifully. He now had five cards in numerical order from the eight to the queen of hearts, he had drawn a ten of clubs, missed a straight flush by one suit. Ace had drawn two, but he seemed a little hesitant in his betting. Pearly decided to sink a sub.

"I'll call you three thousand and raise you five thousand, Ace," Pearly said.

Ace looked at Pearly and swallowed. Adele stood at the side of her husband, not saying a word, not batting an eye, thinking, Shmuck, he's goin' to lose.

Ace's black right hand reached back, and fingered assorted variations of blue chips.

"Call to the five, raise you five."

Pearly tightened a bit and studied Ace. He took two, he wouldn't keep a kicker there for three of a kind. He knows I took one. If he thinks I got two pair, he wins. Odds to make a straight too high. He got four of a kind or a full house. If he had three of a kind he would have raised because he was on the betting side of the Kid. Nothing but a bluff because he didn't open or he went for a straight or flush with three cards. No, not even a schwartzer would do that.

Adele relaxed. She said to herself, and was right, This shmuck is going to lose. So he's got three of a kind, or maybe he had a pair with a kicker, or maybe he's bluffing, because he didn't open, but if he did he's got to have jacks or better. It's tough to tell what a black man thinks.

"Call you, Ace," said Pearly. "I got a straight."

Ace threw over his cards.

"Full house, fives over fours."

"Shit," Pearlstein said, "what a lousy hand to lose to."

As Ace scooped up the chips and started arranging them on his side of the table, Adele stood up.

"Good night, gentlemen." She reached over and kissed her husband on the cheek. "See you later, alligator." Then she left.

If the Kid fucks like he plays poker, he's gonna be in a lot of trouble, Solomon thought. The Kid was out about eighteen thousand by this time. The Kid tried to bluff three hands, Solomon called him twice, and Julie called him once. Pearly had too much compassion, he didn't believe it was right to steal from a man when he was lying down, stooped over, and it was below him to go after someone like Kid Andrew Cody. After all, he was his star. He felt he could wipe him out anytime he wanted to in a poker game. The way he played for the first six or seven hours, you wouldn't think he was the son of a gambling man. His style was clean, though; he checked and raised then raised again. Then bet the size of the ante, which doubled six and made it twelve thousand, and took one card. Ace would have called if he'd had three of a kind, but he didn't. Pearly passed, De Carlo laying back passed on the last bet, Julie checked his openers, Solomon checked, the Kid bet ten grand. Julie was clean but weak. If I had better than nines and fours, I'd call, he thought. He passed. Solomon with three jacks called. The Kid had two high pairs, aces and kings. With those aces and kings and a ticket on a bus, you could get to Pasadena.

"Excuse me for a minute," Solomon said. "I'm gonna relieve myself."

He walked into the next room. Mara was waiting to relieve him. Nine minutes later she was on her way and King Solomon was majestically walking back into the game. There he was, seventy-four, playing poker all night, schtupping and peeing like a kid. King Solomon knew how to be rich and powerful. Slaughter and Sparrow were the only winners so far. The Kid had 'em and decided to bet 'em. Nobody believed him but Julie. Julie opened with three tens, Solomon called with aces, De Carlo had a pair of nines and felt lucky, Pearly was going to try for an outside straight, jack high.

"You can't lose them all," he said.

The Kid had three kings, he called Julie's two thousand and raised it two thousand. Everybody stayed for the draw. Julie didn't improve. He drew an ace and a queen, Harry Ace went for a flush but didn't make it, King Solomon got another ace and a pair of queens, De Carlo didn't improve, and Pearly got his straight. The Kid drew two to improve and did with the last king and a deuce that gave him four kings. He knew he was top dog around the table. Julie checked, Ace passed, Solomon with his nifty full house bet five thousand. De Carlo dissolved and passed. Pearly called with his straight, the Kid called the five and raised it ten. Julie showed his openers and passed. Solomon had beat him three times and was hooked. He was going to beat this fucking cowboy bad and he was happy. He called the ten and raised twenty thousand dollars. Twenty thousand for a straight, Pearly thought. No straight is worth twenty thousand. He threw his cards in, and there they sat, the King and the Kid. It was the Kid's bet. The Kid looked at the King for a long time, then down at his cards. He glanced at Julie for some reason. Sparrow is cool, he thought. Nothing fazes him. He rarely smiled but was friendly enough. He looked like Max. Now if Julie had made that bet, Andrew knew he would have been dead, but somehow with Solomon he felt he had a chance, and besides, he was sitting with a hunch. Four beautiful kings. He cleared his throat, counted out twenty thousand dollars' worth of chips, pushed it to the center of the table, and when Solomon declared, the Kid raised it his last thirty thousand. The butler could feel the tension in the room. Now Solomon with hardly any hair on his head, shining as if he had got his head shined that afternoon at the studio with his shoes, looked at the Kid. Solomon's blue eyes never flickered from the Kid's. He smiled slightly.

"I call you," he said.

The Kid turned over the four kings.

"Read them and weep."

Solomon didn't blink. He counted out thirty and passed

it to the Kid. He turned and took a new deck of cards, slit them carefully, and opened them. They had used four packs by now. The phone rang. They had been playing all night.

"Who could be calling this time of night?" De Carlo asked.

Solomon went to the desk, picked up the phone.

"Yeah, what, cancel all the appointments. I'm playing poker."

Nobody asked the time. A couple of the guys playing knew what time it was. There were still three people from the night watching the game.

"Pearly, your wife is on the phone."

"Lester, when are you coming home? Grace just arrived this morning with Maurice and her two daughters. They're going to stay through the holidays. How much longer do you wanna play?"

"Maybe another hour or so."

"What have you lost so far?"

"I haven't lost much, but that Solomon," he whispered, "he must be out seventy thousand."

"Hurry home, Tatala, it's not a game for you."

"I'll be home soon." Pearly hung up. "Excuse me."

And he went into the powder room and took a leak. They played for one more hour. Julie hooked De Carlo and went for thirteen thousand dollars. De Carlo decided not to chase that straight and folded his cards. Julie quietly bluffed the hand, never showing any of his cards that he had been dealt. The chips were counted, checks were made out for the corresponding amounts, wins or losses, and as quickly as they sat down the night before everybody was gone. The room was empty, stale cigar smoke from Solomon. Diet Pepsi bottles from De Carlo. Empty scotch glass from Pearly. Cans of beer from the Kid. Julie's vodka on the rocks, and the Ace's Bourbon and Coke. It was a beautiful and cold Saturday in California. Each man had won and lost what he had hoped. And they finished the movie.

Randy Malloy

Randy Malloy. The best trick in town. She'd take it any way you gave it to her and came back asking for more. Her appetite was insatiable. Many strong men crawled out of her bedroom. She conned these guys out of every bit of themselves. She wouldn't take no for an answer. She could give an old worn-out priest a hard-on. When you needed a job done it was Randy. The Kid used hookers like some guys use vitamin pills, two a day. By the time he bedded some of these would-be starlets and would-be actresses, he was exhausted from the numbers done. To be in a beautiful girl's pad on a hill overlooking all of Los Angeles, pulling on a joint, wasn't so bad after all. Randy was busy dealing every which way. She handled heavy stuff, light stuff, any stuff. She'd always clear the decks for the Kid. Day or night, she would hang up her no-disturb sign for the Kid. Sometimes they'd fuck and sometimes they didn't. He just had access to her, her house, and the view for that hour or two. He always left two twenties. The minute they met, it was different for both. They didn't know it then. For him just to spend the time with her was enough. She admired him. He was vain and strong and thirty-five now. She found that he wasn't sure of himself, but when and if he ever connected with the power that was his, she would be one of the privileged ones to have been able to spend two hours a day with him. For now he had all the things that she enjoyed as a woman and as a friend. He was tall and graceful, spoke with an easy tongue. Always a smile on his face. He showed absolutely no emotion. He was just beginning to get himself together. He thought that if a woman had ten men in her life, the machinery would wear down in no time at all. Dear Randy had been pounced on, sat on, shat on, dat on, bat on, and any other on you can think of. The kid got hit right between the eyes. Those stone carved figures explicitly showing the different positions in which one human does it to another human, well, these were pikers compared to Randy. The Kid could never want for any new trick. They could live together for twenty years and she still wouldn't be finished with her numbers. She improvised. Things happened in spontaneous ways. Her energies and vitality were only aimed and reflected in one direction, in one stream, on one heat. She felt that she was the goddess of understanding and profound rest. Occasionally, if she were sitting on the right man, she would sense that calm and rest. She could only take a few seconds of that pure joy and then she would swoon and collapse like some rag doll that just got knocked off the top of a bureau. Once in a while she'd meet a guy that could help her attain that, but usually it would only happen once. The Kid could knock her out anytime. She couldn't tell him that, so in their love, she never really sat down hard on him until she was ready and he was half nuts. Then and only then would she plunge down, swoon, and always wake up in his arms. Every time that they made love this happened to her. She didn't tell him, but he was her man. She liked it this way. Among all the other broads he saw, she'd get a call from him every few days. She could sense he really wasn't satisfied. His stable consisted of six hookers that he called pretty regularly. They moved in and out of town in such a hurry, but there was always one good-looking girl asking you if you remembered another good-looking girl and perhaps you could meet somewhere. And then there was Randy.

She hadn't seen him now in three weeks. They spoke on the telephone once. He was just coming off location on a film and would call her later in the week, he said. That was ten days ago. He should be calling any day now. The phone rang.

"Guess who?"

"Prince Philip."

"You bet your ass."

"What's happening?"

"Nothing. Everything's groovy. What's happening? Just back from Lone Pine."

"When you finishing?"

"I'm finished now. Just doing a couple of process shots. I'll have to do the looping in about two weeks, I think. That's it. Another picture bites the dust."

"Don't be so fucking cute. You've only made a few pictures and you're King Shit all of a sudden."

"No, I'm not."

"Then calm down. You still packing that spade with you?"

"Randy, don't talk like that. Yup."

By now she knew everything connected with the Kid. She could see how much Slaughter and the Kid meant to each other and she would goad each man. Each one knowing that they were being done to. Not complaining. She was sure comical, the Ace thought.

"You know I think the Kid's a fag, myself," she'd say to Ace.

"Come on, Randy, don't talk like that about Andrew."

"I think he's got some sailor hid away. I'm tellin' ya, Ace, he's a fag. We were out for dinner the other night, and he threw a kiss at the waiter."

"You mean a waitress, don't ya?"

"No, I mean a waiter. Black Ace. Don't give me any of that Stepin Fetchit. Speak up, will ya? We is all free."

"Randy, you're smart. You sure know how to please a man. But somethin's wrong."

There was a long pause.

"What do you mean? I don't understand. Say it, don't fuck around with love, Ace. Say it."

"Neither one of you are sure that you'd be willing to give up all the other goodies that you call life. Anyway, Randy, I wouldn't worry about it."

"Who's worrying?"

"You are. Take another pull on that joint and feel them muscles relax just a little and you won't be so horny. Then maybe you two will take it a little easier on each other. You're usin' an awful lot of energy to fulfill a small need."

"Are you sure you're a nigger?"

"Another thing. You're still young and your diet's right. Don't go using up that pussy too fast. You use it too much now, it ain't gonna help you later."

"Please, Ace, forgive me for being so rude with you."

She put her head on his shoulder, shuddered, and wept, while Ace stroked her head slowly. Harry the Ace Slaughter had the biggest hard-on he had had in years, and

231

Randy thought it a privilege to help this man come with another burst of life.

"I'll be over in a little while," the Kid said.

"Well, then, I've got dinner to make and clean up."

This voluptuous creature in a robe, barefoot, went into the kitchen and turned out a meal fit for a king. She had bought five cases of wine at a time, twenty cases a year, for the last seven years. They'd have a bottle of red for dinner, Château Lafite-Rothschild '59, of La Tâche, a bottle of Romanée-Conti, every now and then a Château Margaux. She asked him once how it was. Smooth. The Kid wasn't quite sure why she liked him so much. But it was okay. He liked it the way it was.

He got out his Eagle Short Winder, a four-cylinder bike. He kept it in the shed behind the house. Opened it up and found himself sailing upward over a narrow gray ribbon of road. When you thought it's about time, you stopped. He did and there, resting on a point, was this modern glass house, sitting out on arms of steel and concrete, holding it delicately as if on its fingertips like a pastry man holding his pride.

The house looked as if it would just fly off at the slightest disturbance, like a hummingbird just hovering over the earth, not wanting to be contaminated by it. In the winds and in any tremor at all, the house felt it before anybody else in town did. The Kid was scared by it. Randy loved it. She knew the house was built as well as any house could be built in that kind of a position. And, if anything, she was a hell of a lot safer than the bum underneath her who could have it all on top of him. From the street all you could see were wild oleander bushes. There was no opening for your eye to see into the front section of the house. The driveway going in and out was so far at the end of the property that all you saw looking up the driveway were more oleander bushes over what looked like a gravel road. The front of the house was stuccoed white and flat with a high Spanish oak door. Two ten-foot potted fruit trees, one lime, one lemon, sat on either side of the door. He pulled his bike up, got off it halfway up the pathway, and rolled it behind the low hedge. Locked it and came upon Randy's Shangri-La. She called it Randy's. It was her castle and she lived in it alone.

Shandor opened the door. Deaf, Hungarian, and not a hair on him, anywhere. He moaned and sighed his sounds. They were soft and musical and if you knew Shandor, why, he could speak to you. Of course, your thoughts with Shandor had to be quite elementary. Shandor refused to learn when he was a boy to communicate with the outside world. He wanted nobody putting their dirty, filthy fingers on his lips or trying to get him to croak out those ugly sounds. Not for him. Not for Shandor Ernst Kertes. When he came to America and saw television, color television, he knew he would be saved because that's where he spent all of his time between any jobs that he had. In front of a television set. He'd get laid every once in a while by some raunchy old lady and that was enough for him. He loved Randy. All six foot four and eyes of Hungarian goulash. With Shandor, there was no need for anyone else. He was up before anybody. No one could ever remember seeing him sleep. Once Randy had seen him with his eyes closed, coming up from Ensenada, driving hard and heavy. She awoke just as the sun was coming up. The car was pulled off the road. Shandor had his eyes closed. As she opened hers, his did too. And off they sped again back to Los Angeles. He didn't need ears to hear, to tell him what was going on around him. Responding and receiving vibrations were highly developed in Shandor. He was ever alert. Once in a while in his mind, he allowed himself the privilege of fucking around with Randy, but only in the most gentlemanly manner. He would take her in these fantasies and just when it looked as if she was going to come, he'd pop out of her, relieved that he hadn't hurt his mistress. He was a Catholic, Hungarian Church, and asked for forgiveness for thinking in such a carnal and bestial manner. Ten Hail Marys and ten bucks for the church.

As soon as the Kid got into the house, he had to lean against the wall for a minute. Took a good long breath. Shandor murmured. The Kid gestured and walked himself to the one bedroom and Jacuzzi bath that he used. He shaved. He put on a gray and white Egyptian cotton kaftan. Towel-dried his hair. When he was a kid he was always afraid his cock wouldn't be big enough. He slipped into some Japanese sandals, shuffled out of his room and down a long corridor. There were two huge windows embedded, equally spaced from each other, in the wall. Two huge windows with button panels opened by a latch. On a table with slender legs rested four bonsai trees, two Chinese elms, a juniper forest, and a pine. Kid Andrew Cody was a lord. A Japanese lord walking through the corridors of his mind. Observing each incident of his life as an art patron passing through a museum. He passed two doors in the corridor, turned left. He passed into a room whose west wall was glass. One single sheet. All the edges of the glass sat in a rubber-lined furrow that gave a shade more space to the glass than the glass needed. And during the quivers and shakes that rustled the Los Angeles Basin, the glass never shattered or broke, just jiggled in its jellylike compartment. It was slightly curved. The surface curved as in a huge eye. An unblinking pupil gazing out on the valley below, drinking in all the colors of the world. He came and sat two feet from the window on the empty floor and stayed forever.

Vinnie De Carlo

Vinnie De Carlo never packed a piece of anything or anybody with him. He was a loner in the true sense of the word. He was born Vincent Frachetti. He had an attorney in Chicago: Gabroni, Inocenti, and Brown. If you had any inquiries for De Carlo, that was the office you got in touch with. De Carlo didn't advertise in the trades, didn't give a fuck who was the president of the Screen Actors Guild, or whether David Selznick invited him to his latest screening. De Carlo always had something else to do. There was no club, big or small, that was too big or too small for Vinnie De Carlo, if you paid his price. If you didn't know where to find him, then you didn't want him badly enough. When he was a kid he used to do a lot of club dates; two weeks in Vegas, three weeks in Chicago, three weeks in New York. And he was under contract to the same studio as the Kid for a while. As long as he was wanted, name the city in the United States, and De Carlo could work it. You name it and he could pack it. Just call his attorneys and they would arrange everything. They provided the whole package. De Carlo's five-piece band would be augmented by forty-five local musicians who were rehearsed by De Carlo's musical director, Mario Barr, a scholarly classical musician and flutist. The band was not arranged in the conventional manner of five rows of ten musicians each on stage. Nope, Vinnie De Carlo had them all around him. Daisies in a field. A small cluster here, a group to his right, one single girl cellist, and through his whole act, which consisted of singing and only singing, no dialogue of any kind, he strolled as though he were an Italian poet making up poems in some isolated summer field in Ireland, which he was. Oblivious to his surroundings, occasionally stopping to listen to a musician play, he did this for exactly thirty minutes. At the end of nine numbers, he walked offstage and there was a fifteen-minute intermission. When the fifteen minutes were up precisely, Vinnie De Carlo came back onstage and this was the magic of the evening. This was the consummate performer, this Picasso in front of a canvas, sure, deft, clean, melodious, name it and he had it. The second act and the last could go on for twenty minutes or for two and a half hours. He hadn't been doing that too often lately because he was exhausted after it. Vinnie De Carlo was one of the few singers in the world who could do four hours onstage and still have over a hundred songs in his repertoire. They loved Vinnie and Vinnie wasn't too sure about them. His quality and style of singing were exceptional. You couldn't believe those deep notes were coming from such a frail man. And delicate notes, too delicate to come from such a bovine.

If a song moved him, it moved you. He could transmit the emotion of that song like no other singer could. He struck you inside your chest, not in your brain, and made you gag from a sob, laugh hysterically, sigh deeply to yourself. He wouldn't let anyone or anything interfere between him and his voice. He wanted to be obligated to no man or woman. This voice was his and he would run it. His hair started to fall out in his twenties. He never wore a hairpiece or combed it funny. In those earlier days, he used to wear his hair long, maybe to his collar, but now he seemed to cut it shorter and shorter. Onstage, he was an impeccable dresser. His clothes were cut to fit his frame and his frame alone. There was no padding anywhere in the jackets, no embroidery, no outside hand stitching. He wore a black single-breasted suit onstage, a white satin shirt with no double facing on the collar of the shirt, so that the collar just rolled over the black scarf he wore as a tie. He wore a black, simple laced shoe with an inch-and-a-half heel. From the waist to the knee, the trousers fitted just tight enough; from the knee down, they flared ever so slightly. He never slouched. Never sat down because there was no place to sit and didn't ask for tea, scotch, gin, vodka, mother's milk, or Manischewitz Concord Grape. He had the latest in electronic gear, which made it possible for him to stroll among his forest of musicians and always be heard above them. In some places around the world, Vinnie De Carlo could make two hundred and fifty thousand bucks a night with no trouble.

The few romances he had ended up disastrously. In

every city there were four or five guys that were always wanting to be his friend. Influential men in all fields of endeavor, all with girlfriends praying and hoping to get jumped by Vinnie De Carlo. One had a girlfriend who had a boyfriend who wanted to get jumped by Vinnie De Carlo. The only ones Vinnie really liked at all were Kid Andrew Cody and Julie Sparrow. When he worked Vegas, he and Julie spent a lot of time together. They neither gambled nor played golf or tennis. What they did together was fish out on Lake Mead and shoot pool. Vinnie allowed Andrew to drag him around town to meet all the chippies. To and from one Hollywood party to the next. Vinnie didn't have many friends in Hollywood and Beverly Hills. Andrew always had a party or a place that they could go. Vinnie thought Andrew had a knowledge of that kind that no other guy did, and the Kid was always nice with him and gentlemanly, and never presumed and never even asked for a free album. His kind of man. Vinnie knew a lot of people, but none of them knew him. He was a sliver of reflected light in a stream. Here one second, gone the next. No one got close to Vinnie. No one. He wasn't like Julie, who slowly turned and avoided it. Vinnie liked to provoke relationships and then split. He liked to get laid, but that wasn't enough anymore. He didn't want any children. There were a few women around who would have made suitable and beautiful wives, but that was not his number. He wasn't interested in extending his dynasty and being exploited by his children. He didn't know what that meant. He was only interested in perpetuating his voice.

He had a small spread in Ojai Valley. There his life was very rustic and simple. Vinnie had no depth to speak of, whatever that means. He just felt that this was his way of life and he was ordained to it and that he shouldn't do anything too bad to destroy it or hurt it. He was one of the most fortunate men in his profession, for he had it on his terms, and to do that is to have the world. His father, Joseph Frachetti, was alive and well and living on the ranch, always busy with the animals, with the gardens, with the crops. His pleasure and vocation were farming and gardening. There wasn't anything he couldn't get a leaf from. He could plant a nail. All the products of his growing wizardry were around the inside and outside of the house. His ranch house seemed to have been carefully set in an already flourishing garden.

Andrew and Vinnie were driving the Kid's new Jensen —dark blue outside and dark blue inside. It was night. They were roaring up the coast highway passing under the Thelma Todd overpass, whizzing past the Malibu pier, slowing down a little outside the colony, wailing up again almost to Trancis, then slowing for Paradise Cove, cop's paradise, then open again, traveling northwest, but primarily north.

"You know a girl named Marion Pope?"

The Kid reached over and turned down KCLA.

"Who, Vinnie, Marion Pope? Don't know her."

The Kid was wearing a pair of unlined goatskin gloves that all the stunt men used in their work. Both were wearing denims. Vinnie's older than the Kid's. Vinnie's two arms were draped inside of his thighs, hands relaxed, pointed down. He was dressed completely in shades of denim blue. His shirt was denim and so was his short jacket. This American-Italian, Philadelphian, raised as a Catholic, a choir boy brought up in the strictest classical Catholic background, this Jesuit, reflected a moment, rushing past those low-lying hills along the Pacific Coast Highway.

He imagined the background flashing to Cherry Hill around Philadelphia in New Jersey. From the dark brown and black shadows the hills made whipping past his face, he saw Frankie. Too late to do anything about it if he could, and why would he want to? He had done what he thought was best at the time. One day he would tell Giuseppe, but not right now. He was nineteen then when he buried what was left of his brother. Frank, his younger brother. Dead. They had been out shooting pool. They weren't hustlers, they were just good pool players and enjoyed going out to shoot. They would visit parlors all around the state, shoot eight ball with the best of them. They were coming home then. Frankie and Vinnie had won 637 bucks that night in a private club and were heading for their car. They were driving a '47 Mercury coupe, when Frank heard, Hold it. He didn't. He swung his cue sticks, which were finished and enclosed in a hand-rubbed mahogany case, toward the voice behind and to the left of him. An arm reached out and flew around his neck, pulling him backward. When his back was resting against the figure that held him, the right arm and hand of the assailant plunged a seven-inch kitchen knife right through him ending in the middle of his heart. He slumped to the ground. There was no pain, just a spasm as he tried to draw his breath. He saw his brother Vincent looking at him. The knife had been left in his body. The guy who did it had been knocked on the ground. The guy now started to scramble to his feet. There was no way out behind him. The only way would be to pass Vinnie. He hesitated. If Vinnie went for him, he could try to struggle his way past him and down the street. If Vinnie went for his brother, he'd break then. Vinnie leaped over his brother and didn't hesitate. The assailant tried to go and he had fifteen feet in which to maneuver. He got to take one step. Vinnie was on his shoulder. His right arm firmly attached and cradling the assailant's head between shoulder and ears, shoulder and jaw. He applied as much pressure as he could. The assailant's two hands shot up to the arm, for he knew he was in death's struggle. Vinnie, in his anger, frustration, and despair, never let go but dragged the assailant backward until he fell to one knee and looked at Frank. Frank said, Hey, Vinnie, and reached out his hand to touch his brother. His brother took it in his, held it, and started to sob. Frank's eyelids fluttered, ever so slightly, and closed on those brown eyes forever. When the moment of panic disappeared and the agony started to set in, the man in his left arm had died as well, and Vinnie hadn't known it.

Vinnie got up and struck out with his right shoe, which was pointed and made of drawn leather, steel-tipped. A short Western boot. In its short arc, it hit just on the side of the assailant's Adam's apple. There was nobody around. There was a five-foot-by-three-foot grille covering a hole that gave a little light and ventilation to an old deserted garage. The bottom of this well was about two feet below the window. In it were old garbage, leaves, and other refuse swept there by wind and rain. He wrenched it loose in one move and dragged the body and dumped it down. He hid the body with scraps of garbage, wood, some leaves, and empty cartons. The body wouldn't be discovered until early spring, when it would start to smell a bit. He cleaned the scene completely and sat down beside his dead brother. He pulled the knife from Frank's back, surprised to see so little blood on it. He lifted his brother in his arms, carried him hurriedly to where he had parked the car. He didn't stagger or stumble in picking Frank up, as if he weighed nothing at all. He unlocked the passenger side and slipped his brother into the car, then he stopped short and leaped out, went back and found lying in the gutter the exquisitely made mahogany box that held his brother's cue sticks. He picked it up, carried it into the car, and drove off. His despair choked the breath out of him. He broke out in a cold sweat, mouth dry. Only when he looked at his brother sitting there slumped in the seat did he realize the enormity of the experience.

He drove to an area in New Jersey that he knew not far from Philly. He had caddied at this golf club one season and knew the surrounding countryside well. Desolate, moody, lonely, and very beautiful. His sweet brother, Frank. How to explain this to his family. How senseless. Was that an abortion of the mind? Some horrible fantasy nightmare? It had no rhyme, no reason, so therefore it did not exist, he decided. He must not allow it to affect him. It would only destroy his mother and put a pall upon the family for the rest of their lives. He would give them hope at his own expense, his own despair.

He passed a hardware store. He parked the car. There displayed in the window were nine shovels of different sizes beckoning him, drawing him to them. There was a metal milk crate lying discarded by the side of the hardware store, amid garbage cans and refuse from the day's labor, ready to be snatched away in the morning. He took the metal crate and without hesitation hurled it through the hardware store window. The plate glass shattered with an incredible sound. He stepped onto the ledge, into the window, took a shiny four-foot shovel and walked back to the car, threw it onto the back seat, and drove off. He screamed. He parked the car, got out, walked with the shovel to a small cluster of trees on a small slope. He dug feverishly; he dug until it was a seven-foot hole, like a funnel. He went to the car, carried his brother to the hole, and slid him off his shoulders, and, standing over him, legs balanced on the steep side of the funnel, he eased his brother in and held him close. Worn out, he climbed out. He covered the hole. The excess earth he spread all around, leaving the burial spot as close to what it looked like when he first arrived, replacing a dozen or so divots of grass. It was light now and he hardly felt as if he had done anything. He felt refreshed, and somewhat peaceful. He lay down on the dew-heavy grass, looking at the coming day, tears rolling down the sides of his face and joining the new morning dew. He looked around the hillside and couldn't believe anything had happened last night. He took the shovel and threw it in the back of the car, walked about 150 yards to where he remembered a water fountain was, drank some, cleaned his hands, which were blistered and sore, walked back to his car, and took off. All that remained of his brother in the car was in his heart, and that mahogany case.

He called home the next afternoon and said not to be mad, but Frank had run off and enlisted in the Navy, it was no good trying to stop him. He had decided that was what he wanted to do. He would write. His father was a drunk, his mother disinterested in this family of three boys. He told them that he got a job working in a small club as a waiter and a singer. He would be gone for a few days. He then sat down and constructed a letter which he wrote in the hand of his brother, punctuating like Frank would, spelling like Frank would, and writing with that slope that Frank used. It took him all night to compose it. Dear Mother, Father, Vinnie, and Joe, I have gone away. It wasn't fun for me no more around there. I want to travel and see the world. I don't want no ties, sitting around here near Philly sneaking into New York once in a while, shooting pool. I want more from life than that. I always have liked islands, and sand, and beach, warm water all year round. I've never seen it, now is my chance. That's where I'm planning to go. If not, I'll go somewhere else, but I am on the move now. I got a world in front of me and things to see. You'll hear from me every now and then. Love from your son and brother, Frankie.

His mother died, Giuseppe forgot. Once in a while somebody'd ask Vinnie if he ever heard from Frank. Vinnie'd say, Once in a while. He really didn't know what his father thought. He still drank a lot, but that didn't seem to hide the melancholy in his face. Joseph

Frachetti, Sr., thought of nothing but his existence. He never thought of the past or the future, just what was presented to him from day to day. He gave nothing of himself to anyone except cordiality and a smile and an occasional Italian dinner.

Vinnie De Carlo felt that Kid Cody and Julie Sparrow somehow replaced his dead brother Frank. He liked Julie a lot, he didn't like the Kid better than Julie, but he felt more at ease with him. He felt in a way that they were equals and he was more candid with Andrew. With anyone else he was vitriolic and always double-faced and double-tongued. Hey, Charlie, how are ya? Long time no see. Fuck you, Charlie. The longer the better. Edna, baby, you're lookin' great, for an old cunt.

The Kid saw himself getting out of the car. Then he didn't remember anything. There was Vinnie calling somebody an old cunt. Blank. You should be spontaneous in your affections and your love, he heard a voice say. It was soft and melodious. Blank. There was a girl's face, red-haired, full-lipped, full-cheeked, white skin. I don't wanna be hurt again. You wouldn't hurt me, would you? I have so much to give. Oh, please, treat me kind. He saw pink, part of a soft belly, a small bush of red hair. Oh, please, no. I'm not well. Don't. Please. The Kid took her anyway. She'd fight him, then collapse, rally her forces and energy, then try to ward off his passion and drive. Not enough to discourage him, only enough to entice him. He felt nothing. Only the senses of his cock. The two milligrams of Koloxsin was all it took. A short and thin hypodermic needle forced it into his blood, into the side of his buttocks, as he drove himself home again, and again. He sensed it. What was that? An unseen figure disappeared into the shadows of the room, rejoining the party in the other part of the forest. There was no one under him. Where was he? It was all quiet around him. He forced himself to dress. Pops of light. He now remembered pops of light. Short bursts of it. Something hard and coarse holding him. Hard and coarse. Pop. A sliver of light. Out looking for his car. Asphalt. Cement. Bushes. Hanging from somebody's arm. Cigarette smell. Something pulling his hair. Whoosh. Smell of gasoline. Rubber. Something whizzing by. Lying in the gutter. Get up. Ace.

I remember you. You're the one who made my dreams come true. Ages ago. It was his mother. The memory was sharp and clear. Etched in his head. He was looking up. He could see the end of his carriage. His mother pushing him from the handlebars. Click, click, click, click. The sharp sound of her highstepping heels, bouncing on the sidewalk. He felt himself lean forward. The carriage dipping into the street, level again. Somebody whistles. Look at the sidewalk. Click, clack, click, clack. Hair cut to the bottom of her chin. Parted from the center and held back like the curtains on a window in a room. Held back about halfway by two small gold-plated barrettes. Her breasts jiggling in their soft brassiere, looking at him every now and then, smiling. They stopped. She looks and smiles. A man walks up. Light brown hair, cut short. Shirt opened at the neck. Sleeves rolled up above the elbow. Brown belt. Brown trousers.

"I'll meet you at four."

"Uh-huh."

"I can't stop now."

"Later, my love."

A smile. Click, clack, high heeling down the street. Her eyes when she looks seem distracted and pained.

He left his bike at Randy's and went in Ace's rental. He picked up his car at Bonnie's. He had a service that sent somebody every day for five hours to put the Kid's pad in order. With Ace living with him now, there was always somebody at the house or almost always. At the house he rounded up the .38 that he had taken from Farraday and took the shells and put them in his denim jacket pocket while Ace waited in the car. Driving up the hill to Randy's place, he popped the .38 and put one shell in it. It was now in the firing chamber. He took the shell out, waisted the piece underneath his jacket.

"Drive up to Mulholland before Randy's."

He had Ace pull over to the side and from the position on Mulholland that they were in they could see the Valley and Los Angeles. They could see beyond the airport. They could see Baldwin Hills on the left down to the oil refineries, sitting on the outskirts of Long Beach. To the Valley side, they could see the foothills of the Sierras. The Kid got out and stood for a moment. Ace got out and joined him.

"I could've been killed. It was like it was happening to someone else. I was scared, Ace."

"That's okay, Kid."

"Ace, I only mention it because I haven't felt like that for a long time."

"A guy once pulled a shiv on me in Biloxi, Kid. He had me in a corner and he meant business. The only way out of there was past him and he stood there with this knife. Ready to cut me. I started to do a soft-shoe dance. I done a pari-diddle with my right toe and them taps were singing out and when he loved it the most, I kicked him in the balls. I took the knife. I got it somewhere in my stuff. I'm gonna give you all that shit one day, Kid. I got some trunks with some fine-looking suits, shirts, ties and some great shoes. A swell-looking cane, I remember. Let's see, what else do I remember? Oh, and I got a lot of pictures. One day I'll let ya see it all. Anyway, I took the knife with me. I had a drink with this good-looking fox just a few minutes later at a bar. I dropped her off in a cab. The cab then drove me home and while I was upstairs in my room making myself a little dinner, that's when I realized I had shit in my pants. Conscience doth make cowards of us all. Shakespeare could've said that. I don't recollect. Was it bad juice you got last night?"

"No, Ace, had a little vodka, but that was okay."

"Never can tell, Kid, they got stuff now just a few grains, you don't taste nothin', know nothin', or feel nothin'."

"Well, they could have, but I don't think it was the drink 'cause I was holding on pretty good. It was in bed that something happened."

"It always does."

"I got a sore spot on this side of my ass like I could've been shot with something. Or, I don't know if it's just a bruise. Could be that. I just remember doing this redheaded kid, then she wasn't there. There's a stretch where I don't remember anything. Then I'm being held and punched. This guy's screaming something at me, ending in cocksucker."

"Who's B. Shrike Martin?"

"He belongs to Lila London. She packs him everywhere."

"Where did he come from?"

"Out of a cesspool. He's fearless. I was at a party in Malibu about eight months ago, Ace. It was on the Pacific Coast Highway. It was hot that night. He had pulled up in a car with Lila London. He made a gesture to her to stay in the car. He opened the driver's side of the car and stepped out. That Pacific Coast Highway is a busy street. It runs all the way up to San Francisco and down to Mexico. This huge trailer truck was rumbling down the highway. He got to the inside lane because somebody was trying to pass him. The trucker had shifted to the inside lane maybe a little more angrily than he should have, which meant that the trailer's tail end dipped in a little bit closer than you would have liked to see it. The trucker knew it and B. Shrike Martin knew it. He stood there. He didn't move. He glanced over his left shoulder. The cabin of the truck was passing him now, and the further it went, the closer it came. The trailer missed his cheek by four feet."

The Kid saw all of this. B. Shrike Martin didn't flinch or interrupt his flow of movement. As the truck cleared him, he shut the door, came around, opened the door, and Lila London stepped out. The Kid and the Shrike had never met, but had seen each other across a crowded room a half-dozen times. After the second informal meeting they had, the Kid would always raise his finger up to his forehead and give him a half salute and say, Howdy, with a big grin on his face. This didn't change B. Shrike Martin's expression at all. B. Shrike Martin's face was oval-shaped, his eyes were so shaped that the irises were completely exposed like two black marbles in a sea of white. His hair was dark and long. Heavy lashes around his eyes. He was okay looking, that's all. He was obviously strong. You could feel it. His hair was dyed black. The Kid figured him in his early forties. B. Shrike Martin was fifty-six.

"The Shrike is a terrible bird," Ace said.

"Somebody's telling me I can live in this town but up to a certain point, and only in a certain way. I haven't made a lot of money in this town yet, but I've got a good chance, a damn good chance. Who says I gotta hang around here anyway when I'm not working? Ace, we could try Acapulco, Cuernavaca, Mexico City. We could live nicely there. Just come up into town and do my work and split. But shit, Ace, I like this city. Well, I wouldn't have to live all the time out of this city. I could pick anyplace I wanted. Mrs. Pearlstein asked me to do something nice and when I agree I get bumped and dumped. I don't want to live anyplace where someone like Lila London can tell me what to do and what people to see. Ace, whatta you think we oughtta do?"

"You know Mrs. Pearlstein doesn't control this Lila London as much as you think," Ace said. "Neither one is gonna blow the whistle on the other. They'll always get along. I'm sure Mrs. Pearlstein regrets your getting roughed up, but there's nothing she can do about it. Lila London is your key, and while you're working here in this town, you gotta live in this town. You can't travel around afraid to go someplace to eat, afraid to pick up a good-lookin' woman, afraid to go to parties. No! That's no good, Kid."

"I reckon it ain't, Ace."

"I think B. Shrike Martin is the bulb to Lila London's switch."

"What does that mean, Ace?"

"If you tangle with the Shrike and he wastes you, it don't make any difference, does it? But if you waste him, she's only gonna get another. You'll be seein' B. Shrike Martin always somewhere along the line. You gotta get London, Kid, 'cause she's out to get you. Seems to me like everybody's gettin' a little bit nervous. Hole up at Randy's. I'm gonna mosey on down into town and get me some facts and figures. Come on, Kid. I'll take ya up to Randy's."

The Kid got out of the car. Walked to the door, rang the bell, turned around, and bowed low to the Ace. Ace thought, when the Kid got mad enough, they'd stop pushing him around. The Ace smiled, put the car into drive, and waved.

"See ya, sonny."

Book Four

LIKE FATHER, LIKE SONS

Ruth

Julie always invited Ruth and Morrie to come out after the holidays. He would not be busy and he could spend some time with them. He loved them both so much. On their trips to Vegas he took them to Boulder Dam, and fishing in Lake Mead. Once they flew up to Reno to visit a friend of Julie's who had a big club there. Whenever they came to the State of Nevada, they almost felt it belonged to their son Julie. He knew everyone; politicians, hookers, lawyers, dealers. There wasn't anywhere that they would travel with Julie that someone wouldn't come up and engage Julie in some kind of conversation. He'd take them horseback riding. They'd go out in the car to the wide-open desert. That place never ceased to fascinate Julie, Ruth, and Morrie, because the three of them had come from such crowded areas before. Open space to them was truly a mysterious beautiful thing to observe. He had spoken to them a few times on the phone before they came out this time. Ruth did not sound too good. She seemed a little listless, coughing, had a bad cold. If it wasn't this flu it was that flu. Morrie had quit tailoring, tried to occupy himself with his classes at City College, and was looking forward to this long-awaited trip to Las Vegas again.

They flew in; a car picked them up at the airport and brought them straight to the 711 Casino. Julie had put on a dozen deluxe bungalows in the rear of the grounds. There was a golf club whose course ranged along the perimeter of houses that Julie had built. He had made an arrangement with the club so that people staying at his casino could use the golf course and tennis courts whenever they wished. The casino had grown a lot in the years that Julie had taken it over and built it. It was a hide-away in a hideaway city. The bell captain, Art Saper, always at the door when Morrie and Ruth arrived, presented Ruth with some beautiful flowers, picked up their luggage, and escorted them to the bungalow that had been reserved for them. Morrie and Ruth could pay no one any money at all. If Morrie wanted to gamble they gave him money. If Ruth wanted to, they gave her. There wasn't anything they couldn't have.

Art knew it immediately when he saw Ruth. He had seen the same signs in his sister. He greeted them as he always greeted them with great affection and care. Art was a reader and part-time philosopher besides parking cars, checking coats, and assigning hookers to certain rooms and certain people in the hotel. Julie was at the other end of the casino, checking through the gambling receipts and markers that had come before him for his appraisal. From the other end of the casino, Julie saw Ruth was dying of cancer. During the year that Julie had not seen Ruth there was a marked difference in her looks and in her vibrations. This woman was now in constant pain. She took some drugs prescribed by her doctor when the pain seemed to get a bit more than she could stand. The discomfort was mainly in the upper portions of her abdomen. She thought there seemed to be constant indigestion, a constant dull pain that seemed to never really let up except under the influence of the pills she took or under the influence of a short glass of whiskey that Morrie gave her occasionally. This had a unique effect on her mind. Fantasies and dreams would pop into this very straight, contained, and puritanical woman's head, as vivid asleep as when she was awake. At least this indigestion or stomach-ache that she had helped give her some really interesting experiences in the fantasies of her mind. When she saw Julie, her whole spirit seemed to light up. She forgot the ache in her stomach and only remembered this dear young man who always treated her like such a queen. Yet when she searched into his face, into his eyes, into the movements and gestures of his body for that hidden meaning, that mysterious sense that this boy-man carried around him wherever he went, it was more than she could bear sometimes. She kept trying to see if he knew more than he really knew. He seemed so alert when she saw him. They embraced right in the center of the casino. Ruth inquired of one of the dealers how his wife and family were doing. Finally, they made it back to the bungalow. Ruth felt obliged to lie down for a while for she was a bit exhausted. Julie invited Morrie for a steam and a plaitzer in the spa built into the complex. Both men were taking "shivitzes."

"Ruth is dying, Morrie, isn't she?" Julie said.

"Yes, she is."

"What is it, Morrie?"

"Cancer of the stomach, Julie. She'll be dead within three months."

They sat, silent, each deep in his own thoughts. Ten minutes later they were out of the steam, getting a massage, then Morrie was back in the bungalow, Julie was back in the casino, and they were to meet for dinner in about an hour and a half. Dinner was pleasant. Ruth ate very little because her appetite was off from the long trip. She felt that in the next day or two she would be fine, and they could then start on their different trips in and around Las Vegas.

The day before Ruth and Morrie were to leave for Jersey, Julie took Ruth for a ride in his car to Boulder Dam. They parked the car and he walked Ruth all the way to the center of this huge complex of granite and steel. Looking down the huge slope, they saw an expanse of curved concrete reaching down below to a trickle of water which seemed to bubble out of nowhere beneath the conduits that lined the bottom of the dam. Yet looking behind them they would see an immense expanse of clear blue water with stone mountains bursting from its depths. One had the sense that you were at the edge of the earth. In one direction the world going straight up, and in the other, going straight down It was an odd and peculiar feeling that you had, standing there. In Ruth it provoked a sense of clarity and truth. It was as if Ruth, on this very spot, sensed some profound vibration. She turned and looked at Julie.

"I'll be dead pretty soon, Julie," she said. "My life will be over. It's as if I'm talking about someone else. I don't even sense that it's me that I'm speaking of. I don't even know that I exist. All I know is that I have a dull ache in my stomach, and I find my thoughts thinking of you so much, dear Julie. I find it so hard to tell you this, but I love you very much. I'm sorry that twenty years or so stand between us now. I'm sorry that I'm related to you. I wish I weren't. I wish I were a young girl now seeing you for the first time. I wish, dear Julie, that you would take me away from here. You give me courage, Julie. You make me feel young and alive and give me the sense to look forward to something. I think your mother's alive and living somewhere in Los Angeles. I don't know. Stella's never told me who your father was. I've sure asked her a lot of times, but she'd never tell me. I always loved roses, Julie. When I was a girl I used to always love roses. Yellow roses. Oh dear, why should I think of yellow roses here, right now? It must be those pills the doctor gave me. Morrie should have been a teacher at a college now. He has the most exquisite patience with young people. Should be on the campus of some Midwestern college teaching math. Yes, he'd make a wonderful teacher. Where should you be now, Julie? Certainly not standing on the top of a dam talking to a dying woman. I'm sure you wanted more of life. Where do you desire to be now, where should you be?"

Julie looked at this frail, black-eyed woman, looked and saw what the ravages of this disease had done to her in the short year that they had not seen each other.

"Come on, Ruth, I'm gonna take you for a ride."

He walked her back to the car. They got in. Julie reached in the glove compartment, pulled out a small case, opened the top, handmade cigarettes. He offered her one.

"You know I don't smoke," Ruth said.

"This you'll smoke," Julie said. "You're gonna smoke some marijuana."

He lit the joint, started the car, and pulled back onto the road, took a long pull, and handed it to Ruth.

"Just inhale, baby," he said, "just inhale."

By the time they reached the 711 Casino, Ruth didn't have a pain in her body. Couldn't wait to go inside, clean up, and hit them gambling tables. She liked blackjack and that's where she spent the next four hours, sitting trying to beat the bank. When they left, Julie gave Morrie a pack of hand-rolled joints.

"These are for Ruth when it gets a little tough for her. Just give her one of these. Open the window, and join her if you like. If you want any more, the next time we talk, you let me know, Morrie."

When they left, Ruth told Julie that she didn't wanna see him again. She didn't want Julie remembering her in any other way except now. While her beauty was still there. She might have been thinner than she should have been, but she was still a very beautiful, strange, interesting-looking woman.

"Okay Ruth."

They went toward the car. He took Ruth by her hand and walked to the side of the building. It was a lovely night in Vegas cool, nothing in the sky except stars.

"Dear Julie. good-by."

She put her head on his shoulder and shook for a moment. Julie was very moved by this woman.

"Good-by my dear," she said.

"Good-by Mother."

He walked her to her car. She climbed in and they were gone. As fast as that. They were gone. Julie was never the same again. Ruth died the first week of June. Julie was in New York the next day and, with Morrie, helped prepare to bury her. Buried her in a Jewish cemetery in New Jersey. Next to her mother and her brother. Stella was at the funeral. After Ruth had been put in the ground at the grave site, Julie started for his car. When he reached the door of his limousine Stella was standing there.

"I wanna talk to you, Julie."

"Talk."

All around them people were milling, slowly returning to their respective cars to be driven out of the cemetery. Some lingered in groups. talking, occasionally looking at Julie and looking at Stella.

"I think your father was a guy I met on a train. I was sixteen."

"Shut up, Stella," Julie said. "I don't wanna hear anymore from you. I don't wanna know anything more about you or about my father or about where you came from or where he came from. I want no details. Stella. Nothing. Nothing. The best of us is buried here with Ruth."

He walked around her. Opened the back door of his limousine and climbed in, shut the door behind him.

Nobody and nothing moved. He rolled the window down and looked up at Stella.

"Good-by."

"You know, Julie, you're a prick."

She turned, this beautiful woman, walked up the green slope, and out of his life.

Waxie

Julie Sparrow and Waxie Shapiro walked into Domonik's. Julie didn't look around but walked straight to the bar. Waxie, as was his custom, stopped in the doorway and cased the joint, looking for edible griff. Waxie Shapiro got horny looking at nuns. That's one of the reasons why he never married; the thought of having to curtail his natural exuberance about a new piece would have driven him crazy. He had to be free to chase after the warmth of them there private parts.

Waxie Shapiro tried to spend a weekend alone once in Palm Springs and got stir crazy by ten-fifteen Saturday morning. He shacked up with two hookers for three days in town just to get over that experience. He loved being around ladies. Whenever he had had enough and that was usually for a few hours' time, he'd call Julie. Do some business on the phone. Occasionally meet a producer or a writer. Always he was out hunting and why not? He had never asked for anything more than that. And when he did, they wouldn't let him do it. He was a genius and only allowed to use a small bit of his gift. He was an agent who used only two per cent of his head. The other ninety-eight per cent had been turned down when he was a kid starting out. As profound as his genius was, so was his pride. It's your loss, he would say. Let the Cosmos have me, I'm theirs. This very small man, Waxie, had a unique sense of humor, sharp and crystal.

One day he was visiting the set of a Fred Astaire musical. Fred had just finished a three-minute shot of a very intricate, complicated, and beautiful dance number dressed as a sailor, deftly moving from one part of the ship to the other. As the deck rolled, he moved over and under anchors, winches, and clutches. As Fred finished, and stepped out of the lights, Waxie said, Freddie, I knew you could sing, but where did you learn to dance like that?

He and Solomon, these two old cockers, were once sitting nude in the sun in Palm Springs playing backgammon. They played a lot of backgammon with each other, these two.

"I'll double you," Solomon said.

"Not with that cock you don't," Waxie said.

Up to the bar he now strode right next to Jules and Dom.

"Give this friend here on my left, because there ain't no one on my right, a dry martini on the rocks and me my usual."

Dom, half the time, didn't know what the fuck Waxie was talking about. Every time Waxie was in, and that was four, five times a week, Waxie would say the usual and Dom proceeded to give him a different drink each night. In the years that they had known each other, he had tried out all his practice drinks on Waxie and Waxie never blinked an eye. He climbed up on the bar stool next to Julie, who was standing.

"Are you eating tonight?" Dom said.

"You got anybody in mind?" Waxie said.

Dom just showed his teeth.

"Wait."

Waxie looked and spotted Frances Farrell with Kid Andrew Cody.

"Look at that duo, one will and one won't."

"Is that that cowboy?" Julie asked.

"Well, it ain't Randy Reed. That dame can do you a lot of good in this town."

"Nobody can do me any better than I got."

"Well, Julie, my boy, you're one of the rare ones, then, but you're full of shit, you know that."

"Yeah, I know, I know."

"Your problem is you're afraid of life, that's why you're so jumpy and nervous. You've got to learn to calm down, Julie. Take things a lot easier. Now, I mean, look at you. I've never seen a man more tormented, more edgy than you."

Dom and Julie didn't know what the fuck he was talking about, or who he was talking to. Julie looked over his shoulder and turned back.

"You talking to me, Waxie?"

"Julie, what I like about you best is your sense of humor, which is nonexistent."

Julie drank his martini on the rocks, and Waxie drank his Singapore twister.

"And you, sir, where do you think you stand in this conflagration of ideas? Speak up, I didn't hear you."

Dom just listened. Forget it, the world was full of ass-holes. Waxie was a messiah. Nothing he felt was profound. He saw everything logically and cleanly, as a landscape or clouds against a blue sky passing over the rooftops of a city. The sun hot and warm inside the glass. Once he understood the theory, big fucking deal, he was onto something better, or worse, never settling for anything less than a logical explanation. If there was none, he just didn't have enough of the facts, and therefore was not obliged to believe it. Julie and Dom and Solomon were the three guys he liked best. He had a writer, Paul Delaney, who he would see once a year in Europe on one of his annual trips. They had a good relationship because they were both always on the move. After that he didn't want to know from nothing, just beautiful chickies, chicklets, nofkas, babies, birds, whiffers, cuties, lechers, baby janes.

Julie liked the looks of Frances Farrell. No one ever saw him take a look at her. But he got a good one in and no one caught it, and there was Cody. He didn't go to the movies a lot so he wasn't sure what all the wahoo was about. He figured it was a public relations job done by a studio and gave the audience an idol to grab onto. He had seen a lot of those cases in this town before all crumbling away into nothing. If Cody could take the taste for another five years, he could end up a big star. But time alone would tell.

"Waxie, why are there so many Jews in the picture business?"

"No other business would have us, Julie. When I was a kid there were very few firms or companies that I could get connected with. I finished law school in Chicago. I tried to get work at some government agencies, but they wouldn't take a Jew. Then I wanted so bad to be the Attorney General, but four years in Washington proved I was jerking off. I knew I was doomed the first week. As soon as they saw the name, Bernard Shapiro, I knew I was going to end up nowhere. Pictures were starting then and that's when I met King Solomon. The goyim didn't fight over the picture business because there was no way of telling what kind of business it was going to be. They figured it was all going to be a fad, that's why no one bothered with it except us Jews. Fuck 'em and that goes for the schwartzes, too. I don't trust any of them. They treat me like shit. I treat them like shit. These two old Jews were rocking in their chairs on the porch of some very expensive Catskill resort . . ."

"Why do they always have to be Jews?"

"Okay, these two old chairs were rocking in their Jews. One said to the other, 'Where you from?' The other said, 'Philadelphia.'

'How many Jews in Philadelphia?'

'Oh, maybe three hundred thousand.'

'How many goyim?' the other one said.

'Oh, maybe two million. And you. Where you from?'

'New York.'

'Got a lot of Jews in New York?'

'Oh, maybe two million.'

'No kidding? And how many goyim?'

'About ten million,' the other said.

'You need so many?'

"When Kid Gentile over there came to me about me representing him, we bullshitted for about an hour. Then we decided I would be his agent. Just before he walked out, he said to me, Excuse me, Mr. Shapiro, are you Jewish? I said, Not necessarily."

King Solomon
and His Sons

Solomon liked to come up to Vegas and use the 711 Casino. It was a quiet place for him to gamble and a quiet place for him to come to with whatever good-looking lady he was trying to put it to on that weekend. It had no effect on his personal life in L.A. No one knew it. He just liked Vegas very much and would come up whenever he could and spend the time with Julie. Sally was turning out to be quite a regular now. She would be there all the time, coming to see Julie during the week. The studio got a bit concerned. Said she ought to be in town but Solomon said, Fuck her, she likes being with Julie. Let her hang around there. It keeps her out of trouble when she's not working. When she was working, she was back in town or she'd go wherever the locations would take her on films. She and Julie would talk on the phone. She promised she'd come down to see him whenever she could. He tried to see her and their relationship seemed to progress. But then he met a socialite in Los Angeles, Doris Whiting, who tried to keep him quiet. She stuck him away somewhere in the hills of Bel Air, which was then a very isolated area, not allowing anyone to know that she would even imagine having an affair with some kike, Hebe, half-assed gangster who made his living from gambling in Vegas.

One weekend she took him to visit an ex-beau of hers who lived out in Pasadena. The beau was demonstrating his facility with a shotgun, shooting clay pigeons off his back porch into this big yard. He gave the gun to Julie to try. Julie tried once or twice and missed, not badly, but he missed. The ex-boyfriend seemed intent on trying to break Julie's balls because Julie was obviously fucking this very desirable woman that this guy couldn't get to base with. He couldn't understand how she could be fascinated by Julie. So he did everything in his power to try to debase Julie and make him look less than what he was. After Julie had missed the pigeons twice, the ex-boyfriend alluded that maybe Julie had a bit more prowess in bed than he did in the air.

"Now if clay pigeon was as simple as making love," he said, "you would be pretty good at both of them."

Julie didn't blink an eye; it didn't phase him one iota. He just turned with that loaded shotgun and without even really aiming he hand-passed a beautiful hand-carved head of some ancient Roman which sat on the corner of the portico of this very ornately carved fence surrounding the mansion. On the other corner, thirty feet away, was another beautiful head sculpture of some famous historical character. Both expensive and rare, irreplaceable, coming from villas of another time. As Julie panned by with the shotgun, he fired one blast which tore the head of one apart, panned again, and with a second blast tore the head off the next. He looked at his host.

"The pigeons I know don't fly."

De Carlo was singing that weekend and all of Las Vegas and Los Angeles was gearing up. There was an exodus from Beverly Hills by plane, train, and car to Las Vegas to hear De Carlo sing. It was 11:35 in the morning and already the tables were crammed. People were lining up to get the few available seats for the dinner show that were not being held in reservation.

Julie was at the baccarat table bullshitting with Ziggie Earlstein, a pit boss. King Solomon came behind the barrier followed by Kid Andrew Cody. They stopped and watched the action of the game. The smallest bet twenty. You could bet with the banker and you paid a piece if you won, a fascinating doubles game to make that eight or nine. Julie left Ziggie's side and walked over to Solomon and Cody.

"Sam, good evening. Hi, Andrew."

"Hey, Julie, gonna see De Carlo."

"Good evening, Julius."

"How about dinner?"

"You got a date. Hey, Kid Andrew Cody, Julie Sparrow you're so formal."

They shook hands across Solomon. As they shook hands, Solomon held both these young men by the shoulders. These were his tatalas. He loved these two kids. Loved them like they were his sons but never told them. Sol's sons.

Vegas was busting out all over. There were more tits in town than there were chips. Showgirl sizes were big, bigger, and biggest. Monroe and *Playboy* were making knockers popular. Now everybody had to have them, even some of the guys. Some girls were addicted, going back to have them enlarged. There was more silicone in them there hills than there was in all the first-class seats in the new 707s. Everybody was chasing after them. No wonder these poor chickies were pumping up their chests. It was a way of life and a way to make a score.

When Solomon was in town he wanted lots of tits around him. He had three showgirls sent up. The three had to know each other so there wouldn't be any bullshit or any time spent in introductions or any shyness or any numbers. No one really got hurt. They got sucked on a little bit. They would get humped, bumped, and triple jumped. Once in a while some joker would like to poke one of them in the ass and that was okay too as long as she watched her diet. These babes with blown-up tits were better off in Vegas than anywhere else. They could afford their fantasies and their small apartments, stuck away all over the place. Each one's cave unique unto itself, decorated like the costume of a matador, or in early Armenian or like a European health spa, and on top of all of that Vegas housed the research and development foundation clinic for the advancement of tits. With that hustling, bustling, dancing, singing, and winging, a kid could clear two grand a week without taxes. Dear Mother in Chesapeake Bay could get a lot of cha-cha lessons from the local Arthur Murray studio, redecorate her apartment, get her goiter fixed, send her son to a private military school, and put some away for a rainy day on the bread her little dolly sent her from the wild, wild West.

Solomon would hole up with three or four of these beautiful creatures. It wasn't that Solomon was getting jumped on all the time. It was just pleasant and relaxing to be around all those beautiful tits. He'd share one of his chickies once in a while with one or two chums but even then, like the kid who owned the ball, the bat, and the glove, he decided *who* was getting *what* from *whom*.

The moment his flight swooped and landed at McCarran Airport in Vegas, Solomon was the first off, down the gangplank into a waiting limousine, and off he went alone while a secretary, a valet, and a bodyguard went in a station wagon sent by the hotel. He thought of his brother Issy now, who always thought Solomon was a putz and an asshole and would never amount to anything. As far as Issy was concerned, Solomon could never do anything right. When Issy died at thirty-two. Solomon was twenty-two and still hadn't done anything right. Issy, you prick. you think I'm a putz, hah. Look at this limo. Three chickies tonight, beauties. Whenever Solomon showed up at his studio, twelve hundred and eighty-seven people, when it was full, would quiver and quake. Not to mention the other twenty thousand people all over the States; distributors, buyers, agents, publicists, Technicolor people and all the other related arts. And all those waiting customers with their shiny two-dollar bills. waiting for the latest epic from Samuel Solomon Productions, Incoporated, Ltd. He was the epitome of picture making. The best and the worst of it. Countless millions would enjoy over twelve thousand films that Samuel Solomon was involved with in his lifetime When the world became televised. and all those movies were played on television Solomon would still have no rest. While his brother Issy lived, he only thought of Sammy as a putz. Had he lived longer and seen some of the movies that Sammy had made, he would have still called him a putz.

Lila London was there with her entourage of press agents. B. Shrike Martin, one actress and her husband. London had stuck away two hookers for herself. Perry had arranged it for Madame London. so that when she arrived, and was taking her afternoon siesta getting ready for the evening's festivities, she was doing and getting done, with them fifty-dollar numbers.

De Carlo was down in the bowels of the hotel in a sauna, hot room, cold room, steam room, dry room. Pacing back and forth from hot to cold while he waited for what they were calling now the Knight of Nights. Cynical, bruised, and mean he was that night.

Julie, sleek and above it all and troubled by nothing, tried to maintain some decorum and calmness in this forty-thousand-square-foot madhouse.

"Julie?"

"Yeah."

"There's a guy out here from Florida, Kresge is the name, Bernard. Says he knows you. Wants ta bust us for ten-grand credit. Looks like he's straight in every way."

"Kresge's got a son-in-law I did a favor for once. The last time I was in Florida he loaned me his yacht. We cruised to Cuba, to Havana. He laid it on nice. Give him five and five later."

"Yeah, Jake."

"Julie, we've done forty-two thousand since six o'clock and the way I got it figured, give or take some stealing, we're going to do a cool quarter of a million before midnight."

"Jake, get Gretchen out of the apartment for the weekend. Put her in my place. Let Andrew Cody have it for himself. I'll be hangin' in here for the two shows. Tell Gretchen we'll be havin' breakfast at three."

"Okay, Julie."

"Julie?"

"Yeah, Danny."

"There's a guy at baccarat making me nervous. He's been here all night and he's been losin' a lot. He's smokin' a big cigar and gettin' the ashes all over the table. Now when he loses a big score he yells, cocksucker, asshole, mother-fucker, cunty-cards. I mean, Julie, it's bad. He's about eighty-five grand down so I guess he figgers he can talk like that."

"Danny, tell Tannenbaum to tell him to keep quiet. If he gives Tannenbaum any static, tell Itzik to throw him out. I don't need his money or his big mouth."

"Got it, Julie."

"Mr. Sparrow?"

"Yes, Armand."

"Mr. Solomon has asked for the Galaxy Room for ce

soir. Unfortunately it has already been booked by Señor José Catalón of Mexico City. I thought perhaps Monsieur Solomon's party could be held in the Villa Trevi Piazza."

"Armand, you're wrong. Mr. Señor What's-his-name is gonna have his party in the Piazza tonight and Mr. Solomon in the Galaxy. Anything else, Armand?"

"No, monsieur."

"Julie, it's Manny."

"Yeah, what's up?"

"There's a new kid in town, calls herself Brenda, dark-haired, big tits. And her own. You know the one. She was in last night. Nice-looking kid. Fresh, not beat-up-lookin' at all. You know the one I mean."

"Yeah."

"She got a call to do this trick. Went up to the room and it's—er, this—er, woman columnist, writer in Holly-wood, Lila London. You know the one."

"Yeah."

"Well, this kid says this woman asked her to do all kinds of weird things and then when she was finished and waitin' for the fifty, the woman told her to ask at the desk for it. Obviously she's tryin' to beat this kid out of her fifty. From the way she looks, Brenda should be get-tin' five grand."

"Perry Rose's the one that brings her up here, isn't he?"

"Right."

"Does she always get freebies up here?"

"The room and what she eats in the restaurant, that's all. What she eats up in her room she's gotta pay for her-self. That's a joke, Julie."

"I know, Manny. Give Brenda two hundred and tell her to take the night off. Cut down the hot water going to the London broad's room, cut down the air-conditioning, screw up her toilets. If she complains, tell her to get the fuck out. Now get me Perry Rose."

"Right."

"Perry, keep that cheap yenta in line or I'm gonna tear up your credit card."

"Right, Julie, right. Right. There's some trouble?"

"You got room and board for that broad up here. That's all. You pay for her gambling, and her chickies and anything else. I don't wanna see one item on her tab and I'm checking your charges as well. Got it?"

"Right, Julie. See ya later."

"What're ya doin', Julie?"

"Just putting a few things together before I take off. It's gonna be a big night, Vinnie. I'm almost finished. What are you doin'?"

"Come on down, take a swim, take some heat."

"Yeah, Vinnie, I'll be down in about five minutes."

"Sam, come on down and take a shivitz with me. Vinnie's down below."

"Julie, I've got these chicklets."

"I know, I know. They'll hold till later. You got 'em all weekend long, Sam. Don't worry about nothin'. Max is gonna come up and getcha and bring ya down to where we are. Okay. See ya in a couple of minutes."

"Okay, Julie."

"Andrew Cody."

"Yeah, right."

"Julie Sparrow."

"Well, howdy."

"How's it goin'?"

"Wonderful. Thanks for the apartment, Julie. It's really nice. Really don't need all this room for myself."

"That's okay, Andrew. You don't get up here too much and I wantcha to enjoy yourself."

"Thanks."

"Sam Solomon and I are gonna go down to the steam room and pool. Vinnie's down there. Thought maybe if you're free you'd come on down and join us."

"Right, when are you gonna be down there?"

"Why don't you come on down in about fifteen, twenty minutes?"

"Right, okay."

"I'll send somebody to bring ya down."

"That's okay, Julie. I thought I'd walk down to the casino and kinda look around and then drop down."

"Okay. When you're ready to come down to the steam, just look around, somebody'll be there to show you how to get down there."

"Great."
"See ya later."
"So long."

The casino was packed. High rollers, low rollers, top rollers. People lined up for the slots, old ladies, young ladies, bald men, bored men. The crap tables were loaded. Loud suits and no suits, ties and no ties. Loose and swinging ladies pumping on the slots, jerking off each machine, hoping for a come.

Come, baby, come. I need the money.

The Kid moseyed around the casino, checking the action. Come on, baby, dream a dream of me. Love me just the way you dream you love me. People were lined up at the reservations desk, hoping for a room, impatient to put their belongings away and get down and hit them tables. Children sitting up at the top of the steps overlooking the casino. A couple of twelve- or fourteen-year-old girls and an eight-year-old boy playing with a tin TWA toy plane. A two-year-old in a baby carriage with a pacifier stuck in its mouth like some big cigar, being rocked impatiently by his older sister, who happened to be seven and not allowed down in the casino where Mamma and Papa were hoping to hit four the hard way. The only thing really hard was the way these kids had to wait. But looking down into the casino from the raised portion of the steps, these children had the best view of the place.

Kid Andrew Cody stopped at a crap table. The pit boss nodded to him, and he found himself being allowed behind the velvet cord that separated the gamblers from the operation of the pit, where only pit bosses, dealers, owners, entertainers, and visiting celebrities that knew the running crew were allowed. Chips were flying all over the crap table. Bet the come and take all the odds. I wanna buy all the numbers. Come on, baby, Papa needs a new pair of balls. Wham! Seven, eight the loser. Next roller. Andrew watched. His eyes riveted on the crap table, marveling at the swiftness of the caretakers of dice and chips. How quickly money was dispatched and taken in. A good-looking girl with a short mini skirt sidled up to him.

"Can I getcha something?"

Kid Andrew smiled.

"No, thank you, ma'am."

And she left. He glanced up, and as he did, Crimpy was there.

"Mr. Cody?"

"Right."

"Crimpy Lefkowitz."

He stuck out his left hand, his right hand was crimped.

"Julie said when you wanted to go to the steam room, I should take you there."

"What did you say your first name was?"

"Well, my nickname's Crimpy."

"What's your real name?"

"Marvin."

"Well, Marvin, I'm ready to go."

Crimpy turned and Kid Andrew followed him through the caverns, hallways, and banquet rooms of the casino d'élégance. They passed through the casino's big theater and went backstage to a small elevator that only went three floors down. They got out at the bottom, which was the basement. Walking through corridors of pipes and stanchions and wires, they finally arrived at a door and in they went and Kid Andrew Cody found himself in an oasis. You wouldn't think that you were sixty feet below the surface of Las Vegas, Nevada. Potted plants all over the place being fed by the steam heat of this subterranean Garden of Eden. A beautiful girl came forward in a toga.

"I'll take your clothes."

Kid Andrew didn't wait for another invitation. He quickly undressed, wrapped a towel around his waist, and was escorted by this beautiful creature into the guts and bowels of the spa.

Blue square-inch tiles flecked with slivers of silver extended from the bottom of the pool, overflowed the rounded edges of the swimming pool, and covered the entire floor of the room, its walls and ceiling. What light illuminated the room was hidden behind recessed alcoves. With the water reflecting the blue of the bottom of the pool, this huge blue room, shiny and wet, gave Kid Andrew Cody the sense of falling, ready to be sucked through the drain of the pool into a new and meaningful existence. There were two doors on opposite sides of the pool. Through one of these doors, Julie would leave when and if needed, and if he wanted to get out of town in a hurry. You'd be hard put to find the doors when they were shut. There wasn't a mark in the tile that would give you any indication of where the openings were. There were a half-dozen nondescript lounging chairs made of wood and canvas, some towels piled one on top of another, a tray sitting on the floor holding two bottles of water, a large bucket of ice, some plastic glasses. The room's temperature was a hundred degrees. The room's temperature never was less than ninety-eight degrees or never more than a hundred and one degrees. That's how Julie liked it and whatever Julie liked Julie got.

Solomon's body overlapped everything it sat on. His feet were in the water, his arms stretched out like Dali crutches, holding up the ernomous weight of his shoulders, neck, and head. Vinnie De Carlo was sitting cross-legged on a lounge chair, cutting his toenails with a pair of hair scissors. Kid Andrew had been lapping the pool now for about ten minutes, swimming for long stretches underwater. Julie Sparrow was partaking of his daily pleasure: pacing. Like a cat, he prowled around this forty-by-twenty-five-foot pool, stopping occasionally to say something. Once in a while he'd dive into the water. But he would quickly surface and begin his pacing again.

"De Carlo?"

"Yeah."

"How many shows ya doin' tonight?"

"One."

"Good. And don't take too fuckin' long. I got three chicklets waiting tonight."

"Ya know, Vinnie, sometimes when you sing you remind me of a singer I used to know. He's dead now. He phrased beautifully. Buddy Clark was his name. He died in an airplane crash. A private plane fell down on, I think it was Melrose and Western or somewhere, comin' home from a football game or goin' to a football game. Who the fuck knows? The poor bastard. Beautiful singer."

"Fell down in a fuckin' plane, Sam. I remember him."

"I tell ya, these fuckin' actors are crazy. Here we are in Vegas. That Cody could be pulling chicklets left and right up in the casino. He could boff his head off the whole weekend long and what is he doin'? Look. Swimmin' underwater. Present company excluded, that goyisher kup is losin' his marbles."

"Sam, Vinnie is doing his first show at ten tonight. What time you wanna eat?"

"In a little while I'm going up to my room. Come and get me before Vinnie goes on. I need fifteen minutes to dress. After the show, I want the Galaxy Room. I'm givin' a party and I want the best-lookin' quiff in town to be there."

Kid Andrew surfaced just before the word "quiff."

"Quiff, what's a quiff?" he asked, as he submerged again for another lap and a half. The Kid surfaced between the legs of Samuel Solomon. Solomon just watched him.

"You must be the new schoolmarm," Kid Andrew said. What could have been a smile on Solomon's face came and disappeared. And there he sat gazing down at Kid Andrew. This movie mogul giant, towering over him. It didn't unnerve the Kid at all. Kid Andrew Cody was always courteous when he met people. Kid Andrew Cody always admired people older than himself, especially men, because there but for the grace of God go I. The men that he had known, that had made it into their forties, fifties, and sixties, were very few and each one was someone that he admired. Maybe not for his experience with them so much as for the time he had spent in searching for them. Kid Andrew admired Solomon's gruffness and his single-mindedness. He wasted no time in getting his pictures made. If people didn't come up with what they were supposed to, he'd get them bumped off pictures, get rid of them, out, finished. Solomon, the slammer, insisted his pictures be made his way. He wanted his actors and actresses, his stars, to be attractive and real, intelligent and wise, elegant and stupid. Therein lay the magic of it all. He wanted them wholesome and handsome. He didn't care if they were blondes or brunettes—he had no favorite figure in mind. He saw through the smiles and Coke bottles and cheesecloth and diffusions and anything else you could put in front of the seventy-five-millimeter lens. Whoever was in front of it had to be good-looking. He liked stories about guys going after their girls and getting them. He liked stories about race car drivers making their own cars. Starting a new ranch in the West. Building a shipping line between San Francisco and Peru. He wanted all his films to have the proper balance between a little bit of magic and a lot of balls. Once in a while he succumbed to a highly artful piece of mishmash, but he always came back to his first love, his first early images, that each day, each hour, was a moment unto itself. Not to play back or try to recall but to perpetuate that never-ending adventure, that journey in your mind.

Julie was pacing the streets again, lost in memories.

Why can't I find what I'm looking for!

What you looking for?

How the fuck do I know? If I did I wouldn't look for it. Angie. Deader than a doornail. I don't wanna know from nothing any more. Just vanilla malteds and pink candy on the inside and six two and even on the outside. Pull up your collar, Julie, it's cold. Where you goin'? Out, Ma, into the street. How often into the streets, lost, alone, free. Go, come as you please. No one knows you but yourself. And you think you're someone else. Don't pack a piece, putz. Never carry more than you can eat. The cold wind bit his face and rosyed his cheeks. He was shivering, his shoulders drawn up. His white and blue hands deep in his light summer pants pockets in winter. Head down, he walked always with his eyes in the gutter, looking for his ship to come in, in the shape of a fat wallet. Morrie lost his twenty that way. Go give it back, you gutter-fucker. You take everything else anyway.

A sheet covered the small figure in the gutter. Near the corner, cold and windy, a stream of blood ran downhill toward the drain on the corner. From under the sheet it seeped, seeking the lowest ground because water seeks its own level. And, everybody knew blood was thicker than water. Except no one told that kid who got his by that hit-and-run. From where the blood was coming under the sheet, it was redder than farther down near the drain. A small very white hand was sticking out at the edge of the sheet. Never to throw a Spalding high flyer, or jerk off, or write his name in school no more. Or make a model plane or stroke her budding breast.

Julie looked and shivered, shut his eyes hard. And there he was, pacing his blue pool again.

He finally sat down next to Sam.

"Wattss matter, you got tired of walking the streets?"

"What?" said Julie.

"Forget it." Sam said.

Vinnie finished cutting his toenails and moved over and sat alongside Sam, cross-legged like some Italian yogi, in the lotus position, pasta-style. The Kid was floating in the water in front of Sam, three sons in search of a father. Vinnie spoke.

"I've been offered a deal from down the street. Rosebuds Ackermann is offering a five-year deal, four weeks a year, two hundred thousand bucks a year, give me all or whatever I want this year, and two and a half per cent of the business."

"How do you do with Julie?" Sam asked.

"With Julie, he gives me the place and all my expenses, plus a quarter of the take."

"How much time do you spend here?"

"Whatever I want. Makes no difference."

"Hey, Julie, you must like this guinea to do that for him."

"Pass it, Vinnie, here ya got no books. You're not gettin' nickeled and dimed to death."

"I passed already," Vinnie said.

Papa loved them all now more than ever. After a time of silence and peace, Samuel Solomon lumbered to his feet and left. He would be dead seven months later.

Vinnie was gonna sleep until an hour before he worked, so he left through one of the invisible doors. Alone together for the first time, Kid Andrew and Julie. They began to notice each other with the most delicate of tools, sense and emotion. Alone, they realized now how much they were alike in figure and in style. There was something more than brotherly between them and they couldn't figure out what it was, or at least Andrew couldn't. Julie had understood it since the time he was old enough to respond to what he saw. He could recall similarities in people who were not related, didn't even speak the same language, yet held some physical similarity in common that went beyond just coincidence. A particular cut of a nose, the shape of eyes, the neck, all of those elements combine to make some people very much alike. Heavy beard line, cleft in chin, widow's peak hairline. Looking at Andrew, Julie thought he was glimpsing himself from an odd angle. They looked alike but they didn't. Kid Andrew had, if anything, a more quizzical look, a look that broke into a smile very easily. His eyes were set in such a way that his look was one of surprise and interest at everything he gazed upon. He was a bit taller than Julie, but narrower in the cheek. Julie's eyes were more deeply set in his head than Andrew's. Andrew's lips were fuller and Julie's chin was stronger. They both had the same cut of ears, though, flat and shaped to hear with small lobes. Julie's hair was blacker and grayer. Overall, Kid Andrew was more properly proportioned. Andrew felt uncomfortable in the presence of attractive men. He felt threatened, and didn't like to see anyone who he felt was more attractive than himself. Looks to Julie didn't mean a fucking thing except in a very superficial way. He learned right from the first that what you looked like had really very little to do with what you were or how you were. Looks were just another way of getting to know you. Julie liked being in Andrew's company. During the little time that he had spent with him, he liked him. Kid Andrew was friendly and warm and it was especially contagious for Julie.

They looked at each other furtively at first. Not daring to see into each other's eyes. They saw each other in themselves. They flicked at each other and looked when neither was looking. They could bear it no more and like a huge ship easing into a dock they locked eyes. It was like looking into an invisible mirror. A mirror image of their eyes and yet they both feared that furnace of truth.

Where were you from?

New York. You?

Wichita.

How old are you?

Thirty-eight. You?

Thirty-nine, I think.

Why think—

I'm not sure.

What your daddy do?

He's a tailor. Yours?

He was a gambler. Poker player.

Looking for four the hard way. Eh?

Yup. And he got shot for it.

Thoughts unsaid and words unspoken.

You know what dying is?

What?

Going to bed early.

Shi-i-i-t-t-t.

My best buddy, when I was a kid, got shot and killed. His name was Angie.

My daddy's name was Maxwell Boyd Cody.

Maxwell Boyd Cody—that's a nice name.

He was a nice father.

My old man's still alive. Only he ain't my old man. But I love him.

How do you love someone like a father if he ain't your daddy?

He's always been nice to me.

That's not love.

Andy, don't bet on it.

Julie, I won't bet you 'cause I'd lose. You're like my daddy, a gamblin' man. I grew up with a guy that was a cripple, named Slim, for a little while. He was like you. Didn't ask much of me.

You don't have much to offer, except Yup. No offense.

No offense. Julie, you could have been in pictures. You're a good-lookin' guy.

So could you.

Shi-i-i-t-t-t.

I got a boat on Lake Mead. You wanna go fishing?

When?

Tomorrow morning.

Great.

I'll set it up. Some food and some quiff.

That'll be nice, Julie, real nice. When you're in L.A. let's party sometime. I know a lot of grommit.

Andrew, I'll take you up on that.

Julius, I hope you do.

They never did.

* * *

Sally Tarlow was getting to be a pain in the ass to Julie. As her career improved and as she became more popular in films she seemed to become less secure as a person, less sure of herself. At the beginning she was in every way a very vibrant and exciting creature, but she now became more calculating, more into herself. Their relationship shuffered. She became abusive, jealous, fretful, always checking up on him. Julie didn't like it at all. Finally, today she started heaping all kinds of abuse on this socialite girl Julie was seeing. He told her to fuck off. He went out to gig the tables. When he got back to his room to dress for the evening's festivities, he went into his closet in his dressing area and found one sleeve of all his jackets and one leg of all his trousers cut off. All the remnants of these suits sat in a pile in the middle of the room like amputated arms and legs. His shirts had been indiscriminately cut into diamond shapes, his ties, scarves, everything had been butchered. Some had been burned by matches. All heaped in the middle of the room. When he came in, he was so stunned he had no reaction. There was nothing he could do. And there she was standing at the door, one arm leaning against the wall, the other on her hip.

"Well, lover, don't look so shocked," she said, "wait till you see the bathroom, man."

He took a good long deep breath, walked up to her, and smacked her right in the mouth as hard as he had smacked anybody in his whole life. He knocked her halfway across the room. She skidded over a table, knocked over a vase of flowers, knocked over candles, books, phones, cigarette lighters, cigarettes, magazines, papers. Everything went flying around. She lay there very still, very quiet. Julie just walked out of the room, ran into Rosie down below.

"How's it going, Boss?"

"Okay. Let me check the numbers for the night."

"Right."

The gambling bookkeeper was standing alongside of him giving him his figures. He looked up and there coming around the corner of the desk was Sally, really wobbly on her legs. Her face white and ashen. Her eyes almost devoid of anything except fear. The side of her face was swollen and distended. She had difficulty walking. If someone tried to help her, she refused. The bellboy tried to give her a hand. She struck his hand down.

"Put my stuff in the cab," she said.

They put her two pieces of luggage in the car, and

she stopped to get her breath and gather her strength for the last walk to the car. Then turned and looked. A hundred fifty feet away stood Julie looking in the same direction. Their eyes met for a quick moment. In hers there were fear and anguish. A little sadness as well. In his, there was absolutely nothing. They never saw each other again.

This Must Be Love

The Pearlsteins were giving their annual black tie party. They lived on an acre lot. A quarter of that was used up by the house, another quarter for a swimming pool and tennis court. On the other half, Pearlstein had created a miniature forest. No tree was over two feet tall. No leaf bigger than your smallest fingernail. The forest was in scale. There were paths, open stretches of sand, clusters of trees, a small brook. There were prescribed steps to cross this venerable forest that were cleverly hidden by small shrubbery. You could enter the forest and stand in twelve different positions. Squat down and from that position you could see through the trees to the ground underneath. The path railings were no thicker than a kitchen match. Pearlstein had a cardboard telescope that gave his eyes an extra foot of distance. There he would sit on his heels, as if evacuating, holding this black cardboard apparatus between his legs and aiming it down the corridors of the miniature forest. The Kid figured that this was about as nuts as you could get.

When the Kid got to Pearlstein's party, it was going pretty good. He decided to go alone. There was always a good chance he would find some beautiful lady to take out for dinner, then wherever. There were always a lot of strange ladies at these parties, and he'd sooner take potluck. He found he did much better that way than trying to make it any more meaningful. A quick fuck was better than none.

Two hundred fifty people from the picture profession were there. Twenty-five or thirty were invited early for cocktails, between six-thirty and eight. After that, people just started to arrive. There would be no dinner served, just some Jewish-Chinese hors d'oeuvres and drinks. The people who came early were the more important Hollywood dignitaries, and it gave them all a chance to bullshit each other on how good each one was doing. And when they got tired of crapping each other, new people

would arrive and so you could have a pleasant evening.
If you were interested in the size of that girl's tits.
Whether that guy took it in the ass. Whether she was
living with her. Gloating over other people's failures.
Envying those who had some success. You could tell the
quality of a party by what press were invited. They were
all ripoffs, the press. All being deducted. You deduct me.
And together, we deduct them. The Kid met interesting
people at these parties. The Kid's pictures were doing
great. He was a star in movie houses across the country,
but in Hollywood he was an upstart, *nouveau riche.*
Won't last. Morally unacceptable. No education. Ill-mannered, rough and gruff, and a fag. In Hollywood he was
a flop. In the rest of the world, a movie star.

The Kid had eaten a vegetable sandwich at home and
had a joint in the car, coming to the party. A martini on
the rocks at the party, a joint at the Pearlsteins' forest,
and that was all the drugs he was gonna need tonight. He
had a dark blue velvet denim-cut suit. Short jacket and
low-cut trousers. Trousers that sat on the hip with a slight
bell. He wore no tie, just a white shirt, open at the neck.
He met his hosts in a large sitting room that housed a
pool table and a card table that was really a backgammon table disguised as Madame Pompadour's snatch table.
A huge blue couch sat in the middle of the room with an
equally long table along its back. A massive glass stood in
front of the blue couch flanked by five chairs of different styles. The glass held up miraculously by four
slender legs. The table was crammed with silver and gold
boxes of different shapes and sizes, enameled, pearl-
studded boxes of all kinds. The Kid figured when the
rest of the party arrived there would be very few of these
choice pieces left. The Kid didn't know that Chandler,
the butler, cleared away all the boxes from the table and
replaced them with three very sturdy cigarette trays and
a bowl of flowers. The Kid greeted his hosts.

"Perhaps we'll talk later," Adele Pearlstein said.

He left his hosts and started to case the room. He
knew everyone in the room. All somehow connected
with pictures. There was Perry talking with Mrs. Pearlstein. Adele was telling Perry the kinds of items she
wanted to see in the papers the next day and in the
Sunday editions. The photographers were to travel dis-

creetly through the evening taking pictures with their strobe lighted Nikons. Under no circumstances were they to ask to set up shots. Just shoot the party informally. And there was Eric, who worked as head bartender and head server at most of the very chic and exclusive parties around town. There was Snap Barrigan and his snappy five putting down "In a Mountain Greenery" on piano.

"Saw the film you made," said Bracey Tomlin, agent for women. "You're doin' okay, Kid. You've got an easy way of handling yourself. If you don't overdo it, you'll go a long way."

She oughtta know. Here she was, twenty-six, handling a dozen important film people. The Kid didn't have an agent. When he first signed with Pearlstein, Pearlstein recommended he get a lawyer to look over the contract, which he did, and signed. When the Kid figured he wanted to make more money, he'd just go in and ask. He was doing all right. He could make a couple hundred thousand dollars a picture plus a piece. He spotted Billie Jean Jones by the bar. This voluptuous country girl who started out singing for a country Western band and who was now going to try to make it straight. Cut out the singing altogether if she could and just concentrate on acting and giving head. Deep emotion. Well, her tits were deep enough that was for sure.

"Where ya been?"

"Acapulco."

"Oh, holiday?"

"Kinda."

"How was it?"

"Beautiful. Got a new club called Alfonso."

"Oh yeah. Where is it?"

"Right on the beach. You know Georgie's?"

"Right."

"Well, a mile from that you go left on Flippies and right there, right off the beach. Beautiful spot."

"Oh. Wonderful. How long were ya?"

"Nine days. You go down there?"

"Every chance I get."

"I love it."

"What are you doin' in town?"

"I'm not doin' anything now. Just waiting. There's a picture at MCM I might get in."

"You alone?"

"I came with Bracey. Shall we see each other later?"

"Okay."

The Kid leaned forward and brushed her lips.

"See ya later, Billie Jean."

The tip of her tongue touched the corner of his mouth.

"Later, Kid." And the thought of Billie Jean made his mouth water.

The young man parking cars got busy. It seemed as if people were just tumbling in now, as if let off by some impatient express subway in New York. The Kid walked through a library, through what looked like a small sitting room, into a small den and found himself face to face with B. Shrike Martin. They both were so unprepared for the meeting that they smiled and said hello in a cordial manner. But then they froze. There was no questioning the undisguised antagonism between these two men. The Kid wanted to punch him right in his insolent fucking face. And B. Shrike Martin would have loved to kick him right in the balls. The Kid turned abruptly and left him standing. B. Shrike Martin had been standing with about four people. It quieted down in their corner. The Kid got some small slivers of beef on little bamboo shoots. He dipped them in the sauce. He had two or three of these and walked on through an outdoor-indoor room that overlooked the pool. Adele Pearlstein was there. The Kid walked up to her. She turned and saw him.

"They beat up that girl Lynn, you know, Mrs. Pearlstein."

"Very unfortunate. Certainly none of my doing."

"They rummaged me around as well, too, ma'am."

"That's what I heard. Again, none of my doing. I'm a person of my word, and when I told you what I would do, I meant it. I certainly have no idea who could have done anything like that. Whoever did, they were not acting on my behalf and were very irresponsible. You can believe me. But that is all past and forgotten. Let's let it all be where it is—with the past. I hope now, Andrew, we can have a much more stable and interesting relationship. Perhaps, if you wish, you may call me."

She was gone now. Swallowed up by her guests.

"Monica. Jesus, baby, how ya doin'?"

"Kid, I've thought about you a lot."

"How was London?"

"Oh, wonderful. I did that picture and then stayed on for a while. I had hoped I'd see you over there."

"Well. I got busy on that film I finished last week, and kinda stayed around here."

Remembering five months ago.

"How long ya been back now?"

"Just eight or nine days."

"Why didn't you call me?"

"Why, I didn't have your new number, Kid, and I knew we'd run across each other somewhere."

"Sure would like to see ya."

"Well. there's no one stopping you."

"Got a number?"

"Crestview 4-6177."

"What are you doin' later?"

"I've got no plans."

"Didja come with anybody?"

"I came with Bracey. Two down and two to go."

"Monica, stay loose for later."

"Okay, Kid."

He reached forward and kissed her on the lips. The response was warm. His mouth was watering again. And he had a date with Mrs. Pearlstein for later in the week. Billie Jean and Monica would meet him later. B. Shrike Martin and he had sworn their hate. And, he'd been there twenty-five minutes.

Lila London was standing by the mantelpiece, a drink in one hand, a cigarette in the other, standing under a painting by Sisley. She was talking to Bennet Brown, head of publicity for Pacific Productions. Mrs. Brown stood next to him, pissed and smiling. Perry had a new client in tow. The girl's family was paying for her career. They had taken fifteen thousand dollars of their earnings and Lulu Vincent was on her way. Lila London gave her a quick look and lost interest immediately. The Kid walked right up to Lila London.

"Howdy, you must be the old schoolmarm."

Mr. Brown and wife moved off and so did Perry and Lulu, leaving Lila London and Kid Andrew Cody talking under the mantelpiece being lit by the light that was lighting the Sisley.

"I thought I'd come over and iron out our differences." Her eyes narrowed.

"I don't know what you're talking about."

"You racked me up and then you got Lynn rapped. If you'd like to call it an even score, you're gonna have to apologize to me and Lynn first. And if you're not, prepare to fall back into that fucking hole you came from, 'cause I'm gonna shove ya there. I'm not lookin' for any trouble, ma'am. Just tryin' to make a livin'. And I ain't gonna hide out all the time, either. Why don't we just call it square?"

She never lost her smile.

"I'm going to ruin you around here, and I mean it. You shake your masculinity around here like you're salting a steak. You're lucky anybody ever talks to you, let alone uses you in movies. Anybody can do what you can do, so what makes you so high and mighty. You're too sure of yourself, Jacko. When I'm through with you there won't be enough left of you to sell as a deodorant. We don't need the likes of you around here. Now beat it before B. Shrike Martin sucks you up."

She turned and walked away.

The Kid was shooting pool with Vinnie De Carlo. The Kid was chalking up. He could feel it quiet down. People sitting at the bar stiffened a bit. He was looking at the table facing the inside of the room. But through the glass of the window he could see that B. Shrike Martin had entered. Vinnie was leaning over the pool table with a stick in his hand, preparing to put the nine ball in the right corner pocket. He looked around the table. After the nine, he'd go for the four, which was sitting north of the side pocket. The cue ball hit the nine, which it sank, ricocheted off the harsh green felt edge, hit the cushion diagonally to it, bounced off, and stood staring that four ball down into the hole. As Vinnie moved around the table, he saw B. Shrike Martin standing behind the Kid. The Kid was watching the game, watching the table. Vinnie looked up, glanced at B. Shrike Martin, and looked the Kid dead in the eye. Vinnie could tell that the Kid knew that B. Shrike Martin was behind him. Vinnie leaned over the table, sank the four. There were about four other people in the room with other people coming in and out all the time. Vinnie started to chalk his cue.

"There's an asshole round your shoulder," he sang.

"Fuck off, De Carlo, or you'll find that guinea voice of yours singing in the Valley at Toledo Joe's."

Suddenly the room was empty. The last lackadaisical guest in the room was some filly from Philly, tailing De Carlo everywhere he went that night. B. Shrike ushered her out by the elbow through the two sliding doors. He turned and the three of them were alone in the room.

"Go on, De Carlo, you too," Shrike said. "I gotta talk to Kid Shit, here, alone."

The Kid just said it; he didn't even check with Vinnie.

"You wanna talk with me, you talk with Vinnie in the room."

The dead eyes of Martin didn't blink.

"Suit yourself." Shrike shut the sliding doors behind him and bolted the latch.

B. Shrike Martin stepped forward. The Kid took his cue stick, holding it at the felt end and, pointed the blunt end of the stick at B. Shrike's chest.

"That's far enough. What've you got in mind?"

"Lila London doesn't like the way you talk to her."

"Fuck her. Feed her fish."

Both prospects the Kid knew Lila would love. But now was not the time to satisfy anybody's whims.

"You gotta show her a little more respect, Cowboy. She's an important person in this town, Saddle Bum. She doesn't mind you working here, you Shit Kicker, but you gotta show her a little more respect, Asshole. She don't like it when you talk to her crude, you Cocksucker. She wanted me to come here and warn you, Fuckhead. She says you're crude, Fag. She told me what you did to her at the beach house that night, you Crum. After you beg her so she would love you and put your name in the paper, you then punch her 'cause she wouldn't give you money, Pimp."

"Kid, I knew you were raunchy, but to fuck Lila London, you gotta be dead," Vinnie said.

It took B. Shrike Martin a second to get it. Vinnie saw it coming but that was all. B. Shrike struck out with his left hand and hooked Vinnie De Carlo into an unconscious man crumbled at the foot of the pool table. By the time B. Shrike Martin moved the cue stick, and threw his punch at the Kid, the Kid was under it. The Kid swung as hard as he could with the cue stick, which was already in a striking position, and rapped B. Shrike Martin good and hard in his kidney. He dropped the cue stick on the table, turned, and threw a right into B. Shrike's face. B. Shrike fell backward and hit the chromium-plated slot machine and Bam! Bam! The Shrike was out cold. The Kid heard someone rattling the door curiously. He picked Vinnie up under his arms and put him on the pool table, stretched him out like he was stiff. Hands across his chest. He reached down and hauled B. Shrike Martin up to his feet and plopped him onto the pool table and folded his arms as well. Both men were stretched out on this five-and-a-half-by-nine-foot regulation pool table. He turned off all the lights in the room and left only the harsh pool-table light on. He undid the latch, opened the sliding doors. As the doors opened he was confronted by Chandler and about six people. Looking into the room, they saw two bodies stretched out side by side on a pool table. The Kid told Chandler and whoever else was in earshot that it was going to be a double funeral because they wanted it that way and not to disturb anything. He then shut the two doors. He told Chandler that if people would file in one at a time they could view the bodies. With that he opened one side of the paneled doors and Chandler solemnly nodded and gestured for this girl and young chap standing next to her to be the first to enter if they wished. They said, Thank you, walked into the room with their drinks, and went around the pool table and out the door. Chandler sent them in two at a time. He felt that one at a time would take all evening. It was in the presence of the sixth couple that Vinnie came to.

The party was really swinging now. The Kid saw Billie Baby.

"I'll meetcha outside in five minutes," he said.

Saw Monica talking to a writer and a press agent. Walked up behind her, Monica leaned forward.

"Monica, baby, four minutes, out in front. We'll take my car."

Bracey was at the bar with Mike Frankel, the director,

and Lanny Aldrich, who had just played the ingenue in the film *The Miracle at San Stefano,* a religious epic.

"Bracey, you got three minutes to finish your drink and bring this pussycat next to you along and meet me out in front. I'm driving us up somewhere. You're gonna follow me."

"Good-by, Mrs. Pearlstein," he said.

"Call me Adele," she said, looking at Lila.

"Well, Adele, one of your guests hit the jackpot on the slot machine," Andrew said.

"Anyone I know?"

"Maybe."

The Kid turned and looked Lila London in the eyes.

"It was B. Shrike Martin. Good night."

He worked his way through the room. It was then that he saw Vinnie, pale, nervous, and quite shaken up, staggering through the room. The Kid grabbed him by the arm, pulled him over to the side.

"What the fuck was that all about? That prick slugged me," Vinnie said.

"Yeah, I know. Come on, we're going."

"Great. Let's get the fuck outta here. What're we gonna do?"

"We're goin' to a party, Vinnie. We're goin' to a party."

"Shit, I'm not up to any more parties. I've had about all the parties I'm gonna need this month."

"No, you're gonna love this one," the Kid said. "There's gonna be sucking and fucking and wet towels and suppositories and Vaseline."

Vinnie looked suspiciously at the Kid.

"Oh yeah, who's gonna be there?"

They both answered, "You and me."

They were at the door. The Kid nodded at the parking attendant and his car was there and so were Monica and Billie Jean. As the four of them piled into the Kid's car, Bracey Baby stepped out.

"You don't need your car. Pile in with us. Leave your keys with the Pearlsteins and you can pick them up anytime you want, but let's move."

"That was the weirdest thing that ever happened to me," Vinnie said as they were pulling out of the driveway. "I woke up and found myself flat on my back looking up at people walking around the pool table. And lying next to me is this asshole, B. Shrike Martin, out colder than a well-digger's cunt. Oh, er, excuse me, girls. These Hollywood parties get weirder and weirder."

They had been at the Kid's house for an hour now, and the only one dressed was De Carlo. Everyone else was naked. Vinnie asked if he could undress in the bathroom. The Kid showed him where. Vinnie finally came out, towel wrapped around him and a hard-on. He didn't do much outside work, so consequently he was pale and white. Bracey was sitting on the couch with a drink in her hand. The Kid was rolling a joint. Vinnie stepped into the middle of the room and whipped off his towel, wrapped it over his head and eyes.

"Whoever I catch, I fuck," he said.

They all stayed together the whole weekend, sunbathing, making love, swimming, eating Chinese food, reading scripts, chatting, gossiping, and loving. All five of them had an itch that needed soothing. Billie Jean Baby made pancakes. Monica made a *niçoise* salad. That evening, nude, they smoked grass and grilled some steaks. By Sunday at five-thirty he was all alone again.

The Sparrow Flies Again

"Who's calling Mr. Sparrow, please?"

"Mr. Solomon from Los Angeles."

"Just a moment, please."

Lillian's voice rang out. She caught Julie in the dining room having dinner with two gamblers out of Chicago. He excused himself, walked to his office, sat down in an unpretentious, soft leather chair that he used beside a coffee table which worked out to be his desk, picked up the phone.

"I'll talk to the King now, Lillian."

"Julie, I got trouble," King Solomon said. "I don't wanna talk about it on the phone. Can you get down here?"

"I'll be down in the morning."

"Thanks. There'll be a car waiting for you at the airport, bring you to where I'm at. What flight will ya be on?"

"I'll take the first flight outta here, get me in at around nine. Better still, there's a flight leaving here at two forty-five in the morning. It's now eleven. I'll get on that. I should be in L.A. by four-thirty."

"Great," the King said. "See ya later."

Julie left an hour earlier from his club just to take a look at the way Vegas was growing by leaps and bounds. People were descending into Vegas from every possible direction, in every conceivable kind of vehicle. It was truly developing into one of the great cities of the world. No one knew it yet except the people who lived in Las Vegas. There was some talk about a millionaire buying up a lot of land and a huge airport being built outside of the city. There were flights now coming directly to Las Vegas without going to Los Angeles and then to Vegas. Coming in from Chicago, New York, Miami, London. It was fast becoming a very important city and a city that generated an awful lot of bread for an awful lot of people. Club marquees were always lit up, bright and harsh, with the names of players and artists who were in town at the time.

The flight that he was on to L.A. was the latest flight leaving Las Vegas, or the earliest. It would get you into Los Angeles before dawn. For a lot of guys who had to show up for work the next morning, it was a perfect way to sneak up to Vegas the night before, have dinner, gamble, maybe get laid, and back on that plane at two forty-five, with time enough to go home, say good morning to the kids and wife. tell her the trip was quite successful, sold a few more tractors, and in the office by nine. The stewardess was tired, big-titted, and just disagreeable enough to interest Julie. He talked to her almost the whole length of the trip. Her name was Marian Brenner, came from Milwaukee, Wisconsin, and had no strings attached. He got her number in Los Angeles and he gave her his number in Vegas. Somewhere along the line they were gonna meet.

The King's car was there to pick him up. It was a clear night and Julie sat back in the limousine and enjoyed the ride to the King's house in Bel Air. He was driven up that long driveway to the front door. He was ushered in and there was King Solomon. King Solomon was almost five nine, almost two hundred pounds, with a huge head that almost reminded you of Caesar, a dark green robe, initials S.S. over the right-hand pocket; same shade of green were his pajamas, black slip-on slippers.

"Come on in here, kid. You look good, Julie. How do ya feel?"

"Great, Sam, great."

"Thanks for showing up. Come on."

His Majesty ushered Julie into a room that served as his den—fireplace, bookshelves, soft, comfortable leather chairs. There were two other guys in this room. There were Waxie and another fellow, Max Lippert, a man in his early fifties who had worked all the studios in town, starting out as a runner and legman for one of the top female columnists. and now he was running the publicity department at Quality. Julie walked up to the portable bar, fixed himself a vodka over the rocks in an old-fashioned glass, and sat down in one of the leather chairs.

"What's happening?"

"This fucking cunt," Sam said. "She breaks my ass to

give her the part of Mother Cecilia in this picture about a saint with Cody, got the best fucking director in town, Shador Cukor, that crazy Hungarian called Crimson, and she did a great job. I was gonna release the picture at Christmas for the holidays. It would have been eligible for the awards then. It's beautiful, Julie. I sure like that movie. Whatta ya think this cunt does? She gets herself photographed at a motel down by the beach, affectionately known as the Suck Inn, going down on some black broad. She must have been high or something. She doesn't even try to hide or bust out of there. She just nicely obliges the photographer with a dozen of the dirtiest pictures I've ever seen."

Sam handed Julie a small brown envelope. In it were prints of Sally Tarlow in the arms, between the legs, all ranged over, this good-looking black girl, in color yet. Both of them obviously having a good time.

"Max, here, got a call today from some guy that asked for him personally. Well, tell him, Max."

Max cleared his throat and started to talk.

"Well, er . . . I . . . er . . . oh, I would say it was around maybe . . . er oh . . . er . . . ten o'clock or so this morning when . . . er . . ."

"Will you cut out that fucking stuttering and just speak up?" Sam said. "Will ya, for Christ's sake? It's late."

Sam looked at Max with those blue piercing eyes of his; whatever stutters were left in Max, they were driven in even deeper and, like some miracle, they disappeared.

"A guy calls me this morning, doesn't give me his name. Tells me some pictures are coming over that would interest Mr. Solomon, some photographs of Sally Tarlow. The guy says where can he call at nine o'clock. By that time Mr. Solomon had called you, Mr. Sparrow, and when you were arriving, he gave this guy a number to call here at the house. He should call us in about half an hour. He didn't say any more than that."

"Where's Sally Tarlow now?" Julie said.

Max shook his head no.

"She lives somewhere off Coldwater Canyon," Sam said. "Got a house in the hills."

"Is she home?"

"If she is, she ain't answering her phone and her service don't know where she is. She's on a picture but she's off for a couple of days. Haven't heard from her in about five. But I figure everything is all right 'cause sometimes when she's off like this, she goes to the beach to cool down. Who the fuck knows where she goes? I wish you and she hadda worked out a little bit better. At least when she hung out with you, she stayed outta trouble."

Julie thought of their last encounter.

"Thanks, Sam, but no thanks—and fuck you too, Sam," Julie said. "Give me five, will ya?"

"Go ahead, go ahead."

Julie got up and asked Sam where he could take a leak, and he was directed to a beautiful toilet. He was tired and alone. He didn't know quite how to handle this situation yet. He had to think. He had to help out his buddy, Sam, with the people who took these pictures. He knew that Sally Tarlow was the key, if she was vulnerable enough to be caught in these compromising positions. She was either dumber than he thought, which he doubted, or she was deliberately trying to fuck up Samuel Solomon, but why? Envy? Penis envy, or whatever kind of envy you want to call it? She had a touch of destruction in her. It meant he had to tread very lightly and carefully. Now all he had to figure out was how to meet and see what kind of an asshole he was dealing with.

"When this guy calls or whoever calls," he said to Sam, "I wanna talk to him."

"Okay, Julie."

Julie took a pad and pencil from the entry hall table. Sat down with Waxie and asked him how the redhead was.

"The redhead? Oh, gone and forgotten, baby. I got a beautiful blond Polish chick now. Just came into town. She's wearing one of the numbers. I'm letting her wear the mink. Looks like this one's gonna last longer than the others. Maybe even a coupla weeks."

"No shit," Julie said.

"Naw, Julie. I've decided that runs about as long as I wanna spend with any woman, for any length of time."

Waxie sat back composed and quiet. The phone rang. Julie walked over to it, sat down, picked it up.

"Yeah, who is it?" Julie said.

"Did you see the pictures?" a voice husky with booze spoke.

He paused.

"Who am I talking to?"

"None of ya fuckin' business."

Julie said. "What are ya offering?"

"Careful, buddy," the voice said, "or they'll be on Lila London's desk in the morning."

"What do you think that fucking yenta is gonna do with 'em?" Julie said. "Shove 'em up her ass? Are you selling anything? Speak up, prick, whatta you want?"

"I want a hundred thousand dollars cash for the negatives."

"Are you fucking crazy? Now how are you gonna prove that you haven't got any other sets of these negatives right now?"

"Well, I really can't, can I?"

"No, you can't."

"I'll tell you what I'll do. I'll turn them over to you or whoever you wish, personally. But it's gotta be only one guy. I want it in cash fifty- and hundred-dollar bills."

"When do you wanna do this?"

"I'll call you back and tell you when."

"You hang up the phone now, prick, and it's finished. You wanna make the meet, you make an appointment with me now, for today. Get this fuckin' thing settled before noon. I don't wanna wait any longer than that. Where do I meet you? I'll have the money and I want you to have the negatives and whatever prints you've made."

"Okay, it's five now," the whiskey voice said. "When can you have the money?"

Julie put his hand over the phone and looked at Samuel.

"When can I have a hundred grand in fifties and hundred-dollar bills?"

Sam didn't blink.

"We got some at the studio and I got some here. Yeah, I can come up with that."

"By when?"

"I can have it all together in an hour."

"Okay."

Julie looked at his pocket watch.

"How about eight this morning?" he said. "Okay?"

"You be at Coldwater Canyon and Ventura Boulevard at eight o'clock and come alone. I'll know you by the small black valise you'll be carrying which will have a hundred grand. There's a gas station on the corner, bus stop, and a bench. Be sitting on that bench." The voice hung up the phone.

"I'm gonna have a meet at eight o'clock this morning at Coldwater Canyon and Ventura in front of a gas station on a bus stop bench."

Sam called Max, told him to get down to the studio. The combination of the safe was in the head cashier's hands. She was called, rousted out of bed, and told to get to the studio immediately. Max started down in the limousine. Sam went upstairs to his private chambers, opened the wall safe, took out sixty-three thousand dollars, called the studio, told the head police guard there that as soon as Mrs. Franks, the bookkeeper, arrived to call him. Eighteen minutes later, the phone rang; he told her to get thirty-seven thousand bucks in fifties and hundreds and put it in the attaché case that Max had with him. By six-twenty that morning, there was miraculously one hundred thousand dollars in fifty- and hundred-dollar bills. Julie was wearing black leather loafers with a half rubber heel, heavy fabric trousers, a cavalry twill that even if you sat for a long time maintained its crease and seemed unwrinkled. His slacks were gray and his jacket was grayer and short. Shirt was opened at the neck, no tie. In a hidden pocket near his crotch rested his .32, loaded and on safety.

"Can I borrow a car?"

"Sure, kid, sure."

Sam had a dark blue English Jensen rolled out of the garage by his chauffeur, Willard, and sat waiting in front of the main gate of the house. Julie had his license with him. He slipped on a pair of thin gloves from the small traveling bag in the entry hall of Sam's house. The sun was rising in the east, giving parts of the Bel Air hills a mysterious and gloomy look. He stepped in the car and sat down. He rolled the window down and Sam walked around to the driver's side.

"Oh, by the way," Julie said, "I'm gonna get the negatives back and the pictures back and it's not gonna cost ya a fuckin' penny, pal. Nothing."

He started the ignition, smooth. He shifted the car into gear smooth. Julie took off in the Jensen at six forty-five, the attaché case sitting on the seat alongside of him. He went down the long driveway, two minutes, out to the gate, turned left, left again, following Sam's directions. Julie left early for Julie was going to case the whole area before he settled in, before he parked the car somewhere inconspicuously and before he sat on that bench to wait. He drove up Coldwater Canyon, a beautiful road extending from Beverly Hills into the San Fernando Valley. The car rose effortlessly up the canyon road, taking the twists and turns to the crest, where the sun was by now pretty bright, and then down into the Valley side, which got a bit darker. At Coldwater Canyon and Ventura, he saw the bench where he was to wait in front of the gas station. About five minutes after seven he decided to drive around the area. He circled back and forth in a lot of small streets, seeing in which direction the main artery of the Valley went. All of the traffic really went east and west and Ventura Boulevard was by far the major thoroughfare. At twenty minutes to eight, he was back in the neighborhood of Coldwater and Ventura, and found a place to park the car off Coldwater Canyon. He picked up the case and walked to a coffee shop, went in. He wanted an egg cream but settled for Sanka, some toasted wheat bread, buttered, and at five minutes to eight was crossing the street from this coffee shop toward the bench on the corner. He looked at everything around him. He cased everything, cars and people. At a minute to eight, he was sitting waiting at the bus stop. It was now exactly eight o'clock. He had been up exactly twenty-four hours. A Ford coupe pulled up to the bus stop a minute after eight. There was a kid about twenty-two driving the car, Levis, Levi jacket, a kind of scrubby white shirt, pair of low run-down brown boots, insolent black eyes.

"You're supposed to give me that case and I'm supposed to give ya this envelope," the kid said.

Julie said, "Okay," and handed the case through the window of the car. The kid put it down on the seat beside him and opened it, made sure there was money in it, and handed over the envelope to Julie. Julie just as quickly pulled out his .32, quietly, and had it aimed almost nonchalantly at this kid's head.

"Don't move."

He opened the door and got in. They pulled away from the bench and started going east on Ventura. A minute later, driving on Ventura, Julie gestured the kid to pull over and told the kid to keep his hands on the wheel and shut off the ignition, his eyes forward. While holding his piece in his right hand, cocked, he opened the envelope with his left and saw six strips of film and some photographs. He could see right away that they were phonies. The photographs certainly were not of Sally Tarlow and that black chick.

The traffic wasn't too busy at that time in the morning. The window on the kid's side of the car was rolled down. Aiming in front and across the forehead of the kid, Julie fired. The bullet screamed out of the car; it singed all the front hair on this kid and sunburned his forehead.

"The next bullet tears your insides out. Keep your hands on the wheel and your eyes forward. Driving, that's all you're doing. Got it?"

The kid nodded. His forehead stung and now he was even afraid to look in the rear-view mirror at his own reflection and see what damage had been wrought on his forehead. The bullet had imbedded itself across the street in a brick building.

"Take me to your leader, asshole."

The kid pulled out. Went down Ventura Boulevard about six more blocks. Turned north on a cross street. Went to Moorpark, turned right. Went three more blocks, turned left onto a small side street. Went up about a quarter of the way up, on the right, and pulled into a driveway. It was a typical California ranch house, probably two bedrooms, probably cost twelve thousand dollars when it was originally built. There was a fence around the main perimeter of the house so you couldn't see in, and luckily, Julie thought, you couldn't see out. The kid shut the ignition off. Julie reached over and took out the keys, gestured him out of the car, picked up the attaché case and photographs that he had been given, and kept the kid covered with his piece. They started to go through the front door. Julie stopped him. He gestured him up the driveway toward the garage, where the kitchen door would be. Julie lifted the latch, opened the wooden gate, stepped inside, and had the kid follow him. The kid went up to the door, he told him to knock. The kid did. The door opened. The kid started in and so did Julie. He was now in the kitchen and lo and behold, there was that beautiful black chick in a pair of tight Levis, barefoot, a blue sweater that showed her nipples quite distinctly, hair pulled back from her face, her features were clean and dignified. She looked as if she was some African princess. He gestured both of them to walk ahead of him and they started into the next room. As they came through the door, Julie quickly cased the room. Down near the window sitting near a table was a guy, white, about fifty, soft, pudgy, and Irish. Obviously a lot of booze had gone down that gullet. He didn't even look startled. Julie gestured both the girl and the kid to sit down. They did just a few feet away from this asshole at this desk by the window.

His name was Frank Barnett, ex-publicity agent, who tried his hand at writing. No success. Opened his own office, no success. Wrote shit for the movie magazines, no success. He was now at the end of his rope and didn't have the guts or courage to really put anything together. He got these two kids to hustle some old unknown boss of his for some money. He'd given the girl two thousand bucks and a promise of another three thousand when he finally collected. He got the girl, whose name was Winny, a pass to visit Quality Studios. He knew the predilections and tastes of Sally Tarlow. He knew that Winny could make a connection with her if they could just meet. Winny hung around most of the morning watching Sally shooting a film. Sally noticed her immediately because this Winny kid was beautiful. Sally had Winny wait until the end of the day. By eight o'clock they were on their way to the beach, with Sally driving her Karman Ghia. They got to Suck Inn, had joints out, lit up, and, pulling on the grass, popping a couple of downers, they were as comfortable and high as one would ever want to be. Winny had unlocked the door. By nine-twenty this kid with all his photographic equipment, represented by a Nikon with a portable flash attachment, had entered the door of this small suite, having followed Winny and Sally all evening. They were both in bed now, both high and low. Both these beautiful creatures looked so appealing to him that he was taking the pictures with a hard-on. His first impulse was to get that camera off his neck and dive in. But he had a job to do and was picking up fifteen hundred dollars for the night, which wasn't chopped chicken liver. Before Sally knew what hit her, Winny was up trailing this kid out of the door, grabbing whatever clothes she could find that were hers, and they were in the car speeding away at nine-thirty, Monday night. Wednesday morning, Max got the phone call, and the prints. Julie told this character, Frank, to stand up.

"Where's the film and the negatives?"

Before Frank could even answer, Julie fired. The bullet cut a deep furrow across Frank's ass, about four inches long and maybe half an inch deep. Man, that hurt! Frank almost collapsed from the shock of it.

"Where's the film and the negatives?" Julie said again. "If you don't tell me now, pal, I'm gonna put the next bullet right up your ass."

Frank didn't wait. He gestured to a bureau that was in a corner. Julie moved to it, covering all three people with his piece. Pulled open the top drawer and there sitting in the corner were maybe fifteen or twenty envelopes of film, negatives, a camera, and a few other pieces of camera equipment. Julie opened the attaché case, took all the film and envelopes in the drawer, and placed them on top of the money in the case and shut it. He took the camera out and flung it as hard as he could through the window of the house, over the fence, and onto the street. As he flung the camera, this kid picked up a lead pipe that he produced from somewhere and swung it. Julie just barely ducked, but it caught him high on his left shoulder. The pain was deep and long and blinding. From a half-falling position, he threw his right fist so fast that the kid was hit and on the way to the ground before he even had time to lift up that lead pipe again. Julie grabbed the attaché case, told white and pudgy to call that number at nine-thirty, gestured for the girl to go to the kitchen, and he followed her. He backed into the kitchen with the girl, gestured her to go outside, and they went out. He then put his piece away, looked at the girl, and smiled.

"What's your name?"

"Winny," she said.

"I'm Julie. Where you live, Winny?"

"Somewhere in Hollywood."

"Got a number?"

"Why?"

"The next time I'm in Los Angeles, I'd sure like to call ya. Perhaps we could have dinner."

Her face lit up with a sweet smile.

"Man, you're funny," she said.

"Could I call ya?"

"Okay, pal, okay. You got a pencil and paper?"

"I can remember any number."

"It's Bradshaw 4-6987, Winny Bennett."

"Okay," he said, "now come with me."

She came with him. Got in the car; he had her drive. They backed out of the driveway, right over the camera, up to Moorpark, and finally up to Ventura. He had her let him off across the street from the bench on the corner.

"See ya, Winny. I'll call ya the next time I'm in town."

"Later, baby," she said.

It was now ten minutes to nine. He got in the Jensen and at a quarter after nine he was pulling up to Samuel Solomon's mansion. Samuel Solomon, King of Hollywood, almost plotzed when Julie opened the attaché case. There was the money and not only photographs and negatives of Sally's encounter but a half-dozen other people that Sam recognized.

"You wouldn't believe the people that are in these pictures," he said.

"I know a press agent here in town that's pretty much down on his luck," Julie said. "Had a little accident. Lookin' for a job. If I can get him off the bottle, ya think someone can hire him?"

"He's got it," Sam said.

"Okay."

Two minutes later, the phone rang and Frank was on the line. Julie picked it up.

"Call Quality Studios and talk to Max Lippert as soon as your ass is better. Maybe there's a job for ya."

"Thanks," Frank said.

"Forget it," Julie said.

"Max, the guy's name is Barnett, Frank Barnett."

By eleven o'clock, Julie was on a flight back to Las Vegas. By a quarter to one, he was taking a steam and a plaitzer at his club. He had been gone exactly ten hours and twenty-two minutes. And his fucking shoulder hurt.

Long Time No See

One night, Joey Vittucci stood in his club, right out of the past.

"Hey, Julie. Julie, man, you look great, pal. You look just great. Okay, Julie, okay. I'm here for a couple of weeks, thought I'd stop in and hit some of your tables."

"Okay, Joey, come on in. Have ya eaten, want anything?"

"No, pal, just a little gambling, and maybe, if ya got a few minutes later, we can have a talk."

"Okay, Joey, anything you want. Rosie, see that Joey here gets everything he wants."

He did. At two that morning Joey searched out Julie. The club was quiet now. Julie and Joey walked over to one of the blackjack tables that had been closed up for the night.

"Get a pack of cards," Joey said. "We'll play some blackjack."

"Okay."

"What's the limit, Julie?"

"Whatever you want, Joey. Put your money where your mouth is."

He put out five hundred bucks, and Julie dealt Joey the first hand.

"If this is the way it's gonna go tonight," Joey laughed, "I won't even have to buy this place. I'll own it in the morning."

Julie paid Joey the money he had won.

"Deal again," Joey said, looking at Julie.

Two hours later, Joey Vittucci was out twenty-three thousand dollars.

"That's it, Julie," he said. Joey pulled out a wad of bills from the inside of his jacket and peeled off twenty-four.

"Julie, why don't you let me be your partner? For old time's sake, for sweet Angie's sake. I like it out here. I'm tired of the East. I don't wanna come out here and try to get settled. I'm a little old for that. I'd like to tie in with somebody that I can trust, somebody that I know. Give ya anything ya want. Any partnership you want. Let me buy a piece of the action, Julie, just a piece of your action."

"Joey, I can't do that. I built this club on my own, and I don't want to share it with anybody. Come and use it anytime you want. Feel free to come and go as you wish. You got any kind of credit you want. Tell your friends to show up, but I'm not gonna give you a piece."

"Julie, I never took no for an answer in anything I ever wanted. I'm not taking yours. I'm gonna be here for a few more days. I'll call you before I leave. You can tell me what you think."

"Okay, Joey, call me before you leave. We can say good-by."

Joey laughed and stalked out of the 711 Casino. As he got into the back seat of the car waiting for him, "That kike don't know who he's fucking with," he said to Vito.

Two days later at about seven o'clock, a gunsel nonchalantly walked up to the bar in the 711 Casino. Rosie was talking with one of the guards, making sure that the back doors were carefully patrolled because there had been one or two petty robberies in one of the bungalows. Joey strode in.

"Where's that asshole Julie?"

The club quieted down immediately. Everything stopped cold. Rosie didn't like the looks of this. Rosie kept his Colt always ready to fire, ready to pull out of the short holster that sat on his hip.

"I'll tell Mr. Sparrow you're here."

"Didja hear that, Vito?" Joey said. "Mr. Sparrow, that's a funny name for a Hebe."

Julie heard that last line that Joey spoke. He was out of the office and in the lounge looking directly at Joey.

"Why, you guinea prick."

That somehow froze the smile on Joey's face. No one ever called Joey anything but Mr. Vittucci, the head of a small and organized mob operating out of New York, whose one strength was his unpredictability. They were staked out like some early Western. No one will ever really know what flicker started it, because before Joey could even get his hand near his waistband, Rosie's Colt was out and fired. Blew a hole right through Joey's heart. Vito fired in Julie's direction. Julie wheeled around, shot Vito through the right eye, and as he turned to the third gunsel who was retching at the bar, the man was crying.

"No, no, please don't, please don't shoot. I'm not carrying a piece. I'm not carrying a piece."

Rosie slammed him up against a crap table but not enough to knock him down. In the excitement of it all, Julie didn't feel the hit, he forgot it immediately.

"Get rid of all of them, clean up this place quick. You all right?"

"I'm all right."

He walked toward the bungalows. He heard Ruth call his name. J.U.L.I.E. He was so surprised that he was bleeding, even more surprised that he had been shot. For a minute, it was some kind of fantasy that he had had. Closing up now. Bungalow. Get a few hours' sleep before the count at eleven o'clock. Not a bad wound but it frightened Julie. It felt different. He'd never been shot before, but if he had, he would have known that this was different. The bullet had shattered his pancreas. Things that should not have passed through his blood were now rushing through the vital organs of his body. Into his immaculate room, almost stumbling a couple of times, but he was determined to stay on his feet. There was a dullness now around the right side of his abdomen and thigh. Maybe he'd better lie down but not before he took a shower, which he did. Towel wrapped around his waist, he lay down on his bed, and waited for the doctor to come. Didn't seem to be much bleeding. For a moment he felt relieved and the pain wasn't too bad. As if it was just superficial, nothing really serious. The next thing he remembered was being awakened. There was René a waitress he used to ball and this doctor that he had been using up there, Dr. Gershon.

"Julie, we're gonna get you to a hospital," Gershon said.

"Bullshit. You're not taking me anywhere. You got anything to do to me, you do it to me here."

"They'll look after you much better at the hospital."

"I'm going to no hospital. Now you look after me here or get the fuck out of here. One or the other."

"All right."

He got on the phone and immediately barked out the instruments and equipment that he would need. He gave Julie a shot to kill the pain. J.U.L.I.E. An antibiotic to kill the infection already surging through his wound. Something to sleep. And René sat alone with him for a while. By that time, a nurse and the equipment the doctor wanted had arrived. Julie drifted off. René started to leave, but he pulled her back and made her sit down.

I feel good. Angie, wait for me. I'll be back in a couple of minutes. You shoulda seen Ruth when she was young. She sure was beautiful. They tried to break into Morrie's store once. Came down through the roof and tried to break into the transom. We lived in the back of the store then—lunch—he lost his week's salary—twenty bucks once. Fell out of his pocket or some prick stole it from him. Don't kiss with your mouth open. I don't know. Morrie discovered it when he got home. Ran outta the house the same way he had come from work. Tracing every step to see if he could find it in the streets. Castor oil. I followed him. Morrie. Knowledge is power. Bet your wife is an elevator operator somewhere now. Ringa-leevio-ko-ko-ko. I love you.

He finally fell asleep. René looked at him for a long time. She could see his eyes fluttering and moving underneath the closed lids. Once in a while, he would mumble. Then he was off into another world. To another place, to another time He could feel a pressing on his chest. If he called in the doctor, they would just give him some other medication and he would go out cold, maybe never wake up again. that's gonna happen eventually, but it ain't gonna happen in any bed. That's for sure. He was feverish. They gave him another shot.

J.U.L.I.E.

It started him off again, he was out of the room, he was out of the bed, moving, hoping that this room would miraculously disappear and this would turn out to be nothing more than just a nightmare on his fire escape bed, or just a bad dream or even just a dream. It was a warm and breezy night. He felt free and not connected to any pain, not even connected to his own body. He walked onto the green, well-manicured lawn, a putting green which was just twenty feet from the front of the bungalow. There was a small stone bench. He felt that he had to sit down but when he sat the pain was bad. He lay down on the stone bench straight out flat extending his arms down along his sides, taking a deep breath. The pain eased. He heard someone call him Julius. He sat up and there was his father. He knew it was his father by the way he was dressed. That's the way his father would have dressed. In a pinstripe suit, a vest, cuffs on his trousers, pointed shoes, soft shirt with a tie bar holding a maroon tie, a cigarette hanging from his lips.

Are you my father?

Well, I ain't your mother, kid.

You died when I was born.

I'm here, ain't I?

Is that all it's about, being alive?

What are ya asking me for? I'm only nineteen years old.

Can I call you Father?

Can I call you Son?

I'd like to have known you when I was younger.

I'd like to have known you when I was older.

Those stars in the sky—those hills, this valley—somehow I feel it's gonna last a longer time, and yet we are it.

I love to dance, said his father. Didn't get enough dancing when I was younger, kid, beautiful, beautiful, nice.

Father . . . who are you . . . where did you come from? Tell me, dear Father. Tell me.

Son, I am death.

He reached and pulled his face as one would open a door. There was nothing beyond it except a part of the blue sky. When they found him finally, he was dead, lying on the stone bench, an offering to the gods.

Alone Again, Naturally

The city was stretched out below him. It was night and the city lights glittered. The Valley of the Tears was smog-ridden and noisy. He had broken out in tears and sobbed as he did when his father died. When he heard that Julie was dead. Those countless nights in the orphanage, what happened to them? If anything, he felt stronger for his father now than he had when he died. Julie. He could sense it then, but he knew it now. He had lost the company of a great man.

Max, am I doin' okay?

Come on, Kid, I'll take ya to Charlie's for dinner.

Take me, baby, take me.

Who knows the way out of here?

You're gonna be on the cover of *Life*.

Seven hundred thousand dollars cash, plus ten per cent of the gross from the first dollar. We'll pick up all your checks. Pay all your bills. And when we find some kind of proposition that we think is good, we'll ask you to invest in it. For that, we want five per cent of all your gross earnings.

I'll make out all your contracts and give you corporate advice. For that I want seven per cent of your gross income.

Throw that punch as hard as you want. It's okay. I'm set for it.

Julie's dead. Did he take it lying down?

They want Ram Cochran for the part. If he passes on it, you got it.

Did he think of me before he went?

The exhibitors' poll will give you third spot if you take out full pages in both trades.

Julie's dead and Cody's got him.

I made you what you are in this town and don't you forget it. I can break you just like that.

I'll give you worldwide representation, which includes a

bedroom flat in London, and I'll negotiate all your deals. I get ten per cent of the gross of your earnings.

The only thing you can rely on the Academy for is the free movies at the end of the year.

I love you and I'll see you at four.

Max, what would you have done with B. Shrike Martin? Don't ask me. My license expired.

He got up, put on denims, a white T-shirt, jacket, gloves, short boots, and got on his bike. He pulled out of his driveway like a bat out of hell. B. Shrike Martin had his eyes on him the minute he left the house. He started following the Kid up Coldwater Canyon. The Kid saw and knew it was the Shrike. He was taking those curves at forty and climbing all the time. And the Shrike wouldn't let him out of his sight. The Kid pulled up to Mulholland and turned east. As he cleared a turn, he could see in his rear-view mirror the Shrike's car coming into view and then disappearing behind a slope and reappearing again. He let the Shrike shorten the distance between them just to see what he had in mind. All he could see was hate glaring at him through the rear-view mirror. He was using a Chrysler Imperial as his weapon. From the way he took those turns, the Kid knew the Shrike knew something about cars. To his left lay the San Fernando Valley below, with a two-hundred-foot ridge sloping drastically down the northern side of Mulholland Drive. The Kid swung his bike into the left lane. He pulled his bike over short and sweet onto the edge. He never let the Shrike off the hook. The Shrike was always a second away from getting him, splattering him and his bike, smashing him to a pulp, finishing his stubborn existence. The Kid could hear the growl of his engine and feel the vibration that the Chrysler made behind him, like the end of a vacuum cleaner, sucking in all that was in front of it. The Kid was still in that left lane. He'd have to move quickly, that car in the opposite lane was long overdue. The Kid's bike and the Shrike's left wheels were a foot from the edge. They were doing sixty miles an hour, screaming around the top of Mulholland Drive. The Kid feinted to his left with his shoulder and so did the Shrike. It was just enough. The Kid broke hard right, forcing his bike to scream to the right-hand lane, the G-force pulling on him and the bike, keeling them over. He forced the machine out of its spin with his own balance, weight, and strength. He started to come out of it. When he turned his head, B. Shrike Martin and his Chrysler Imperial were skimming out over the ledge as if tossed by some giant hand. It didn't nose or tumble, it just sailed down. When it hit, everything stopped, the engine stopped, the clock stopped, and so did B. Shrike Martin.

Where Do We Go
from Here?

The Kid was buried up to his neck in sand on the beach of the west shore of Catalina Island. Whitey sat alongside, his hand holding a two-foot-square cardboard box with one side cut out. It framed the Kid's head like the proscenium in a theater, gracefully enclosing the actors below. Inside the box alongside of his head sat a club soda over the rocks in an old-fashioned glass with a bent-over and white stripe straw. They had waited almost an hour now for the shot.

"This fucking company is crazy, I tell ya. They knew an hour ago it was going to take 'em two hours to get this shot. Why the fuck bury you in there until they're ready? What assholes."

"I don't mind," the Kid said.

The thought of being buried like that and not being able to move frightened Whitey. Whitey couldn't understand why either. Maybe it had to do with taking it in the ass. Why not? That was being blamed for everything else. All the noncombatants had to fall back. The camera was on a ridge shooting down and took in almost the whole beach from one end. The director thought the effectiveness of the shot would be this isolated head in this immense vastness of space, water, and sand. He was going to zoom from the widest possible angle, and continue zooming in until he disappeared in the Kid's eyes. The film would end that way. The Kid was a bit sore around the edge of his neck, and he started to sweat almost immediately. He peed; he could feel the hole it left below in the sand. He was facing the sea. From his eyeline, he couldn't see any living creature. He was told to look straight forward and straight forward he looked. Whitey came running over after rehearsal and put the box around his head again. He put his drink in the right-hand corner of the box and bent the straw so all the Kid had to do was turn his head and pull on the straw and instant drink.

"Whitey, you out there?"

Whitey was just three feet away.

"Yeah, Kid, what can I do for ya? Do ya need anything?"

"Take the box and the drink away, will ya? I don't mind being in the sun. Every little bit helps."

"Okay, Kid. If ya need me, yell."

"Okay, Max."

Whitey didn't hear it. The Kid heard.

The cameraman, Johnny Anderson, had his eyes screwed into the eyepiece of the Mitchell. He had had it on a F32MM zoom lens. The glass had been polished in Holland, mailed to England, assembled in Canada, and ended up in California. Through the eyepiece all you could see were sea and sand and a speck in the center of the frame. The number one camera was placed just where the waves were breaking. The camera was on a tripod, held in place by five fifty-pound lead weights, stacked one on top of the other, surrounding the center pole of the camera which sank below the lead weights, and held it in place on the platform. The camera was as steady there as anywhere. In the wide angle position of the zoom lens you could see, on your right, the waves just breaking on the shore, and, on your left, the sloping beach and hills of Santa Manuela.

He was being bombarded by invisible probes and he knew it. By moving his eyes slightly to the right, he could see the group of six men huddled around a black object popping out of the surf. They were busy with their calculations and measurements. Sircazzi told him they were getting different shots of him with his head stuck out of the sand with three cameras. He didn't bother looking behind him to the sloping hills. It had all faded away by now. He only vaguely remembered any of them. Here he was, stuck. His picture was the biggest success of the year. Lila's power had now receded like her hairline. She was told by Adele in no uncertain terms to lay off Kid Kosher. B. Shrike Martin had died under unfortunate circumstances. What was he doing way up there on Mulholland Drive, all alone anyway? Adele told her she could write one more book about Hollywood and then she'd have to get out of town. They replaced Lila with Lynn, Miriam's nofka, who was getting successful, and who gave up her half-assed film career to become a half-assed Hollywood columnist waiting for the next belch from the stars like Cleopatra waiting for Antony. The Kid was stuck. Where would it all end? Ten years later write a book about himself?

Sircazzi, the director, came walking over to the Kid. So did Whitey. They brought over the cardboard box and fit it over the Kid's head. He now had a little shade.

"We'll be ready in a minute, Kid. You're doing a fine job."

"Thanks, Sirgay."

And he was off.

"I don't need this box on my head, Whitey, let the sunshine in, I don't mind."

"That's okay. I'm not goin' anyplace."

Whitey left him there. The propman moved off with his shovel. And there he was, stuck, going no place. They were all gone and everything was a memory. All memories. He was earthbound, that was for sure. As fanciful as your dreams could be, you ended up getting stuck. Where to go, what to do? As lonely as ever. Getting lonelier all the time.

Max, how could you leave me in such a predicament? Where are you now that I need you? If I can figure out what I'm after, I'll go after it tomorrow.

"Hold it, we're getting ready to do it."

"You ready to let me see it, Jean?"

"Okay, Sirgay. Have a look. Crammer, rack it over, I wanna look through the lens. Okay, Phil, you set?"

"Set and ready, J.J."

"Wally, the reading again? We're at eleven, Sirgay, we're going to do three of them at different speeds, twenty-four frames, twenty frames, and sixteen frames. Okay."

Sircazzi sat down in a metal seat that was upholstered in light blue vinyl. Sircazzi was enjoying the picture. He liked everybody. Everyone seemed delighted to be working and doing their best.

"Es ed a mossyie," Sircazzi said in Hungarian to no one

in particular, took his sunglasses off and nestled his right eye into the eyepiece of the Mitchell.

"All right, Jean, may I see it, please?"

"Let's see it," Anderson barked to the zoom operator.

"Ready. Start pulling."

With that, the operator rotated a circulator ratchet. As he circled, the glass of the lens seemed to seek out something. You didn't know what. You just knew you were being drawn to something. Still in the width of the angle it was difficult to determine or discern anything of interest. From what you could see, it was all sand and sea. But somehow you were attracted finally by something in the center of the screen. As the lens rushed past innumerable dried wood bits, snails, shells, stones, rubbers, all discards of both land and sea, you seemed drawn to the center. The lens paid no attention to any of it, just raced past everything. You finally could see a head. The lens was slowing down and you could see this head on the sand. The lens didn't stop, it kept going. The landscape had changed and became a face and still you were moving, disappearing into it. It seemed to center around the eye now. It went past the lashes into the eye. You were passing through blue, then dark green, and then to black. Gone, gone forever.

About the Author

Tony Curtis, one of the screen's most successful and best-known actors, has appeared recently in "The Last Tycoon," based on the book by F. Scott Fitzgerald. KID ANDREW CODY & JULIE SPARROW is Mr. Curtis' first novel, and he is currently at work on his second.

More Big Bestsellers from SIGNET

- [ ] **FRENCH KISS by Mark Logan.** (#J7876—$1.95)
- [ ] **COMA by Robin Cook.** (#E7881—$2.50)
- [ ] **THE YEAR OF THE INTERN by Robin Cook.** (#E7674—$1.75)
- [ ] **MISTRESS OF DARKNESS by Christopher Nicole.** (#J7782—$1.95)
- [ ] **SOHO SQUARE by Clare Rayner.** (#J7783—$1.95)
- [ ] **CALDO LARGO by Earl Thompson.** (#E7737—$2.25)
- [ ] **A GARDEN OF SAND by Earl Thompson.** (#E8039—$2.50)
- [ ] **TATTOO by Earl Thompson.** (#E8038—$2.50)
- [ ] **DESIRES OF THY HEART by Joan Carroll Cruz.** (#J7738—$1.95)
- [ ] **RUNNING AWAY by Charlotte Vale Allen.** (#E7740—$1.75)
- [ ] **THE ACCURSED by Paul Boorstin.** (#E7745—$1.75)
- [ ] **THE RICH ARE WITH YOU ALWAYS by Malcolm Macdonald.** (#E7682—$2.25)
- [ ] **THE WORLD FROM ROUGH STONES by Malcolm Macdonald.** (#J6891—$1.95)
- [ ] **THE FRENCH BRIDE by Evelyn Anthony.** (#J7683—$1.95)
- [ ] **TELL ME EVERYTHING by Marie Brenner.** (#J7685—$1.95)

THE NEW AMERICAN LIBRARY, INC.,
P.O. Box 999, Bergenfield, New Jersey 07621

Please send me the SIGNET BOOKS I have checked above. I am enclosing $_____ (check or money order—no currency or C.O.D.'s). Please include the list price plus 35¢ a copy to cover handling and mailing costs. (Prices and numbers are subject to change without notice.)

Name_____

Address_____

City_____ State_____ Zip Code_____

Allow at least 4 weeks for delivery

SIGNET Bestsellers You'll Want to Read